# HOME:
## THROUGH A FIELD OF STARS

*Book three of the*
***Through a Field of Stars***
*trilogy*

BRIAN JOHN SKILLEN

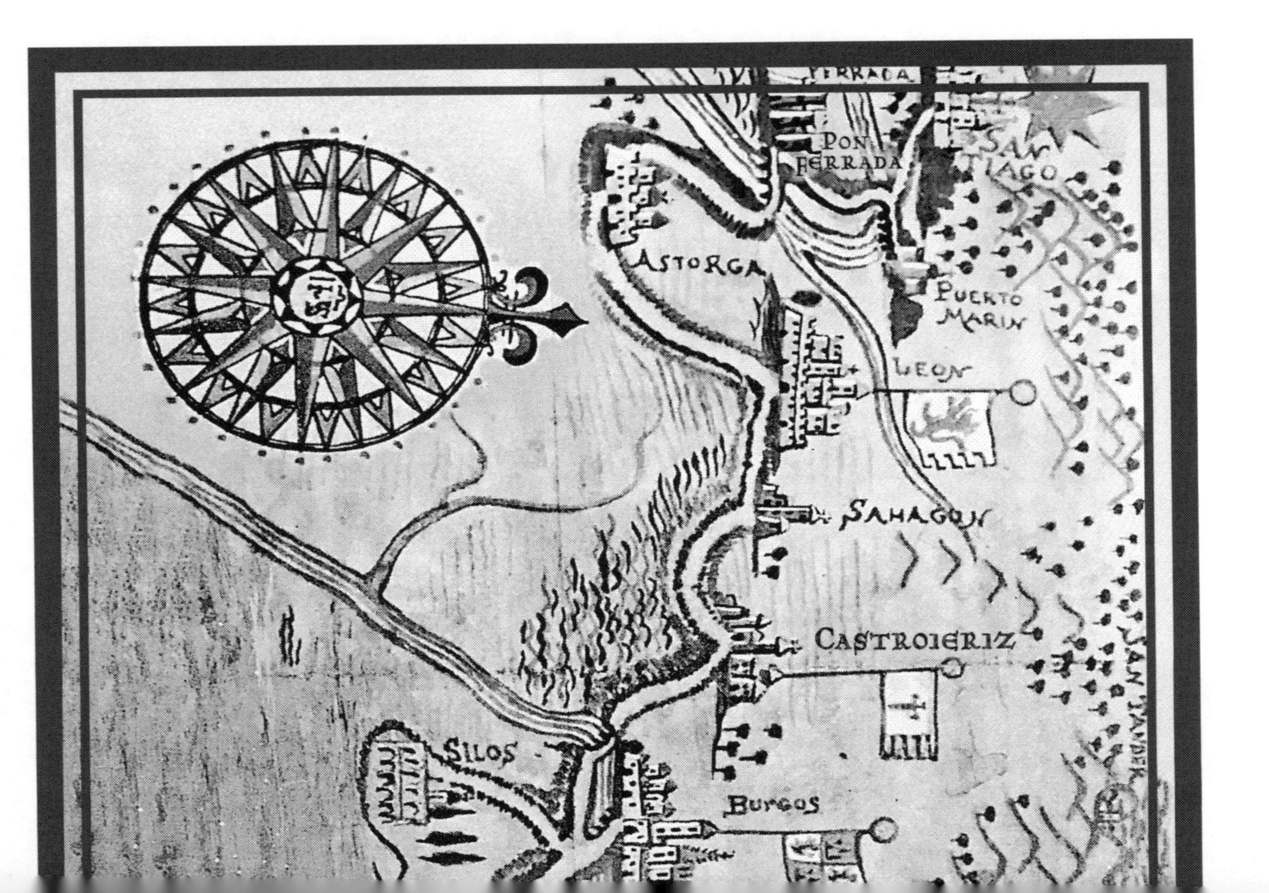

PON FERRADA
SANTIAGO
ASTORGA
PUERTO MARIN
LEON
SAHAGUN
CASTROIERIZ
SAN TANDER
SILOS
BURGOS

LOGROÑO
ESTELLA
OTEIZA
PUENTE LA REINA
PAMPLONA
TAVIER
JACA
RIO EBRO

Published by: 1881 Productions
Arvada, Colorado, USA

Paperback ISBN: 978-1-7353036-3-5
Hardcover ISBN - 978-1-7353036-7-3
Ebook ISBN - 978-1-7353036-8-0



Design and formatting by Valeria Fox
Edited by Librum Artis Editorial Services

Printed in the United States of America

November 2022

www.throughafieldofstars.com
throughafieldofstars@gmail.com

This book is dedicated to all the pilgrims from
the Camino de Santiago
who inspired

***Home: Through A Field of Stars,***

especially my wife Chelsea.

I hope reading this novel inspires you
to take the adventure of a lifetime.

Buen Camino!

# AUTHOR'S NOTES

On April 8, 2017, in the small town of Castrojeriz, I was first told about a secret code of the Knights Templar on the Camino de Santiago. This code inspired me to write the Through a Field of Stars series. As I hiked the Camino across Spain, the story for this novel played like a movie in my head. The things I saw, the people I met, and the experiences I had all wove together into the perfect narrative. Since that day, I have walked more than a thousand miles doing research for this book series.

The first novel in the series, The Way: Through a Field of Stars is set in the year 1306, one year before the Knights Templar mysteriously disappeared, along with their treasure. The novel follows Princess Isabella of France on a fictitious pilgrimage along the Camino de Santiago as her father, King Philip, plots to disband the Templars. Join Isabella and her companions as they travel through foreign lands, unlock the Templar's secret codes, avoid immortal Shadows, and discover the wisdom of the Camino de Santiago.

The second novel, Back: Through a Field of Stars was inspired by a return trip I took to the Camino de Santiago in 2018. Just like the first novel, the pilgrims I met on this Camino became characters in the novel, and experiences I had on this journey weave their way into the pages you are about to read.

The third novel, Home: Through a Field of Stars was inspired by a return trip to the Camino in 2019. This trip was taken with my wife, Chelsea, and we researched the remaining information I needed to complete the third and final book in the trilogy.

Being a historical fantasy, many of the characters are historical figures, like Princes Isabella of France and the Knights Templar. Though these characters are actually historical figures, I've altered certain things about them to fit the narrative. To learn more about the factual history of these characters, refer to the appendix in the back of the novel. Being a fantasy, there are also some supernatural entities you can expect along the way.

I have walked the miles my characters have walked and learned the lessons they have learned. All of the characters in the novel that aren't based on historical people were inspired by pilgrims I met on my Caminos. This book is dedicated to them. "Buen Camino!"

# TABLE OF CONTENTS

# CHAPTER 1

***Paris, 1307***

Isabella[1] gasped awake as a hand wrapped around her mouth, stifling her scream. Her eyes scanned the dark room. She wasn't in her quarters at the palace. Where was she? Isabella tried to shed the last layers of sleep, willing her mind to remember, but it was difficult to think of anything as she struggled to free herself. Who was doing this to her?

The last thing Isabella recalled was the ball. They had been dancing and then...the castle was overrun by the insurgence. Grand Master Jaques de Molay[2] had offered them protection at the Templar[3] Commandery.

*My God, are they here as well?*

Isabella's hand searched frantically for the dagger under her pillow—Etienne's dagger. Strong fingers wrapped around her wrist like a vice-grip, momentarily freeing her face. Isabella gasped for air, but it was choked off by a cloth forced inside her mouth, followed by a gag securing it tightly. Bile rose in Isabella's throat as she tasted the salty sweat from her captor's hands still lingering on the fabric.

An itchy bag was placed over Isabella's head, and her hands were bound. Her captor lifted Isabella from the bed and placed her on her feet.

"Walk," his soft voice requested. The gentleness of the stranger's voice was a drastic contrast to the actions he had taken.

Isabella reached for the leather of her captor's boot with her bare foot, and she slammed her heel down hard. Her captor's grip loosened, and Isabella ran blindly. A searing pain thundered across Isabella's head as she ran into the sharp corner of the mantle. Isabella's stomach rose into her throat as she fell backward, and the same hands that imprisoned her saved her from hitting the floor. Her captor lifted Isabella into his arms and cradled her. As Isabella's consciousness faded, she heard the rumble of stone moving, and the stale cool air of a tunnel kissed her face.

Isabella's eyelids felt like two lead weights as she forced them open. She raised her brow to help with the task. *A fire.* Her eyes drooped closed again. Isabella's eyes fluttered open again. *A man in a chair. A circular room.* Her hands gripped wood beneath her. *A chair.*

"Welcome back, Your Highness," a powerful voice said.

Isabella blinked a few times and raised her brow. As she did, a warm liquid ran down her forehead to her temple. She brought her fingers to it. *Blood.*

"Let me help you with that." The wooden chair creaked as the man rose.

Isabella closed her eyes again, their weight was too much. The sound of heavy boots approached, and a soft fabric gently blotted her forehead.

"Where am I?" Isabella managed.

"You are still in my commandery."

*My commandery?* Isabella forced her eyes open and was met by a Templar cross on a white mantel staring back at her. Her gaze moved up past a long gray beard to Jaques de Molay's face. The corners of Grand Master's mouth was turned up in a smile, which accentuated the deeply carved lines chiseled into his skin from both war and old age. Even though he smiled, his hazel eyes masked any true emotion.

A surge of adrenaline pumped through Isabella's body, and she slapped him.

Molay stepped back and rubbed his cheek.

Isabella's world came back into focus, and she caught a glimpse of herself in a decorative shield on the wall. Youth still hung around her face, but tonight she looked older than she ever had before. Her long hair was disheveled and parts were matted with blood. Her cheeks, which had been full since childhood, now revealed her mother's high cheekbones. Isabella's arms were strong, but she had lost some of the definition she had gained on the Camino[4]..

*My arms?* Realizing she was still in her night dress, Isabella frantically tried to cover herself. Molay unlatched his cape and handed it to her. Isabella snatched it from him and cocooned her body behind it.

"I suppose I deserved that. My apologies for bringing you here like this."

"You deserve much more than that! What were you thinking? Kidnapping?" Isabella stood, and the circular room with the fireplace spun. Molay caught Isabella and redirected her momentum back into the seat.

"It wasn't my intention to injure you. I needed to speak to you in private without anyone knowing."

"There are other ways to do that than kidnapping!"

"Yes, perhaps I will use different methods next time, but what is done is done, and we are running out of time. It will be morning soon, and I will need to get you back to your chambers." Molay tried to dab Isabella's forehead again, but she took the handkerchief.

"What is so important that you had to resort to kidnapping?"

"I wanted to talk to you someplace where others couldn't hear; for what I am going to say next would be considered treason." Molay's eyes locked with hers. "Isabella, I want you to kill your father." Molay intercepted Isabella's hand as she tried to slap him again. "He gave you these, didn't he?" Molay held open Isabella's palm and stared at the scars.

"That is none of your business." Isabella pulled free from his grasp and cradled her hand.

"If your father was that cruel to you—one of the people he loves most in the world—how do you think he would act if he ever got his hands on the treasure? You saw firsthand the destructive capabilities of what protects it. The treasure is even more powerful." Molay took a deep breath. "Isabella, if you do not kill your father, we will be forced to. The threat he poses is too great."

"If you think he is such a threat, why don't *you* kill him tonight?" Isabella crossed her arms and raised an eyebrow. She felt the blood trickling down her face again, but she didn't care.

"We do not want a war with France, nor the Pope[5]. Your father is the only one who poses a threat. If I were to kill King Philip[6] tonight as he sleeps in the safety of our halls, it would spark this war, and many lives will be lost. No matter how much I would like to do it—I can't take that risk. That is why I have brought you here, to propose an alternate option. An option where only one life is lost.

"Should you accept my offer, the Templars would support your claim to the throne. You would be the queen of France. You could marry Etienne. I know you love him and can never be with him. I also know he would die for you."

Isabella slumped in the chair. She couldn't kill her father, but Molay was right—he couldn't possess the treasure. If she did this, she wouldn't have to marry Edward. She would be free. She and Etienne could be together. Isabella rubbed the scars on her hands; she couldn't believe she was even considering the idea.

"What about my brothers?"

"They will be unharmed and won't pose a threat to your rule. We will make sure of that."

Isabella's father had asked her to get close to Molay. Was pretending to accept his task the way to do this?

Molay presented a small vial from his sporran and placed it in Isabella's hand. "I know you will make the right choice." He smiled and clasped her fingers around the poison.

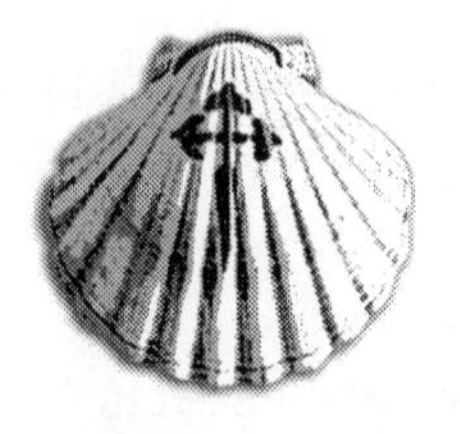

# CHAPTER 2

"She said my waking up to reality would lead others to do the same..."

Etienne listened intently as Mariano spoke, hoping that he would give him a clue as to what to do next. Etienne was in charge now. He needed to have a plan. They only had three days in Santiago de Compostela[7] to find the Templar treasure before they had to leave to rescue Sister Fransie's friends. The deranged priest had told Etienne that he was holding them captive in Hospital de Orbigo. He warned that he would start killing them one by one, unless Fransie gave him the secret message that Molay had given her to deliver to Etienne.

Etienne had promised Fransie that he would save her friends, and intended to keep it, but time was running out for him as well. He needed to find the treasure before King Philip made his move against the Templars. Molay was risking his life to buy Etienne more time.

"When you first entered the chapel, you said you knew the way home. What did you mean by this?" Etienne interrupted. He studied Mariano, whom he hadn't seen in months. His friend's Spanish skin had browned in the summer's sun, making him almost as dark as Etienne, and the worry lines had completely disappeared from his face. With his hair pulled back, Mariano's green eyes shone like emeralds that contained a reservoir of deep peace.

"I cannot tell you. I can only show you—as she did for me. It will take time."

"That is the one luxury we do not have. Much has happened since you left." Etienne kept his eyes on his companions. Everyone was there in the small alcove chapel of the great cathedral of Santiago de Compostela: Gerhart, Clair, Andy, Sister Fransie, and Gabriel; all gathered around Mariano.

"Don't worry, we are all in this together." Sister Fransie placed a reassuring hand on Etienne's shoulder.

"Aye, laddie, don't ya ken; we are a fellowship now." Andy winked at Etienne.

What an unlikely fellowship they were. Sister Fransie still wore her nun's habit even though she was pregnant. Granted, her child was conceived without a father and seemed to be connected with the Holy Grail, which was one of the seven keys to unlock the One True Treasure.

Fransie had brought Gabriel with her, a tall, brooding, tattooed Druid with a heavy forehead and the look of a prince. They both possessed True Senses, which to the best of Etienne's understanding meant that they could sense virtues and sins in a way that no other human could. This ability would be too much for them to bear, but they both had found an animal that acts as a filter. Rosalita, Fransie's mouse cleaned herself on Fransie's shoulder, and Sephira, Gabriel's dog, sat obediently at his side. This gift was difficult for them at times, but also a huge asset, as the seven keys that unlock the One True Treasure are guarded by the seven deadly sins.

Etienne smiled at Andy, Clair, and Gerhart. They were the closest thing he had ever had to a family. When he had first met Andy, he would have never guessed that the short, bald, stalky, Scotsman would become his best friend, nor that his sister, Clair, would become the matriarch of the group. She had a fire inside of her that Hell would be jealous of.

Gerhart the destroyer and Mariano the mercenary had come a long way from when they had first met as well. Gerhart had turned from a destroyer into a protector and the strength of their group. His sheer size led him to these roles, and Mariano had gone from swindling pilgrims on the Camino to this enlightened state. They had met them at the boathouse when the Shadows had first attacked. Etienne's blood went cold remembering the first of the Seven Deadly Sins they had faced.

"Etienne?" Fransie placed a hand on his arm.

"Sorry…" Etienne shook his head. "So, where do we start then?"

"Ya can start by telling us what you and my brother were doing down in that passage below the altar." Clair crossed her arms and shifted her gaze between Etienne and Andy.

"She is right," Fransie said, exchanging a nod with Clair. "As a fellowship, we should each have all of the information."

"Well, I was born in the wee town of Glasgow…" Clair's side glance stopped Andy mid-sentence. "What? I was just trying to lighten the mood."

"They are right, Andy," Etienne said. "We need to give them all of the information. Show them the papers and the code."

Andy reluctantly took the papers from his bag and spread them out on a pew.

"What is all of this?" Gabriel asked, leaning in for a closer inspection.

"There are two parts to finding the Templars' most valued treasure." Etienne took a deep breath. "The first is unlocking and overcoming the challenges of the seven doors. As we have come to discover, these trials are the Seven Deadly Sins. If you don't die from the challenge, you will receive a gift like this." Etienne patted the flaming sword. "We believe that these gifts are the keys to unlocking the One True Treasure—"

"And the second is this," Andy interrupted, motioning to the papers. "The Templars left a hidden code on the Camino de Santiago that leads to the location of their greatest treasure."

Gerhart scrunched his brow. "Why would they do that?"

"In case they were ever in a situation like the one we now face." Etienne looked gravely at the others. "The Templar line of succession has been interrupted, and Jaques de Molay, the only person who knows the location of the treasure, is trapped in Paris. I'm assuming this treasure is something too important to be lost to time forever."

"Ya don't have ta find it," Clair said, wrapping her arm around Gerhart. "We could all just forget that we ken of its existence."

"I would like nothing more," Etienne said, sincerely. "But, as you know, Isabella's father, King Philip, is searching for the treasure as well. If we were able to locate the hidden doors and overcome the trials that protect the Templars' greatest treasure, then so can he."

"Are you sure? I cannea see him overcoming the trials of the seven sins; that Acedia was a piece of work. She was like a spider that sucked the life out of ya." Andy shook as if he was trying to shed the memory of facing the deadly sin of Sloth in a physical form.

"Yes, I am sure. Philip's thirst for power will drive him, and he has a whole country of people at his disposal," Etienne said sternly. "And, the trials we have all faced will pale in comparison to the power of the One True Treasure. If it fell into the wrong hands, many lives would be lost. I can't take the chance of King Philip finding it."

"*Where five become one, here I lay under a field of stars, at the feet of the saints*," Gabriel read aloud. "I take it this is the riddle that leads to the treasure's location?" His tattoos raised as his forehead crinkled.

Etienne and Andy nodded in unison.

"I can see why you think it's here in the Cathedral of Santiago de Compostela," Gabriel continued.

"Why is that?" Etienne asked.

"It is believed the word Compostela comes from the Latin *campus stellae*, which translated means field of stars."

"Of course, we knew that." Andy crossed his arms defensively.

Etienne smiled at Andy's intellectual pride. They hadn't even thought of that.

"This still doesnea explain what you were doing in the passage below the altar," Clair said.

"'Tis obvious… *At the feet of the saints*." Andy shook his head.

"Last time I checked, Santiago[8] was only one saint," Fransie said gently. "Plus, why would you think his remains are down there?"

Andy shot Etienne a look, and everyone else followed his stare.

"I know he is." Etienne took a deep breath. He didn't like people to know about his personal spiritual life, but he had to tell them. "When we first came to this cathedral, Santiago appeared to me in that space below the altar. I know his remains are there."

Andy didn't expect everyone to come down into the passage below the altar, but it seemed all seven of them wanted to be treasure hunters now. He could barely breathe or see anything with everyone flitting about. The light from the staircases on either side of the passage helped aid the torchlight, but the others, especially Gerhart, kept blocking his light. How was he supposed to find anything under these conditions? Andy wasn't quite sure what they would find, but he wanted to be the one to find it. He didn't like that Gabriel had figured out the Latin for *field of stars*. He was supposed to be the smart one. Andy squinted one eye at Gabriel.

*Who does this guy think he is anyway with his tattoos and big shaggy dog?*

"Are you well?" Fransie asked, noticing his glare.

"Aye, I just 'ave something in my eye." Andy rubbed his eye and continued to push on random stones, hoping that one of them would lead to a secret passage.

"And what are you all doing down here?" A commanding voice filled the small passageway. Andy recognized Joseph, the Grand Master of the Knights of Saint James[9], descending the stairs.

"Joseph, I don't have time to pretend that we aren't searching for something," Etienne said. "It is of great importance that we find what is hidden down here. Can you help us?" Etienne stood tall as he made the request.

Andy had noticed a change in Etienne since he was made Seneschal of the Knights Templar. Andy didn't understand how a title could change him so much.

"Ask and it will be given to you; seek and you will find; knock and the door will be opened to you." Joseph smiled at Etienne then turned to where Andy was standing. "Excuse me."

"Ah, right." Andy removed his hand from the brick he had been pushing. The Grand Master knocked three times on it, and the stone recessed, setting off a chain reaction on the wall opposite where Andy was standing. Bricks turned and moved like a jigsaw puzzle coming apart, revealing a dark passage.

"You asked, you sought, but you forgot to knock." The Grand Master winked at Andy and took the torch off the wall.

Andy's blood boiled as they followed the Grand Master into the passageway. He knew he would have found the trigger for the door eventually.

"What is this?" Sister Fransie asked.

"Before the Knights of Saint James were formed, this cathedral was looted several times. These passageways were added so the priests could escape to a safe location with the most precious relics." The Grand Master took a torch from the wall. "Follow me."

Andy batted a spider web away from his face. "'Tis been a while since these have been used."

"It has. Not many people know of their existence. How did you know to search for them?"

"'Tis a long story, but in short—Saint James told Etienne."

"Andy!" Etienne hit Andy in the arm.

"Would you like to pay your respects?" the Grand Master asked.

"You mean he is really down here?" The bright excitement in Sister Fransie's voice cut through the darkness of the tunnel.

The Grand Master led them to a larger open space and lit a few other torches that lined the walls. In the middle of the room, a silver sarcophagus glinted back at them.

"Well, I'll be." Andy made the sign of the cross.

Both Etienne and Sister Fransie dropped to their knees in prayer. Andy placed a hand over his heart and bowed his head. But even in this sacred moment, he couldn't quiet his thoughts, nor his curiosity. His eyes scanned the room for any signs of a treasure or code.

"Is this all that's down here?" Andy asked after enough time had passed.

"What do you mean *is this all that's down here*? We are standing on holy ground. This is where Saint James, the disciple of Jesus, is buried." The Grand Master narrowed his gaze.

"I didna mean any offense. I just donna think 'tis what we are looking for. Where does that tunnel lead?"

"Etienne?" the Grand Master said.

"I'm sorry about my friend. I don't know why he is acting like this."

The Grand Master shook his head. "It leads to the place of safety."

"Do you mind if we—"

"I am not your tour guide." The Grand Master's sharp tone cut Andy's sentence in half. "If you want to continue on you can. I don't think the others have finished their prayers. You can't get lost. There is only one place it leads."

"Fine." Andy took a torch from the wall and walked down the tunnel by himself.

The passage was even dustier and cobwebby than the last. Andy held the torch in one hand and waved the other in front of him to clear the passage.

*"If you want to continue you can,"* Andy mimicked in the Grand Master's voice. He didn't realize it before, but he preferred figuring out the code alone. He had solved the hard part. The others were just standing on the shoulders of his work.

*That's it...you don't need them.* Andy wasn't sure if he had thought that or if the tunnel was whispering to him. He peeked over his shoulder, cautiously. The light from the room where the others were was gone. He was alone.

"Ach!" Andy screamed, brushing a spider off his head. Another set of legs crawled up his legs, then another on his arms, and soon his whole body was covered. He patted himself vigorously and dropped the torch, leaving himself in total darkness.

Andy was turned around; he had spun in circles batting off the little eight-legged beasties. A growl echoed up the chamber, and the hairs on Andy's arms stood on end. The sound was ferocious and closing in quickly.

"Spiderwebs be damned!" Andy ran in the opposite direction from the terrible noise, barreling down the tunnel. He kept one hand on the wall and the other outstretched in front of him. The sound was gaining quickly, but ahead there were pinpoint shafts of light coming from above.

Andy's hand knocked something metal—it was a rung of a ladder. Hand over hand, he climbed the ladder. Andy heard teeth snap below him as he continued upward. At the top, Andy pressed hard, moving a metal covering. He quickly covered the hole again, leaving the beast below. He lay on his back panting.

"Well, I'll be." High on the ceiling above was the Cross of Jerusalem[10]. The passage had led to San Fructuoso—the church where Andy had found the severed head.

# CHAPTER 3

Isabella awoke with her head throbbing. Not that she really had slept; her conversation with Molay had kept her up. She couldn't kill her father. There had to be another way. She studied the small vial of poison, which Molay had concealed in a necklace he had given her.

*I have to tell my father immediately.*

The fabric of Isabella's gown swished as she dressed. She fastened the corset, the best she could without help, and walked to the door. It creaked open, and Matilda almost fell through. She took one look at Isabella's dress and giggled uncontrollably.

"What happened to you? You look a mess," Matilda said, clearing the tears from laughter. "We can't let anyone see you like this."

Isabella turned toward the mirror and laughed a little. Her dress was unfastened and tucked in strange places; her hair was disheveled; and she had a small goose egg on her head from hitting it the night before. She looked more like a common prostitute than a princess. Her cousin, on the other hand, looked immaculate. Matilda's blue eyes shone on her porcelain skin, and her black hair was pulled back tightly.

"You are right, Matilda. I look ghastly. Will you help me?"

"That was just what I was coming to do. I'm happy I made it in time." Matilda produced a brush.

"Where did you find that in a Templar Commandery? Most of these men have more hair in their beards than on their heads." Isabella stopped Matilda's hand. "Please tell me that isn't a beard comb." Matilda and Isabella both burst out laughing.

"No, it is my spare. I never go anywhere without it." Matilda spun the comb in her hand.

Isabella sat and waited. "Well, are you going to help me or not?"

"Isabella, what happened to your head? I was so busy laughing at your dress, I didn't realize you were injured."

"I ran into something in the dark last night. I will need you to style my hair so it is covered. Can you do that?"

Matilda let out an unsatisfied sigh, and brushed Isabella's hair.

"I hate it here, Matilda."

"It is dull and could use a woman's touch. The only thing they decorate with is the Templar cross. They need to have more imagination." Matilda picked up the necklace with the poison and fastened it around Isabella's neck before she could protest. "I don't remember you wearing this last night—"

The door slammed open. "Leave us," Isabella's father commanded. His features were sharp and to the point just as his words were.

"As you command, Your Majesty." Matilda curtsied and left the room.

Philip closed the door and sat on Isabella's bed. "Daughter, join me." Philip patted the bed next to him. The light shining through the window made his auburn hair glow

Isabella clutched the necklace and sat next to her father. "Father, I have something—"

"It worked." A large smile crossed Philip's face. Isabella had never seen her father smile this widely before. "I have done my part, now it is time to do yours."

"What do you mean, Father? What worked?"

"My child, I raised you to be cunning. You disappoint me." Isabella's heart sank, and her mind raced to come up with the right answer.

"The attack on the palace last night...you orchestrated that?"

Philip nodded.

"But, why?"

"So we could be sitting in this very room. What do you see out that window?"

"I see the wall surrounding the Commandery, a courtyard... some Templars."

"You want to know what I saw out my window?"

Isabella nodded.

"I saw what time the guards on the wall changed shifts. I saw how many guards were stationed. I saw where their defenses were the weakest. I saw where the heaviest fortifications are. Now I need you to do your part. Did you gain the trust of Molay last night?"

"Father?" Isabella's heart skipped a beat. Did he know about the secret meeting?

"I had you dance at the ball. I wanted you to gain his trust. Did you succeed?" His tone was sharp and impatient. "What happened to your head?"

The corners of Isabella's mouth turned down. With those words, she realized her father hadn't even looked at her since he entered. He hadn't seen her. He hadn't listened to her. The small weight of the necklace pulled heavily on her.

"I fell out of bed." Why hadn't she told him? Was she considering what Molay had offered? "I have Molay's trust." Isabella's words felt like ice coming out of her mouth.

"Good, good. Now it is time for you to do your part. I want you to request that Molay show you his treasury. I need to know where it is. He will think that you are just a naive girl impressed with fancy things. You can convince him of this, right?"

"You know me, Father...I am just a shallow girl who likes shiny things." Isabella's words had a sharp edge that would have cut anyone, except her father, who was as oblivious to them as he was oblivious to her.

"There is nothing wrong with liking treasure. Soon, France will possess the most powerful treasure in the world; if you do your part. You would like that, wouldn't you, daughter?"

Isabella nodded.

"What a pretty necklace that is."

# CHAPTER 4

Etienne rushed down the dark tunnel, following Sephira's barking. How could have he let Andy go off by himself? He hoped the dog hadn't attacked Andy. The huge dog looked ferocious as it darted out of the chamber with its gray fur bristled.

"Andy, are you all right?" The echo of Etienne's voice was consumed by the barking of the dog.

"Sephira!" Gabriel yelled, but the dog continued to snarl and bark.

Ahead, pinpoint streams of light landed on Sephira. Her gnashing fangs were the size of a finger.

"Sephira!" Gabriel called. The dog whined. "Here! Now!" Gabriel ordered. The dog lowered her head and walked to Gabriel's side. He reached down to pet her. "What has gotten into you?" Gabriel turned to Etienne. "She has never behaved like this."

"I…" Fransie took some heaving breaths. She placed her hands on her knees. "I...have seen her act like that once before…" Fransie stood. "Gabriel, it was when Pride attacked you in Burgos."

"Andy!" Etienne stormed down the tunnel and quickly climbed the metal rungs. He couldn't lose his best friend, not now, not when they were so close. Etienne pushed the metal covering, but it was slammed right back down. Etienne pushed again, but the weight on top was too much.

"Andy!" Etienne yelled desperately.

"Etienne? 'Tis that you? Did you kill that monster?"

"Yes, it's me." The metal covering moved, and Andy helped Etienne up.

"Thank God you are all right." Etienne awkwardly hugged Andy.

"Did ya kill that beast?"

"That beast was Sephira."

"Well, did you kill her? The damn thing nearly ate me."

"She wasn't trying to hurt you—she was trying to protect you," Sister Fransie said, struggling to climb the rungs. Both Andy and Etienne reached down to help her out of the hole.

"Ya shouldnae be climbing in your condition, and that didnea feel like protection." Andy crossed his arms.

"Did anything happen to you in the tunnel before Sephira started barking?" Fransie asked.

"Well, some spiders were crawling on me, and I may have screamed like a wee lassie."

"Nothing else?" Etienne raised a questioning brow. He could tell when Andy was holding back.

Andy shook his head. "Just keep that animal away from me," he said to Fransie, then turned to Etienne. "Anyway, I 'ave something ta show you."

"What is it?" Etienne asked.

Andy smiled and pointed up; carved in the domed ceiling was the cross of Jerusalem. Etienne recognized the symbol with one large Templar cross surrounded by four smaller crosses immediately.

"So, it is the Cross of Jerusalem?"

"Don't you see, laddie? Where five become one. Five crosses all one. I found the severed head below this very symbol." Andy pointed to the ground directly below the image. "Here on the floor was a Flower of Life. I unlocked it, and now there is nothing—the symbol is gone. At the time, I thought I had found the one true treasure. Maybe it was down there with the head? Maybe I did something wrong? Fransie, do you sense anything in this church?"

A small mouse crawled to Fransie's shoulder and twitched its ears a few times then started cleaning itself. "I don't sense anything here. Etienne, what is the significance of the Cross of Jerusalem?" Fransie asked.

"It's the—" Etienne's jaw dropped, and his laughter filled the church. "Of course."

"Are ya gonna let us in on the joke, laddie?"

"Andy, it's the sigil for Castrojeriz. The treasure is there."

"Now, let's not jump ta any conclusions. Besides the sigil, why do you think 'tis there?"

"There are five Templar commanderies in the town. Why would a town so small need five Commanderies? There is only one Templar Commandery here in Santiago, which is at least ten times the size of Castrojeriz."

"*Where five become one, here I lay under a field of stars, at the feet of the saints.* Ya might be on ta something." Andy patted Etienne on the shoulder.

"We have to go back there anyway to collect the treasure from the door Isabella opened. I can't believe we will be returning to the place where… If Isabella hadn't shown up that day…" Etienne shook his head. "I never thought I would see Castrojeriz again."

"Well, what are we waiting for? Let's go save Fransie's friends," Andy said, a little too robustly.

# CHAPTER 5

The food in Isabella's mouth was almost as bad as the conversation she had just had with her father. She pretended like she was enjoying it, just like her father and Molay were pretending to be friends. This whole breakfast was a lie, and it turned Isabella's stomach. Before her Camino, Isabella had no problem lying. She didn't see the harm in it, but her pilgrimage taught her that one lie can cause the death of many lives—so many deaths hung on the edge of Isabella's lies.

The weight of the small necklace holding the poison pressed heavily on Isabella's chest. Molay had seen it the moment she entered the room and smiled broadly. If only he knew it wasn't her who placed it there. Isabella took another bite of the bland food and wished the breakfast would end quickly.

"That is a beautiful necklace, Your Highness." Isabella couldn't believe what she was hearing—Molay was gloating.

"The princess likes beautiful things. I'm surprised she hasn't said anything. Usually, when we visit a palace, Isabella asks to see its treasures. Isn't that right, daughter?"

"Actually, it is usually some young prince that wants to show off the size of his...wealth. And father, this is not a palace, and the

Grand Master is definitely not a young prince. I'm sure his wealth isn't very big, nor that exciting." The others at the table snickered at Isabella's remarks, but her words had no effect on Molay.

"You are right, Your Highness, I actually have no wealth. A Templar swears an oath of poverty, chastity, and obedience. I don't even own the clothes on my back, nor my sword. All that I am, and all that I once had, belongs to the Templars. It is the same with a monarch—isn't it so, Your Majesty? All that you have belongs to France?" King Philip tightened his grip on the table at Molay's remarks.

"Now you have made me curious, Grand Master," Isabella's words cut through the tension. "I would love to see what treasures have been turned over to the Templars by men like yourself. What a noble sacrifice."

Molay looked at Isabella's necklace once more. "As you wish; follow me." Molay stood and beckoned for the others to join him.

Isabella hadn't lied, but she was angry that she had resorted to manipulation. Both Molay and her father manipulated people, and she didn't want to be like either of them. She just wanted to be honest. She admired Etienne for his honesty. On the Camino, he had helped her to push away the veil of dishonesty. There was so much to Jesus's words. "the truth will set you free." She was free on the Camino—why had she left? Why had she come back to all of this? She had told herself it was to protect her friends and the treasure, but she hadn't been able to do either. It was all for nothing. Perhaps she would just leave again.

# CHAPTER 6

Andy sensed his head and cheeks flush. He was furious that Etienne had figured out the riddle. He was the one who did the hard part. How was he supposed to know the Cross of Jerusalem was the sigil for Castrojeriz?

"Andrew Sinclair! Don't ya ever scare me like that again." Clair climbed out of the hole into the church and squeezed Andy so tightly that he almost passed gas.

"'Tis all right, Clair. Ya can let go now. If ya squeeze any harder ya might regret it." Andy cocked an eyebrow, and Clair released her grip.

"Hee-haw." The bray of a donkey filled the church.

"Was that Blueberry? I'm surprised we can hear him all the way over here," Etienne said.

"Aye, I think 'twas. I cannea say I'm gonna miss that donkey. He was the most stubborn a… Clair, why are ya looking at us like that?"

"Blueberry is comin' with us."

"But, ya hate that donkey!" Andy said as another loud bray entered the chapel.

"I just couldnae leave him… We put the severed head inta Chelsea's cart ta bring ta the cathedral with our things. Plus...well, let's just say the cart and the head are one now."

"Does Chelsea know that you took Blueberry and the cart?" Etienne asked.

Clair shook her head.

"One of us will have to return Blueberry, and we can pay Chelsea for the cart." Etienne pulled out some coins from his sporran.

"Blueberry is commin' with us." Clair placed both hands on her hips. The donkey brayed loudly again, and Etienne and Andy exchanged a look.

"Clair, are you sure ya want ta take Blueberry?"

Clair narrowed her gaze at Andy, and he raised both hands.

"We will only take Blueberry if Chelsea will accept payment for him." Etienne took a few more coins from his sporran.

"Actually, we need ta pay Chelsea for the back rent we owe as well," Andy said. "She has been so good ta us. We canna steal her donkey and leave without paying her what's due."

Etienne shook the remaining coins from his sporran into his hand. "It's a good thing I am Seneschal now. The Templars can provide the money we need for our journey. Why don't you go, Andy? We are halfway between the cathedral and her house. Plus, I'm sure you would like to say goodbye."

Andy took the coins from Etienne and his whole face flushed. He avoided eye contact and hurried out of the chapel.

The crispness of autumn was in the air, and a sense of change was carried on the wind. Andy had often thought about leaving Santiago, but now that it was happening, he wasn't sure if he wanted to go. Life would be different after he left.

Andy gazed adoringly at the bar across the street from the church and thought of all of the evenings he and Etienne had spent inside. They weren't necessarily the happiest of memories, but they were his memories nonetheless.

"Goodbye, bar. Thank ya for all of the drinks." Andy waved as he passed.

In the sun the air was warm, but the moment Andy stepped foot into the shade of the buildings, the warmth melted away. There was no doubt summer had passed.

The creases on Andy's forehead softened, and he inhaled deeply. Andy finally had a moment to himself. The others were so ungrateful for the work he had done on the code. They all just waltzed in and figured out the easy things. How was he to know that the sigil for Castrojeriz was the Cross of Jerusalem?

*What is going on with me?*

Andy shook his head and changed his thoughts to what he would say to Chelsea. He would miss her more than Santiago. He had loved her from the moment he saw her, and she had no idea how he felt. He always seemed to be running away from her. This would be his last chance to tell her his feelings.

Andy licked his thumb and index finger and then tried to flatten his eyebrows. He always had one rogue eyebrow hair, and he wanted to tame it before saying goodbye. He breathed into his hand and smelled his breath and cringed at the odor as he walked up the small alley leading to Chelsea's front door.

"Ach, 'tis terrible." He picked some mint to chew on. "That should do the trick." Andy wasn't going to run away this time. He may never have another chance.

On the landing, Andy straightened his cloak and knocked on the door. It was answered by a tall, handsome man with blond curly hair and spectacles.

"Who are you?" Andy asked, looking the stranger up and down.

"I could ask you the same thing." The stranger stared down his nose at Andy.

"I live here...well, I lived here," Andy said.

"So did—*do* I." The corners of the stranger's mouth raised. Something about his smile was familiar to Andy.

"Oh, Tyler, get out of the way. It's just Andy," Chelsea said from inside the house. The pixy of a woman, with the kindest smile Andy had ever known, pushed her way past the stranger. "Andy, I would like for you to meet my brother Tyler. He has just returned from university. I know the two of you will have much to talk about over dinner tonight."

"Brother?" Andy thanked God Tyler was her brother. "'Tis nice ta meet you."

"Nice to meet you too. I have heard a lot about you and your friends… Although you look a little different than I expected."

"That's enough, Tyler." Chelsea and Tyler exchanged a smile.

"Chelsea, 'bout dinner. We won't be able ta come."

"That's fine. Tyler will be living here now. His studies are over. You will have plenty of time to get to know each other."

Andy lowered his head. "See the thing is...there won't be any more dinners. We are leaving." Andy's face scrunched, and his heart dropped. Those words were so hard to say.

"What do you mean? You can't go."

"It's not that we want ta, but that we have ta."

Chelsea's body drooped like a flower on a cold day. "You don't have to do anything, Andy. There is always another option."

"I'm afraid in this situation, there isn't."

Tyler cleared his throat. "Andy, it was nice to meet you. I will let you two say goodbye."

"Nice ta meet ya too."

Tyler disappeared inside, and Andy raised his eyes to meet Chelsea's. Even with her sad features, Chelsea's eyes sparkled like rays of light playing on the ocean. He held out his hand with the coins.

"I came here ta say goodbye and pay ya what we owe ya."

Chelsea shook her head and clasped her hands around Andy's.

"Andy, there is something I have been wanting to tell you."

"There is?" Andy's hands fidgeted. Chelsea bit her lip and nodded. "I 'ave something ta tell ya as well, but ladies first."

Chelsea took a step closer drawing Andy in with her eyes. "Andy...thank you for saving my life."

"What?" Andy's shoulders slumped.

"I remember everything. Had you not gotten rid of Acedia, she would have killed me. I felt it and knew it for sure. There wasn't anything I could do. But, you saved me, and I have wanted to thank you ever since."

"You're welcome. Acedia was a nasty piece of work." Andy pretended he was grateful for her words, but he was hollow inside.

"What was it you have to tell me?"

"Well, it seems kind of silly now. But...I may never see ya again..."

"Don't say that." Chelsea smiled kindly at him.

"I love you." The words just came right out of Andy's mouth. "Andrew Sinclare, you idiot." Andy shook his head. "Well, now that the cat is out of the bag... Chelsea, I have loved ya since I first came here. See, that's why I always tried ta avoid ya. I was often too ashamed ta even look at ya. I mean, what could you ever see in a—"

Chelsea's lips cut off Andy's words. They felt like two down pillows gently pressed against his mouth. Andy's knees wobbled, then his legs completely gave out.

"Andy! Andy! Are you all right?" Chelsea said, standing over him.

"Aye, 'tis the best day of my life."

"Here let me help you pick these up." Chelsea bent down and collected the coins that had fallen out of Andy's hands. "This is too much for what you owe, Andy."

"Aye, well, ya see...Clair wants ta take Blueberry."

"You want to take my donkey?"

"I know, I donnae ken what Clair is thinking. He is a miserable beast."

"It's true, but don't talk about him like that. This is a tough situation." Chelsea lay next to Andy on the ground and they both stared at the sky. "I'll tell you what. I'll let you take Blueberry on one condition."

Andy propped himself up on his elbow. "And what is that?"

"That you promise to bring him back here to me yourself."

# CHAPTER 7

Isabella stared at the necklace on her nightstand as she sunk deeper into her covers. The weight of the blanket shielded her from the plight that this simple piece of jewelry had brought upon her. She couldn't kill her father, but she also couldn't let him possess the Templars' secret treasure.

Isabella picked up the necklace and took out the vial. It was amazing that something so small could do so much damage. The door swung open. Isabella fumbled with the necklace, but she couldn't get the small vial back inside, so she concealed it in her fist.

"I didn't know that opened," Matilda said as she barged into the room, followed by a maid servant. "Actually, I have never seen that necklace before yesterday. Where did you get it?"

"How many times do I have to tell you to knock before you enter? I am your princess."

"Apologies, Your Highness." Matilda and the maid curtsied in unison. "I bet Etienne gave that to you and that's why you have kept it secret from me. Can I see it?"

"If you weren't like a sister to me, I would have you punished."

"But, I am like a sister to you."

Isabella shook her head and handed over the necklace. "You know, Matilda, one of these days your curiosity will get you killed."

"What do you keep inside?"

Isabella slipped the vial of poison under her pillow as Matilda fiddled with the hinge.

"Matilda, there are some things I can't even tell you." Isabella held out her hand, and Matilda returned the necklace. "What are you doing here anyway?"

"Your father sent me. He has a surprise for you."

"No need to do that now!" Isabella chastised the servant for straightening the bed. She couldn't let the vial be discovered. "One thing I learned on the Camino is that we are all equal. If my father has a surprise for me, we should all go enjoy it. You will accompany us..."

"My name is Floure, Your Highness," responded the mousy maid servant as she curtsied.

# CHAPTER 8

"Sir Richard, Sir David, what are you doing here?"

"Your Highness." Both knights from England bowed at the entrance to the throne room. Sir David was broad shouldered with sandy blond hair, and Sir Richard was tall and barrel chested.

"Or should we call you, Your Majesty," Sir David smiled at her, coyly. "We were just discussing your marriage arrangements with your father. All seems to be in order. I believe you will be a great match for our Prince Edward. Perhaps your lady will be joining you as well." His full attention turned to Matilda, and Isabella felt the animal magnetism of his eyes pulling her in.

"Perhaps," Isabella said, demurely.

"I do hope so." Sir David kept his eyes on Matilda.

"You must excuse me. One doesn't keep my father waiting."

"We will keep your companions entertained while you speak to your father," Sir Richard said, raising an eyebrow at Floure, the handmaid who had accompanied Isabella and Matilda.

"You're right, one doesn't keep your father waiting, Your Highness." Matilda gave Isabella a look urging her into the throneroom.

"Very well. I shan't be long. Matilda, remember, you are a Lady of the French Court." Matilda smiled and nodded.

Isabella shook her head and entered the throne room. The last time she had been in here, Etienne's mother had held a knife to her throat. Marble pillars lined the walk from the door to the throne where her father sat raised above the world. Light gently streamed in through the windows and landed softly on Isabella's face.

Isabella stopped in front of the throne and curtsied. "Your Majesty."

"You may rise, daughter. You have done well." Her father's eyes revealed a momentary glint of kindness.

"Thank you, Your Majesty—" Philip held up his hand, stopping Isabella before she could continue.

"You may call me Father." These words fed her need for her father's approval and a warmth grew inside her.

"Thank you, Father." The word glided out of Isabella's mouth. "What do you mean, I have done well?"

"The way you handled Molay was superb. You found that pride was his weakness, and you played it excellently, just as I have."

"What do you mean?" Isabella asked, even though she knew of her father's plans and had been the one to warn Molay about them.

"Of course, I shouldn't expect you to have figured it out."

"You mean your plan to keep the Templars here under the false pretenses of a crusade?" The words slipped right out of Isabella's mouth. She wanted to show her father she was intelligent. She wanted that warm feeling that his praise gave her.

"Who told you?" Philip gripped the arms of his throne tightly.

"No one, Father." Isabella needed to think quickly. It was never a good sign when her father gripped the throne. "I figured it out on my own. When I returned to Paris, the captain of our ship told me Molay was here for that reason, and that extra guards were stationed at all entrances to the city. I quickly figured out the guards weren't stationed there to fight off a threat; they were stationed there to keep Molay in."

Philip loosened his grip, and the blood returned to his white knuckles. Isabella's body exhaled at the sight.

"Very good. Truly, you are your father's daughter. If only your brothers were as smart."

"Speaking of brothers, I haven't seen Charles since my return. Where is he?"

"I sent Charles to the Camino to accomplish the quest I sent you on. But, he is failing just as miserably. However, he found your Etienne and killed him."

Isabella's whole body went numb. He couldn't be dead. Surely her father was lying. Isabella tried as hard as she could to not betray any emotion.

"Good, I see this news doesn't affect you. I knew some time in the palace would cure you of that childish love." Each of her father's words cut into Isabella's heart.

"Yes, it has, Father." Isabella stared out through vacant eyes.

"This will make your marriage to Prince Edward much easier. Thanks to your manipulation yesterday, Charles has more time to accomplish his task. I had heard a rumor that Molay had discovered my plan and was evacuating the Templars and their treasure. As we saw yesterday, this rumor was false. Molay and all of the Templar treasure is still here in Paris. I have prepared a surprise in the courtyard to thank you for getting Molay to show us his vaults. Take Lady Matilda and enjoy picking out the fabric for your wedding dress. You are dismissed."

Isabella forced a curtsy. Her body left the throne room, but her true self was frozen in the moment before her father had told her of Etienne's death. It was only a shell of Isabella leaving the throne room—empty and hollow.

# CHAPTER 9

Etienne sat in meditation and prayer on a pew in front of the ornately decorated altar in the Cathedral. It was the first time in as long as he could remember that he had done his morning routine. What once was habitual had now become foreign to him. Seeing the tomb of Saint James had awoken something inside him. He wanted to be connected to the spiritual part of himself once more. His morning routine had been that bridge. It had connected him to the most important thing in his life—God—and it focused him for the day ahead. He had become so lost, but now, he couldn't be lost anymore. He needed to lead the others. They were leaving the protection of Santiago today. This was his first true test as a leader, and he wasn't ready for it.

"You look like something is bothering you." Grand Master Joseph said, sitting next to him.

"It's that obvious?" Etienne raised his eyebrows, and Joseph nodded.

"What's on your mind?"

Etienne scanned the room. Out of all the people in the cathedral, Joseph would understand his feeling. "I'm not ready to be a leader."

Joseph placed a hand on Etienne's shoulder. "None of us are, but for some reason, we are chosen. I know that you can follow orders—that is one key aspect to leading. But, do you know how to dance?"

"Dance?"

"Yes, there are many similarities between being an excellent dancer and an excellent leader. I see by the look on your face you don't believe me."

"I just can't see how being good at ballet could make you a good leader?"

"I'm not talking about ballet—I'm talking about partner dancing. In partner dance, there are leaders and followers, just like in life. In both, I never ask my followers to go where I am not willing to go first. In dance, I initiate the movement and ask my partner to follow. I then lead with precision and clarity, not with strength. When I was a young man, I used to swing the girls around with my brute strength. Sometimes they enjoyed it, but eventually, they got hurt. I soon learned that I didn't need to use force. If I was precise with the movement and clear with the direction, they would move as if a breath of wind was pushing them. It was almost as if it was their idea. It is the same with leading; you have to be precise with your directions and clear with your why, and soon your followers will believe it is their idea. Lastly, in dance, I always lead my movement from my core."

Joseph tapped his abdomen. "Your partner will feel a difference in movement lead from your core versus lead from your arms flailing around. It is the same when leading in life—move from the core of who and what you are, and others will follow. I am happy to see you are connecting with the core of who you are again."

Joseph's eyes glowed like Santiago's eyes had.

"Are you—"

"One last thing—make sure everyone else is fed before you eat, that they are rested before you rest, and that you follow your followers." Joseph placed a hand on Etienne's shoulder again.

"Aghh!" Etienne lurched back into the pew. Instead of Joseph's hand on his shoulder, he saw Andy with a confused expression on his face.

"Sorry, laddie. I didnea mean ta scare you. Everything is sorted with Chelsea. We can take Blueberry and the wagon. Everything is packed and ready ta go when you are."

"Have you eaten?" Etienne asked, heeding Joseph's last words.

"Actually," Andy placed both hands on his belly. "I was just thinking about a small meal before we left."

"Perfect. Gather the others and let's feast before we depart."

# CHAPTER 10

Isabella entered the courtyard with Matilda on her arm. It was lined with merchants' wagons with fabrics strewn between them. It was a kaleidoscope of colors and life, which was the antithesis of what Isabella felt. Matilda didn't know it, but she was Isabella's life support system—the only thing holding her up.

"Look at all of these fabrics, Isabella. I could burst with excitement! Of course, your father would order the very best for your wedding."

Isabella's legs went weak. "Matilda, I must sit for a moment."

"You do look pale; what did your father say to you?" Matilda asked as they found a bench. "Or is it because you are picking out fabric for your wedding dress? I know you love Etienne, but—"

Isabella pushed off of the bench with all of her strength and ran.

"Isabella!"

Tears blurred Isabella's vision as she darted between the wagons. She didn't want anyone to see her. Her father couldn't know that she was crumbling inside. Her forward momentum was the only thing stopping her from collapsing on the ground.

Isabella tore through a hanging fabric and ran straight into someone. They both nearly toppled.

"How dare you stop your princess!" Isabella demanded.

"This is not my land, nor you my princess, but you are my dear friend."

"Katsuji!" Isabella cried, wrapping her arms around her friend from the Camino de Santiago. Isabella's body heaved with tears.

Katsuji pulled down the hanging fabric and wrapped it around Isabella.

"Come, we have to get you inside my coach before anyone sees you."

Isabella didn't know if she was dreaming. She had first met Katsuji and his caravan at Santa Ana, where she had met Sister Caroline and Sister Fransie. The last time she had seen him, he was recovering from his injuries at the Templar castle in Ponferrada—the injuries he had sustained while saving her and her friends.

Katsuji ushered Isabella into the same wagon they had ridden in as they crossed the Meseta. She hugged him tightly and wept. Katsuji remained silent, his arms wrapped around her. She didn't have to explain anything. She could just be, and that was all she needed at the moment.

"He's...he's dead." Isabella tried to choke back her tears, but it did no good.

Katsuji remained silent and continued to be present.

"Are you really here?" Isabella asked.

Katsuji nodded.

"I'm sorry." Isabella nodded to the wet splotches her tears had left on his tunic.

"No need to apologize." Katsuji took a piece of fabric and tied it to one side of the wagon and then to the ceiling. "Do you mind?" He handed Isabella another piece of fabric and nodded for her to fasten it. "When I was young, I used to make forts from my blankets when I was upset. Being inside always made me feel better. I was safe inside, and the world outside ceased to exist. I welcome you to join me in making our fort."

Isabella accepted the strange invitation and together they made an acceptable fort from the fabrics. The task took Isabella's mind off of Etienne for a few moments. When they finished, they sat across from each other on pillows inside the creation.

"Now, tell me, how is that?"

"Cozy," Isabella responded.

"It is safe here to speak. The world outside does not exist."

Isabella appreciated the safe space they had created. It was true, inside the fort, she wasn't trapped at the palace, but back on the Camino with her friends. She imagined Etienne passing by the window at any moment and reveled in this bliss.

"Katsuji, he is dead… Etienne is dead!" Sorrow welled inside Isabella.

Katsuji waited patiently until Isabella continued.

"My father just told me my brother has killed Etienne."

"And you know this for sure? Things are not always as they appear."

His words struck Isabella. She hadn't for a moment considered that her father had been lying.

"You're right! I don't know for sure! My father told me once before that Etienne was dead, and it was a lie." Isabella's mind reeled. The emotions of sadness, anger, and hope all mixed into a hurricane inside her.

Reading her eyes, Katsuji said, "This fort can protect you from the storms out there, but not the storms inside."

"There is only one way to know for sure. I must leave and try to find him myself. There is nothing here for me now. The only reason I came back was to try to convince my father—" Isabella stopped herself. She wasn't sure how much Katsuji knew about the treasure. "To convince my father to stop searching for something, and I have failed. Katsuji, you must help me to escape the castle."

# CHAPTER 11

"Did you sense it?" Gabriel asked Fransie as she rode Cash. "In the tunnel?" His eyes met hers from below the horse.

"I heard something faintly. But Andy said nothing else happened to him down there. He thought Sephira was a beast trying to kill him." Fransie repositioned herself in the saddle. It was hard to get comfortable with her pregnant belly.

"Sephira was just trying to protect him. Pride was in that tunnel with him. I know it. Sephira got close enough for her to smell it."

"Are you sure? I don't want to scare anyone unless it is absolutely necessary. If she was down there with him, why would he lie about it?"

"Maybe he doesn't know it was her. You didn't know in Burgos. You thought she was me."

"True, we must speak to him about it. We should speak to all of them about it."

Gabriel nodded. "There is one other thing that is troubling me. I don't sense anything coming off of that man."

"You mean Mariano?"

"Yes. I don't know if it is the same for you, but usually, I sense a low level of either a sin or a virtue coming off everyone I have ever encountered—except him."

"This all is still new to me, and I don't have the experience you do—but no, I don't sense anything from Mariano. It is as if he is nothing or a part of everything."

Thunder rolled across the sky, and the clouds opened up. Fransie pulled her hood over her head. The rain brought the smell of the eucalyptus and earth up to her perch on Cash's back. The horse shook his mane, sending little droplets of water in all directions.

"We need to find shelter!" Etienne yelled from ahead.

"I know a place. Follow me," Mariano responded.

They veered off the Camino and followed a little stream upriver. The trees grew narrower and Fransie touched the multi-colored bark as she passed. The dry parts felt like paper; it had the same chalky dryness.

"Over here!" Mariano shouted as the sky rumbled. From her position above, Fransie could see the trees open up onto a rock outcropping with a tunnel, into the hill, wide enough for her to ride into.

Gabriel helped Fransie dismount. It was becoming more and more uncomfortable to move. Her feet were swollen and her back hurt. But, it was all worth it. She cradled her belly.

"Gabriel, feel right here." She took his hand and placed it to the left of her belly button. "Did you feel it kick?" Gabriel smiled at her and nodded.

"Come on, Blueberry. Let's get you inside too." Gerhart unlatched the donkey from the cart and tugged on the reins. Blueberry brayed loudly and shook his head obstinately.

"'Tis alright, Blueberry." Clair moved a hand to pet him, but the donkey snapped at her. Andy laughed robustly, and Clair stared him down.

"What? 'Twas your idea ta bring him." Andy started whistling and followed Mariano and Etienne into the cave.

Gerhart gave the donkey one more tug and looked at Clair pleadingly.

"Fine, tie him up out here." Gerhart tied Blueberry to a tree and joined them at the mouth of the cave. He took off his cape and wrung it out with his massive hands.

Fransie walked to the small fire they had started in the middle of the enormous cavern. As her eyes adjusted, she saw hundreds of cave paintings, and her mouth gaped.

"What is this place?" Fransie asked

"My prison and my salvation." Mariano's eyes shone brightly.

"What are you talking about, my old friend?" Gerhart put his large hand on Mariano's shoulder. "This is no prison."

"The only prison was in my mind." Mariano patted Gerhart's hand. "I took it with me everywhere I went. This place is where I broke free of all the thoughts that were keeping me trapped. I died in here and woke up to reality." Gerhart tentatively removed his hand, and Mariano let out a laugh that reverberated throughout the cave.

Fransie's eyes met Gabriel's and saw that he was having the same thought; if Mariano was dead, that explained why they sensed nothing coming off of him.

"My body didn't die, only my beliefs about reality. The Alchemist gave me a system that set her free. It is called *The Work.*[11]"

"I donnae ken what type of work she gave you, but if I can be at peace like you; I will take two helpings of it." Andy warmed his hands by the fire.

"It is actually really simple. It is just four questions and a turnaround."

"What is a turnaround?" Andy rubbed his chin as he paid close attention.

Fransie didn't know if she should listen or not. Was this *work* blasphemy? Did it go against the church and belief in Jesus Christ?

"Jesus is the way to salvation," Gabriel said, almost reading Fransie's mind. "If the message you are about to preach goes against that, I would rather wait in the rain."

"What I am about to say doesn't go against the church, nor that belief. If anything, it will bring you closer to God, closer to the way things were before man fell from Eden. The way things were before we started to believe the lie that most people call reality."

"Very well."

Gabriel made a clicking noise, and Cash lay down by the fire. He took Fransie by the arm and helped her to sit with her back against the horse. The heat coming off him and his rhythmic breathing created a soothing feeling.

"I need ta try that trick with Blueberry," Clair said as she sat. Everyone else followed suit, and soon all sat comfortably around the fire.

"How many of you have ever had the thought 'I'm not good enough?'" Mariano asked.

Andy's hand shot up in the air. He turned to the others and raised his eyebrows. "I ken I'm not the only one." Slowly, everyone else raised their hands.

"And how many of you have ever had the thought 'I don't belong?'" Everyone kept their hands raised. "Thoughts like these have been passed down from generation to generation since the fall from Eden. The world and everyone in it suffers because they believe these thoughts that aren't true."

"What are you talking about? Those thoughts are true," Gabriel said, positioning himself cross-legged.

"When was the last time you had the thought 'I don't belong?'"

"Right now." Gabriel's eyes scanned the cave and rested on Etienne.

Fransie's heart sank. "You don't really feel that way, do you?"

"I feel that I belong with you." Gabriel nodded at Fransie. "But I don't feel that Etienne has ever accepted me."

Etienne's body went rigid across the fire. How could Fransie not know Gabriel was feeling this way? He had been so good to her, but he was carrying this burden feeling like he didn't belong.

"This is perfect!" Mariano said, joyfully. "So, 'Etienne thinks I don't belong,' is the thought that has been causing you to suffer?"

Gabriel nodded and stared at the fire. Fransie wished she could comfort her friend. She took his hand and patted it.

"The first question is: Is it true?"

"Yes. It is true. The way he acts towards me proves it again and again—"

"I forgot to mention the first two questions are just a simple yes or no. Anything else is just a thought fighting for its survival."

"Yes." Gabriel continued to stare at the fire blankly.

"Very well, that leads us to the second question: can you absolutely know it's true beyond a doubt?"

Gabriel laid one palm on top of the other in his lap and took a moment. "I suppose there is no way I could know beyond a doubt that that is what he thinks. I have never asked him." Gabriel looked directly at Etienne.

"How do you react when you think that thought?"

Gabriel focused back on Mariano.

"I give Etienne the cold shoulder, I avoid him, I close up, I feel unwanted, and I get angry. I also don't connect with the others. I want to leave with Fransie. I feel a hollowness inside me and a longing to belong."

Fransie touched Gabriel's arm with sympathetic eyes. How could she have been so blind to his feelings? Perhaps he had mentioned it; had she just ignored it?

"It must be very painful for you to believe that thought."

Gabriel nodded again.

"That brings us to question number four. Who would you be without that thought?"

Gabriel shifted his gaze from Fransie to Mariano with questioning eyebrows.

"What if there was no way for you to think the thought: 'I don't belong here.' Who would you be in this moment?" Mariano elaborated.

"If there was no way I could think that thought…" Gabriel took a large breath. "I would be at peace. I would feel like I belonged—like I had friends. I would be happy."

"Can you think of any sane reason to keep the thought 'Etienne thinks I don't belong here?' When you believe that thought you are closed off, alone, angry, and don't do the one thing that you long most for—connecting with the others. Without that thought, you would feel like you belonged. It is only this thought that is stopping you from belonging, not Etienne. That brings us to the turnaround. Now, we turn the statement around to the opposite, the other, and the self."

"I think you'll have ta explain that one more," Andy said.

"Let's turn the original statement around to the opposite first. Gabriel, what is the opposite of 'Etienne thinks I don't belong here?'"

Gabriel scrunched his forehead. "Etienne thinks I do belong here."

"Yes, very good. 'Etienne thinks I do belong here.' Can you give me three examples of how this is as true—or truer—than the original statement?"

"The obvious one is I am here." Gabriel switched which hand was on top. "Etienne could have told me to stay in Santiago." Gabriel shifted his gaze to Etienne. "Etienne had me take the oath along with the others." Gabriel shook his head and chuckled.

"Let's keep going," Mariano said. "Turn it to the *other*. In this case, the *other* would be Etienne."

"I don't quite get that."

"*Etienne thinks I don't belong here,* becomes: *I don't think Etienne belongs here.* Can you give me three examples of how that statement could be as true, or truer?"

"That one hurts. I have thought that one many times. I have thought that I would be accepted if Etienne would disappear. I have thought about leaving with just Fransie. Etienne…" They locked eyes across the fire. "...I'm sorry." Etienne smiled and nodded at Gabriel.

"It is amazing what happens when these thoughts unravel themselves and you see them for what they are. Let's move to the last turn around. the self," Mariano said.

"I think I don't belong here..." Gabriel looked around the fire at each of them and rested his gaze on Fransie. "I have been telling myself that I don't belong here. That is so much truer than the original statement. All of you have been so accepting and kind to me, and I have just been closed off, ready to leave." A large smile spread across Gabriel's face.

"Can you see how untrue your original statement was?" Gabriel nodded. "It would be insane to believe the thought, *I don't belong here,* because you are here. The reality of the situation is that you are here. To believe you belong anywhere else only causes an internal war. If you were meant to be somewhere else, you would be there."

"I am happy you are here, Gabriel." Fransie took his arm and rested her head on his shoulder.

"So am I."

## CHAPTER 12

Andy sat at the entrance of the cave under a rock out-cropping and played with a small pebble. It was his turn to keep watch as the others slept. He thought it was pointless to keep watch; their plan had worked. Etienne had ordered a decoy caravan to leave Santiago with a heavy Templar guard. The Hospitallers had taken the bait and followed the caravan toward Finisterre. It was a good plan—of course it was, he had come up with it—but Etienne had gotten the credit. Andy threw the pebble and it landed perfectly in a small hole in a tree stump.

"Bullseye! You still have it, Andy Sinclare," he murmured.

*Andrew Sinclare.*

Andy shook his head; did he hear that? Or think it? Why would he repeat his name? Andy started to feel claustrophobic, just as he had in the tunnels below Santiago. He pulled back his hand sharply as something crawled over it. Andy stood so abruptly, he almost hit his head on the rocks. Where his hand had been was a centipede with all of its legs scurrying. Andy wondered what he ate; for no reason, he tasted bile in his mouth.

*Andrew, I called you in the tunnel. I showed you how to find the treasure.*

"Is that you, creepy head?" Andy peered warily at the wagon, where the severed heads lay hidden. Thoughts were entering his mind that were not his own. But, it wasn't like before when the head told him how to defeat Acedia. This was different.

*You are the chosen one.*

"Who are you?"

*Do you not know my voice? I have been guiding you the whole time. I am every intuition you have had, every right path you took. I have put everything into action for you to end up at this spot. You are the chosen one, not them. Why does Etienne still carry the shard of the cross that you earned?*

"How do ya ken about that?"

*I led you to Charity.*

The taste in Andy's mouth continued to worsen. Andy screamed as he felt one hundred tiny legs crawling up his pants. He shook his leg vigorously and fell backward. It was worth the pain of the fall; the little beastie scurried away with all of its legs.

*The shard of the cross is yours, the Grail is yours, the head is yours, the flaming sword is yours. You must take them and step into the destiny that is yours.*

"You are right. It is my destiny. I was given the cross. I figured out the codes. I am meant to find the Prisca Sapientia[12], the ancient wisdom God gave to Adam and Moses. I have felt it in my jibblies since I was young."

Andy brushed himself off and formed a plan. The cart would be easy enough to take. Blueberry liked him. Andy always used the carrot method over the rod. All he had to do now was get the shard of the cross, the sword, and the Grail.

*The sword and the shard should be easy to get,* he mused. He had shared a room with Etienne, and knew his sleeping patterns perfectly. Andy chuckled, Etienne thought he slept like a cat ready to pounce at any moment. But the truth of it is, Etienne could sleep through anything. *Right, I'll start with him first then grab the Grail[12] and make my getaway.*

Despite his size, Andy had always been light on his feet. He attributed it to all of the dance lessons he had taken when he was young. He quietly darted to and fro through the cave as if he was doing the Ghillie Callum. He bent down over Etienne, unnoticed, and took the small shard from his sporran. Andy quickly put it inside his own and looked around to make sure no one had seen. He unlatched Etienne's grip around the sword, one finger at a time. Etienne stirred momentarily and rolled on his side. Andy smiled at his friend sleeping like a baby.

Andy tiptoed to Cash, Fransie, and Gabriel. He loosened the straps of the saddlebags.

*That's it. It is meant for—*

Snarling and gnashing teeth meet Andy's face, and paws scratched his chest. Andy stumbled backward, and Sephira pinned him against the wall.

"Sephira!" Gabriel commanded. The dog snapped its jowls one more time and sat obediently at Gabriel's side.

"What are you doing, Andy, and why do you have my sword?" Etienne asked.

"I grabbed it to protect myself from that thing." Andy pointed at the dog. "I was coming in to wake Gabriel for his watch, and she nearly bit my head off." Andy grabbed his chest to slow his heart.

Etienne was right though—what was he doing? Why had he taken these treasures and tried to leave the others? What had gotten into him? One thing was a relief though, the awful taste had left Andy's mouth.

"Give me the sword," Etienne demanded.

Andy cocked an eyebrow at Gabriel. "Are ya sure 'tis safe?"

"I don't know what has gotten into her. I will keep her on a leash when we sleep."

Andy handed the sword to Etienne. "Do ya still believe she wasnea trying ta kill me in that tunnel?"

# CHAPTER 13

Isabella warmed her hands by the fire in her quarters. The evenings had turned cold, and the humidity from the rivers added an extra bite that penetrated deep into Isabella's bones. She would miss this semicircular room with the best view of Paris. After dinner, she had packed a few things, but she still couldn't do this on her own. She would need help. There was only one person she could turn to. Isabella pulled the fur blanket tightly around her and poked her head out of her door.

"Fetch me Lady Matilda," Isabella ordered a servant as she passed. The servant curtsied and scurried away.

Isabella sat at her nightstand and unfastened her necklace. *I am done.* Isabella slammed the necklace down hard, hoping that the force would shatter the vial inside. Seeing no liquid, Isabella began to open the necklace, but the door opened first.

"Your Highness, you summoned me?" Matilda said.

"Close the door."

"Isabella, what has gotten into you?" Matilda said, as soon as they were out of earshot of anyone. "Is all well? You ran away in tears and have been avoiding me all evening. Did I do something to displease you?"

It was true she had avoided Matilda, but only because she needed to pack. She loved her cousin, and she was the only one she could trust in the castle—even with all of her faults and flirtations.

"Matilda, I need your help."

"I would be happy to help you into your nightclothes," Matilda said, unfastening Isabella's corset. Isabella stopped her hand and led her to the bed.

"No, I need your help with something else."

"Isabella, you have that look in your eyes."

"What look?"

"The look that tells me you are going to ask me something I will regret."

Isabella cracked a smile. Her cousin knew her too well.

"The task will be easy. I promise."

"What is it?"

"I need you to pretend you are me for a few days."

"What! No one would mistake me for you."

"No one will see you."

Matilda held her hand to Isabella's forehead. "Are you running a fever? You are talking as someone who is delusional."

Isabella removed her hand and patted it.

"I am well. Matilda, my father told me Etienne is dead." Isabella fought to hold back tears.

"What… Isabella, I am so sorry—"

"I don't need your sympathies, at least not yet."

"That is why you ran away this afternoon; but, that doesn't explain why you have been avoiding me. You should have told me earlier." Matilda crossed her arms and pouted.

Isabella pointed to the bag she had been packing, and Matilda's mouth gaped.

"I don't believe my father. I can't believe him. I need to see it with my own eyes. He lied to me once before about Etienne's death. For all I know, Etienne is leading the Templars now."

"I want no part of this. Your father would kill me if he knew I helped you to escape."

"You won't be helping me to escape... You just will be pretending you are me for a few days—enough time to give me a head start. No one will know."

"Once again, I don't see how I could be mistaken for you."

Isabella jumped under the covers. "Leave me! I am sick!" Isabella faked a cough. "Get me a glass of water!" Isabella pulled the suffocating covers away and smiled at Matilda. "See, no one will know it is you. Think of it, you could be a princess for two days—that is all the time I would need."

"Princess... I suppose under the covers our voices would sound similar."

"Especially if I am sick." Isabella raised hopeful eyebrows. "Please, Matilda. You know my father wouldn't punish you too severely—he needs the grain that comes from your father's lands. The last thing he would want to do is lose the support of his nobles."

"You know, sometimes I hate you." Matilda threw a pillow at Isabella.

"So does that mean you will help?"

"How could I say no to being princess for a few days...and helping my best friend?" Matilda climbed under the covers. "I will need to practice being bossy."

They both laughed. Isabella captured a picture of this moment in her mind. This could be the last time she saw her dear cousin. Isabella wasn't planning on ever returning to the castle.

# CHAPTER 14

Isabella ran her hand along the coarse stone wall as she traversed the intricate tunnel system in the castle. The tunnels had been installed should the royalty ever need to escape a siege. Her father had made sure she and her brothers knew them inside and out. Isabella never thought she would be escaping her own father. Even with all of his faults, she still felt for him—he was her father. There was no way she could kill him, even if he had taken Etienne's life. How could Molay ask her to do such a thing?

Isabella wrapped her fur-lined cloak around her tightly and pulled her hood low as she exited the tunnel into Notre Dame. She was grateful that the church was still under construction. It meant that there would be less people around. The passage led from the palace to a confessional inside the church. Isabella quietly slid open the wooden panel and slipped into the wooden box. She was about to pull back the curtain, which kept people's sins secret from the outside world, when she heard the sound of footsteps echoing toward her. Isabella stole a glance through the curtain—it was Pope Clement. Isabella ducked back into the confessional and pulled her black hood low over her face. If Clement saw her this would all be for naught. He would return her to the palace. He was thick as thieves with her father.

The footsteps stopped right outside the confessional. Isabella pulled the hood even lower over her face and huddled on the floor. It was dark enough that just maybe she wouldn't be seen. Isabella flinched as the rungs of the curtain screeched on an iron bar; then footsteps, wood creaking, and the metal grate separating her confessional from the other compartment slid open.

*My God, Clement is waiting to hear someone's confession.*

Isabella glanced at the panel hiding the secret tunnel she had just come from. Did she dare to move it? Surely he would hear.

"Bless me, Father, for I have sinned. My last confession was yesterday." Clement said from the other wooden compartment of the confessional. They were less than a foot apart with a thin piece of wood and a grate between them.

Isabella couldn't believe she was hearing the Pope's confession to himself. She breathed shallowly and held as still as she could.

"Father, these are dark times with sinister deeds. I cannot believe the person I have become. He has changed me so much and pushed me to these actions. I confess to the murders I have ordered to fulfill your purposes. Their blood is on my hands. And all of the deceit. Surely King Philip is the devil. Look at what he has turned me into: a cowering, lying, murderer. Help me to stop this madness so I will sin no more. Father, I also pray that you will forgive me for my plans to take King Philip's life should he find Etienne and the Templars' treasure before I do. This is all I can remember. I am sorry for these and all of my sins. I pray you will help Father Alexander complete his task in Hospital de Orbigo."

*The Pope is planning to kill my father?* Isabella clenched her fists.

"For my penance, I will pray ten rosaries. My God, I am sorry for my sins with all my heart. In choosing to do wrong and failing to do good, I have sinned against you, whom I should love above all things. I firmly intend, with your help, to do penance, to sin no more, and to avoid whatever leads me to sin. Our Savior Jesus Christ suffered and died for us. In his name, my God, have mercy."

The wood creaked as Pope Clement rose. He pulled back the curtain and the sound of his footsteps was devoured by the immense cathedral. Long after he had left, Isabella sat in the small confessional. She was torn. She needed to see if Etienne was still alive, but she also wanted to warn her father. She pulled her knees in tightly and rested her forehead on them.

The bells rang through the church as the hour reached midnight. This was the appointed time she was to meet Katsuji. She needed to make a decision. Her heart and her gut were at war with each other. Isabella peered out from behind the thick velvet curtain. No one was there. Now was her chance. Isabella's body made a decision for her. Before she knew it, she was moving across the cathedral as quietly as a shadow.

The metal hinges of the door screeched as she pushed it open. But it didn't matter; her salvation lay on the other side. The brisk cool air of the night and a thousand stars met Isabella outside. In the middle of the plaza, in front of the church, was Katsuji's caravan as promised.

Among the stones of the plaza was a scallop shell marking The Way of Saint James. Isabella had nearly forgotten that this is where she had started her journey before. Even though she was still in Paris, Isabella was free. She was back on the Camino de Santiago.

# CHAPTER 15

"I think Andy was trying to steal the Grail last night." Etienne overheard Gabriel whisper to Fransie as they walked eastward on the Camino through a eucalyptus forest. "I sensed it again," Gabriel continued. "It was faint just like in the tunnel. I know Sephira would never attack anyone unless they were trying to harm us."

"Gabriel, I didn't sense anything. I was deep asleep. I believe you, though." Gabriel searched Fransie's face for reassurance, and she touched his shoulder from on top of the horse. "I do."

Etienne approached them. "I do too. But why would Andy try to steal the treasures? It doesn't make any sense." They turned, visibly surprised.

"Why would you believe me over your best friend?" Gabriel asked. Etienne looked at Andy and Claire driving the coach, laughing and teasing each other.

"Because each one of us is equal in this group." Etienne locked eyes with Gabriel and gave him what he hoped was a reassuring smile. "And because Andy is my best friend. I can tell when something is wrong with him—and something is going on."

"Thank you for believing me." Gabriel avoided eye contact with Etienne.

"Thank you for being so honest with Mariano yesterday. I apologize for any of my actions that have made you feel unwelcome. I am new to being a leader, and to tell you the truth, I'm not sure if I am cut out for it."

"I'm sorry for being aloof. I realize now that I was pulling away; you weren't pushing me. After doing *The Work* with Mariano I realized that this was a pattern I have held for many years, and it goes back to being exiled from my father's kingdom. That sense of rejection has haunted me ever since. It was amazing to see that thought unravel before my eyes."

"It was amazing for all of us to experience as well. Although I do wish you would have told me you were feeling that way," Fransie said, looking at Gabriel compassionately.

"What should we do about Andy?" Gabriel asked.

"Knowing Andy, he would never confess." A spark twinkled in Etienne's eyes as he leaned in toward Gabriel and lowered his voice. "We need to catch him in the act, and I think I know how."

It was late in the evening when they arrived at what Etienne and Andy called the Keystone Church. It was a lonely, gray church with a simple circular stained glass window. It was here that Fransie had first found Etienne after her long Camino. She had been so relieved that she had found him and completed her mission.

Thinking of it made her miss her friends. Raphael, Auriel, Emanuel, Michael, and Luca had all risked their lives to help her achieve her quest. Now it was her time to help them. She needed to save them before the priest executed them one by one. If she didn't make it in time, their blood would be on her hands, just like Stephano's and Sister Caroline's. She would turn herself in in exchange for their lives. Etienne had the information now and knew what to do. It wouldn't matter if the priest knew the information as well; Etienne and the others would get to the treasure first.

Thinking of the others made Fransie's soul yearn for Sister Caroline. She wished she could have one more day with her best friend. They had been inseparable at the convent. Sister Caroline had taken her under her wing when Fransie had arrived. She had been so nervous, and Sister Caroline made that all go away.

Fransie glanced at Etienne and shook her head. Etienne must be feeling conflicted; if Fransie was laying a trap for Caroline, she would be overridden with guilt. Fransie didn't like being deceptive. She would have rather asked Andy directly, but Etienne knew him better than any of them, so she deferred to his judgment.

"Etienne, my boy. It is you!" Brother Philip, a kindly looking older monk, said as he stepped out of the church. "Andy, you have brought help. Gerhart, I can't tell you how excited I am that you are here. There are things that need reaching, and things that need moving, and you are the perfect man for the job." Philip hit Gerhart's bicep and shook his hand as if he had just punched a metal wall. "You are all welcome to stay as long as you want."

"You know there is more to me than just muscle," Gerhart grunted.

"I know, I know. Forgive me," Brother Philip said. "There are just so many things I can't do myself anymore. Come, come."

Brother Philip ushered them into the church. Sephira followed Gabriel, but Bennie and Moira blocked her path and bared their teeth. Fransie remembered the last time the canines had met; they hadn't gotten along.

"It's all right, girl. You keep Cash company tonight," Gabriel said. Sephira's eyes pleaded with him, but she followed orders and curled up by the coach.

This was all part of the plan to catch Andy in the act. They would all pretend to sleep with the treasures just far enough away that Andy could get them. If he tried to make his escape, Sephira was to block the door. It would work perfectly.

After working for their room and board, everyone gathered for dinner. The food was simple but incredibly nourishing. Fransie took a sip of the potato and cabbage stew. The warm liquid traveled down her throat and warmed her to the core. She cradled the wooden bowl, heating her hands. She was grateful for the food and to be in good company. Andy had been in true form over dinner. He had made Gerhart laugh so hard that soup came streaming out of his nostrils.

"If you will excuse me?" Brother Philip stood. "I will retire for bed a little early. I am not as young as I used to be. Do you all mind—"

"We would be happy to do the dishes," Fransie said.

Brother Philip smiled and left the room.

"Ach!" Andy yelled, flinging a centipede onto the table. Everyone pushed back as the thing scurried and hid beneath a bowl.

"Do you sense it, Fransie? It smells terrible." Gabriel pinched his nose as his eyes watered.

"I don't," Fransie replied.

"I smell it. That food stank and tasted worse than it smelled." Andy held his nose, waving his other hand in front of his face. "If we stay, I'll do the cooking tomorrow. I am the best cook. So much better than Brother Philip. Actually, better than all of you."

"And I am the best at smashing." Gerhart brought down his mighty fist on the bowl that the centipede was hiding behind. The bowl shattered, and the creature scurried away. Gerhart smashed the table again. The force of the impact flipped the table, sending its contents flying across the room. The centipede landed on Mariano's chair between his legs, and Mariano smiled at the repulsive thing. He stood just as Gerhart's fists broke the chair.

"I am the best at smashing!" Gerhart said, picking up Mariano by the tunic.

"I agree you are the best at smashing," Mariano returned.

"Gerhart, stop!" Fransie cried, "What has gotten into you?"

Fransie wheezed as a sharp finger poked her chest.

"Donnea tell Gerhart what ta do! I'm the best at bossing him around." Clair's eyes burnt like embers. She went to poke Fransie again, but Gabriel intercepted her hand.

"I'm the best at protecting Fransie. I have saved her life, and I will do it again." Gabriel's wild eyes glinted in the candlelight. They all looked like they were possessed, except herself and Mariano.

"You should all follow my orders." Etienne stood with his hand on his hips. "I am in charge. Listen to me. I am in charge. Mariano, I am in charge. You're not in charge."

"You're right, Etienne. You are in charge and doing a fine job." Mariano patted Etienne's shoulder.

"Good, I will tell the others." Etienne walked to Gabriel and Clair, who were wrestling on the ground. Clair sunk her teeth into Gabriel's forearm, and he let out a yelp.

"I order you to stop!" Etienne said.

Clair looked at him and yanked him into the tussle.

"Gerhart will destroy it!" Gerhart yelled as he chased the centipede right to Andy.

"Look over there." Andy pointed to his left, and Gerhart turned. Andy crawled right through Gerhart's legs. He took the saddlebag with the Grail and Etienne's sword on his way to the door. "See, I am smarter than all of ya. 'Tis why I will win."

Fransie noticed the centipede on the scabbard of the sword as Andy ran out. Fransie stood in disbelief; how was this happening? Sephira ran right past Andy to Gabriel, and Gabriel immediately regained his senses.

"Pride! It's Pride—she is here," Gabriel said as Sephira stood between him and the others.

Seeing her gave Fransie an idea. "Andy, the centipede is your animal. Let it help you!" she called as Andy disappeared into the night. "So much for our plan."

Andy sped away in the wagon—well, he went as fast as Blueberry could go, which in actuality wasn't really that fast. The others would catch up to him soon once they returned to their senses. Andy wondered what had happened back there.

*You were the smartest. I told you. This quest was meant for you. Not them. The perfect knowledge will belong to you alone.*

"See, Blueberry. 'Tis all right. The voice of God just told me we are doing the right thing. Don't feel guilty for leaving the others. We are supposed ta do this."

In the valley below, Andy saw the merry lights of Portomarin twinkling by the river.

"We need to hide, Blueberry. That's what we need ta do. 'Tis just you and me now. We need to rely on each other." The donkey brayed loudly. "Shhh." Blueberry stopped and examined him skeptically. "If ya are good, I'll give ya this carrot when we arrive." Andy produced a carrot from his cloak, and the donkey continued down the hill.

Andy found lodging at a local tavern with a barn large enough to house Blueberry and the entire coach. He sat at a table by himself with a mug of beer. Everyone around him was laughing and having a great time. Here he was by himself. He took another large gulp.

"Hola, peregrino, you look lonely. Do you mind if I join you?" a pilgrim about his age with sandy blond hair asked.

"Be my guest." Andy motioned to the stool across from him.

"My name is Marko." The pilgrim extended his hand, and they shook as he sat.

"Andy. What is that ya 'ave there?"

Marko swung an instrument from his back. "It is a Guitarra Latina. I am a minstrel."

"I don't 'ave any money ta pay ya for a song." Andy looked up from under his brow.

"I didn't ask you for any," Marko said, plucking a few strings. The sound was quite soothing. "You looked distressed, so I figured I would join you to see what's troubling you." Marko strummed the instrument, and it seemed that the whole bar quieted down.

Andy scanned the room. "I donnae know ya. Why would I share what's on my mind?"

"Exactly, because you don't know me. I may never see you again. If you want I can go join my friends over there and leave you be. But sometimes, it helps to tell a stranger what ails you."

"Well, since I will never see ya again. It doesnea matter if ya think I'm mad." Andy surveyed the room once more, glancing over both shoulders. "I 'eard the voice of God, and it told me ta steal from my friends." Marko stopped strumming. "Ya see, I had worked so hard and... I donnae ken why God would ask me ta do such a thing. I feel mighty guilty and alone for it."

"How do you know it was the voice of God?"

"Well, see, 'tis complicated."

"Be careful to think you know the will of God." Marko started to strum again. "The hubris of man has led many men astray. All we can do is humbly ask for guidance and help, and then do the absolute best we can with the purest of intentions. If it then be God's will to reward the fruits of your labor during your lifetime, then it will be. I highly doubt it was God who asked you to steal."

"Yeah, I didnea think so either. But it was so compelling. Now, I donnae ken what ta do." Andy's large cheeks drooped, and he stared at his mug.

"I know just the thing to cheer you up. "Marko strummed the strings loudly, which quieted down the bar, and he sang:

*Oh, the Camino's ahead of us, the Camino's behind,*
*My friends walk beside me, stepping in time.*

The whole bar was clapping their hands to his music.

*There's pilgrims on the Camino,*
*They have blisters on their feet.*
*They do the pilgrim shuffle,*
*When their legs are beat.*

Everyone in the bar, including Andy, joined in for the chorus.

*O, the camino's ahead of us the Camino's behind,*
*My friends walk beside me stepping in time.*

The bartender took the next verse:

*The pilgrims on the Camino*
*Walk amongst the stars,*
*Then they stop for breakfast*
*At the local bars.*

The bartender held up tortilla, a breakfast dish Andy had come to love, which is made of potatoes, eggs, and so much goodness all cooked in a skillet.

*O, the Camino's ahead of us, the Camino's behind.*
*My friends walk beside me stepping in time.*

The song went on and on. Marko encouraged other pilgrims to make up verses. He was right, the music did make him feel better.

Marko played the last notes, and the bar erupted in applause.

"I see ya 'ave done this once or twice before." Andy took a large gulp, and nearly spit it out as Etienne appeared at the door.

"I take it that is your friend?" Marko asked, and Andy nodded. "I will let you take it from here. Remember, beware of hubris, my friend." Marko left Andy and joined his friends.

"Etienne, over here!" Andy shouted. Etienne gave him a death stare, and he shut his mouth. A hand pushed Etienne all the way into the bar, and Andy saw that Etienne's hands were bound. The hand pushed Etienne again and the owner of it appeared—it was Prince Charles the Fourth of France,[13] Isabella's brother, with billowy pantaloons and all.

"This cannea be," Andy mumbled.

Following the prince, an escort of ten soldiers entered, all warhardend and grizzly. Andy pulled his hood low over his head as the prince led Etienne to the table next to his.

"The infamous Etienne LaRue," Prince Charles said, loudly. "I have captured the most wanted person in France." The prince forced Etienne into a seat and slapped him across the face. "That was for humiliating me in Santiago."

Andy heard his soldiers snicker, and the prince gave them a sinister glare. Charles slapped Etienne again.

"That was for making my sister fall in love with you." Etienne smiled, and Andy wasn't sure if it was at the comment or the slap—it didn't look like it was very effective. "What, why are you smiling?"

"Your sister fights better than you, and hits harder."

The prince's soldiers snickered again. Andy smiled as well and took another sip of his beer. His face puckered. All of the sudden, his beer tasted terrible.

"You think you are so tough, but you are nothing without the Templars or Knights of Saint James to protect you. What were you doing in the forest by yourself unarmed?"

A lump formed in the back of Andy's throat as he reached for Etienne's sword on his lap. He touched the scabbard and felt something crawl up his arm. He yelped, abruptly standing from the table as a centipede crawled on his forearm.

"You!" Charles said. Andy scrambled for his hood, but it was too late. He had been recognized.

"Me..." Andy said. "Right, it is I!" He tried to summon all the gusto he had. "He was looking for me. I am a powerful wizard." Andy waved his left arm and cautiously looked at the centipede on his right. It almost seemed as if the wee beastie was copying his movements.

The prince and his soldiers burst into laughter. They were right to do so, he looked ridiculous. What in the heck was he doing? Andy stole a glance at the centipede and the little, not so little, fella continued to move with his hand. He recalled Fransie's words as he left the chapel. *The centipede is your animal. Let it help you.*

"If you are a wizard, prove it." Charles cleared a tear from his eye from laughing so hard.

"Marko, play me a jig!" Andy yelled. Marko strummed his instrument loudly. Dancing was the only way Andy had to test his theory. Andy's feet twiddled to and fro as he did a jig. Everyone was too busy laughing to notice the little centipede dancing as well. Andy was thrilled it was working. Andy did one last twirl. "I summon a centipede," he said, straightening his arm, and the little bugger went flying onto the prince's face.

The whole bar went silent, and the prince stared cross-eyed at the centipede.

"Get it off! Get it off! Get it off!" Charles ordered. A soldier moved.

"I wouldnae do that if I were you." Andy raised his arm as if he was making a duck shadow, and the centipede raised as well. Andy turned his hand to the left and the right and so did the centipede. The soldier moved again, and Andy positioned the centipede into a biting position.

"They are deadly poisonous, you know," Etienne said. "I wouldn't do that if I were you, unless you want to return to France with a dead prince." The soldiers shifted their weight, unsure what to do. "What do you think King Philip will do to you if Charles dies?"

"Untie Etienne!" Andy ordered. "Do it now!" Andy opened his hand, and the centipede readied its pinchers.

"Do it!" Charles ordered.

Andy loved seeing the look of terror on the prince's face. He bet he had soiled those pretty pantaloons. The soldiers followed orders and loosened Etienne's bonds. Etienne joined Andy, and Andy handed him his sword.

"They look like they need more proof you are a wizard," Etienne said.

Andy cleared his throat and waved his free hand over Etienne's sword. "Blade forged in fire, burn with might."

Etienne gave Andy a half-smile and drew the sword. The flames coming off the blade were blinding. The whole bar took a collective gasp, and all of the prince's soldiers drew back.

"We will take the prince prisoner!" Andy said, in his most authoritative voice. "Tell King Philip we are holding him ransom. If we see you again, I will 'ave a centipede for each of you."

"Are you sure you want to do that?" Etienne asked, but it was too late. The soldiers all ran from the bar in terror, leaving them with Prince Charles.

"Mariano, why was it that you were unaffected by what was going on?" Sister Fransie asked as she stitched up Gabriel's arm from where Clair had bitten him. "I watched you, and you just agreed with each of them."

Mariano smiled as he pulled splinters out of Gerhart's fist. "You really showed that chair, my friend." Gerhart shook his head. "And as for your question, I could have tried to prove I was right, or I could have been at peace. If I were to argue with their reality, I would have been creating a war between myself and them. A clear mind sees this."

"Why didn't you help to calm things down?"

"Would my help have actually been useful in the situation, or would it have added more fire to the flame? People will give their lives just to prove that they are right. People choose this suffering, and start this war, all the time. Plus, Gerhart smashes things much better than I ever could." Mariano pulled another splinter from Gerhart's knuckle.

"Ouch! Be careful," Gerhart said.

Fransie knew he was right. It seemed that anytime someone disagreed with the reality someone was believing, it just started more strife.

"The other question," Gabriel said, "is why weren't you affected by Pride, Fransie? Why couldn't you sense it in the tunnel, nor the cave, nor here? We possibly could have stopped this all from happening," Gabriel asked.

"I have wondered the same thing, and I think I know the answer—I was given the cloak of humility—it isn't one of the treasures, but Humility thought I would need it."

"Ach, she was right," Clair said. "None of us would have ken what happened if ya weren't there ta pull us apart and talk some sense inta us. Sorry 'bout the arm." Clair nodded at Gabriel's arm.

"How is it that you don't have a scratch?" Gerhart asked.

Clair shrugged then grinned. "I'm scrappy."

"Etienne should be back by now. I wonder what is taking him so long. Andy couldn't have gotten too far."

"Not with Blueberry." Clair laughed and put a hand on her stomach.

"I should have gone. Cash isn't always the friendliest to new riders."

"Gabriel, you were in no condition to ride. I am sure they will show up at any moment. If not, we will go search for them after everyone is stitched up."

The doors to the chapel flew open, revealing Etienne and Andy with their arms wrapped over each other's shoulders.

"Did ya see them, laddie, when ya pulled the sword?" Andy's whole face stretched into a smile.

"It seems that everything is well." Fransie continued to sew. Gabriel nodded to the door, and Fransie stole another glance. Behind Etienne and Andy, a young man was being led by a rope.

She turned back to Gabriel. "Maybe not."

Etienne and Andy rejoined the others and recounted the tale.

"Fransie, thank ya so much for your warning. I donnae ken I would have understood that this little beastie was my animal without ya." Andy tickled the centipede under the chin, and everyone eyed him warily.

"Andrew Sinclair, ya 'ave 'ad a lot of pets over the years, but this one?" Clair raised her eyebrows.

"It's not a pet, Clair, it's his animal, his filter. You must have true taste, Andy."

"That explains so much. I just thought I had bad indigestion." Andy pounded his chest with one hand. "Every time—Pride, was it?—came around, I tasted bile."

"You should experiance how Pride smells," Gabriel said, scrunching his nose

"Or sounds." Fransie smiled at both Andy and Gabriel.

"Speaking of sounds, where is Philip? I'm sure he would have been woken by all of the noise we were making."

"I haven't seen him." Fransie's eyes searched the small chapel. "I guess he is still in his room."

"This isn't like Philip." Etienne rushed to his bedroom door and knocked. He knocked again and there was no answer. Etienne opened the door and Fransie could see from behind him that Philip was still lying in bed. He slowly opened his eyes.

"Oh, I wish I could have joined the party, but it seems I wasn't able to get out of bed."

Fransie placed a hand on Philip's forehead.

"He is burning up."

Etienne sat all night at Philip's bedside. He had given them so much and never really asked for anything in return besides help

with some small chores. He sat with him for himself, but also for Isabella. Philip had helped her immensely the last time they were all there. It was because of her conversation with Philip that Isabella had finally been honest with him. Brother Philip was a mentor and guide, just as Ronan and Nazir had been. He didn't know if he could take losing him as well.

"I must be cursed," Etienne said quietly.

He had lost every male role model he had had in his life. He never met his father; he was taken away from Gaston at a young age; Ronan had died; and most recently Nazir. A pit formed in Etienne's stomach. He wanted to ask them all for advice. The weight of leadership was on his shoulders, and he wished he could have turned to one of these great men for advice. Now, Philip was leaving him too. Why did this happen to him?

Philip's eyes fluttered open. "There is no such thing as being cursed."

"Sorry, I didn't mean to wake you."

"I am happy you did. This could very well be the last time these old eyes open. I feel this body dying. Etienne, I would like to see the garden one last time. Will you take me there?"

"You should rest. You can pull through this."

"I will ask Gerhart to take me if you won't." Philip smiled gently at Etienne.

"Why don't you just phase into another time and place? You told me the butterfly moves in all directions."

"Who's to say I'm not? Now, take me to the garden."

Etienne draped Philip's arm around his shoulder and scooped him up in the blankets. Philip was much lighter than Etienne expected him to be. Etienne carried him quietly across the chapel with Bennie and Moira at his heels. All of the others remained asleep as they snuck out the side door to the garden.

"I love it," Philip said as Etienne sat him on the log. Bennie stood behind Philip so he could rest on him and Moira placed her head on his lap. He petted her head gently. "I will miss you, my friends. Etienne, can I ask you one thing?"

"Anything."

"Will you take care of Bennie and Moira for me?"

"They can take care of themselves. Have you seen them hunt?"

"I'm asking you to take them for your sake, not for theirs."

Etienne nodded.

"Good." Philip patted Etienne's leg. "That is very good."

Etienne tucked the blankets tightly around Philip, and he fastened his own cloak.

"You know, you can never step into the same garden twice. You think you are, but it is never the same."

"What do you mean?" Etienne asked, looking over the garden.

"It is one of the many tricks of the mind. What you are seeing in front of you isn't the garden that is actually here. The mind creates a mental image saved from a thousand memories to create the picture of the garden you are experiencing. It is a shortcut for your mind.

"It is the same thing with every person you have ever met. You can never experience the same person twice. They are created anew in every single moment by the mental pictures you hold in your mind about them; but the image is incomplete, even when you are looking right at them."

Etienne had to smile. Even in his last moments, Brother Philip was trying to teach him something.

"You have an experience of me, and I have an experience of you, and we each have an experience of ourselves. We have never actually met."

"What are you talking about? Has your fever returned?" Etienne placed a hand on Philip's forehead.

"You have only met the story of who you think I am, and I have only ever met the story of who I think you are. Every person has an experience of us based on their assumptions and past experiences. The mind works this way so you can make quick decisions. But these assumptions aren't always what you think they are. They are just interlaced memories, missing the whole."

"I'm pretty sure I have met you before."

"I know you don't want me to die."

"No, I don't. I have lost every mentor I have ever had."

"Did you ever lose them?"

"Yes, they are dead, and soon you will be too." Etienne put both hands on the log and pressed.

"Can anyone ever really die? Or have we ever really lived? You may never experience me like this again, but others may experience me over and over again. After all, we are just made up of memories and beliefs. I will be alive and with you every time you remember me.

"A memory isn't the same thing as you sitting here with me."

"Etienne, look at the garden—really look at it."

Etienne gazed out over the garden and realized it was no longer a garden. It had been overtaken by weeds and grass. Many of the plants were dead, and nothing was bearing fruit. If this was his first time seeing the garden, Etienne wouldn't have guessed that it had ever been a garden.

"It's not a garden anymore."

Philip nodded. "It hasn't been a garden for some time. But, your mind created a garden from your memories of it. I haven't been able to care for it since the last time I saw you, and now it looks like this."

Etienne let the lesson sink in. How many other times in life had he not seen things for what they were? How many other times had his mind played tricks on him, clouding his mind to the truth?

"It's the same with people. You may not know who they truly are. You have your experience and expectations, but often these can change. Remember, everyone is the hero of their own story. I am the hero in the story of my life, and you are the hero in this one."

Philip pointed to Etienne's chest. "Even then, do you know who and what you truly are? 'In the beginning, was the word, and the word was with God, and the word was God.'"

Philip made a laboring noise.

"My Lord Jesus, take me home."

Philip's body went limp, and Etienne caught him. He placed an arm around his teacher's shoulder and held him as Bennie and Moira howled. His body seemed so frail now, but his words were more powerful than ever.

Andy was the first to come running out of the chapel, followed by the others.

"I'm sorry, laddie." Andy placed a reassuring hand on Etienne's shoulder.

"Andy, out of all of our adventures we have had together, who would you say the hero is?"

"'Tis a strange question at a time like this."

"Brother Philip would have wanted me to ask it."

"Right then, don't take any offense, but... I am, of course." Etienne smiled and patted Andy's hand.

They toiled for most of the morning to dig a grave for Brother Philip in the middle of the garden. What once was a beautiful garden, turned to weeds, was now the final resting place for one of the best people Etienne had ever encountered.

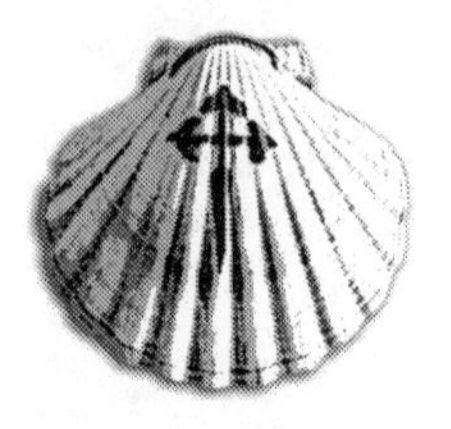

# CHAPTER 16

It had been three days, and no one had come looking for Isabella. The ride, and the company, had been pleasant. Katsuji and she had recounted their adventures on the Camino de Santiago. It was so nice to talk to someone who knew her friends and knew the life-changing effects the Camino has on one who travels it. No one is ever the same after walking the Camino de Santiago—it has a way of working on you.

The twilight painted the sky pink, purple, and orange as Isabella sat next to Katsuji on a log by the fire that was crackling away merrily to its own tune.

"Katsuji, I feel guilty asking you for your help."

"There is no need for your guilt. They are my friends as well. The moment you traveled with our caravan, you became a part of our Camino family, and family protects one another at all costs."

Isabella's heart ached at his words. She longed for that feeling of belonging she had had with Etienne and the others. It was the first time she truly had a community—the first time she was surrounded by people who loved her for who she was, not her position. Except Matilda. Isabella glanced over her shoulder in the direction of Paris and reassured herself that she had made the right decision.

Isabella was sure if Matilda was found out, her father wouldn't punish her severely. He couldn't, he needed all of his nobles behind him with his lofty plans, and Matilda's family was quite powerful in their own right. Anyway, the plan seemed to be working. Here they were, three days later, and not a single soldier from the palace after them.

"Katsuji, what is that?" Isabella pointed to the glass container that Katsuji kept at his side.

"This is my most valuable possession. When we first met, I told you about Akari." Katsuji's eyes became distant, as if he was reliving a dream. "Her father told me the only way he would grant me permission to wed his daughter was if I left my home country with nothing and returned a rich man with sand from the end of the world."

"Is that the sand?"

Katsuji nodded. "After we parted ways, I continued onto Finisterre and collected sand from the end of the world. I am also a rich man now, as you can see." Katsuji motioned to the caravan. "But, none of that matters if I do not have my Akari. I sometimes wonder if she has already wed. It has been many years since I have left." Katsuji's eyes turned sad and he stared longingly at the glass bottle.

"And now I am detaining you even longer." Isabella felt so selfish. She was depriving Katsuji of returning to his love as she searched for Etienne. The guilt began to gnaw at Isabella's stomach, along with the feeling she shouldn't have left.

"As I said, we are family. It is my honor to protect and help you." Katsuji feigned a smile.

"Katsuji…" Isabella wrapped her arms around him. "...continue home. Go find your—"

Isabella's head jerked back as she was ripped away from Katsuji by her hair. Isabella wrenched herself free and stumbled over a log. As she tumbled, Katsuji popped his sword and flourished it around his body.

The attacker drew a sword—it was of the same make as Katsuji's. In a beautiful display of skill and elegance, the stranger matched Katsuji's flourishes and speed. Isabella's assailant was dressed from head to toe in black. The only thing exposed were eyes that matched Katsuji's.

"Did Akari's father send you to kill me? I must warn you, others he has sent have tried and met their fate on the edge of this sword. I offer you the opportunity to walk away now, and no harm will come to you."

The stranger advanced and with a turning kick that sent Katsuji flying into his wagon.

Katsuji bowed. "Very well then."

The two met swords, and to Isabella, it looked more like a dance than a fight. Movement and countermovement intertwined, a rhythm created in perfect time with the clashing of swords. Isabella was in awe. She had never seen fighting like this before. Katsuji was leading with his strokes and the stranger followed perfectly, matching his every movement.

Snapping out of her admiration and recovering from her fall, Isabella ran to the fray, only to be met by the handle of the stranger's sword in her gut. The wind was knocked out of Isabella, and she stumbled back.

"I will deal with you next," the stranger said.

This momentary distraction gave Katsuji the upper hand. He grabbed the attacker by the arm, and in one movement he flipped and pinned the stranger to the ground.

"I must look upon you before I take your life," Katsuji said as he pulled off the stranger's mask. Katsuji stumbled back and placed his forehead to the ground. "Akari, forgive me, my love."

The most beautiful woman Isabella had ever seen stood over Katsuji and held her sword to the back of his neck.

"You have dishonored me and the vow we made to each other, Katsuji. I brought shame to my family by leaving to search for you, and I find you in the arms of another woman."

"It wasn't what you think it was—" Isabella intervened, but Akari's glare silenced her.

"My life has always been and will always be yours, Akari. Do with it what you will, but Isabella is just a friend. I am helping her to find her true love. She was consoling me for the sorrow of being away from you. Remember the quest your father sent me on?"

"Yes, how can I forget the day my heart was caged, and the tears ran from my eyes like the spring snow melts from Fuji San?"

"I have completed that impossible task. Look to where we were sitting." Akari glanced in the direction. "That is sand from the end of the world, and as you can see, I have become a rich man. Akari, I was coming home to you, a worthy man."

"Then why were you heading east?"

"To find my true love," Isabella said. "He was taken from me by my father as well. Katsuji has told me your story many times, and it parallels mine. Now, I don't know if my Etienne is dead or alive. I am running away from everything just to find him."

Akari glanced back at the container of sand, and in one swift movement sheathed her sword. She bowed and said, "Katsuji, I believe you and will accept you back on one condition—she does not join us."

Isabella's heart dropped into her stomach. "Why?"

"What you are sacrificing is too great. Today you may be fine with your decision, but a year from now, when you are in a strange land by yourself, and unsure if your family will ever accept you again for leaving—then you question your decision. If this Etienne is a person of merit like Katsuji, he will return for you no matter the consequences—and you will have your honor, family, and the one you love."

"But—"

"Isabella, I will keep my promise to you," Katsuji said. "I will find Etienne, but you must return home. The dishonor you would bring on yourself and your family would be too great. If he is still alive, Etienne will come for you. If he is dead, I will bring news. There is no need to sacrifice as Akari has for me."

# CHAPTER 17

"Bloody cold," Andy muttered as they ascended the steep climb to O'Cebreiro. He donned his hood and crossed his arms, placing his hands in his armpits. He should have ridden in the wagon, but no, he still felt guilty for what had happened at the Keystone Church. Now he was stuck in the rear with Bennie, Moira, and Prince Charles.

"'Tis easy for you—isn't it?"

"Actually, silk is quite warm—"

"I wasnea talking ta you. I was talking ta them."

Andy nodded past Prince Charles to Bennie and Moira. The two wolves looked as if they were smiling, with their tongues loosely hanging out of their mouths. They were built for weather like this, and Andy was not. The pair had followed them from the Keystone Church, taking up a position at the rear—guarding the young prince.

"Just because I am your captive doesn't mean you have to treat me so poorly. Back at the palace, I am actually quite popular."

"I'm sure ya are, laddie. I'm sure ya are."

"I am! I am! I am!"

A foul taste appeared in Andy's mouth. He took a drink to try to clear his palate, but the taste remained.

"Anyone in Paris would die to be me. That is how popular I am." Charles stomped his feet loudly.

Andy caught a snowflake and almost tasted the words, *You are the most popular.*

"Ach, no! Not here. Not now." Andy turned around.

"Good, I knew you couldn't resist my charm." Charles smiled broadly.

"I'm not lookin' ta ya. I'm looking at them." Andy made eye contact with Bennie. "Watch him."

The wolf growled, and Andy hoped Bennie wouldn't eat Charles. But, it didn't matter, he had to warn the others that Pride was here. Andy edged alongside the wagon, watching the sheer cliff drop to his left. One wrong step and he would tumble over just as Isabella had. The cart jerked, and Andy felt his heels go over the edge. He swung his arms frantically in circles trying to keep his balance. He closed his eyes and scrunched his face. He knew this was the end.

Two hands grabbed Andy's cloak, pulling him forward. Andy opened one eye and then the other.

"See that is why I am so popular at the palace—I save people. I am a good archer. I am the best dressed; did I mention silk is extremely warm?"

"Right, right ya did. Excuse me." Andy ducked past the prince to the other side of the cart. He figured it was better to be crushed against the wall than to risk falling off the edge again.

With each snowflake that hit him, the taste in his mouth worsened. He knew he needed to hurry. The wagon lurched again, and Andy ran past it narrowly avoiding a broken foot from it's front wheel.

"What are ya doing?" Andy asked Gerhart and Clair, who were both seated on the drivers bench of the wagon.

"Don't you know women can't drive?" Gerhart pulled hard on the reins, trying to pry them from Clair. Blueberry lurched and so did the wagon, but Clair didn't give up her grip.

"How dare ya!" Clair put one foot on the bench and the other in

Gerhart's chest. She took the reins in both hands and pulled in the opposite direction. Blueberry brayed loudly and pulled to the edge of the cliff.

"You're gonna kill yourselves!" Andy took out his dagger and cut the reins. Both Clair and Gerhart flew back into the coach, but the arguing continued. Andy hurried up to Blueberry and calmed the donkey. He took him by the bit and led him forward.

The wind was howling now, and Andy could barely make out the others in the blizzard forming around them.

"Etienne! Fransie! Gabriel!" Andy yelled.

Fransie was the first to appear through the flurry of snow.

"Andy, can you sense it?" she yelled.

"Yes! 'Tis in the snow. I taste it."

"I hear it on the wind. Her voice is everywhere."

"Where are Etienne and Gabriel?"

"Gabriel and Sephira are trying to catch Etienne to put the cloak of Humility over him." As Fransie finished, the two men appeared from the whiteout. Gabriel's nose was bleeding, and Etienne avoided his eyes.

"It seems that our animals are filtering Pride out for us. We should put him in the cart with Clair and Gerhart and wrap the cloak around all of them. The last time I saw them, they were trying to kill one another."

"What about the prince?" Etienne asked, holding the invisible cloak around him.

"Ach, no, the prince. You donnae think that the wolves would eat him?"

"They might," Etienne said.

"Fransie, do ya mind?" Andy handed Fransie the remainder of the reins, and he ran to the back of the coach, followed by Etienne.

"By the looks of it, we made it just in time," Etienne said.

He was right; Charles was pinned to the ground by Bennie, who was edging closer to the young prince's face.

"Ya donnae think Pride affects animals as well?" Andy raised questioning eyebrows.

"No, but I think arrogant young princes are quite affected." Etienne shook his head.

Andy watched in disbelief as the young prince tugged on Bennie's fur.

"You are unworthy to wear that fur. It will look much better on me—made into a coat."

"Bennie, it's all right," Etienne said, approaching with two hands raised. "He doesn't know what he is talking about."

Bennie snapped his jaws and stopped an inch from Charles's face. The massive wolf looked behind him—followed by Moira. The pair quickly turned, and the hairs on their backs bristled.

"Awoo!" A wolf's cry pierced the gale-force wind.

"Andy, help me." Etienne rushed to the prince, and they lifted him into the wagon. "We have to help Bennie and Moira."

Andy spotted seven sets of yellow wolves' eyes, cutting through the snow.

"Etienne, ya canna." Andy placed a hand on Etienne's chest. "If ya lose that cloak, Pride will control ya. She already has all of them," Andy pointed to the others in the wagon, "and they will kill each other if that cloak doesnea cover them as well. I donnae like it, but that is the way it has ta be."

"You're right." Etienne's shoulders slumped as he climbed into the coach.

Andy pulled his blade and joined Bennie and Moira. The other wolves lowered their heads as they approached. A massive black wolf led the pack. Small icicles had formed on his fur, making him look like he was wearing armor.

Andy turned as he heard the sound of paws racing to them from behind. It was Sephira. She slowed her pace as she approached and flanked Moira. Together, Bennie, Moira, and Sephira blocked the narrow road. The sight reminded Andy of a Roman phalanx.

These brave souls would hold the pass, just as Leonidus held Sparta from Xerxes. The number of attackers didn't matter; there was no way for them to pass with the cliff on one side and the rock wall on the other. Andy hoped their strength would hold until they reached the safety of the city.

One wolf attacked, then another, but they broke like waves on solid rocks. Bennie, Moira, and Sephira gave no ground. The pack of wolves tried to go over and under, but each advance was met with a counterattack. Howls and gnashing of teeth echoed on the wind.

Andy walked with the coach as the titans guarding their rear became smaller and smaller until the whiteout devoured them.

A whistle cut through the wind and a dark dot appeared in the snow. The dot turned into a mess of fur, blood, and fangs. Andy held his sword shakily waiting for an attack, but it never came. Sephira darted past them.

Two more shapes appeared racing toward the coach. It was Bennie and Moira—the line had been broken. They stood on either side of Andy, and yellow eyes gleamed through the snow. There was blood on both wolves, but Andy couldn't tell if it was their own or not.

A wolf lunged at Andy, but before he knew it, he was airborne. Two large hands had lifted him into the coach. The wolf latched onto Andy's cloak and was clawing at the coach to gain its balance and enter.

Gerhart set Andy down and thumped the wolf on the head. The beast whined and dropped like a stone.

"Thank ya," Andy said, catching his breath.

"I had to save my brother." Gerhart rubbed Andy's bald head. Even though Andy didn't like the rubbing, he smiled. That was the first time Gerhart had called him his brother.

"Andy, take this." Etienne handed him his sword. "We can't leave this cover, otherwise—"

"I am the best at thumping wolves!" Gerhart threw Andy into the side of the coach.

Things went black for a second. When Andy opened his eyes, he saw Etienne and Clare tackling Gerhart. Etienne wrapped the invisible cloak around the three of them.

"Otherwise that happens," Etienne said.

"I'm sorry," Gerhart said. "I didn't mean to."

"'Tis nothing." Andy rubbed his forehead where a goose egg had formed.

Andy heard a wolf whine. He wrapped a cloth around his hand and pulled Etienne's sword. The flames lit the wagon. Andy peered over the edge and saw a white wolf on Moira's back. Andy thrust the sword and it made a sizzling sound as it made contact. The wolf whined loudly and tumbled to the ground.

The attack stopped momentarily. The pack looked to its leader for guidance. The large black wolf let out a howl, and the other wolves gathered around him. Andy brandished the sword wildly, and the beasts kept their distance.

"We are here! Thank God!" Fransie cried from the driver's bench of the wagon. Moments later they passed two giant pillars on either side of the coach.

"We made it!" Andy said merrily, smiling at the others.

"No, we haven't." Etienne pointed out the front of the coach. He was right; instead of retreating, the wolves split down the streets of the village. They were trying to surround them.

"Run, Fransie! Run!" The coach picked up some speed but not enough.

"This way!" Andy heard Gabriel call.

With the rear of the coach being well guarded by Bennie and Moira, Andy climbed through the coach to join Fransie on the driver's seat. Just as he exited, a wolf lunged at Sister Fransie.

Abandoning all of his instincts for self-preservation, Andy jumped from the coach and tackled the beast mid-air. The wolf and Andy tumbled to the ground. The beast stood on top of him. Its saliva dripped on his face, warming his cheeks from the cold.

*'Tis it; this is how I die.* Andy grimaced, waiting for the inevitable, but the beast was pulled off of him.

"Thank you, Gerhart—" Andy stopped mid-sentence. Instead of seeing Gerhart wrestling with the wolf, Blueberry had the beast's tail in its mouth and was swinging it around and around—thrashing it on whatever was closest. The donkey flicked its head, and the wolf went flying through the air. The donkey stamped his hooves and brayed loudly.

Andy got to his feet and took the sword.

"Thank ya," he said, petting Blueberry's muzzle. He shook his head and touched his forehead with Andy's.

"This way," Gabriel called.

Ahead was a lonely church surrounded by a wall. Andy led the coach in, and Gabriel shut the gate behind. Andy hoped everyone in the back of the wagon was still in one piece.

Fransie clutched her stomach and feared the worst. A searing pain had shot through her abdomen as she had fled from the wolves.

"Fransie, are you well?" Gabriel raised his heavy brow.

"I don't hear it, Gabriel. I was running and there was pain, but I couldn't stop. I may have…"

"Breathe." Gabriel took a large inhale, encouraging Fransie to do the same. "Calm yourself and focus."

Fransie tried to push past her fear. She focused on slowing her heartbeat. After a few breaths, her heart regained its steady pace, and Fransie heard the quiet hum inside her.

"I think it just kicked." Fransie knew the child was inside her, but this sensation made it real. "Gabriel, you have to feel this." Fransie took Gabriel's hand and placed it on her belly.

"I feel it," Gabriel said, smiling.

Their eyes locked, and Fransie had the thought that Gabriel would make a good father. What was happening to her? Was she developing feelings for Gabriel? She had sworn her life to Jesus, and she would keep that vow, but her child needed a father. She didn't want to raise it by herself.

"I hate ta break this up, but we need a plan." Andy leaned against the gray stone of the chapel's covered entrance, where they had parked the coach. "We cannea stay out here in this weather, and we cannea trust our friends. I still taste something foul on the air."

"Yes, the smell of Pride is pungent."

"I ken Pride wants these treasures. When I was under her spell, she was controlling me ta steal them; and I bet she will do the same ta our friends in the wagon."

"Why would Pride want these treasures?" Fransie asked.

"I wouldnae want ta be trapped for seven hundred years, or however long 'tis been. Perhaps if she gets the treasures, she will be free. Maybe they will all be free ta do what they like ta this world." Andy read the worry on Fransie's face. "'Tis just a theory though," he said reassuringly.

If Andy was right, they had to stop Pride; they had to collect all of the treasures first. Fransie had opened two of those doors. What had she been thinking? She had to remind herself that she had been under the influence of True Sound without a filter. She doubted anyone would have been able to resist.

"We can't let her have them." Fransie was surprised at the resolve in her voice. "How many of the treasures do we have?"

"I have the Grail in Cash's saddlebag," Gabriel said.

"And I 'ave the shard of the cross and the sword."

"I thought Etienne had the shard of the cross?" Fransie crossed her arms.

"I stole it from him the night in the cave, and, well, I never gave it back. What? It is working ta our benefit now."

"True, I suppose it is all part of God's plan. That just leaves the head."

"I donnae ken it is going anywhere without Blueberry, and I donnae think she is moving again tonight except ta a stable." Andy was right; the donkey looked exhausted.

"What about Mariano?" Fransie asked. "Do we trust him?"

"He seems unfazed by Pride. For that matter, he seems unfazed by anything. It looked as if he was going to start petting one of the wolves when we were under attack." Gabriel looked around. "Where is he now?"

"I was the last one in through the gate," Andy said. "Mariano! Where are you?" Andy yelled. He ran to the gate, but Gabriel stopped him.

"We don't have time to worry about that now," Gabriel said. "I'm sure he can take care of himself. We must figure out how to protect the treasures from the others. If they slip out through the cloak, they could easily overpower us."

"I think we should hide them for the night," Fransie said. "There are three of us and three treasures. Andy, give Gabriel the Shard. If we each hide one without the others knowing where it is then we have a better chance of retaining more treasures should anything happen. "

Andy hesitantly reached into his sporran and placed the shard into Gabriel's hand. "Take good care of this. Etienne would kill me if we lost it again."

Andy went in one direction and Gabriel in another. Fransie held the Grail in her hand and entered the church. She walked briskly to the altar and bowed.

"Forgive me, Lord." Fransie made the sign of the cross. She walked around the altar to the tabernacle and switched the Grail for the cup inside. The chapel was just as cold inside as it was outside. She fastened the cup to her belt and walked outside. She had hoped that maybe they could stay inside, but the church was just too cold.

The wind outside the chapel bit at Fransie's face. She tried to shield herself from it, but it did no good. It was the type of wind that burrows right through the flesh and heads straight to the bone.

"Mariano, thank goodness you are here," Fransie said, noticing the Spaniard propped against the coach.

"This was the only place I could be." He flashed her a charismatic smile. "We have been offered shelter."

"What about the wolves?"

"They have left. I saw them chasing after Gabriel. He rode out of the city a few minutes ago.

Fransie looked around desperately. It was true; Gabriel, Cash, and Sephira were all gone.

Andy came whistling around the corner. "Hi, Mariano. I'm 'appy ya made it. Why the long face, Fransie?"

"Gabriel abandoned us. We gave him one of the treasures and he left." Fransie's heart sank into her stomach.

"Is it true?" Mariano asked.

"I can't process my feelings now. We need to figure out what to do."

"Tie us down," Etienne's voice came from inside the coach. Fransie opened the flap and saw all of them cuddled together holding the invisible cloak. "We can't stay like this all night. Take us back to the lodgings Mariano has, fasten the cloak around Gerhart, and tie the rest of us down in our beds.

"Aye, 'tis a good idea, laddie. There is some rope there." Andy pointed to a large bundle of rope.

Mariano led them down the narrow streets between the gray-stone buildings. Fransie was relieved she wasn't the one who had to make the decision. She didn't like being in control—she would much rather follow.

Mariano stopped and knocked on a wooden door with black hinges.

"Pilgrims, welcome, come, get out of the cold," a nun with sharp features said as she opened the door.

"Thank you, sister." Fransie's face was numb, and the heat from inside almost hurt her skin as she approached. "Our friends in the coach have been temporarily taken by madness. We will need to restrain them for the night. This storm has had an effect on them."

The nun scanned Fransie up and down then glanced at Mariano. He returned her gaze with a peaceful smile.

"Your friend has told me of your situation. Our convent has never turned away a pilgrim in need, and we never will. Let me know if we can assist you in any way."

Fransie's hands and toes tingled from thawing as the nun led them to the sleeping chambers. The tension in her shoulders loosened, and a smile crossed her face at the sight of Gerhart, Etienne, Clair, and Prince Charles all moving as one mass behind her. They were stumbling over their feet all trying their best to ensure that the others were fully covered by the cloak. She hadn't sensed Pride since they were inside, but she didn't want to take any chances. Fransie's shoulders tensed again, and with wide eyes she touched her ear. Pride wasn't here. She hadn't sensed Pride at all, not even after she had given her cloak to the others. Was she losing her True Sound?

They tied their companions to the beds one by one. Gerhart was the last, they fastened him down with the cloak still on him. If Pride got to him, there would be no stopping him.

The door opened, and Fransie's heart skipped a beat. "Where would you like me to put these?" A matronly looking nun nodded to the bowls of soup on a tray. "What is going on—"

"I'll take those," Andy said, quickly taking the tray from her and ushering the nun out. He closed the door and put a chair against it so no else could come in.

Fransie enjoyed feeding her friends hot soup. It reminded her of being with the ill—serving them was her true calling in life. Fransie blew on a spoonful and fed Etienne.

"I think this is the first time I have been spoonfed," Etienne said, resting his head back down on the pillow.

“’Tis na true, laddie. Isabella and I fed ya for several days in Hospital de Orbigo when ya had been poisoned. We had ta do other things for ya as well.” Andy pretended the spoon was a bird and flew it around Prince Charles’s head.

“Is that necessa—” The prince’s words were cut off by the spoon going into his mouth.

“Aye, ’tis.”

The mention of Hospital de Orbigo was like a slap in the face to Fransie. Her friends were still held prisoner there. If she didn’t reach them in time, the priest would start killing them one at a time.

Etienne read Fransie’s longing eyes. “What’s on your mind?”

“My friends… I have to reach them before that priest starts killing them. I don’t have time to be stuck in this storm. I don’t have time for Pride to stop me. Regardless of what happens tonight, I must leave in the morning.”

“You still have plenty of time.” Etienne looked at her with his soulful eyes. “We had a two-day buffer. Something else is bothering you as well.”

“I can’t believe he left.”

“What do you mean he left?” Etienne refused the bite that Fransie was giving to him.

“Gabriel. I gave him one of the treasures to protect, and he rode off, along with Sephira.”

“Do you realize what you have done?” Etienne struggled with his ropes. “Only the chosen are supposed to have them. We are the chosen. I am the chosen. Not any of you. Untie me so I can retrieve what you have lost.” Etienne struggled harder, and the ropes binding him turned his skin red.

“I’m royal. I am the chosen one, not some peasant. Untie me at once. I am the chosen one, and I command you!” Prince Charles pouted his lips.

“Ya men always thinking ya are the chosen one. Women are much superior ta men. Untie these ropes and I will show ya.”

"Fransie, it looks like Pride is back. It tastes terrible. I donnae ken how ya can sit there unaffected." Andy took a bite of the prince's soup and spat it out. "Well, that didnea work."

"I can't sense it. If I didn't see the way it is affecting our friends, I would never know it was here. I thought I couldn't sense it earlier because of the cloak, but I was wrong. I don't sense Pride at all." Fransie looked down at Rosalita on her shoulder. The small mouse was sitting peacefully cleaning herself. "Am I losing my True Sound?"

The question struck fear in Fransie's heart. What she once thought was a curse had become such a blessing to her. She didn't want to lose it. She couldn't lose it.

"Maybe it gets better with time?" Andy rubbed his tongue with both hands. "I sure hope so."

"No, this is different."

"What did Humility say to you when she gave you her cloak?" Mariano asked, smiling contently. If Fransie didn't know better she would think that he was actually enjoying this, as if he was a conspirator of a joke.

"She said the cloak would help to protect us from Pride."

"Why did she give you the cloak?" Mariano continued.

"She gave it to me because the treasure was missing... She gave it to me because I defeated my Pride." The realization pushed Fransie back into her chair. She couldn't sense Pride because she had defeated it, not because of the cloak.

"How did ya defeat your pride?" Andy poured the jug of water down his throat. "I donnae ken how much more of this I can take."

Fransie thought back to the claustrophobic tunnel that Pride was chasing her through. The sound of the insects chasing her was almost visceral.

"I gave up... I admitted that I couldn't do it on my own, and I called for God's help."

Fransie turned to Andy; his tongue was swollen. He tried to

speak, but only a jumbled mess came out. Fransie clasped her hands and closed her eyes.

"My Lord Jesus Crist, we are nothing without you, but we know we can do all things with you. I pray that you will enter our hearts and help us to overcome our pride. Help us to approach this world with a humble heart that only yearns to do your will."

"God, help me to overcome my pride. I am just dust without your life in this body," Etienne said

"God, help me! I cannea do this on my own!" Andy cried, finding his voice again.

"God, I know we haven't always been on the best terms, but I can't do this on my own. Amen." Gerhart awkwardly crossed himself.

"Amen," Clair said.

"'Tis gone. I donnae taste Pride anymore. Thank the Lord 'tis gone."

"Are you sure?" Etienne asked. All eyes turned to Fransie.

Fransie shook her head. "I… I don't know." She looked at Rosalita. "I think I have lost my True Sound."

# CHAPTER 18

Isabella's mind was at war as she raced back to Paris. She wanted to continue on the Camino—she was free—but there was truth in Akari's words. When Isabella had left, she had made peace with the idea of not being a princess anymore. She had even made peace with not seeing her father, but not seeing Matilda or her brothers again—that would be difficult.

*What a terrible friend I have been.*

Matilda did get on Isabella's nerves sometimes, but she was always there for her—being supportive in her own way. Now, she had convinced Matilda to take the fall for her. Isabella promised herself that she would be better to Matilda when she returned.

Sneaking out of the palace was one thing, but sneaking back in was something completely different. There were too many variables. On the long ride back, Isabella had devised a plan. When she arrived in Paris she had confused the guards at the entrance of the city. None of them knew she was confined to the palace, and who would they be to argue with a princess? The harder part was getting back into the castle.

Isabella's horse's hooves clacked as they crossed the bridge leading to the Isle de la Cite. Instead of turning left to the palace,

Isabella turned to the right to Notre Dame. The horse neighed as it came to a stop in front of Notre Dame.

"Steady, girl. I don't like them either." Isabella examined the gargoyles perched on the roof of the cathedral, and they stared back with their menacing eyes.

Isabella entered unnoticed along with other parishioners. The jewel-colored light from the round stained-glass window bathed her as she passed.

"I must speak to the Pope," Isabella demanded as she looked impatiently at the guard.

"The Pope isn't here."

Isabella pulled back her hood.

"I am Princess Isabella of France. I know the Pope is here, and I have a message he will want to hear." Isabella raised an eyebrow.

The guard tugged at his collar, and his eyes glinted from side to side searching for help. Isabella continued to stare him down.

"Very well, wait here."

The guard disappeared behind a door, and Isabella smiled. It was a gamble she had taken. There was no guarantee the Pope would still be there, but there was no other way Isabella could think of to get back into the palace unnoticed.

The door opened slightly, and the guard motioned for Isabella to enter. The guard led Isabella past all of the holy jewels on display to the private chambers reserved for the Pope. The room was opulent. It could have rivaled any chamber in the palace. At the far side, the Pope sat by the fireplace in a golden chair with red velvet.

"You may leave us." The Pope nodded to the guard, and he quickly disappeared, closing the door behind him.

"Come, my child, join me." Isabella traversed the room, knelt, and kissed his ring, then sat on the chair opposite the Pope. "How is it that you know I am here?"

"God led me to you." It was true; her escape plans had led her directly to the confessional that Clement had used. "Just as everyone else, I thought you had left Paris after the castle was overrun."

Clement placed his fingers together and leaned back into his chair. "So, you are the only one who knows I am here?"

"To my knowledge, yes." At her words, the worry lines on his face softened, and he eased back into the large velvet chair.

"How can I trust you? How is it that God has led you to me?"

"I was escaping Paris when God told me of your confession. He heard you. I was on my way to Santiago de Compostela, but God showed me how I can be the answer to your prayers."

"Once again, how can I trust you?"

"God showed me that you gave this confession: 'I confess to the murders I have ordered to fulfill your purposes. Their blood is on my hands. And all of the deceit. Surely King Philip is the devil. Look what he has turned me into—a cowering, lying, murderer. Help me to stop this madness so I will sin no more. Father, I also pray that you will forgive me for my plans to take King Philip's life should he find Etienne and the Templars' treasure before I do.' You then prayed ten rosaries for penance."

Clement's face turned white. "How could you possibly know..."

"As I said, God led me to you. I am here to help you stop this madness so you will sin no more."

Clement grasped Isabella's hand. "Oh, my child, surely you are blessed." Tears formed in Clement's eyes. "Thank you. I am a good person...thank you."

Isabella looked Clement directly in the eyes. "I know you are...I know... My father has a way of making people do his will. That is why I was fleeing the castle. I was done with his wicked plans as well, but I couldn't bring myself to kill him. That is not the way. Together, though, we can stop him. God also told me that should you find a Templar named Etienne La Rue, you are not to harm him. He has a divine task that he must complete."

"How do you know about him? He is the key to finding the treasure."

"The search for that treasure only brings death and destruction. Believe me, you want nothing to do with it. Look at the sins you have committed already."

Clement bowed his head in shame.

"And how do you propose we stop your father? He is a powerful man, obsessed with this treasure."

"First, I will need you to sneak me out of Notre Dame and back into the castle unseen. There is nothing I can do from out here."

"Doesn't anyone know you are gone?"

Isabella shook her head, and the Pope leaned back.

"Don't worry. If you take me into the castle in the papal carriage, it won't be searched. You will say that you are there to hear my confession in San Chapelle, as is customary for royals. And there is one other thing we must do."

"What is that?"

"We must get Jaques de Molay to join us."

# CHAPTER 19

Fransie had spent a sleepless night watching over the others. Even though it appeared as if they had overcome Pride, Fransie didn't want to take any chances. She knew from personal experience that Pride was tricky. Sometimes, you don't know it is there until it is too late. Fransie shifted her weight in the wooden chair and it creaked.

What was troubling Fransie more than Pride was that Gabriel had left them. The moment he had one of the treasures, he rode off. Fransie wanted to believe he had a reason for leaving, but Etienne's original suspicions about him kept creeping into the back of her mind. She placed her hand on her belly where Gabriel had felt the baby kick. Fransie thought they were a family of sorts—at least they could have been.

"Ya look as rough as I feel." Andy stood and stretched his back. "I mean, ya donnae look bad, just tired." He shook his head. "I mean… You are glowing."

Fransie smiled at Andy gently.

"What do ya reckon we should do with this lot?"

"You should untie us immediately," Prince Charles said.

"I wasnea talking ta you."

"I agree with the prince," Etienne said. "Andy, do you sense Pride?"

Andy tasted the air and smacked his lips. "Ach, 'Tis terrible."

"Is Pride here?" Etienne put his hand on the hilt of his sword and scanned the room.

"Na, I just taste morning breath, but 'tis usual."

"Very well. We need to get an early start. I must reach my friends before the priest starts…" Fransie's words trailed off and she bit back a sob.

"We will reach them in time, Fransie. I promise you." Etienne's eyes were sincere, and she believed in him.

"Mariano, will ya untie them? Fransie and I have a little errand ta run before we leave," Andy said.

"As you wish," Mariano said, stretching.

Outside, the air was so cold it hurt to breathe. Fransie wrapped a scarf around her face tightly to shield herself from the whipping wind. Little flurries of snow flew here and there down the small streets.

"I'll see ya in a few minutes," Andy said, at the entrance of the church.

Fransie nodded, and Andy disappeared around the side of the building. She gripped the metal door handle, and the frozen metal stuck to her hand, tearing off a layer of skin as she pulled away. Inside the church, it was almost as cold as it was outside. Had they stayed there the evening before, they surely would have frozen. Fransie was glad Mariano had found them shelter.

Fransie bowed at the altar and made the sign of the cross. She said a quick prayer for safe travels, for her and her companions, as well as for Gabriel. Just as she was about to enter the side sanctuary where she had exchanged the grail for the Eucharist cup, the door to the left of the altar was unlatched. Without knowing why, Fransie ducked out of sight behind one of the large stone archways.

"Why am I the one who has to come into this freezing church... As if anyone will show up to Mass anyway... If they do show up they are a fool," a monk muttered as he prepared the altar for Mass. He lit the candles around the altar and warmed his hands.

Fransie didn't know what to do. She needed to retrieve the grail, especially before anyone drank from it. She hoped that the priest was right and no one would show up for Mass.

The priest rang the bell for Mass and waited for a few moments.

"See, not worth getting out of bed for." The monk blew out the candles and walked to the door he had come from.

A gust of wind entered the chapel, and Fransie pulled her cloak around her tightly. She peered from behind the archway to see a lone figure in the doorway. The parishioner walked to the front pew, knelt, made the sign of the cross, and sat.

"What are you doing here Juan Santin?[14] Aren't you a resident of Barxamaior?"

"It is so," Juan answered.

"Why come to Mass at the church of Santa Maria le Rea? Why not attend Mass in your town? You are a fool for braving the storm. This Mass will be wasted on your presence."

"The only presence that matters is the presence of our Lord. Will you perform Mass or did I make the long walk for nothing?"

The monk muttered to himself and relit the candles. Fransie silently attended Mass from behind the pillar, careful not to be seen.

"You came all this way for a little piece of bread and some wine," the monk said, before the consecration of the Eucharist. The monk shook his head and held up the Grail and the bread to finish the prayer. "Through him, with him, in him, in the unity of the Holy Spirit, all glory and honor are yours, almighty Father, forever and ever. Amen."

"Amen," Fransie said, under her breath.

"Amen," Juan said, and the Host turned to flesh, and the wine in the Grail turned to blood.

The priest put down the Grail and flesh on the altar with shaky hands. The church bells rang, and the monk dropped dead to the ground. Fransie sensed the presence of the Virgin Mary. She looked at the statue of the Virgin, and it had moved from a standing position to a kneeling position. Fransie crossed herself and praised the Lord.

Juan dropped his head and prayed hard with closed eyes. Fransie knew this was her chance. She rushed to the altar—the sound of bells covering her footsteps. She poured the contents of the Grail into the communion cup and ran back to her hiding place.

The doors to the chapel flew open and numerous townsfolk entered, including Andy. Fransie took him by the arm as he passed and they disappeared into the crowd.

# CHAPTER 20

“What Shadow is attacking you, my friend?” Mariano’s comment pulled Etienne out of his deep thoughts. He was so angry at Gabriel for abandoning them and stealing the Shard of the One True Cross that he hadn’t been able to think of anything else. He hadn’t even been able to enjoy the sweeping views as they descended the mountains from O’Cebreiro.

“It’s Gabriel,” Etienne said, understanding Mariano’s reference to the Shadows they had overcome in what seemed like a lifetime ago. The Shadows were the first of the seven deadly sins they had encountered. The creatures were composed of every painful thought from the past or fear of the future. They were Wrath in a physical form, and they had all almost lost their lives to them. After saving Fransie’s friends, in Hospital de Orbigo, they needed to get to Castrojirez to collect the treasure from the door the Shadows had protected.

“What about him?” asked Mariano

Etienne stared at Mariano in disbelief. “What do you mean ‘what about him?’ It has been two days since he abandoned us and stole the One True Cross.”

“Is it true that Gabriel abandoned us and stole the cross?”

"Of course it is. If he didn't abandon us, he would have returned by now."

"Can you absolutely know it is true beyond any doubt?"

Etienne picked some pine needles from a tree as they passed and broke them piece by piece. He threw away the remainder of the needles and answered. "No."

"Good. Now answer me this, how do you react when you think the thought, 'Gabriel abandoned us and stole the cross.'"

"I get angry…" Etienne hesitated; he wasn't used to sharing his feelings with others. The compassion in Mariano's eyes encouraged him to continue. "The anger is all-consuming; it is as if I see the whole world through a lens of that anger. I get angry at myself for letting him go. It robs me of enjoying this beautiful landscape and my friends. It makes me scared that I have failed as a leader and that we will fail in our mission." Etienne shook his head.

"Who would you be without that thought? If there was no way possible for you to think the thought that 'Gabriel abandoned us and stole from us'?"

"I would be present. I would be able to think clearly about what our next steps should be. I would be able to enjoy the company of my friends and the smell of the pines." Etienne brought his fingers to his nose, the sap of the pine needles still clinging to them.

"It must be really painful for you to believe that thought. Can you see any reason to keep the thought as it is robbing so much from you?"

"Holding onto that thought and anger makes me feel like there is still something I can do about it—like I still have some control over it. But, that is just an illusion, isn't it?"

Mariano nodded. "Yes, the only thing that holding onto that thought is causing you to do is to be at war with reality. It is a war you will lose every time. Gabriel is gone and so is the shard of the cross. To believe anything else *should* have happened is insanity. If it *should* have happened, it would have. In this present moment, it isn't Gabriel, nor the loss of the shard that is causing you to suffer; it is just your thinking about it."

Etienne could see that now. Who was he to judge what should or shouldn't have happened? The reality is it did happen. No matter how much anger he had, nor how many different scenarios he ran in his head, it wasn't going to change the fact that both the Shard and Gabriel were gone. The only thing holding onto that thought did was make him feel bad, and steal him from the present moment. The scowl Etienne had worn for the past few days lifted from his face.

"Good," Mariano said, joyfully. "Let's turn it around."

"Turn it around?"

"Yes. There are three basic turnarounds: the opposite, the other, and the self. Let's start with the first one. What is the opposite of the thought 'Gabriel abandoned us and stole the cross'?"

"Gabriel didn't abandon us and steal the cross?" Etienne raised questioning eyebrows.

"Wonderful." Mariano gave Etienne a charismatic smile. "Can you give a few examples of how this can be as true or truer than the original statement?"

"I don't know that Gabriel actually has the Shard of the Cross with him. For all I know, he hid it someplace before he left. Also, as I heard him gallop off, I heard the wolves leave as well. They were chasing after him. Had he not left, we wouldn't have been able to find shelter. We may have frozen to death." Etienne's eyebrows pulled together. "I never thought about that before."

"Let's go to the next turnaround—the other. Exchange your name and Gabriel's."

"I abandoned Gabriel and stole from him." Remorse struck Etienne as the words left his mouth. "That sure is true. Gabriel was right; I never fully trusted him or accepted him into our group. I shut him out and stole from him the sense of belonging. So much so, that he had to do *The Work* on that thought in the cave. I didn't even realize I was doing it. But looking back now, there are many subtle actions I did to shun him. I would have left too, if I was treated like that. What is the third turnaround?"

"The third one is to the self. So in this case it would be, 'I abandoned us and stole the Cross.'"

"My Pride incapacitated me. I also haven't been stepping into my role as a leader. I have been too busy brooding about Gabriel. I haven't been present with you all since he left. We need to form a plan. We are only a couple of days away from Hospital de Orbigo. As for stealing the cross, I did exactly the same thing. Charity gave Andy the shard of the One True Cross. I took it from him for safekeeping, because I didn't think it would be safe with him. I also left the others when I was with the Knights of Saint James and took the shard with me."

"Can you now see the Shadow that has been attacking you?"

"I see it for the lie it is, and I am ready to start making a plan to move forward."

# CHAPTER 21

The fading light of the setting sun lit the bricks of the Templar castle in Ponferrada aflame. Etienne was unsure of his decision to come here, but he needed help to free Fransie's friends; the days were growing short until their execution. He thought his plan to assert his authority as Seneschal of the Templars was a good idea—he couldn't see a way to save Fransie's friends without help—but as he walked up the drawbridge and stared at the two imposing turrets on either side of the gate, he was questioning his decision once more. He glanced over his shoulder at his companions walking up the drawbridge. They all seemed relaxed, except for Andy.

The Templars on the other side of the wall would see him and Andy just as he had seen Gabriel—a traitor. He had abandoned them—and all of the Templars—to save Isabella. These were the very Templars who had hunted him and Andy for so long. Etienne shook his head at the comparison and hoped that Gabriel's reason for leaving was as valid as his had been.

"Who comes here?" a voice shouted from one of the turrets.

Etienne looked at his companions. It was time for him to step up as a leader.

"Etienne LaRue, Seneschal to Grand Master Jaques de Molay!" Etienne was surprised at the authority those words gave to his voice. Standing in silence, he hoped these Templars had gotten the message about his promotion. If not, he had just condemned Andy and himself to death. Etienne resisted the urge to fidget and held his ground.

The massive wooden doors swung open, revealing the courtyard filled with Templars at arms. Etienne breathed deeply and entered. These were his soldiers, and he needed to show that authority.

In the place where he had first seen Molay stood a tall, slender Templar with Brother Andre at his right.

Brother Andre adjusted his glasses and turned to the slender Templar. "Yes. That is him, Commandery Master. His companion Andrew Sinclair is with him as well."

"Thank you, brother." The slender Templar said, placing his hands behind his back. "So you are the infamous Etienne LaRue and Andrew Sinclair. We have been searching for you since you abandoned the Templars."

"Who are you to address your Seneschal like this?" Etienne wasn't going to take the bait. He outranked this man, whoever he was.

"Seneschal? Forgive me for not bowing." A wave of laughter crossed the courtyard. "I am Commandery Master Christian Rivera, and you are an imposter who is not worthy to wear the title you claim."

"Did this castle not receive the orders from Jaques de Molay?"

"Yes, we did. But, do you really expect us to follow the orders from someone who has gone mad?"

"He is not mad! How dare you speak like that about your Grand Master." Etienne never thought he would be defending Molay.

"That is the only explanation for his order to disband the Templars and to make you, a traitor, into his Seneschal. We should have you and your friend hanged for your treason."

"What you are saying now is more treasonous than any wrong I have committed against the Templars."

"Perhaps, but this castle will not be abandoned, and we most certainly will not follow your orders. Out of respect for the great man that Jaques de Molay once was, we will grant you sanctuary for the night, but you must be gone in the morning. Brother Andre, you will attend to them." Brother Andre bowed, and the Commandery Master left the courtyard followed by his escort.

"If you will follow me," Brother Andre said, without making eye contact. "Your companions will stay in the guest house, and you and Andrew will stay in the Templar compound."

"They are Templars as well." Etienne's words stopped Brother Andre in his tracks. He looked Etienne's companions up and down.

"They are no Templars."

"They have taken the oath."

"But two of them are women," Brother Andre said, adjusting his spectacles. "And one of them is pregnant—definitely not Templars."

"Very well then. If they can't stay in the Templar compound, neither will we. We will all stay in the guest house. I am sure more than half of you no longer think that Andy and I are Templars."

"You said it, not I. I do have one question for you though."

"What is it?" Etienne asked

"Was she worth it?" Brother Andre's words nearly knocked Etienne over. "Princess Isabella, was she worth abandoning your brothers and your oath? I don't see her with you now."

"Yes, she was worth it," Etienne said, without missing a beat.

"Hmmph." Brother Andre continued on to the guest quarters.

"What 'appened ta him?" Andy said, plopping down at the table. His feet were sore and were threatening to blister at any moment.

"He is just following orders," Etienne said. "Although, they are the wrong orders."

"Did ya think it would be easy, and that all of the Templars would accept you as Seneschal? If ya did, ya were kidding yourself, laddie."

"Ya two can keep jabbering; I'm gonna find my bed." Clair stared at Gerhart, who was paying no attention. She cleared her throat. "I said, I'm gonna find my bed." She winked at Gerhart.

"Oh, oh yeah." Gerhart faked a large yawn. "I'm tired too." He winked back at Clare conspicuously.

"Ya donnae have ta hide it; you're married now. Although, I still donnae want ta think about it. I'm gonna take a wee walk ta the library ta say hi ta Puna and Brother Bernard. Do either of ya want ta join me?" Andy asked Mariano and Etienne.

"I don't feel like seeing another Templar tonight," Etienne said. "I would rather—" The sounds of Clair and Gerhart in the next room stopped Etienne mid-sentence. He shook his head. "I hope these walls are thick."

"How about ya two?"

"I will stay with Etienne," Mariano said.

"As will I." Fransie walked to join Etienne at the table. "We have to come up with a new plan to free my friends as it looks like we won't have the support of the Templars."

"Suit yourselves." Andy heard a bed creak, and he rushed out of the room.

Andy climbed the stairs to the second story and walked along the wall of the castle that led to the library. Below the castle wall, the townspeople appeared as small as mice, and the gray slate roofs stretched off into the distance. Andy wondered what it would be like to be a normal person again. Even in Santiago when they were leading a *normal* life, the knowledge of the Templar treasure had hung over their heads.

The smell of beeswax candles and old books met Andy as he

entered the room. Andy loved that smell. For him, it was the smell of knowledge. It was his happy place. Even though Andy hadn't liked being a Templar very much, he had loved this library. It felt exactly as a library should—cozy. The ceilings were low, and books lined the walls. The two desks had great piles of books stacked; each one looked more tantalizing than the last. He wanted to spend a decade discovering all of their secrets. Without the book with the Keystone Church that he had discovered previously, they would have never been able to decode the secret message in the cathedrals.

"Puna! 'Tis good ta see a friendly face!" The gray cat with stripes peered up at him from Brother Bernard's desk. Andy went to pet Puna, but she hissed and walked away.

"Now, donnae be cross with me. I know I left without saying goodbye, but I didnea have a choice. I was kidnapped." The cat scowled over her shoulder with squinted eyes. "Will ya ever be able ta forgive me?"

"Of course, we will." Andy jumped back and placed his hand to his chest. Behind him, Brother Bernard laughed so hard he started wheezing.

"'Tis good ta see you too, Brother Bernard," Andy said as he caught his breath.

"We know that you were kidnapped by the Hospitallers, Brother Sinclair. It is good to see you alive." The old monk walked past Andy and scratched Puna behind the ears. The ferocious cat melted and purred like a kitty. She flopped on her back and playfully batted at Brother Bernard's hand.

"Good ta see some things haven't changed around here. Puna is still as temperamental as the wind."

"But, much has changed, and not for the better. Och!" Brother Bernard pulled his hand away from Puna's deadly claws. She looked up at both of them innocently and jumped off the table.

"Aye, we met Brother Christian. He is worse than Molay."

Brother Bernard stared down his nose. He pushed up his spectacles. "Shut the door."

Andy closed the door and latched it, then sat opposite Brother Bernard at his desk.

"There is a faction growing in the Templars who think Molay has lost his mind. Brother Christian is part of this faction. They want to break away from Molay's command. Most of the castle agrees with Brother Christian, but there is a resistance." Brother Bernard scanned the room. "And we will help you to escape."

"'Tis good, 'tis good. What do ya mean, escape? Commandery Master Christian said we could leave in the morning."

"Brother Christian knows whoever controls the secret treasure controls the Templars."

Andy's body tensed, and he sat back in his chair.

"We donnae ken anything about a secret treasure." Andy crossed his arms for emphasis.

"Did the book I left for you to find last time help you to decode the riddle?" Brother Bernard raised his eyebrows.

"Ya mean the Keystone Church?" Andy leaned forward. "Ya left that for me ta find?"

Brother Bernard smiled and nodded.

"But, I thought you didnea like me that much."

"I was actually quite fond of you and was sad when you left. This library can be quite lonely. The younger Templars don't study as much as they should." Brother Bernard shook his head. "But I didn't help you because I liked you. I helped you because Molay ordered me too. He saw the designs of Brother Christian and a few other very powerful Templars. He called you, *insurance*."

"Well, I'll be. I didnea think Molay liked me either."

"Brother Sinclair, liking is beyond the point. Making sure the Templar treasure is safe is the only point. And right now, you and Etienne are the best chance for that. God help us all."

Brother Bernard laughed and started wheezing again.

"Right. Let's get back ta this escape and resistance thing. Why do we need ta escape?"

"Have you not been listening? He who controls the secret of the treasure controls the Templars. Brother Christian and the others suspect you have this secret. My guess is he will try to get Etienne and you to join them through reason at first, and if that doesn't work—through torture."

Andy sat back and slumped in his chair. They had only made matters worse by coming here. Puna jumped on his nether regions, and Andy was frozen in excruciating pain. She blinked at him with her big eyes, circled a few times, and sat comfortably on his lap. Andy didn't know if he should pet her or kick her off. Her claws were deadly, and he didn't want to make any wrong moves.

"So, how big is this resistance?" Andy noticed his voice was an octave higher.

"Well, it's myself and Brother Andre."

"'Tis it? There are at least a hundred Templars in this castle."

"It's more like five hundred."

"Five hundred." Andy shook his head in disbelief. "How are we ever going to escape?"

"Well, the plan is working so far. You are here, aren't you? There are advantages to age; you become wiser than most."

"Ya mean what Brother Andre said was meant ta get us ta stay in the guest quarters instead of the Templar quarters? He was so rude."

Brother Bernard nodded.

"And how did you ken I would come here?"

"I knew you couldn't resist being around all of this knowledge again." Brother Bernard spread his arms wide. "And, I knew you would want to see Puna again."

Andy stroked the cat in his lap. Her purr was so strong it was vibrating his thighs. "So what are we waiting for? Shouldn't we get ta this escape?"

"All in due time. But first, I have to give you something." Brother

Bernard unlocked a desk drawer and handed Andy a beautiful book. "Molay had me make this for you. He wanted me to give it to you when the time was right. But, you disappeared before I had a chance to. So, I think now is the right time."

The smooth leather covering was a stark contrast to Andy's rough hands. He thumbed through the pages. It was the book of Genesis and the gospel of John.

"Thank ya. A book 'tis the best present I could ever receive. Why did Molay want you ta give this ta me?"

"He said it would help you to find what you are looking for. He also wanted me to tell you, 'It helps to start at the beginning.'"

"Thorough, isn't he?" Andy raised his eyebrows and smiled. "So, do ya ken what this treasure is?"

Brother Bernard shook his head. "No one does. Not even Molay. The secret died with Grand Master Arnold of Torroja. No one has unearthed it since it was moved from the Holy Land. We only protect the secret of its whereabouts."

"So, how are we going ta escape?"

## CHAPTER 22

"Was that a knock or the headboard again?" Etienne asked. He regretted his decision to not go with Andy; they hadn't been able to make much of a plan with all the noise Gerhart and Clair were making.

"No, I think that definitely was a knock," Fransie said. "Would you like me to—"

Etienne stood before she finished and strode across the room. He answered the door just as Brother Andre was going to knock again.

"Ahh, good, Brother LaRue, you will accompany me. The commandery master wishes to speak with you."

Etienne looked back at his friends, and both Mariano and Sister Fransie nodded for him to go. Etienne sighed heavily. He had no desire to see the commandery master again. He just wanted this night to end so they could be on their way.

Brother Andre and Etienne walked through the halls of the guest quarters silently. They crossed the quad of the guest quarters, through another hallway, and out onto a large green open space.

"Beautiful, aren't they?" Brother Andre motioned to the stars. "A thousand writers have tried to capture their beauty, but words can't do justice to a sight like this."

"I didn't know you were a poet." Etienne wasn't expecting this from Brother Andre. He had always taken him for a nose-in-a-book, follow-the-rules, sort of a guy. However, he always had that mischievous twinkle that hid behind his old eyes.

"I'm not, but I needed it to look like we started a conversation. It will take us exactly two minutes to cross the green to the commandery master's chambers." In the distance, the black silhouette of the large stone Templar quarters blotted out the sky. It always amazed Etienne just how immense this castle complex was. A whole village could fit inside its well-guarded walls.

"Why is that important?"

"Because this is the only place where we can speak unheard, and that is exactly how much time I have to tell you something very important. So I need you just to listen and not speak."

Etienne nodded.

"Commandery Master Christian knows Molay entrusted you with the knowledge to find the one true treasure. He has summoned you here tonight to try to convince you to give him that information. You must not give in. Hold your ground and remember that you are the Seneschal to Grand Master Jaques de Molay. You are rightfully in command of the Templars, not him.

"Actually, I'm not surprised Molay picked you as his Seneschal. You remind me of him when he was younger. You also possess many of the qualities that make a great Templar. Brother Sinclair on the other hand... Well, that isn't important. You will be an excellent leader, Etienne. You are brave, loyal, and intelligent. Look at all of the dangers you have survived and brought your friends through. I would like to see your command one day... However, that isn't important."

"Later tonight, we will help you to escape. Prepare the others." Brother Andre pointed at the sky as they came within earshot of a Templar. "And that is Orion's Belt. You can tell by the three stars. Do you understand?"

"That constellation has always given me hope," Etienne responded as they entered the Templar quarters.

"Commandery Master," Brother Andre said as they entered Christian's quarters. "I present to you Brother Etienne LaRue."

"Thank you, Brother Andre. You may retire for the evening. Your services are no longer needed. I am sure Brother LaRue can find his way back to the guest house."

"As you wish, Commandery Master." Brother Andre closed the door behind him and left Etienne and Christian alone.

"My apologies for the way I treated you earlier. I needed to make a point."

"And what point is that?"

"The point that I am in control here, and you have no power. Neither does Molay. He has gone mad."

"I think your lust for power has made you go mad, and you are taking all of these Templars with you."

"You foolish boy, I am not in power. I am just following orders. There are many others that hold the belief that Molay is unfit to command. Disband the Templars? What is he thinking?"

"Molay is risking his life to buy us time."

"Time to what? Feel like cowards?"

"Time to avoid bloodshed. Time to avoid killing those we have sworn to protect. Do you not know that King Philip has the Pope on his side? Who are you to go against the might of the Holy Roman Empire?"

"We are the future of the Templars. We are the New World Order. Plus, there is no proof that the Church is with King Philip."

"There is proof in your very own guest quarters. Sister Fransie can confirm that the Church is against the Templars. She was nearly killed by the Hospitallers delivering—"

"We know that Molay has entrusted you with the secrets of the One True Treasure. But, we didn't know this nun—Sister Fransie, is it?—was carrying the Master's Word from Molay."

"Join us, Etienne. Do you want to see the Templars disbanded? Think of the chaos it will cause in this world. We are what keeps it balanced. You mentioned the might of the Holy Roman Empire. Don't you know that the Templars are that might? The church would be nothing without us.

"Your pride will destroy you," Etienne said. "I will never join you."

"'Never' is a strong word. At sunrise, we will start torturing your friends as you watch, unless you join us. We will begin with Sister Fransie. Sleep on it. You might sing a new song in the morning, little bird. You don't even have to join us; all you have to do is give us the information we need. Tell us where to find the treasure."

# CHAPTER 23

Sister Fransie tapped her fingers on the table. She couldn't help herself. Etienne and Andy were taking too long. They needed to make a plan to save her friends. Etienne had promised that the Templars would help, but they hadn't; they were on their own. How would they ever be able to set them free?

Sister Fransie made eye contact with Prince Charles, who was sitting opposite her. Fransie didn't like that he was tied to the chair. He was a prisoner, just like her friends. Etienne thought it was best, but Fransie didn't see what harm he could do. His soldiers were far away, and he was just a boy.

"Would you like some water, Charles?"

"Yes, thank you for being civil."

Fransie walked around the table and lifted a glass to the young prince's lips.

"If we released you, what would you do?"

"I don't know. I suppose I would make my way back to Paris—even if I had to beg the whole way." Charles's face scrunched in disgust.

"There is virtue in humility. It has taught me some of my greatest lessons in life."

The prince let out a laugh.

"The disciples gave up everything to follow Jesus. Do you think yourself greater than them?"

Charles smiled and stared at her. For a moment his eyes were no longer his. They reminded Fransie of… Pride. Had she possessed him? Was it here in this very room with them right now? Fransie backed away as the young prince continued to stare.

The door flew open, and Etienne and Andy rushed in at the same time.

"We have to pack. Now." He walked over to the sleeping chambers and banged on the door. "Clair, Gerhart, It is time to go."

"Is it morning?" Gerhart said, groggily

"No, but 'tis time ta go," Andy said, as he stuffed a bag with their food.

"What's the plan?" Fransie asked as she helped Andy pack up.

"I donnae ken, but we have inside help." He winked at her.

Moments later, the room was packed and everyone was in their traveling clothes.

Clair crossed her arms. "Now what?" Fransie could tell she didn't like being woken up.

"Now we wait," Etienne said.

"Are you sure they are coming?" Gerhart asked, after an hour. Clair was fast asleep on his shoulder.

"They will come. They will come," Etienne said, trying to will it into existence.

The door handle turned, and Brother Andre entered the room. "Good, I see you are ready."

"So what's the plan?" Etienne asked.

"I'm not sure if you are going to like it," Brother Andre responded, staring right at Fransie.

"Why are you looking at me like that?" Fransie clasped her hands on top of her belly.

"I am going to need you to pretend like you are going into labor."

"Excuse me?"

"You are about eight or nine months along, aren't you? Well, the actual number doesn't really matter that much. We just need the guards at the gate to believe you are going into labor. I'm sorry about this."

Brother Andre picked up a jug of wine from the table and spilled it on Fransie's lap. The cold sensation sent a shock through her body, and she lurched to her feet.

"'Tis the best plan ya could come up with?" Andy said. "Brother Bernard was going on about how wise ya two are."

"Well, we didn't have much time. And this plan will work. If we are going to do this we must do it now."

Fransie's wet clothes clung to her as Gerhart carried her across the great lawn to the front gate. She was thankful for his heat; without it, she would be shivering. As they walked under the archway that led to the courtyard in front of the main gate, Brother Andre gave Fransie a nod.

"Ooo!" She moaned. She thought she had done well, but the others stared at her. She took a deep breath and wetness streamed between her legs. Her water had actually broken. She was really going into labor. Her body let out a guttural cry as she experienced her first contraction. The sound reverberated under the archway and into the courtyard in front of the gate. Two guards came running—weapons at the ready.

"Who goes there!" a guard with a spear-pointed ax yelled.

"Clair, I—" Fransie had another contraction, and she let out a cry.

Clair took one look at her and inhaled deeply. "Breathe, just breathe."

Fransie followed her instructions and breathed in deeply.

"I said, who goes there?"

"Lower your weapons. It's I, Brother Andre, with the pilgrims. Pilgrim Fransie has gone into labor, and I need to get her to the midwife in the village."

The guards looked at the scene and then at each other. Their weapons lowered a little, but they held their ground. Fransie let her head fall back as another contraction came along with a scream.

"We have orders to not let them leave. Why don't you take her to our healer?"

"And just how many babies has he delivered? I don't know of any Templars who have gotten pregnant. I'm guest master in this commandery, and I won't have any of my guests dying."

Fransie let out another cry as the next contraction came.

"Do you want this child born in this courtyard? If she, or the baby dies, their blood will be on your hands."

"What about the Commandery Master's orders?" One of the guards lowered his weapon. "Why would they need to go?" The guard nodded at Andy and Etienne.

"I will take full responsibility. Just open the gate, and get me their cart so I can get her to the midwife immediately!"

"As you command," the guard who lowered his weapon said. The other guard looked at him. "I don't want innocent blood on my hands; do you?" The second guard shook his head. Within moments, Blueberry and the cart were ready to go.

Gerhart climbed into the wagon and laid Fransie down. Clair jumped in as well, sitting beside her. Clair took Fransie's hand and patted it reassuringly. Fransie had another contraction, and she screamed. The cart moved quickly, vibrating Fransie's body.

"Take off your belt!" Clair demanded.

"Clair, I don't think it is appropriate—" Gerhart turned red.

"Ach, no, you fool. She is actually in labor. The wee bairn is comin', and she needs something ta bite down on."

Fransie let out another scream.

"We are far enough away from the castle now. You can stop pretending," Brother Andre said from outside the cart.

"She isnea pretending. The bairn is comin'," Clair said, loudly.

"We have to get her to the midwife," Etienne said, from outside the wagon

"We can't. We will be caught if we do," Brother Andre responded from the driver's seat of the wagon. "This is your only chance of escape."

"We should take a vote," Andy said from next to Brother Andre.

"We don't have time," Etienne said.

"Enough!" Clair bellowed, sticking her head outside the wagon. "I will deliver the bairn. I've been through it once, and I helped ta birth many a goat back in Scotland." Clair rolled up her sleeves. "Right, Fransie, 'tis going ta be like nothing ya 'ave experienced before. Just remember ta breathe, bite down hard on the belt, and ya can squeeze Gerhart's hand as hard as ya like."

"What do you mean, Clair? I can't—" Gerhart's words were cut off as Fransie squeezed Gerhart's hand hard.

"Fransie, look at me," Clair said as her eyes scanned the wagon. "Now I need ya to lean over that barrel and squat. 'Tis a holy child, how hard can this be?" Clair pointed at Gerhart. "And, you—no lookin'."

Gerhart turned the same direction as Fransie, took her by the hand, and stroked her hair.

"Now, 'tis time ta get ta work. Push!"

The labor lasted into the morning as the wagon climbed the steep mountains. Fransie was so grateful for Clair and Gerhart. She had never been so exhausted in her life, nor in so much pain.

"That's it, lassie. Just a few more pushes."

"Look at me," Gerhart said. He took some large breaths, and Fransie matched them.

Another contraction came, and Fransie let out a scream. She squeezed Gerheart's hand so hard, that she was afraid she had broken it.

"Push as hard as ya can!" Clair yelled.

Fransie pushed with all of her might as the contraction continued.

"A head! I see the head! Keep pushing, lassie."

Fransie pushed even harder, and then she heard the most

beautiful sound she had ever heard in her life—the cry of her child. Fransie's body collapsed down, utterly depleted.

"Gerheart, hand me tha' dagger—Gerhart!"

Fransie looked up just as Gerhart fainted. He was white as a ghost.

"Seeing the birth musta been too much for him, Men!" Clair sat next to Fransie. "How would you like ta hold your daughter?"

Clair handed Fransie the infant. The feeling was indescribable. To use a word to describe it would be to do an injustice to the experience. Clair cut the umbilical cord as Fransie held her daughter.

"There now, lassie, ya can rest—both of ya." Clair wrapped them in blankets and placed her arm around Fransie. "Now, quit your staring!" Clair chastised Andy, Etienne, and Mariano, who were all trying to see into the wagon. "Fransie and the bairn need to rest. Brother Andre, we need ta clean up. Do you ken a friendly place we can stop?"

"I know just the place," Brother Andre said.

## CHAPTER 24

"Thank God they are all right," Etienne said, hearing the baby cry inside the wagon.

"What does she look like?" Andy asked Gerhart as they walked up the mountainside, carrying supplies from inside the wagon. They each had something to lighten the load for Blueberry as the donkey struggled up the steep incline.

"She… She… She is like looking at the sun." Gerhart stumbled to find the right words.

"Ya mean she is glowing?"

"What? No… She just is too beautiful to look at for a long time. It just kind of turns your insides into mush."

"I never knew you had such a soft side." Etienne hit Gerhart in the arm.

"Just seeing her makes me want one of my own. Do you think Clair would? You know…"

"Want ta have a child? I donnae ken. It still might be possible."

"I hope so."

Etienne's heart winced. When he had married Isabella in secret, he imagined them having a family and growing old together. He never knew he had this desire until she awoke it inside him.

Etienne stared at the top of the mountain. It had been just on the other side of the peak where they had said their vows in that small church and celebrated their wedding night under the stars.

"What's gotten inta ya? Donna tell me ya want a bairn as well?" Andy asked, reading Etienne's face.

Etienne shook his head and carried on in silence.

"We are here," Brother Andre said from the driver's seat of the wagon after a good few hours of climbing.

Etienne shielded his eyes from the sun, which was just peeking over the mountain top. To the left, there was a small road leading off of the Camino. Brother Andre pulled on the reins slightly, and Blueberry strutted onto the side road.

"I donnae ken how he does it," Andy whispered. "I had ta bribe Blueberry to even move. He makes it look so easy."

"I guess with age comes wisdom," Etienne said.

"Was that a thank you? I heard, 'With age comes wisdom.'"

Etienne and Andy exchanged a smile.

"Aye, thank ya, your plan worked—except, we left behind Brother Bernard. I donnae ken how I feel about that."

"He will be fine. It will look like I acted alone to help you escape. Plus, I couldn't convince him to leave his precious books. He wants to die in that library, with them prying a book from his cold hands."

"I can understand that," Andy said.

Andre led the cart up a steep climb to a door built into the side of the hill.

"Welcome to Brother Julian's hermitage. We should be safe here. He is still loyal to Molay and the true order of the Knights Templar. The last time I saw him, he tried to convince me to leave the castle and join him out here."

"I'm happy you finally took up my invitation." A large man ducked out of the hermitage door and stood almost as tall as Gerhart.

"Brother Julian! You are a sight for sore eyes. Help me down, Brother Sinclair." Andy rushed to the cart and clasped both hands for Brother Andre to step on. Brother Andre took the step, and Andy wobbled. Brother Andre's arms swung around a few times then found a home on Andy's face.

Brother Julian let out a laugh that was so infectious Etienne couldn't help but join him.

"Brother Sinclair, always doing things wrong. I should have asked Brother LaRue." Brother Andre awkwardly found his way to the ground.

"So, you are the infamous Etienne LaRue?" Brother Julian crossed his arms and lowered one eyebrow.

"Yes, that is me. But I don't know how infamous I am."

"Oh, you are."

"What about me? I'm infamous too," Andy said, puffing out his chest.

"I have heard of you as well, Andrew Sinclair. So Achilles hasn't caught the two of you yet?"

"Who is Achilles?" Etienne placed his hand on the hilt of his sword. "Is he the leader of this New World Order that Christian was talking about?"

"No," Brother Julian shook his head. "Achilles is the world, my friend, and you are the tortoise." Brother Julian let out another infectious laugh, and Brother Andre joined in. Etienne suppressed a chuckle, but he couldn't help smiling.

"So they are." Brother Andre nodded.

"Let's get your cart out of sight, then all of you must come inside for some tea and breakfast."

"One of our members just gave birth in the back. I seem to remember you have a well around here. Do you mind if they—"

"By all means. They can go around back to clean up, and we can give them some privacy by going inside."

The hermitage was small and cozy. A large black cauldron was merrily boiling away on the fire. And in the corner was a well-used altar dedicated to the Virgin Mary. Brother Julian offered them a seat around a wooden table with various makeshift chairs.

"You must excuse the accommodations. Being a hermit, I don't get many visitors. Actually, my last visitors were here a few weeks ago; the ones before that a few months ago; and the ones before that nearly a year ago. Do you know what they all had in common?"

"I do," Brother Andre said. "That is why you made the reference to Zeno's paradox of Achilles and the Tortoise."

"They all had you in common, Etienne. They all asked me if I had seen a black Templar by the name of Etienne LaRue. And yet, here you are, unscathed, sitting at my table. That, my friend, is why you are the tortoise."

"What is this paradox?" Andy asked, always hungry for knowledge.

Brother Julian held up a finger and walked to the fire. He retrieved boiled eggs from the cauldron and placed the bowl in the middle of the table.

"Zeno was a Greek philosopher who came up with the paradox of Achilles and the Tortoise. In the story, a tortoise challenges the great hero Achilles to a race under the condition that the tortoise has a head start. Achilles accepts—sure that he will win."

Julian took two eggs and placed them on the table, one on the edge and the other ten inches in front of it. He pointed to the egg on the end of the table. "Meet Achilles." He pointed to the other egg. "And the tortoise." He smiled at Etienne.

Etienne didn't like being compared to a tortoise, but he was interested in what Brother Julian had to say.

"The race starts, and Achilles reaches the point where the tortoise started." Brother Julian moved one egg to reach the other. "But, by the time Achilles reaches that point, the tortoise has moved forward." He moved the other egg forward by five inches. "Even though Achilles is faster than the tortoise, the tortoise will always be in the lead." Brother Julian moved Achilles' egg to reach the tortoise's egg then moved the tortoise's egg forward by two and a half inches.

"How long does this go on for?" Etienne asked.

"Eternity."

"Surely he has ta catch the tortoise at some point?" Andy sat back and crossed his arms.

Brother Julian's face turned hard. "Take your things, and go out the back entrance—now."

"I didnea mean ta offend ya—" Etienne placed his hand over Andy's mouth. He followed Julian's gaze. Out the front window were two Templars, approaching the hermitage.

"Go now. It is amazing what a little headstart can achieve." Brother Julian walked to the front door and the others walked to the rear.

Etienne made sure everyone got out, and as he was closing the door he overheard Brother Julian saying, "Welcome, brothers."

"Brother Julian, have you seen a wagon pass this way? We are looking for a fugitive named Etienne LaRue."

"I haven't seen a wagon pass." Etienne heard the half-truth—not quite a lie, but not quite the truth either. He listened at the door to see if Brother Julian needed assistance. There were only two Templars and several of them.

"What's with all of the eggs?" one Templar asked.

"I was doing an experiment. It gets lonely being a hermit. Have you ever heard of the Paradox of Achilles and the Tortoise? Come in and I will show you..."

# CHAPTER 25

It was just after lunch when the coach left Notre Dame. Isabella sat across from Pope Clement, once again on a red velvet seat. Clement kept looking nervously out the window. The ride was short, and Isabella didn't have much time to steady him.

"Your Excellency, are you well?" Isabella took his hand and patted it.

"I don't want to lie, nor cause my men to lie."

"It is not a lie. You will hear my confession in Sainte-Chapelle. I fully intend to confess all of my sins. It has been too long since my last confession." Clement eased at her remarks, but his eyes darted outside the coach again.

"What if you are seen exiting my coach?"

"I won't be. I will enter the chapel from another entrance. No one will know." Isabella sat back in the seat and crossed her ankles. As the coach slowed, Clement searched Isabella's face for reassurance, and she smiled.

"His Majesty wasn't expecting the Pope today," a husky voice called to the driver.

"His Excellency has been called for Princess Isabella."

There was a long pause, and Isabella held her breath. She locked eyes with Clement and mouthed the words, *It will be fine,* to calm his bouncing leg.

"Very well. You may pass." The guard's voice was somber. "I will inform the King that he has arrived. I am sure he will want to speak with the Pope. But how did you—? Oh, never mind."

The coach skirted the chapel to its lower entrance. Adjacent to it was a door to the kitchen that Isabella could slip into unnoticed.

The coach door opened, and Isabella nodded at the Pope. Clement breathed deeply and descended the stairs. Isabella pulled her fur-lined hood over her head and darted to the left. She ran quickly through the kitchens, up the spiral staircase, to the large hall above. She nearly ran into a servant on the landing—the girl just stared at her as if she had seen a ghost.

"You didn't see me," Isabella said to the young servant. The girl continued to stare with wide eyes and nodded.

*Good, at least one person has seen me.*

She could make up any number of stories as to why she was in the kitchens. That encounter would work to her advantage. Isabella continued down the corridor and entered Sainte-Chapelle. She basked in the ruby reds and emerald greens streaming in through the stained-glass windows. Isabella was probably imagining it, but each shade of light felt different.

"I am in here already, my child," Clement's voice came from within the confessional box.

Isabella pulled back the half-door of the confessional and slid open the small piece of metal covering the grate. Before she spoke, wood banged and Clement yelped as he was pulled from the confessional.

"How did you know?" Her father's voice boomed through the chapel. He rammed the Pope hard against the wood, and Isabella heard him wheeze. "Answer me!"

"Father! Stop!" Isabella yelled as she burst from her side of the confessional.

Philip looked at her with wide eyes then back at Clement. He released his grip, and the Pope crumpled to the ground. Isabella had never seen that look on her father's face before. It was a mixture of shock and horror.

"Daughter, is it you? Is it really you?" Isabella slowly nodded. "But...I saw..." Isabella had never known her father to be without words.

"It is me, father. What did you see?"

"I saw you dead in your bed. With these very eyes—I saw you. Are you a ghost come back to haunt me?"

"No."

Philip rushed to her and wrapped his arms around her. His embrace nearly suffocated her. Isabella had never received this kind of affection from her father before. She didn't know how to react. Her mind was so clouded with emotions. What was happening?

*I saw you dead in your bed.* The realization hit Isabella and nearly knocked her to the ground. He had seen Matilda—she was dead.

## CHAPTER 26

After leaving the hermitage, the company reunited with Clair and Fransie at the well, then circled back to the Camino undetected; except for Brother Andre, who decided to stay at the hermitage with Brother Julian.

Etienne took the rear to protect the others, but he kept finding himself peeking into the coach to get a glimpse of Fransie's child. Gerheart had been right, she was dazzling.

It wasn't long before they reached Cruz de Ferro, the highest point of the Camino. The last time they were here, they had followed the custom of placing a stone at the foot of the cross as a symbol of some pain or hurt they wanted to leave behind on the Camino.

As they passed, Etienne could tell his stone had long since been covered by hundreds of other pilgrims' stones. Etienne had left behind the guilt he felt for breaking his vow as a Templar by choosing his love for Isabella over the order. Etienne, reflecting on the decisions he had made since then, and standing there as Seneschal of the Templars, knew every decision he had made had been the right one, even if he couldn't see it as each event occurred.

On the descent, the sweeping landscape and rolling mountains opened in front of them, but Etienne's mind was fixed on the small town just ahead. The memory that town held for him was bittersweet—it was where he had married Isabella in secret.

"So why didnea ya try ta escape at the Templar castle?" Andy's question to Prince Charles broke Etienne out of his thoughts. He blinked a few times and shook his head to get back into the present. Etienne had been wondering the same thing and turned his attention to Charles. He also needed the distraction.

"Being held captive by the Templars would be much worse than being held captive by you. They are my father's enemies. I could only imagine what they would do if they found out I was his son. Plus, I imagine the ransom they would ask would be much larger than what you will ask. Obviously, you don't have expensive taste." The prince looked at Andy's clothes with contempt.

"We're not holding you for ransom," Etienne said.

"We're not?" Andy scratched his head.

"No, Charles is the brother of the woman I love… The woman we all love. When we get to Astorga you will be free to do what you like. It is a town large enough for you to be safe and get word to your father. I'm sure he is anxious to hear from you."

"Why the change of heart?"

"Andy, he is my brother-in-law." The words seemed to slip out of Etienne's mouth.

"'Tis right. Sometimes I forget that you two wed in secret in that small mountain town… That small mountain town that we just passed. Oh, laddie. I'm sorry. How insensitive of me. I forgot, and ya never talk about your emotions—"

Charles stopped in his tracks."Brother-in-law? You married Isabella?"

"Yes, technically we are family. But, I have accepted that Isabella must fulfill her destiny, and I must fulfill mine." Etienne tapped the sword he had received for overcoming his envy. "It was very painful, but I accepted it."

"Laddie, I once heard the saying 'Love is like a butterfly, if ya let it go and it comes back ta ya, 'tis yours; but if not, 'twas never yours ta begin with.'"

"That was really poetic of you, Andy. But, I am fine."

Andy gave Etienne a questioning look. He had known Etienne long enough to know he wasn't fine. No matter how hard he tried to hide it, Andy always seemed to have a way of seeing right through him.

"Do ya think we should visit Charity when we reach Astorga?" Andy asked, changing the subject.

"Why would we do that?" Etienne stopped and narrowed his gaze.

"Ya ken with Gabriel gone and taking what he took, maybe she would give us another piece of you know what."

Etienne shook his head. "Andy, we shouldn't be talking about this in front of you know who." Etienne glanced at Prince Charles.

"Right," Andy said, and they continued on in silence.

The whole way down the mountain, Andy rehearsed what he would say to Charity. They needed to get another shard of the One True Cross, and Astorga was the only place to do that. They had to have all seven of the keys to unlock the one true treasure; he knew it. How could he have let that one slip away from him? Charity had entrusted him with it, and he had lost it several times; now it was gone for good. The last time they were here, Charity had been kind and sweet. Andy was sure she would help them out.

The multicolored rock wall surrounding Astorga was just as impressive as it had been the last time they had entered the city. Andy craned his neck up to see the tops of the walls. He was happy they were entering the city from this direction. At the other entrance, he remembered the steep stairs that they had to climb. They had almost killed him—although he was a lot fitter now than he had been. Andy tapped his fingers on his stomach.

They followed the shells inset in the cobblestones. He loved that this city marked the Camino so well. Pilgrims passed them on either side, continuing on to Santiago. Andy felt like he was a salmon swimming upstream. Walking the Camino this way was a much different experience than walking to Santiago. The places were the same, but he had changed so much.

"Do ya think we should stop at the cathedral now or later for prayer?" Andy asked Etienne, who answered his question with a sharp look. "Right, later then."

They passed through the town square, and Andy's stomach rumbled at the smell of pinchos laid out for the evening. As they arrived at the albergue, Andy felt an overwhelming sense of guilt. It was here that he had first lost the papers with the code on them to those Italian Hospitallers. Andy resolved that he would make up for his mistakes. He would visit Charity, even if Etienne didn't come with him.

"Peregrinos, you have returned!" José, the owner of the albergue said, with his arms spread wide. The older Spanish gentleman still had a curled mustache and adventure in his eyes.

"I'm surprised you remember us," Etienne said.

"How could I forget all of the theatrics that happened last time you were here? I see you have some new friends." He smiled at Fransie and Charles. "But, where is the young lady who took such good care of you? She loved you so much. That isn't something you find every day."

"She is at her father's house."

"Good, I hope you two are reunited soon. You are meant for each other."

"Right," Andy said, noticing Etienne's discomfort. "We will need some rooms."

After everyone was settled in, Andy decided he would take a little walk. This was the perfect opportunity to go see Charity. Etienne was at the Templar Commandery getting more gold—Brother Andre had assured them that the Templars in Astorga were still loyal to Molay as well; Clair was with Sister Fransie and the baby in the room; and to Andy's delight, it was Mariano and Gerhart's turn to do the laundry. That left only the prince, who was already gone. Andy didn't know if they would ever see him again, and he didn't really care either way. The young man could find his own way back home.

Andy skirted the main square of the city opposite of where the Templar Commandery was. Just as he was reaching the far end of the plaza, he spotted Etienne leaving the Commandery. The other Templars saluted him as he left. Andy quickly turned to the bar to his right.

"Una vino tinto y una tortilla," Andy said, to the barman.

The barman disappeared and moments later placed the red wine and Andy's favorite pincho, tortilla, in front of him. Andy nibbled on the egg and potato wedge as he watched Etienne traverse the square. Before he knew it, both the tortilla and Etienne had disappeared. Andy swigged down the wine in one gulp.

"I needed that," he said, wiping his lips.

Andy wove in and out between people as he followed the shells up the main thoroughway to the cathedral. He veered right to the entrance with the red Virgin Mary statue. Andy stopped dead in his tracks. The door with the stairs leading down to Charity's lair was wide open.

The last time they were here, Charity had met them in this very spot and opened the door for them. She wasn't here, which meant she must have led someone else inside.

Andy squirmed as the centipede crawled across his stomach. Andy still wished he would have gotten a different animal. All those legs crawling over him creeped him out sometimes. But, the little guy had helped him more than once.

"I suppose I should give ya a name. I'll call you Bartholomew." Andy nearly giggled as the centipede ran up his chest. "All right, Bart. Let's do this."

Andy took two steps forward and had to stop. His mouth became oily. *Maybe I shouldnae gotten that tortilla.*

"Run!" Prince Charles shouted as he came tearing out of the doorway. He bumped Andy's shoulder as he passed and dropped something. Andy bent down to pick it up, but when he saw what it was, he left the large ruby on the ground. This was part of Charity's hoard. Charity was the embodiment of the virtue of her name, but she was also the deadly sin of Greed, and Prince Charles had chosen Greed over Charity.

"You foolish boy! What have ya done!" Andy called after the prince, who was heading for the back gate of the wall that surrounded the cathedral.

A pair of glowing green eyes appeared in the dark stairwell, and Andy ran after the prince. In a single bound, Greed leaped from the doorway and landed on Charles— knocking him to the ground.

"Mine, you are mine," Greed said, lifting its terrible claws to strike.

"Ah, Charity." Andy couldn't believe what he was doing. The beast in the form of a small girl looked over its shoulder. Greed's glowing green eyes sucked Andy in. He felt like his essence was being drawn into her, and the oily fatness in his mouth was increasing.

"Charity is gone."

"See, I met Charity before, and I ken she is in there someplace."

Greed turned back to Prince Charles and stared at him with those terrible eyes.

"He is just a wee lad and doesnea ken what he is doing. Charity would give him a chance to give her something. I know that Ronan gave his life, as he had nothing to give. But this young prince has more to offer than just his life."

"Prince." Greed stepped off and cocked its head from side to side as Charles scurried back.

"Make it stop!" Charles screamed. "Make it stop!"

"Only ya can do that. You have ta give Greed something that is more valuable than what you stole."

"But, I don't have anything."

"You do have one thing, Your Highness."

"No. I can't."

Greed jumped back on Charles like a raven who hooked its talons around its prey.

"'Tis either that or your life. And even if I don't like ya, I don't want ya ta die. You did save my life once. I am only returning the favor," Andy shouted.

Greed leaned forward.

"Stop!" Charles yelled. "Very well then. I give you my claim to the French throne."

Greed straightened up from its animalistic crouch, and the part in the back of its head split, revealing Charity's face. Her clothes turned from black to white and her whole demeanor turned soft and kind.

"What a wonderful gift," Charity said, running in place. "Your charity has set you free, young man. I will do wonderful things with this." She helped Charles to his feet.

"What have I done?" Charles shook his head.

"Andy! I'm so happy to see you." Charity ran to Andy and wrapped her arms around him. "Let's go play, all three of us."

The room at the alburgue was cozy, with a bed for each of them, a fireplace, and two windows at the far end. Fransie lay in bed and held her child close to her chest as she nursed. She couldn't stop admiring her. She was the most beautiful thing Fransie had ever seen. Her little hands and feet were perfect; her little nose was perfect; she was perfect. Fransie loved her child so much. The pain from the birth was still present in her body, but the memory of it was long gone.

Fransie had never imagined she would have a child. When she

became a nun, and gave her life to God, it just wasn't an option. Now, holding her little one in her arms, she couldn't imagine a life without being a mother. How could she have given this up?

"Have ya thought of a name for the wee one yet?" Clair asked, from her bedside. The others had all gone out, and it was just the three of them in the sleeping chamber.

"I have. Her name is Roslyn. It was Sister Caroline's given name."

"No, ya donnae say. I didnea ken that ya got a new name when ya became a nun."

Fransie nodded. "You give everything to God when you become a nun—including your name."

Clair reached out a finger, and Roslyn grabbed it absentmindedly as she continued to suckle.

"Clair, this is the happiest I have ever been."

"I felt that way with my wee Heather."

"Where is she now?"

"She's dead." Clair's eyes became vacant. "She 'ad the Fire of San Antone. We brought her ta the Arc of San Anton ta be healed, but she died before we reached it. These wee ones can be your greatest joy and your greatest sorrow. A mother's love never dies. I didnea think I would ever go back ta Castrojeriz. We didnea even get a chance ta give her a funeral."

Clair buried her face in the covers, and Fransie felt the blankets become damp from her tears. With her free hand, Fransie stroked Clair's hair as she wept. She had never seen Clair express her emotions. She was tough as a sword, but even swords shatter sometimes.

Clair sat up and wiped her nose with the back of her forearm.

"I donnae ken that I can go back there. I cannea face that loss again. I buried my emotions because I couldnae bury my wee one."

Fransie's heart went out to Clair. She wished there was something she could do to help her. Perhaps there was. Maybe Clair was afraid to share her emotions in front of the boys. She was always so tough;

maybe she didn't want them to see her as weak. Lord knows she wasn't. Maybe all Clair needed was for someone to hold space for her.

Clair's head went back into the covers again, and she cried for a long while until she went to sleep. Fransie continued to stroke her hair, and she hummed a lullaby for both Roslyn and Clair.

"Are there any more clothes to be washed?" Mariano said merrily as he entered the room with Gerhart.

Clair looked up with bloodshot eyes. "I need ya ta do that thing ya do ta me. I cannea stop the pain."

"Clair, are you—"

"Go away, Gerhart! I cannea see ya like this."

"But—"

"Go!"

Roslyn stirred and started to fuss. Seeing this, Gerhart raised his arms and backed out of the room. He shook his head as he closed the door behind him. Fransie bounced Roslyn to settle her down. Roslyn let out a large burp and smiled at Fransie.

"Are ya just gonnae stand at the door, Mariano? I need you. I've fallen ta pieces, and I donnae ken if I can shove this sadness back in ta its little box."

Mariano sat on the edge of Fransie's bed and took Clair by the hand. "My dear friend, what Shadow is causing you so much pain?"

"Shadow?" Clair cleared her nose again with her forearm.

"What is the thought that is causing you to suffer?" Mariano asked.

"My wee bairn, Heather. She shouldnae died. She had so much life ahead of her."

"It must be very painful for you to believe that thought." Mariano looked at Clair with kind eyes, and his stare was met with fury.

"It would be painful for anyone!"

"Clair, please," Fransie said, trying to calm Roslyn. "You are scaring her."

"Sorry, lassie. I'll control my temper." Clair looked back at Mariano. "Yes. 'Tis painful."

"This process can seem cruel, and I may seem insensitive as I am doing *The Work* with you. It's like pouring alcohol on a wound so it doesn't fester. It hurts like hell for a moment, but it saves you from losing a leg or worse."

Clair nodded.

"Is it true that Heather shouldn't have died?" Mariano asked.

"Who the 'ell are ya ta ask such a question?" Clair knocked over the chair as she stood, and Roslyn started to cry. "Sorry lassie, it willnea happen again," Clair said to Fransie.

"If it does, I will insist that you leave," Fransie said.

Clair sat back down. "I ken that ya are just tryin' ta help, but—"

"But, you are fighting to hold onto a thought that is causing you to suffer. Is there anything causing you to suffer in this present moment besides the thought Heather shouldn't have died? You are sitting in a beautiful room with friends and a miracle child. The world is perfect, but this Shadow is robbing you of this perfect moment. It is turning heaven into hell. This Shadow is fighting for its existence by causing you to act out—to yell, to scream, to cry, anything to make you believe it is real. So I am going to ask you again, and I only want a yes or no answer—is it true that Heather shouldn't have died?"

"Yes," Clair said, coldly.

"Can you absolutely know beyond a doubt that she shouldn't have died?" Mariano asked.

"I suppose there is no way ta ken beyond a doubt. But—"

"That is just the Shadow fighting for its survival. Anytime you try to justify or make an excuse that causes you to fight with reality, it is the Shadow trying to fight for its life. Let's go onto the next question; how do you react when you think the thought that Heather shouldn't have died?"

"I get angry." Clair's eyes filled with tears. "Really angry. Not at her, but at myself, for being a terrible mother. I shove the feeling inta a little box where it punches and kicks me all day—everyday."

"Who would you be if there was no way possible to think the thought that Heather shouldn't have died?" Mariano asked.

"I suppose I'd be here with this wee child—caring for it, not scaring it—enjoying the company of my friends. I'd be able ta breathe."

"Can you see how there is nothing in this present moment causing you to suffer, besides this thought that is causing you to fight against reality? Every time we wage war with reality, we lose—and create suffering for ourselves and others.

"Heather only died once, but you continue to kill her in your head again and again, by fighting with the reality of her death." Clair nodded as he spoke, but Fransie saw skepticism in her eyes.

"I'm not asking you to give up this thought—this Shadow. There is no way you can. However, when you hold it up to inquiry, it loses its grip on you, one question at a time. Let's turn it around. What is the opposite of Heather shouldn't have died?" Mariano asked.

"Heather should have died," Clair said, through clenched teeth.

"Good," Mariano seemed unfazed by the anger radiating off of Clair. "Can you give me three examples of how this is as true or truer than the original statement?"

Clair seethed for a few minutes, then, almost as if she was ice melting, she sat back.

"Because she did die. 'Tis truer than the thought that she shouldn't have died. She did die. 'Tis the reality of it no matter how hard I fight against it."

"Can you find another?"

"She was suffering and in pain. I see her wee face now, covered in sores—every inch of her was covered in sores. She was in so much pain. In its own way, death was a mercy for her."

"Good now turn it around to the self."

Clair raised questioning eyebrows.

"I shouldn't…" Mariano encouraged.

"Oh, I see. I shouldnae have died. 'Tis true. I shouldnae died. That day a piece of me died, and I havenea been able ta recover it. My compassion died, and I became angrier and angrier—always lashing out at others. I've been so mean—especially ta Gerhart."

"Can you see any reason to keep this thought that Heather shouldn't have died? It is causing you so much pain and causing you to hurt others."

"I think I'm being a good mother by keeping the thought—by punishing myself for her death. But that doesnea accomplish anything—does it? It doesn't bring her back. It just makes me mean ta all of ya. I have to go find Gerhart and apologize. I need ta talk ta him about all of this."

Clair nearly knocked over Etienne as she flew out of the door.

"What has gotten into her?" Etienne asked, entering the room.

"She just defeated one of her Shadows," Mariano said.

"The gift the Alchemist gave you is amazing." Etienne patted Mariano on the back.

"It is only four questions and a turnaround."

"Your daughter is beautiful, Fransie." Etienne said, taking Clair's seat.

"Thank you, Etienne. Her name is Roslyn." Fransie felt so proud as she said her child's name.

"We are only a day away from Hospital de Orbigo now." Etienne said, sitting. "We need to come up with a plan. Are you well enough to travel tomorrow? We still have two days until the date the priest set."

Before Roslyn was born, Fransie would have happily traded herself in exchange for her friends, but now things were so different. Her priorities had changed from helping her friends to protecting Roslyn. She would give her life to keep her safe.

Fransie nestled Roslyn tighter in her arms and sighed. "I have been thinking about—"

"You should have seen your face when she was perched on you."

Andy said, as he and young Prince Charles entered with their arms around each other's shoulders. "I nearly wet myself just watchin'!"

"What happened to you two?" Etienne turned in his chair to face them.

"We went ta go see Charity... Actually, I went ta go see Charity, and Charles here beat me to it. By the time I arrived, he had awakened Greed. She was just as terrible as Ronan had said."

"How are you still alive?" Etienne asked Charles.

"Andy saved me."

"'Twas nothin'. I just was repaying the favor. Ya saved my life once. And as to how he saved his life, he is no longer a prince. He gave Charity his claim ta the throne. He is just plain old Charlie now." Andy rubbed his knuckles on Charles's head.

"That is enough," Fransie said. Charles looked like a poor scared child, unsure what to do. He was just going along with Andy, as he had no other choice.

Andy released Charles and sat on the bed opposite Fransie's.

"What is this I heard about a plan?" Andy sat on a bed, and tweedled his legs in the air. "If ya are scheming, I have some ideas that I know will work!"

"Before we get to any plan, Prince Charles has some explaining to do," Etienne said.

"It's just Charles now," the youth said timidly.

"Right, how did ya know about the cathedral, Charlie?" Andy tweedled his legs again.

"Andrew Sinclair," Fransie chastised. "Stop calling him Charlie. I can see that he doesn't like it. You are better than being a bully. Do you want to be a bad influence on Roslyn?" Fransie was surprised at her words, but Charles seemed so unsure of himself. The poor child was petrified. She could see it in his eyes.

"Sorry, Sister Fransie. I was just 'aving a bit of fun."

"It isn't me you should be apologizing to."

"Sorry, Charles. I know 'tis been a hard day for ya, and the last thing ya need is someone poking fun at ya."

"I accept your apology." Charles joined the others around Fransie's bed.

"So, Charles, how did you know about Charity?" Etienne asked.

"I overheard you and Andy talking about visiting her to recover what Gabriel had stolen."

Fransie's heart sank as she heard the young prince accuse Gabriel of stealing. Fransie didn't want to believe that he had been planning to leave the whole time. He had to have a reason for leaving.

"But that isn't the reason I went," Charles continued. "There was a voice putting thoughts into my head. It told me how powerful I would be if I possessed what Charity had. It told me my father would respect me… Everyone would respect me, including all of you." Charles avoided eye contact with the others.

"Charles, respect can't be bought, nor forced, it is something that has to be earned. It won't come from the clothes you wear, the money you have, nor the title you possess. It starts with you respecting yourself first—soon, the rest of the world will follow your example." Sister Fransie had wanted to say that to Charles since they first met.

"I guess I have none of that to hide behind anymore. Even my clothes are torn now. Greed has taken it all away from me." Tears formed behind Charles's eyes.

"It sounds like Pride caused this as well," Etienne said. "It must have been what was whispering to you to visit Charity. You must not have accepted that you can't do this alone in O'Cebreiro."

"I am alone now and have nothing." Charles placed his head in his hands and sobbed.

"You have us." Etienne placed a hand on Charles's back. "I don't know how, but we will ensure that you make it home to your father. Just because you gave up your claim to the throne doesn't mean that we have to give up on you."

The music played merrily in the bar attached to the albergue, and mixed with the chatter of pilgrims from all nations. Andy didn't know if he was more excited about his food or about sharing his plan with the others. Being in a bar with a pint in his hand was his natural element. The laughter, glasses clinking, and general merriment made Andy feel alive.

"Now that we are all together—" Andy took a large gulp of ale and wiped his mouth. "'Tis time ta go over the plan." Everyone watched Andy as he cleared a space on the table. He was the center of attention and he was loving it. "This is the front entrance to the Hospitaller Commandery." He took a carrot and placed it in the space he had made. "Here is the infirmary." He placed his cup to the right of the entrance. "The medicinal garden 'tis here." He made a square out of chicken bones. "This is the library and Hospitaller quarters." He took Etienne's mug and Clair's plate and placed them in the appropriate places.

"How do you know this?" Fransie asked.

"I had a lot of time ta wander the halls when Etienne was recovering from being poisoned by that dagger."

"So what's the plan?" Etienne leaned in closer to get a better look.

"Well, the way I see it, we have two options." Andy placed his fingers on the table as if they were legs and started walking to the carrot that represented the entrance. "Option A: Fransie walks to the entrance and turns herself in. She tells the priest what she knows as 'tis useless without the rest of the code." Andy tapped his satchel with the coded pieces of paper. "Then the priest either keeps his word by releasing her friends and the Harp, or he doesn't. From what I ken of the priest, I don't think this plan will work."

"And what's plan B?" Etienne asked, crossing his arms.

"Plan B is my favorite." Andy linked his fingers and stretched them out, cracking his knuckles. He looked at Gerhart. "This plan will require muscle." He looked at Etienne. "Speed." He looked at Charles. "Deception." Andy smiled widely. "And, of course, brains."

"In plan B, Mariano and Clair take Roslyn and the wagon safely across the bridge and set up camp by the lake." Andy took a roll and placed it by the water jug.

"When enough time has passed, and we know they are safe, Fransie and I will walk to the front entrance." He placed the index finger and middle finger of both hands on the table and walked to the carrot. "We will pretend that I have captured Fransie and am turning her in. This results in one of two possibilities: one, they think we are lying and throw us both in prison; or two: they throw Fransie in prison with the others and they give me a guest chamber for the night—and some gold for my trouble." Andy winked.

"I don't see how either of those options help!" Fransie said.

"Have you met my little friend?" Andy's centipede scuttled onto the table and everyone drew back. "What? 'Tis just Bartholomew."

"Bartholomew?" Etienne asked, and Andy nodded. "What good will he do?"

Andy flicked his head and the centipede jumped off the table and crawled up the door that led to the locked ale storage room. The centipede disappeared into the keyhole. Andy made some jerky movements with his hands; and moments later, the door opened. Bartholomew scurried across the floor and up Andy's pant leg. Andy squirmed around as the little critter climbed his hairy legs. He still hadn't gotten used to it.

"That's amazing!" Gerhart said.

"We have been practicing for just such an occasion." Andy crossed his arms smugly. "Whether 'tis just Fransie locked or the both of us, it doesnea matter. Either way, we will get out."

"So where do we come in?" asked Charles, excitedly.

"I take it, at the palace, you had many pages and servants?" Andy raised his eyebrows.

"Loads of them."

"Good. I will need ya ta pretend you are a servant. Do you think ya can do that?"

"I think so, but how does that help?"

"I will go ta the medicinal garden." Andy walked his fingers to the chicken bones that represented the garden. "And will make a tea that will put our priest friend ta sleep for a good long while."

"You aren't going to kill him? If so, I want no part in this." Fransie sat back.

"No, just a good long sleep. He will wake up feeling wonderful."

"So, you want me to pretend I am a servant to give him that drink?"

"Yes." Andy held up his two fingers. "'Tis you now." Charles nodded. "Ya take the tea to our priest friend and put him to sleep. The Harp will either be with him or in the library. If 'tis with him, ya take it ta Etienne, who will be waiting outside the Commandery with a really fast horse. Then Etienne rides off into the sunset. He will draw away the majority of the Hospitaller force. When they are away, we will break out Fransie's friends and escape to the lake, where Etienne will meet us."

"Wow," Etienne said, rubbing his chin.

"Where does the muscle come in?" Gerhart leaned both forearms on the table, causing everything to slide.

"Ya will know if we need it. But, let's hope it doesnea come ta that. 'Tis the perfect plan."

# CHAPTER 27

“Philip, what is the meaning of this?” Pope Clement said as Isabella watched him struggle to his feet.

“Isabella was found dead this morning. I saw her disfigured corpse lying in her bed, wearing her dress, and her jewels.” Philip looked at Isabella in disbelief once more. “We found this on the bed stand next to her.” Philip produced the necklace and an empty vial of poison. “There was a note that said Isabella had taken her own life because she couldn’t bear to live without Etienne.”

“This is my fault… This is all my fault… God, forgive me.” Isabella placed her face in her palms and leaned against the outer wall of the confessional.

“Daughter, this is joyous news. You are alive!” Philip said, spreading his arms.

“But, Matilda is dead.” Isabella slid down the wall and pulled her knees in tightly. “How could you not see it was her?”

“The poison had contorted her face beyond recognition, but I did recognize the clothes and jewels. Tell me daughter, why was Matilda in your bed wearing your things? And why is he here?” Philip pointed at Clement. The joy disappeared from her father’s face like a cloud passing in the sky.

Isabella pulled her knees in tighter.

"Answer me!" Philip hit the confessional hard. "If you won't answer, perhaps he will." Philip turned menacingly to the Pope.

"I ran away," Isabella said, clearing her blurry eyes.

"See, that wasn't so hard. Why would you do a thing like that?"

"Because you told me Etienne was dead." Isabella shot daggers out of her eyes "I needed to see for myself. So I asked Matilda to pose as me to buy me time for my escape. I was going back to the Camino de Santiago to find Etienne."

"Why would you think I'd lie about his death?" Philip asked.

"Because you have lied about it before." The words just slipped out of Isabella's mouth, and the world moved in slow motion.

Philip laughed uncontrollably, and Isabella pulled her knees in tighter.

"You mean, Etienne is the same boy that I put to death all of those years ago?" Isabella didn't respond. "This will make finding him so much easier. He must be the only black Templar."

Isabella rested her forehead on her knees and wanted to disappear. Her best friend died because of her, and now, he would find Etienne.

"Wait, this means Etienne is alive?" The realization dawned over Isabella's whole body and culminated in a smile.

"So, why are you with him?" Philip lifted a suspicious eye at Clement.

"As I said, I was on my way to find out about Etienne, but I had an overwhelming urge to give Pope Clement my confession. He convinced me to come home."

"I'm happy you are home," Philip said. "There is much to celebrate. This means your wedding to Prince Edward is still on."

Isabella had no words for her father. Someone had killed Matilda thinking it was her. Matilda was dead! The killer was still out there! And all he could think about was how her wedding would benefit him!

"Leave us!" King Philip commanded Clement.

"I am the Pope. You will respect my station."

"And this is my house and my country; you will respect my wishes."

Pope Clement glanced from Philip to Isabella.

"The Lord giveth and the Lord taketh away," Pope Clement said. "I am sorry for your loss, my child." He shook his head and left the chapel. Isabella knew that his words were as much a warning for her father as condolence for her.

After the Pope was gone, her father laughed hysterically. The sound bounced merrily to the vaulted ceiling, playing amongst the shafts of light.

"You can quit pretending now." Her father's words shook Isabella from her grief.

"What?"

Her father produced a scroll and read. "'Dear father, I am sorry you have to find me like this. I have decided to take my own life rather than live in a world without Etienne. When you killed him, you killed me as well. Pray for my immortal soul.'"

Philip crumpled the paper and threw it at Isabella's feet. "You had us all fooled."

Isabella read the scroll. It was true; this was a suicide note. She had no words; she just stared at her father, blankly.

"Ingenious, daughter, you faked your own death by killing Matilda so that we would never come searching for you. I commend you for this."

Isabella began to speak, but Philip cut her off with a sweep of his hand.

"It is all right, you don't have to confess or apologize. I think it was absolutely brilliant. I even grieved for you. This is a great thing. This means you are ready to lead, Isabella. I now know you will do anything possible to achieve your goals—just like me. You have earned my trust and respect today. I do have one question though. Why did you return?"

"I discovered that someone was planning to kill you, and I had to stop them. I used the Pope to get back into the castle." Isabella answered truthfully. Even though she wished the poison had taken him instead of Matilda.

"Thank you for the noble gesture, but that is what being a royal is. Every day someone is plotting or trying to kill you. Haven't you figured this out yet? That is why I need people I can trust around me. People like you. Come, there is much to discuss."

# CHAPTER 28

Andy never thought he would return to Hospital De Orbigo, but here they all were standing on the edge of town. So far the plan was working well. Mariano and Clair had passed with the cart in the night, and to the best of his knowledge, they were already at the lake. Etienne had bought a fast horse and was at the ready for his signal. Their man on the inside, Charles, was in position. Gerhart, the muscle, was also in position should they need him. Now it was up to him and Fransie.

"Ya ready for this, lassie?" Andy asked.

"Andy, I don't know if I am making the right decision. What about Roslyn?"

"The wee bairn is safe with Clair and Mariano. They will look after her."

"But, what if something happens to me?"

"We are a family, and we will all look after her together, but nothing is going ta happen ta you."

"Are you sure there is no other way?"

"You are the only one who can do this, lassie. No one else. 'Tis up to you, though. Do you want ta leave your friends and continue on? We could just try ta steal the Harp."

Fransie shook her head. “I can’t leave them.”

“Right then. Let’s go. ’Tis getting late.” Andy took Fransie by the arm and walked her down the empty street, their shadows stretching with the setting sun. They stopped at the main door to the Hospitaller Commandery, and Andy took a deep breath.

“Andy, I’m happy I’m not doing this alone. No matter what happens in there, thank you for coming with me.”

Fransie nodded at him, and he knocked loudly on the door. Moments later, a large Hospitaller answered. He wore all black and had the silver eight-pointed Hospitaller cross on his chest.

“Can I help you?” The Hospitaller looked at them up and down then narrowed his gaze.

“I have a present for the priest visiting you from Paris.” Andy shook Fransie by the arm slightly. He thought some theatrics would help sell their story.

“Well I’ll be… He has been expecting you… He said it would happen today, but none of us believed him. God is good.” The Hospitaller moved out of their way. “He has been waiting for you in the medicinal garden all day. Page!” the man barked.

Andy almost started laughing as Charles came trotting their way. He was doing his best to disguise his noble upbringing, but he stood too straight, and he was too well groomed.

“Yes, sir.” Charles made a flourished bow that took way too long. The Hospitaller shook his head as he waited.

“You must excuse him—he is a noble runaway. He is getting used to the whole page thing,” the Hospitaller side-whispered to Andy as Charles was finishing his bow. “Boy, can you remember where the medicinal garden is?”

Charles nodded.

“Good, escort our guests there.”

“As you command, sire.” Charles flourished some more.

When they were out of earshot of anyone, Charles asked, “How am I doing?”

"You are doing just fine." Fransie answered as she and Andy exchanged a look.

Andy was glad that she had answered. He didn't know if he would be able to keep it together.

Charles opened the large doors to the garden and led them in. This had been Andy's sanctuary the last time he was here. It had also been the biggest help in figuring out the code from the Cathedral of Leon. Had it not been for that sundial, he may not have figured out the code.

"Father Alexander," Charles said to the tall slender priest, who was sitting on a bench with his arms outstretched and head tilted back.

The priest opened his eyes and smiled. "Thank you, My Lord," he said in his raspy voice, as he made the sign of the cross. "That is all, you may go, page."

Charles bowed and flourished the whole way out of the garden.

"'E is a strange one, isn't 'e," Andy joked. The priest didn't smile; he continued to stare at Fransie.

"I have been expecting you." He switched his piercing gaze to Andy. "You, on the other hand, I was not." Father Alexander clasped his long, cruel fingers together.

"See, she is my prisoner—"

"You do not matter to me. You may go." The priest signaled at the door with his eyes.

"Now wait a minute. Isnea there a reward or something?"

"Doing God's will should be a reward enough for you, my son."

"But, aren't ya even interested in why I brought her?"

"No."

"Well, the least ya could do is offer me a bed for the night. The sun is setting, and 'tis a long road back."

"Very well, charity is a virtue. Page!"

Charles reappeared at the door.

"Summon the Mother Superior," Father Alexander said, not taking his eyes off of Fransie.

"There is no need, Father. I am... You! You? How dare you come back here?"

Andy turned to see the nun who had caught him taking herbs for Etienne.

"Father, this man is a thief and a liar. He must be thrown in the prison for rehabilitation. Where are your friends? You travel like a pack of rats: the giant, the murderer, the invalid Templar, and the woman who loved him so much. Her love for him was sickening."

Charles glanced at the nun with surprised eyes at the mention of Isabella.

"If she is with him," the nun pointed to Fransie, "I would throw her in the prison as well." Father Alexander silenced her with a look.

"Sister, let me be clear. This woman is a guest of the Pope. No harm shall come to her. If it does you may suffer the fires of hell. Him, on the other hand," the priest nodded toward Andy, "you can do whatever you like with. He doesn't matter to me, only her."

"Guards!" the Mother Superior called.

Several Hospitallers entered the room.

"Take him to the prison with the others in rehabilitation."

"'Appy ta see ya got promoted since the last time I was here," Andy said as he was dragged out of the room. He smiled smugly at the nun as he passed. He also took note of all the herbs as he passed, and just as he remembered it, he saw what he needed to make the sleeping tincture. This was going exactly as planned. Well, almost exactly as planned.

Fransie stared in disbelief as Andy was dragged out of the gardens.

"Sister Fransie, isn't it? Come, sit with me." The Priest patted the bench next to him.

Fransie stood firm. The priest made her flesh crawl. She didn't want to be anywhere near him.

"How do you know my name?"

"Your friends told me. Actually, your friends told me many things."

"Like what?" Fransie crossed her arms.

"Come sit with me."

"No!"

"That is no way to treat the person who saved your friends."

"What do you mean *you saved them*?"

"They would have died had we not shown up in Logrono. But, more importantly, he would have lost his soul to the devil that possessed him. Luca, show yourself."

Fransie's blood turned to ice, and her hands shook uncontrollably. She expected anything but this. She couldn't face Luca, not after what he had done. Fransie stared at the ground and heard Sister Caroline's screams. Luca had fallen prey to the deadly sin of Gluttony. He had drunk from the Holy Gail, which gave him eternal life, but it also gave him the Curse of More.

Fransie closed her eyes to shield herself from the horrific sight, but his cursed appearance haunted her thoughts. The large mouth protruding out of his stomach, devouring everything in sight including Sister Caroline… She squeezed her eyes tighter, in the hopes that the image would disappear.

"You have nothing to fear. He is well restrained."

Fransie heard chains pulling, but she didn't dare to look up.

"Come now, Sister Fransie. That is no way to treat an old friend. One who sacrificed so much for you."

"Fransie," Luca said, weakly. "Fransie, help me." His voice was so pained.

Fransie shifted her eyes hesitantly over her shoulder. Opposite of where the priest was sitting, Luca was stretched out in an X, chained between two pillars. He was pale and his head hung low. She looked back at the priest, and he was smiling.

"You are a monster!" Fransie said. The priest had been sitting there all day, watching Luca suffer. He was enjoying it.

"He is the monster, Sister. Had we not arrived and subdued him, he would have killed your friends and devoured that whole city. Luckily, I am well versed in exorcisms; the power of Jesus saved him."

"Well, why is he still chained?"

"The exorcism was only temporary. So we are starving the devil out of him. The man hasn't eaten in many days, yet he won't die. However, I'm training the beast to do God's will. If only I was making better progress with the witches. They are harmless to others, but nearly deadly to themselves. It is as if they are going mad, especially when I play this."

The priest lifted the small Harp and strummed a few chords. Fransie's mouth salivated and her pulse raced, but Rosalita stirred in her pocket to remind her she wasn't alone. With Rosalita's filtering, she was able to resist its call. In Pamplona, Fransie's lust for the music of the Harp almost got them all trapped in the trial of Lust. Fransie had opened the door, but it was Michael who saved them. Each one of her companions were held captive for what they lusted after most, but Michael overcame the challenge with his chaste heart.

"It is interesting that it makes them go mad, yet it calms this beast." The priest nodded at Luca, who seemed to be in a stupor.

Fransie's heart heaved. He was torturing all of them. She knew at that moment that she had made the right decision coming back. Even if something happened to her, she couldn't let him treat her friends like this.

"I wish I had more time to study them."

"What do you mean, 'had more time?'"

"Since you are here, we will depart immediately for Paris, to see the Pope. The road is long, and finding you has taken more time than expected."

"What about my friends? You said you would kill them if I didn't come. I am here now. What will happen to them?"

"I'm thinking of taking him with us. It would be risky, but a possession like this hasn't happened since biblical times. I'm sure my colleagues would like to study him as well."

"And the others?"

"I will order the Hospitallers to let the Italians go after we are a safe distance away. But the witches, they are too dangerous. They must be burned at the stake. Surely you know that."

This wasn't part of the plan. Fransie's stomach turned in knots, but she straightened and stood more firmly.

"No," she said, "I won't go with you. I won't tell the Pope what I know. The deal was that you wouldn't kill them if I came."

"Very well then, life in prison. I don't see why you would care about the lives of two witches, Sister."

"That is not ideal…but better than death. Very well then, but one last thing."

"What is it?"

"We have to wait until tomorrow to leave. I have traveled many days to get here, and I need to rest. I would also like time to say goodbye to my friends."

The priest placed the tips of his long fingers together and tapped them a few times.

"Very well then. We will leave at first light." The priest took a scrap of food and threw it at Luca. The mouth in his stomach opened wide and caught the food.

Fransie turned away at the sight of those terrible teeth, and her knees went weak.

"But, if you try anything, I will send him after you." The priest threw another piece of food at Luca, and Fransie heard those gnashing teeth.

Fransie prayed silently that Andy's plan would work. She had bought them some time, but there would be dire consequences if they failed.

Andy didn't offer any resistance, or help, as he was dragged through the Hospitaller Commandery. He took note of the layout—it was exactly as he remembered.

*Left at the library; then right; and finally, down some stairs.*

"Meet your new friends, and good luck with the witches," a guard said as they threw Andy into the prison, slamming the door behind him.

"Witches? No one said anything about witches!" Andy banged on the door loudly.

"Should we put him in manacals?" a second guard asked.

"Nah, he seems harmless," the first answered, and the sound of their footsteps disappeared up the stairs.

Andy looked around the cell, and as far as prisons go, this one seemed nice enough—except for the witches, wherever they were. There was hay, one lonely barred window, and of course, that lovely musty dungeon smell.

"'Ello," Andy said, timidly.

"Who are you?" a voice with an Italian accent said from behind a large pillar.

"That depends, who are you?" Andy asked, cautiously.

"You-a answer first." Another thick Italian accent answered back, from the opposite side of the pillar.

"I'm a friend of Sister Fransie. Now show yourself. I prefer to talk ta people instead of pillars." The light was too dim for Andy to see the pillar clearly, and for that matter, the whole prison. Those witches could be anywhere.

Andy heard a heated discussion in Italian. Finally, the first voice said, "We can't show ourselves. You have to come to us. We are friends of Sister Fransie as well."

"Ya must be Michael and Emanuel. I'm Andy Sinclair. Surely Sister Fransie talked about me and Etienne?" Andy took a few cautious steps to the pillar.

"She talked about Etienne, but never mentioned you. I'm Michael," the first voice said.

"And I'm Emanuel."

"Nice ta meet ya—" Andy cautiously rounded the pillar and found both men chained to the pillar. They were emaciated, and their hair and beard had grown long. The manacles had dug deep into their wrists and blood had crusted around the cruel iron. "I see why ya couldnae come ta me." Humor was Andy's coping mechanism. He sometimes wished he could turn it off, but the words just came out.

Michael managed a weak smile.

"Donnae ken? I came here ta get ya out. We have a foolproof plan." Andy winked. "Now, what about these witches? Should I be worried?" Andy discreetly pointed over his shoulder.

"Witches! Witches!" Emanuel said, passionately.

"They are not witches. They are our friends. The priest has tortured them every day. They can't resist the Harp without their animals. They have beaten themselves nearly to death against the bars to reach it."

"Where are they now?"

Michael motioned slightly with his head to a pile of straw to the right of the window. Peering closely, Andy saw two women badly beaten and bruised. One had porcelain skin and red hair. She was wrapped in the embrace of the other, who had dark skin and a warrior's body.

"That must be Raphael and Auriel."

"It was… I don't know how much of them is left." Michael shook his head.

"Damn that priest!" Emanuel struggled with his chains.

"Donnae worry. We are here ta get you out."

"How? You are just as trapped as we are." Michael's head slumped.

"I have Bartholomew." Andy extended his hand, and the centipede scurried to his palm.

Both Emanuel and Michael started laughing like madmen.

"Sorry, sorry, this prison must be making us go insane. Are you really here?" Michael said.

Andy nodded.

"And did you just say that that centipede will help us to escape?" Emanuel raised both eyebrows.

"Well, I said Bartholomew would help us to escape."

"You're serious, aren't you?" Michael asked.

Andy nodded.

"How?" Emanuel asked, skeptically.

"Like this."

Andy started to walk his fingers and the centipede crawled up Michael. Michael squirmed as Bartholomew went on his expedition. Andy continued to walk the centipede to Michael's wrist. When it got there, Bartholomew stopped and shook its head. Andy leaned in for a closer look; the lock on the manacles was too small for the centipede to fit.

"The hole—'tis too small," Andy said as Bartholomew jumped back into his hand. "Who has the key ta these?"

"Mother Superior, keeps them on her at all times," Michael said.

"Right then. We will 'ave ta adjust the plan, but 'tis still possible. I 'ave ta go; I 'ave a date in the medicinal garden. I will come back for you though. Can they walk?" Andy nodded to Auriel and Raphael.

"I don't know. I'm not sure if we can, either."

"You will 'ave ta." Andy patted Michael on the shoulder. "Right then." Andy walked to the door, and within seconds, Bartholomew had picked the lock.

Fransie sat at a long table opposite Father Alexander. To the right, a fire crackled in a hearth that was large enough for Fransie to stand in. With each pop of the wood, Fransie couldn't help but think of Raphael and Auriel burning at the stake, if Andy's plan didn't work. Fransie didn't have an appetite; the thought of her friends in the dungeon while she sat in such opulence was sickening. She moved the food around on her plate, but not a morsel met her lips.

"Are you finished, sister?" Fransie did a double-take. It was Charles who had asked the question. She nodded, and he discreetly winked at her as he cleared her plate.

"Father Alexander," Fransie said. "Would you join me in having a hot drink to help settle the food? I always find warm peppermint helps me to sleep better."

"No." Father Alexander took the last bite of his food.

Fransie's body tensed. How would they get the Harp from him now? How would she save her friends? Would she have to kill him? Fransie eyed a knife to her right, but she knew she couldn't kill anyone.

Father Alexander cleared his mouth with his napkin and folded it neatly next to his plate. "I will have anise. I find it to be more soothing. Boy, go fetch us our drinks."

Charles bowed and left the room.

Fransie took a deep breath and sunk back into her chair. This was going to work—Andy's plan was going to work.

"We will need a good night's sleep. We will be traveling straight to Paris, stopping only to resupply. The coach we will be traveling in should be more than adequate to sleep in."

"Father Alexander, why must I go with you? Can't I just tell you the message and you deliver it to the Pope? What good does it do any of us for me to see the Pope in person?"

"Must you really ask that question? Receiving an order from the Pope is like receiving an order from God himself. The Pope ordered me to bring you back to Paris, so I will bring you back to Paris. I do not care what information you have. I only care to follow orders and do the will of God."

"Are you sure this is the will of God?"

"It is the will of the Pope. Jesus said to Peter, the first pope, 'Truly I say to you, whatever you shall bind on earth shall have been bound in heaven, and whatever you shall loose on the earth shall have been loosed in heaven.' This power has been handed down from pope to pope. So yes, Sister, I know it is the will of God, because the Pope commanded it. I will follow his instructions to the letter and will bring you back to him in Paris." Father Alexander continued to straighten things on the table as he spoke, until all was in perfect order.

"But, what I have to say would make more sense to you than to the Pope. It has to do with the Fibonacci sequence."

Father Alexander looked up from the table. "Sister, do not tempt me."

Their eye contact was broken by Charles re-entering the room with two steaming mugs. Fransie took hers, and Charles winked at her. The warmth from the cup quickly spread through her body. She inhaled deeply. The ribbons of peppermint steam cleared her sinuses and opened her lungs. Fransie felt as if she could breathe clearly for the first time since she entered the commandery. The plan was going to work.

Fransie sipped her tea calmly and stared at the fire. The flames danced on the logs, and the embers glowed brightly. She jumped as the sound of a large thud and shattered glass broke the tranquil moment. Father Alexander had passed out.

The door behind Fransie burst open, and she thought they were done for.

"What are ya doing, just sittin' there? We 'ave ta go!"

"Andy, thank God it is you!"

"Quickly, we donnae have much time." Andy rushed past Fransie to the far end of the table where Charles and Father Alexander were. He hooked one of Alexander's limp arms around his shoulder and Charles did the same. "I'm happy ta see ya too, lassie. But, we have ta move."

Fransie joined them and took the priest's feet as Charles and

Andy took the larger portion of the priest's weight. Fransie kept her eyes on the door expectantly.

"Andy, where are the others?"

"There was a problem." Andy read the look on Fransie's face. "But we can fix it. We have ta get him ta his sleeping chambers first, or we are done for. Charles, which way?"

Charles led them through a small passage and into the simple sleeping chambers of Father Alexander. Fransie was relieved it was a short walk, not only because of the risk of being caught, but because she didn't know how much more stress her body could take. She had given birth only a few days before, and her body was nowhere near recovered enough to carry so much weight.

"Somethin' tastes really good." Andy smacked his lips.

"Ignore it, Andy. You have to fight it. Let Bartholomew help you."

Andy dropped the priest and moved toward the desk where the Harp sat.

"Charles, take it and run!" Fransie ordered.

Charles dropped the priest and jumped past Andy. He took the Harp and narrowly avoided Andy's grasp as he darted out of the door. Fransie stuck out her foot and tripped Andy before he reached the door. Andy shot Fransie a murderous look then shook his head.

"What happened?"

"You just met Lust," Fransie said.

Father Alexander groaned, and his eyes fluttered.

"Help me get him into bed!" Fransie ordered.

Andy dusted himself off, and together they placed Father Alexander in his bed. Alexander's eyes shot open, but he couldn't form words nor move.

"Andy, how long will this last?"

"I donnae ken, but we have ta go quickly."

Father Alexander's eyes burned with rage, shifting back and forth between Fransie and Andy. Andy pulled the covers over the priest, and they hurried out of the room.

"Andy, where are my friends?"

"See… well… They are still in the dungeon."

"What!" Fransie stopped in her tracks. "How could you leave them?"

"I didnea have a choice. Michael and Emanuel were chained to the wall. Poor little Barty couldn't fit inta the lock."

"What about Raphael and Auriel?"

Andy shook his head. "They are in a bad way, lassie. Nearly beaten ta death. All self-inflicted. That priest has been torturing them with that Harp. By the way, thank ya for stopping me in there. I can only imagine the power of that thing without an animal ta filter it." Andy shuddered. "Will Charles be all right?"

"Yes, The Harp only affects those with True Senses."

Shouting came from outside the commandery followed by bells ringing out. The whole commandery came to life.

"Quickly, in here." Andy pulled Fransie into the medicinal garden.

The sound of armored soldiers filled the corridors outside the door. Andy's plan was working once again. Charles must have gotten the Harp to Etienne and told the Hospitallers that it had been stolen. Etienne would ride west toward Astorga, and the Hospitallers would pursue him. With the commandery empty, Fransie and the others could escape east to rendezvous with others at the lake. There was only one problem though.

"Andy, how do we save my friends?"

Andy fell to the ground and pulled on his cape with both hands. The mouth in Luca's stomach had gotten ahold of a corner of the cape and was dragging Andy to his death. Fransie took Andy's dagger and frantically stabbed at the cloak in the hopes that it would tear. She stabbed again and again until her hopes came true. Andy's cape ripped and he fell face first on the ground. The mouth happily chewed through Andy's cape as if it was nothing.

"What in the 'ell is that?" Andy panted from the ground.

"That is my friend Luca, who has become consumed with gluttony."

"Give me that dagger. We have ta kill it."

"No! My friend is still in there."

"Kill me… Please, kill me," Luca moaned as the teeth gnashed at the cloak.

"See. It wants ta die." Andy reached for his dagger, but Fransie pulled it away.

"Luca, look at me. I know someone who can help you. He has suffered the Curse of More, as well, and is healed. Do not give up hope."

Luca nodded.

"Andy, who has the keys to release my friends?"

"Mother Superior."

Etienne tucked the Harp tightly under his arm as he tore down the Camino, back toward Astorga. He had never ridden a horse so fast before. The merchant had sold him the steed at a bargain price as he had nearly given up on it. He wasn't able to break her, nor was anyone able to ride her. But, the moment Etienne met eyes with her, it was almost as if she was pleading with him to take her. He still remembered the warm feeling of her muzzle as she allowed him to press his face to hers. That was the moment he knew she was the one.

"I'm sorry I'm putting you into danger right away," Etienne whispered to thc horse.

As Etienne climbed the hills west of Hospital de Orbigo, he saw a serpentine line of Hospitallers zig-zagging up the Camino after him. Their armor reflecting the light of the torches made them look like the scales of a giant dragon—all moving in unison. Etienne hoped that he had drawn away enough Hospitallers for Andy and Fransie to save her friends. He didn't like putting other people's lives at risk. He would have preferred to be the one inside.

Etienne tore past the shack of the man who had fed them when they had had nothing. The man who had told them about his good life. A life where the whole world came to him.

The flat mesa opened up, and the horse moved even faster. Etienne was sure they would reach the descent on the other side long before the Hospitallers reached this point. Etienne hoped to disappear in the streets of Astorga, then quietly slip into the Templar Commandery.

Etienne reached the edge of the mesa, and the valley opened up below with Astorga nestled in its heart. Etienne skidded to a halt. A line of knights was ascending the steep hill below. Etienne couldn't fathom how the Hospitallers had beat him to this side of the hill. There was no way. Etienne strained his eyes. The banner the knights were carrying below was a Templar banner.

Etienne didn't know what to do. Were these the Templars that were loyal to him, or the Templars loyal to the New World Order? The light from the Hospitallers' torches lit the horizon to the east. They had reached the top of the mesa and were closing in quickly.

Etienne's horse reared up and kicked as a black object darted in front of them. Etienne squeezed his thighs tightly and leaned in. The horse circled as two more black objects joined the first. Etienne was surrounded and the horse turned in circles. A piercing howl cut through the air.

"Bennie! Moira!" Etienne cried.

A black silhouette appeared in the night sky as a single rider approached from the north. If this was Bennie and Moira, then the third shape must be Sephira, and the rider, Gabriel. Etienne strapped the Harp to his back and grabbed his sword. Had Gabriel been following them, waiting for the perfect moment to strike and take more of the treasures? Etienne urged his horse forward, but was blocked by Bennie as Sephira and Moira stood on either side. Had Gabriel turned them against him? The two wolves had disappeared along with Gabriel the night of the storm and hadn't returned.

"Gabriel, stop!" Etienne ordered as the rider approached.

"Etienne, that is no way to greet a friend."

"Friend is yet to be determined."

"After all of this time, and the miles we have traveled, you still don't trust me?"

"No! You stole one of the treasures and abandoned us."

A fiery arrow landed a few yards behind them.

"You don't have the luxury of trust now. You can come with me and remain free or be captured."

Etienne studied the Templars climbing the hill.

"If you think those Templars are friends, they aren't. I can assure you of that. They are from the Templar castle in Ponferrada. Come with me, and I will explain everything." Gabriel nodded to Sephira, Bennie, and Moira. "They will cover our tracks."

Etienne looked at the two armies approaching. "Seeing as I have no other choice—I am forced to trust you."

Gabriel led the way, and Etienne followed.

Andy was pleased that his plan was working—well, sort of. He and Sister Fransie waited until the hall was quiet to peek their heads out from the garden. Andy's head swiveled left then right; the coast was clear.

"Where do you think the Mother Superior is?" Fransie asked, clutching onto the door.

"If I was here, there is only one place I would be."

"And where is that?"

"Guarding the prison." Andy grabbed Fransie and pulled her back behind the door as torchlight filled the corridor to the right. He put his fingers to his lips, and they pressed their backs to the wall.

Footsteps echoed toward them and stopped right outside the door. Andy drew his dagger slowly. He lunged at the torchbearer as he stepped into the garden. They wrestled to the ground, and Andy's dagger sunk into his foe.

"Stop!" Fransie cried.

Getting his wits about him, Andy looked down; he had just stabbed Charles! The young prince whimpered and held his wound.

"Oh, Charles. I am so sorry. I didnea ken 'twas you."

Tears formed in Charles's eyes as he placed both hands on the dagger in his gut.

"Don't pull it out," Fransie protested.

Charles lurched and stifled a scream. His eyes were pleading with both of them.

"No this cannea be happening." Andy cleared his face with the back of his sleeve. "I'm so sorry. You're just a wee bairn yourself."

"Andy, pull yourself together," Fransie said, helping him to his feet. "I will stay with him. You have to go get that key and my friends; otherwise, all of this was for nothing." Fransie motioned to the young prince.

"Aye, that I do. I have ta make this right. But, I cannea do this alone."

"You won't be alone. You have Bartholomew." Fransie looked at her shoulder. "And Rosalita." The small mouse perked up at the sound of her name." Fransie took Rosalita from her shoulder and held her in her palm in front of her face. "I need you to help Andy." The small mouse cleaned herself. Fransie placed her on Andy's shoulder. "Take good care of her."

"I cannea take her."

"You have to. As you said, you can't do this alone, and I can't leave him."

"Right." Andy nodded and took off out the door.

Andy cleared his face as he made his way to the dungeons. He couldn't believe he had just stabbed Charles. What if he died? Andy couldn't have his blood on his hands.

After a few minutes, he arrived at the stairs leading to the dungeons. He had been right; below he heard the Mother Superior and several Hospitallers talking. He took Bartholomew in one hand and Rosalita in the other.

"Right, you two have ta work together. I need ya ta scare that nun so badly that she runs up here. Now, I ken that you aren't scary, just misunderstood, but I need ya ta do your best." Andy placed them both on the floor, and they disappeared down the steps.

"Ahh! Get them off! Get them off!" The shrill cry of the Mother Superior came echoing up the staircase, followed by a lot of commotion and laughter. The sound of the screams, footsteps, and jingling keys came closer and closer up the stairs.

Andy casually put out his foot, and Mother Superior, in all of her piety, came tumbling to the ground. Andy quickly unlatched the keys from her belt and the two animals jumped onto his arm.

"Good work!" Andy said, running down the corridor.

"Guards!" Mother Superior yelled. "Get him!"

This part of the commandery was shaped like a square, with the medicinal garden in the middle. Andy was hoping to run around the garden and double back to the dungeon on the other side. He was running as fast as he could, but the sound of footsteps were gaining on him quickly.

Andy was out of breath; then the side cramp came. He knew he was done for. It would be only a matter of seconds before he wouldn't be able to run any longer. Perhaps if he could reach the entrance to the gardens, he could hide, and the guards would pass him by.

Andy pushed past the pain from the cramp and rounded the corner. He was startled from his feet, and his body reflexively tumbled through the legs of the person in front of him. He skidded on the other side, panting on the floor. Andy closed his eyes, expecting the death blow to come at any moment, but instead came the sound of several bodies hitting the ground behind him.

"Is now a good time for the muscle?" Gerhart said, standing over Andy with a large, puppy dog smile.

"Aye, that 'tis. Thank ya." Gerhart helped Andy to his feet and they ran back to the dungeons.

"It took you long—" The Mother Superior's mouth gaped as she realized it wasn't her guards returning.

"If ya would come with us." Andy motioned down the stairs. "Oh, and sorry for tripping ya."

Gerhart held Mother Superior as Andy rushed to Michael and Emanuel. He unlocked their shackles, and both men nearly dropped to the ground.

"Thank you," Michael said, weakly.

"Can you walk?"

"We will manage, but what about Raphael and Auriel? We can't possibly carry them." Michael pointed to the haystack where the sisters lay.

"We cannea, but he can. Gerhart, will you get those two?"

"Sure, but what about her?" Gerhart nodded to Mother Superior by his side.

"Sorry 'bout this as well." Andy took her hands and put them in the shackles. "I'm sure someone will come by ta get ya in a few hours when they return."

"Hey, don't I know you?" Emanuel said, staring at Gerhart.

"I don't think so, I'm Gerhart." Gerhart extended his hand, but Emanuel just stared at him, scrunching his brow.

"I'm Michael." Michael shook Gerhart's hand "And this is Emanuel."

"Did you prepare what I asked you ta?" Andy asked.

Gerhart nodded, and smiled broadly.

"Good, let's get this lot there first and then come back for Charles and Fransie," Andy said. Gerhart swooped up Raphael and Auriel into his massive arms, and led the way.

Andy lifted his arms in relief as he stepped into the cool air outside the commandery. He had worked up quite the sweat running around. As he entered the stables, it was even better than he had imagined. Gerhart had commandeered the most elegant coach Andy had ever seen.

"*Momma mia*. This is just like… Is this real?" Emanuel's mouth gaped open.

"Sure is. This coach belonged to Father Alexander himself, whoever that is." Gerhart placed Raphael and Auriel on the velvet seats inside. He took the reins and handed them to Emanuel. "You can even drive, if you like."

"You mean… I can…" The look of shock on Emanuel's face was almost comical. This man sure loved his coaches. Life instantly seemed to return to his body.

"We will be ready to go when you return," Michael said.

"Let's get Fransie, and that poor wee lad Charles," Andy said.

Gerhart nodded and they stormed back into the commandery. They ran through the empty halls, and Andy kept wondering where all the guards were. They had to have left more guards than the ones at the dungeon.

"Fransie, we're back—" Andy stopped dead. The medicinal garden was filled with Hospitallers, one of which held Fransie by the neck.

"I knew you would return for this one." The Mother Superior stepped out from behind the first row of Hospitallers and pointed to Luca. "I was pleasantly surprised to find these two as well."

"Where is Charles?" Andy said.

"Right where we left him, behind Luca," Fransie said, struggling with her captor.

"Ach, no!" Behind Luca, Andy could make out the young prince clutching his wound. He rushed to him. "I'm sorry, so sorry." Andy knelt to Charles and the keys clanked. "You will let them go." Andy stood. "Or I will—"

The guards erupted in laughter.

"Or you will what, little man?" a larger Hospitaller said.

"Or I will release him." Andy leapt to Luca and placed a key into his right manacle. A hush fell over the garden, and the Hospitallers ground their feet. Andy's heart was trying to escape his chest, but he was resolved to save his friends one way or another. He had to make up for what he had done to Charles.

"You wouldn't dare," the larger Hospitaller said.

"Watch me, little man."

Andy clinked the lock and all hell broke loose. Luca wrenched his other hand from the manacle and the gruesome mouth in the stomach opened wide. It ran full speed at Fransie with Luca's top half trailing behind. Gerhart knocked a Hospitaller in Luca's path and the mouth chomped him. Fransie's captor drew his sword, giving her a chance to escape behind Gerhart. Andy lifted Charles and met them at the door. Luca stood between the companions and the Hospitallers. Andy waved, and they ran out the door. On the other side, Gerhart placed an iron candlestick between the handles so no one could escape.

Gerhart took Charles from Andy, and they ran down the hall as quickly as they could. Within a matter of minutes, they were at the stables. Emanuel sat atop the coach with the reins in hand. Even though his clothes were haggard and his body was frail, Emmauel was smiling from ear to ear. Sitting in the luxurious coach had given him new strength. Andy would say he was almost beaming.

"Wait! Wait!" a cry came chasing after them. It wasn't a command. It was a cry of desperation. "Wait for me."

"I know that voice," Fransie said.

A man with a broomed mustache came bounding out of the commandery.

"Joshua!" Fransie ran to the man and embraced him. "Thank God you are here."

"Thank God *you* are here."

"I hate ta break up the reunion, but we donnae have time for this." Andy ushered Fransie and Joshua into the coach. Manuel cracked the whip, and the team of four white horses took off like a shot. Andy sank into his seat; the plan had worked.

Etienne and Gabriel circled to the south through a grove of trees as Bennie, Moira, and Sephira ran behind them, obscuring their tracks.

"Where are you taking us?" Etienne asked.

"To a forgotten way."

Behind them the mesa glowed with torchlight. The two armies had met, and appeared to be at a standstill. Etienne didn't see any signs that they were being followed, but he couldn't be sure.

"What is this place?" Etienne asked as they entered the ruins of a city.

"It is an alternate route of the Camino. It once was a thriving town, but when they diverted the Camino, the town died and has been all but forgotten. The pilgrims are like blood; if they stop traveling to a place on the Camino, it will die. From here we can loop back around to Hospital de Orbigo and pass before their forces return. They won't expect us to go that way." Gabriel rode up to Etienne and held out his fist. "Here, I think this belongs to you."

Etienne extended his hand, and Gabriel dropped the shard of the One True Cross onto Etienne's palm. Etienne examined it and placed it into his sporran.

"My apologies, it seems that I misjudged you once again."

"We need to resolve this issue, Etienne. You need to trust me. The only thing I desire to do is protect Fransie and her child. As long as she decides to join you, I will be there."

"I don't trust many people," Etienne admitted. "And it did look suspicious that you dissapeared the moment you possessed the shard of the One True Cross."

"As I said, my only goal is to protect Fransie and her child."

"The child's name is Roslyn."

"What?" Gabriel stopped his horse. "She gave birth?"

Etienne nodded.

"I will never forgive myself for missing it."

"If it was so important for you to be there, why did you abandon her when she needed you the most?"

"To save all of you." Gabriel pulled ahead. "You would have all frozen to death if I had done nothing. With Sephira, I could resist the pull of Pride. I let her think she had gotten to me. She was whispering in my ear to take the treasures—that they were mine. So I took one and fled. I was right to do so. The moment I left the safety of the church wall, the pack of wolves pursued me, along with Pride. This gave you a chance to find shelter, and a chance to figure out how to defeat your own pride."

"You mean you were willing to sacrifice yourself to protect us?"

"To protect Fransie and Roslyn."

"How did you defeat the wolves?"

"I had a little help from these three. Having a common foe to fight against brought them together. They bought me some time to find shelter. The moment Pride realized I wasn't under her control, she left. However, the wolves stayed. Two days they waited for me to leave my shelter, until they finally gave up."

"How did you find me?"

"I sensed what is tied to your belt; what is it?"

"It is a Harp." Etienne loosened the Harp and strummed it.

Gabriel jumped from Cash's back and tackled Etienne from his horse. The fall knocked the wind out of Etienne, but he kept a firm grip on the Harp. Gabriel would have to pry it from his dead hands if he wanted it. Gabriel punched Etienne, but he wouldn't loosen his grip. Gabriel raised his fist again, but Sephira bit his forearm and dragged Gabriel away.

"Give it to me!" Gabriel yelled. "I have to have it!" He struggled with Sephira, but Bennie and Moira pinned him as well. Etienne looped the Harp on his belt again and jumped onto his horse.

"I was right about you." Etienne spat. "Yah!" he yelled, and his horse took off down the abandoned Camino.

"Apply pressure here," Joshua ordered.

Fransie placed both hands around the dagger in Charles's stomach. The boy was stretched out across Gerhart, her, and Andy on the bench inside the coach. It was cramped, but comfort wasn't the important thing at the moment.

"Thank God you didn't take it out," Joshua said. "This poor boy would have bled to death if you had. We still might have a chance to save him if the blade didn't pierce any organs. How far away is your camp? Do you have supplies there?"

"We have some things; what do you need?"

"The most important thing is honey."

"Honey?" Andy and Fransie said in unison.

"It prevents the wound from festering. Everyone thinks that the battle is won the moment the bleeding stops, but that is just the beginning. If the wound isn't treated properly, the boy could still die.

"Andy, did I earn your respect…?" Charles deliriously moaned.

"Aye, that ya did, laddie, that ya did." Andy stroked Charles's hair and the boy closed his eyes again. "Ya have ta save him. 'Tis all my fault," Andy said as tears welled in his eyes.

"I will do my best." Joshua pushed his broom mustache from side-to-side. He kept looking at Charles's wound, but also at Fransie's stomach, which was right behind it. His eyes had a question inside of them.

"What about them?" Fransie nodded to Auriel and Raphael, who were on the other bench, leaning against Michael. Joshua turned from his position on the floor to face them. He expanded their eyelids and examined their pupils. He then gently ran his hands over the wounds on their heads.

"They need some sal-ammoniac."

"What is that?" Fransie asked. She had been around a lot of

remedies, but had never heard of that before.

"It is a salt-like substance that revives people who aren't conscious. Is there a cave near where we are going?"

Fransie turned to Gerhart and Andy. They were the only ones who had been to the lake before.

"I donnae ken if there was a cave, but I do recall some bats."

"Perfect. That is exactly what we need. Sal ammoniac can be found around bat dung." Joshua straightened himself and looked at Fransie. "Sorry for my language. I didn't mean to offend."

Fransie smiled gently. She had been around much worse words than dung.

The carriage came to a halt, and a wooden panel slid behind Fransie's head. "Where do we go from here?" Emanuel asked, poking his head through the slot.

"I'll be right out," Gerhart said, gently placing Charles's legs on the seat as he stood.

The carriage moved again, and the terrain became bumpy. Sister Fransie did her best to stabilize Charles, but it was nearly impossible to do.

"Clair!" Gerhart shouted. "Clair!"

"Quiet ya down, ya big oaf!" Clair yelled back.

"Thank the Lord we are here," Fransie said.

"Agreed." Joshua glanced between his patients. "Let's gently lay him flat. I'll support him when you slide out, Fransie." He looked at Andy. "Then I will need you to gently put his head down and find me some honey as soon as possible. You seem to know this place."

"What about us?" Michael asked, with both Raphael and Auriel propped on him.

"Have the big fellow—Gerhart, was it?—help you take them out of the coach, we will need room to work in here. I will also need a blade heated so we can seal this wound."

Everyone followed Joshua's instructions, leaving him and Fransie in the coach.

"I'm sorry for your loss." Joshua looked at Fransie kindly.

"What? He isn't dead, is he? We can save him, right?"

"That is yet to be determined. I was referring to…" He nodded to Fransie's midsection.

"Roslyn…? She is fine. I gave birth a few days ago."

"What—?"

The carriage door swung open, and Andy's swollen hand reached through with a glob of honey.

"Is this enough?"

"Andy, you are soaking wet," Fransie said.

"I had ta jump in the water ta get them little beasties off of me. Donnae ask me ta get more; it hurts."

"That will be quite enough." Joshua took the golden blob from Andy's hand and applied it around the wound.

"You should soak those stings in some vinegar as you say ten Our Fathers," Fransie offered. "It should help."

Andy nodded; and as he disappeared, Gerhart appeared with a red-hot dagger.

"Good, we will have to do this quickly. As I pull out this dagger, I want you to press that one down to stop the bleeding. Can you do that?"

Gerhart nodded.

"Good." Joshua took the hilt of the dagger and made eye contact with Fransie and Gerhart. "On the count of three: one, two, three!"

Joshua pulled the dagger out as Fransie removed her hands and a fountain of blood poured out. Gerhart placed the glowing dagger on the wound and it hissed as Charles let out a pained scream. The smell of honey mixed with burning flesh made Fransie feel faint. She covered her nose and pushed past Gerhart and out of the carriage. Fransie took a few breaths of fresh air, but she still felt faint.

"Fransie, you are bleeding," Michael said.

"No, it is just Charles's blood." Fransie's eyes went in and out of focus.

“Look down.” Michael walked to her side and took her arm.
At Fransie’s feet a pool of blood was forming.
“Michael…”

# CHAPTER 29

The pipe organ shook the numbness from Isabella's body. She hadn't slept, nor eaten, since Matilda's death. Isabella stared at the coffin which was ornately decorated with roses—Matilda's favorite flower. It should have been her in that coffin, not Matilda. That poison was meant for her. Someone was trying to kill her, and Matilda was a casualty of it.

*I am so sorry...* Isabella placed her face in her hands. Guilt was ravishing her insides. *Had I not left, you would still be alive, my friend. I vow to you, I will find whoever did this and destroy them.*

Anytime Isabella mentioned to her father that they needed to find the killer, he just gave her a coy smile. He believed that she had killed Matilda to cover her own escape. He admired Isabella for the cleverness of it. The thought made Isabella want to retch. There was no justice for Matilda—at least not yet—and she most certainly didn't feel safe. Isabella looked around at the throngs of people filling Notre Dame; it could be any one of them.

The cathedral was still under construction in parts, but the main chapel looked immaculate. Matilda's funeral was the first of this scale and notability that the church had seen so far. Matilda would have never guessed that the Pope would be the one presiding over her funeral; she wasn't the most pious person, but at least she lived life to the fullest. Matilda was unashamedly herself at all times, even when it annoyed Isabella. What she wouldn't give to be annoyed by her one last time.

Isabella dabbed her tears under the long black veil covering her face. She thought it was fitting that the clothes she escaped in were black; she was dressed for mourning long before she knew what had happened.

"Amen," the congregation said in unison.

The organ blasted once more, signaling the processional to the casket. Isabella walked forward. This was it, she was really saying goodbye to her best and only friend in court. More tears streamed down Isabella's face as she touched the casket.

"Matilda, I'm sorry... It should have been me...goodbye."

"Here, my child, take my handkerchief." The Pope urged Isabella with his eyes.

"Thank you, Your Excellency. Mine is filled with tears for my dear friend." Isabella took the piece of fabric and returned to her pew. Isabella felt tears forming, again, and she unraveled the handkerchief the Pope had given to her. She closed it quickly to make sure no one else had seen. Inside was written:

*Stay behind to meet me.*

Isabella watched hundreds of people say their goodbyes. She wondered how many of them actually knew Matilda, and who was here just to be seen.

"Isabella, it is time to leave," King Philip said.

"Father, I need more time to grieve. You go on without me."

Her father gave her a conspiring smile. "Right. I will send another carriage for you. Take as much time as you need to *grieve.*"

Isabella couldn't believe her father. Her rigid body collapsed on the pew as he disappeared out of the doors at the rear of the church. Isabella rested her head on the pew. She didn't pray, nor weep; she just sat, as an emptiness filled her numb body.

"Your Highness, the Pope wishes to see you in his chambers," a young priest said as he extinguished a candle nearby.

Isabella stood, but she felt as if she was leaving a piece of herself behind. She passed the large stained-glass window and was escorted to the Pope's chambers. Inside, matching golden chairs with red velvet were facing the cozy fire. Pope Clement stood from one and Jaques de Molay from the other. Isabella's fingernails dug into her skin from her clenched fists as a white fury rose inside her.

"I hate you! You killed her!" Isabella ran to Molay and pounded him hard on the chest. Soon the pounding became wailing, and her head unwittingly sank onto his tunic despite her rage. Molay stood there and held her as she cried. He was the last person she wanted to console her, but he was here. It was his poison that had killed Matilda. The poison he had given her to kill her own father. Isabella composed herself and stepped back.

"I didn't kill your friend. I am sorry for your loss." Molay's eyes were soft, and he almost looked grandfatherly.

"It was your poison that killed her." Isabella wiped her face with the back of her wrist.

"What?" Molay's eyes widened.

"Yes, it was your poison. The one you gave me to kill my own father. I wouldn't do it. I couldn't... So, I left. I left the castle, I left my father, and I left that poison behind. I never wanted to come back here."

"But then God directed you back here. Isn't that so, my child? I was just telling the Grand Master about how you were shown my prayers." The Pope clapped his hands in excitement.

Isabella just nodded her head. She didn't have words at the moment, only a ball of raw emotion inside of her.

"Right." Molay raised doubting eyebrows.

"I'm happy you will be gone soon." The words came reflexively out of Isabella's mouth.

"Gone?"

"Yes, Grand Master Jacques de Molay. You will be gone soon one way or another."

"What do you mean?" Molay's expression quickly turned from condensation to concern.

"I won't kill my father. You don't want to start a war with him. I'm not sure if it is because you want to save the lives of many or because you are afraid you will lose. Either way, my father isn't going to wait for you to decide. He plans to attack you next week."

"That is too soon. We need more time."

"Why? The battle will come sooner or later."

"Because, unlike your father, I am trying to avoid war at all costs. Even at the expense of my own life. And because we need to give Etienne more time." Molay was trying to press Isabella's soft spot, and it was working.

"You don't care for Etienne. You never have. You only care about his mission and submission to your command."

"Isabella, I made Etienne my Seneschal. When I am gone, he will lead the Templars."

"What?'

"I know you may hate me, and I have asked you to do terrible things, but there are some things that are bigger than us. Some things that you must sacrifice for. I have dedicated my whole life to protecting and serving others. I won't stop that now."

"What are you talking about?"

The Pope placed his hands together and said, "I have told the Grand Master all of your father's plans—at least all that I knew of. Philip plans to justify his actions by charging the Templars with heresy for the actions they do in their initiation ceremonies. I have already given your father my official Papal decree, giving him the go-ahead."

"So why are you both smiling?"

"We have come up with a plan to save many lives by risking only a few." Molay took a deep breath. "Since you failed to kill your father, my plan was to leave with the treasure in the Paris commandery on the twelfth of October. When I first learned of your father's plans, I ordered the Templars to disband in secret by that date, taking all they could with them to… Well, that isn't important. After the twelfth of October, the Templars will be no more. I was to remain here in Paris until the task was done and then go join them. However, I fear Etienne will need more time. I am sacrificing myself to give him that time."

"Well, it won't be a complete sacrifice," Pope Clement said, looking at Molay as if they were old friends.

"Yes, the Pope has agreed to find me not guilty eventually and set me free. I will have to endure torture and prison, but it will be worth it to help Etienne succeed."

"We only need one thing from you, my child." The Pope clasped his hands together.

"What is that?" Isabella asked, caught up in the whirlwind of plans these two were hatching.

"Isabella," Molay said earnestly. "We need you to buy us more time. Tell your father directly, or start a rumor, saying that we will be moving the Templar treasure on the thirteenth of October and that that will be the best time to attack. Make him believe that we have a way of permanently closing the vault here so it will never be opened. If your father wants that treasure, he will have to attack on the thirteenth, when the time is right. His greed will get the better of him, and he will attack then. We need you to do this, and you will get your wish. I will disappear, and so will the Templars. You will be free to be with Etienne, if that is something you choose. And yes, he is still alive, in case you are wondering. I just received a report about his progress yesterday."

"Etienne's alive?" Her father had confirmed it, but hearing it from Molay made it that more real.

Molay nodded.

A sigh of relief passed over Isabella's body. She felt guilty for the smile that crossed her face, under her veil.

"I wouldn't celebrate, just yet. There is one other matter to attend to. If that poison was meant for you that means the killer is still out there. Be careful, Isabella. We need you in order for this plan to work."

The joy of the news about Etienne had momentarily plucked Isabella from reality, but Molay's statement sucked her back in. She was surrounded by men who didn't care about her, except as a pawn for their plans, and he was right—that poison was meant for her. Her father wouldn't be any help in finding the killer. She would have to do it on her own.

# CHAPTER 30

Etienne sped past the Hospitaller Commandery and hoped that his friends had escaped. He was tempted to stop, but he continued on to the rendezvous point. If his friends weren't there, he would circle back and pray he reached them before the Hospitaller forces returned.

Etienne couldn't believe Gabriel had tried to take the Harp from him. After all this time, he had been right about him. Etienne had tried to repress his feelings about Gabriel, but this just showed that he needed to trust his gut. He was a leader now; other people's lives were in his hands. He didn't have the luxury of making a mistake like that again.

Etienne followed the Camino to the point where he knew it split off to the lake. In the morning light, it was clear that a coach had traveled that way recently. Why hadn't his friends taken the time to cover their tracks? Something must have gone wrong. Etienne did a rudimentary job of covering their tracks, and his. If all was well at camp, he would return and finish the job properly. There wasn't any time now.

He continued on to the lake on foot. He wanted the element of surprise should he need it. He ducked behind a tree. In the distance was a Papel coach. Was he too late? Were the Hospitallers and the priest already there? A falcon screeched overhead, and before he could spot it, a blade dug into his back.

"Do not move," a woman's voice said. Her accent was beautiful, but the words were sharp and the force behind them strong.

Etienne spun quickly, took the blade from his attacker, and pinned her to the tree, holding the blade to her throat. The woman was Moorish—her features similar to his own. Was she an Assassin?

The woman smiled. "So, we shall meet our fate together."

The sting of a blade dug deeper into Etienne's abdomen. He realized she must have taken his dagger.

"Or ya could just be friends," Andy's voice came from behind him. "Etienne, meet Raphael; Raphael, meet Etienne."

Etienne dropped the blade and picked Andy a few inches off the ground in a bear hug.

"Now donnae hurt yourself. Put me down, laddie."

"You made it? Your plan worked?" Etienne said.

"Like a charm." Andy's eyes gleamed with pride. "Do ya have it?"

Etienne lifted the Harp and strummed it.

"Keep that thing away from us!" Raphael yelled as a falcon swooped out of the sky onto her shoulder. "Auriel can't—"

Etienne was knocked to the ground by a blur of red. Raphael and Andy took off after a barefoot woman with the Harp in her hand. He pushed himself up and joined in the pursuit. Andy stopped and put a hand on his side. Etienne slowed as he reached him, but Andy motioned for him to carry on.

"'Tis just a side cramp."

The red-haired woman was nimble. She moved as if she was a creature of the forest. Etienne knew he wouldn't be able to catch her on foot. He veered right and ran to where he had left his horse. When he arrived, the beast was pulling at its reins and whining.

"Calm down. I am going to untie you." Etienne pet her muzzle and looked the horse in the eye. "First I need you to calm down." Slowly, the horse calmed, and Etienne mounted the steed.

"Auriel! Fight it!" Raphael's voice darted through the trees.

"Yah!" Etienne yelled, and they followed the sound of her voice.

It wasn't long before they caught up to Raphael. Her eyes widened as Etienne passed. His horse whinnied loudly, and Auriel stopped abruptly, causing Etienne to nearly fall off. Auriel dropped the Harp and turned with tears in her eyes.

"Thank God you are here." Auriel ran to Etienne's horse. "Binah!" She shouted, wrapping her arms around the horse's neck.

"Go pick that thing up and never play it again," Raphael demanded. Unsure of what was going on, Etienne dismounted and fastened the Harp to his belt once more.

At camp, Clair, Gerhart, and Mariano rushed Etienne. He was wrapped in a large embrace. There was only one face missing.

"Where's Fransie?" Etienne asked.

"She is resting," a man with a broomed mustache said, stepping out of the carriage.

"What happened?"

"Etienne, meet Joshua; Joshua, Etienne," Andy said.

"Sorry," Etienne said.

"It is quite all right," Joshua said. "I would be concerned as well. Fransie put too much strain on her body after giving birth. She has lost quite a lot of blood. Truth be told, I'm not sure if either of my paticnts will makc it through thc night." Joshua wipcd thc blood from his hands with a rag and tossed it aside.

"Either of your patients?" Etienne raised questioning eyebrows.

"Charles was injured as well." Andy's eyes glazed over with tears. "I…"

"It wasnea your fault." Clair wrapped her arm around him. "'Twas an accident."

"I need to see them," Etienne demanded.

"You may see them, but keep it short. They need their rest."

Joshua pushed his broom mustache from side-to-side for emphasis.

Etienne nodded and brushed past Joshua into the carriage. Inside, it looked like something out of a battle scene. There was blood everywhere—Charles was sprawled out on one bench, and Fransie was on the other. Both of them were white as ghosts. Etienne shook his head. Charles was just a boy, and Fransie was a mother. He couldn't let them die.

"Etienne," Fransie said weakly as her eyes fluttered open.

"I'm here, Fransie." Etienne knelt at her side and cupped her hand in his.

"Take care of my baby if I die."

"You're not going to die."

"Promise me." Fransie looked up at the ceiling. "I'm going home." Fransie shut her eyes.

"You are doing no such thing." Etienne took the shard of the One True Cross and placed it on her abdomen. Fransie gulped for air again and again as her body convulsed. She writhed in pain, then she went limp.

Etienne's heart moved to his throat as warm tears rolled down his cheeks. Had the cross killed her? Etienne turned; he couldn't bear to see her lifeless body.

Fransie gasped again and squeezed his hand tightly. Etienne turned and embraced her.

"You're not dead... Thank God you're not dead!"

"What did you do to me?" Fransie asked, sitting up. "Whatever it was, do it to that poor boy as well. I couldn't bear to live and see him die."

Etienne placed the shard on Charles's wound. Nothing happened. Etienne thought back to the woods. The shard had only healed James's wound. It didn't bring back Nazir. Was Charles already too far gone? Etienne clenched his jaw. Why would God only heal some people and not others?

"Why isn't it working?" Fransie asked.

"I don't know." Etienne shook his head and sat to face Fransie.

"What is that?" She pointed to the shard in Etienne's hand.

"I guess you never saw this, did you?"

Fransie shook her head.

"It is a shard of the One True Cross."

Fransie crossed herself.

"It is one of the seven treasures. Charity gave it to us in Astorga."

"Wait, that means you saw Gabriel? This was the treasure he supposedly stole. Is he here too?" Fransie glanced out the window.

"No!"

"What do you mean, no?"

"Gabriel did steal this treasure, and no, he isn't here. He also tried to take this from me." Etienne pulled back his cloak to show the Harp.

Fransie's whole demeanor changed. Her right hand reached for the Harp, but her left pulled it back. Fransie turned away from Etienne slowly, as if she was fighting against a great force. Rosalita squeaked from her shoulder, and Fransie shook her head.

"Get that thing away from me. Do not tempt me."

Etienne covered the Harp once more, and Fransie's body relaxed.

"Was Sephira nearby when Gabriel tried to take the Harp from you?"

"No. Sephira, Bennie, and Moira were covering our tracks. I showed it to Gabriel, and as I strummed it, he attacked me."

"What happened next?"

"Sephira knocked him off of me, and I rode away."

"You abandoned him! He helped you, and you abandoned him. Didn't you stop to question why he gave you the Shard then tried to take the Harp?"

"I thought it was a ploy to get me to show the Harp to him."

"No, he couldn't control himself. That thing on your belt is cursed with Lust. We can't resist it without our animals. Raphael and Auriel nearly killed themselves trying to get it. The priest tortured them with it."

"That explains why Auriel tried to take it from me."

"Without Binah here, she is a liability to the whole camp. She will stop at nothing to get it."

"Binah is here too. Apparently, the horse that I bought was Binah."

Fransie laughed at the strange coincidence.

"Why isn't it working on him?" Fransie's eyes shifted back to Charles.

"I don't know."

Fransie rose to leave the coach, but Etienne stopped her.

"I don't want the others to know that I have the Shard. I need you to spend the night in here and be magically healed in the morning."

"Etienne, how do you expect others to trust you, if you don't trust anyone? Give people some grace." Fransie's words struck Etienne and sank in deeply.

"I will tell them, but not tonight with so many new faces."

Andy was thrilled to be sitting by the lake with a book in his hand. He couldn't remember the last time he had felt the smooth leather of a book cover and the pages on his fingertips. But, it was the smell—the smell of knowledge—that got him really excited. He took a deep breath and opened to the first page.

The Book of Genesis

*1 In the beginning God created the heaven and the earth.*

*2 And the earth was without form, and void; and darkness was upon the face of the deep. And the Spirit of God moved upon the face of the waters.*

> ***3** And God said, Let there be light: and there was light.*
>
> ***4** And God saw the light, that it was good: and God divided the light from the darkness.*
>
> ***5** And God called the light Day, and the darkness he called Night. And the evening and the morning were the first day.*

"What are you reading there?" a voice said.

Andy looked from the pages of his book to see Joshua cleaning the blood from his hands in the lake. He was so engrossed in his book that he hadn't noticed him. All Andy wanted to do was read and be left in peace. He needed a little escape after the chaos of the night before.

"'Tis the first book of the Bible, Genesis." Andy closed the book and sighed heavily. He didn't want to talk, but he also didn't want to be rude to the person who was saving the lives of his friends.

"You mean the first book of the Torah." Joshua raised an eyebrow. "There is a lot of light in there." He chuckled to himself. "I can see you don't want to talk; so I will let you be." He shook off his hands and started back to the camp.

"No, wait. Ya can join me if ya like. I ken that we are all strangers ta you. Let's start over. I'm Andrew, but my friends call me Andy." Andy didn't want to be rude, but Joshua's comment had enticed him to make the offer.

"Joshua." He smiled, and his broom mustache raised. "Thank you for the invitation." Joshua joined Andy on the rocks just above the sandy shore.

"Thank you for saving our friends."

"Fransie is my friend as well. I only knew her for one day, but she left a lasting impression. It was hard to see her like that."

"Do you think they will make it?"

"It is out of my hands now. All we can do is pray. Would you care to join me in a moment of silence for them?"

Andy nodded and closed his eyes. He listened to the little waves of the water lapping against the shore as they prayed silently.

"Amen," Andy said, crossing himself.

"Amen." Joshua looked out over the water with wise eyes.

"What did ya mean when ya said there was a lot of light in here?" Andy held up the book. "I ken in the beginning God said *let there be light*, but I somehow don't think that is what you were talking about."

"I was, and I wasn't." Joshua pushed his broom mustache from side to side. "It depends on how you interpret it. Read the first passage."

Andy opened the book and read, "*In the beginning, God created the heavens and the earth.*"

"Good, I'm happy it's the same." Joshua patted Andy on the shoulder and laughed. "Would you like to hear how the story of creation relates to Kabbalah?"

Andy's body perked up. "Kabbalah?"

"Yes. Kabbalah is the Jewish tradition of mystical interpretation of the Torah. It is very popular in Burgos now, which is where I was from before I was kidnapped." Joshua shook his head. "I see that you are a man of learning, and since you saved my life, I want to give you something to say thank you. Right now, my wisdom is all I have."

"'Tis the best gift anyone can give me." Andy's eyes gleamed.

Joshua picked up a stick and drew in the sand. "So, imagine spirit floating in the void, in the darkness…nothing continuing on in all directions for eternity. The first thing consciousness does is create a sphere around itself, which gives it a boundary for the first time. It now has an awareness of what's around itself for three-hundred and sixty degrees." Joshua drew a dot with a circle around it. "Continue reading."

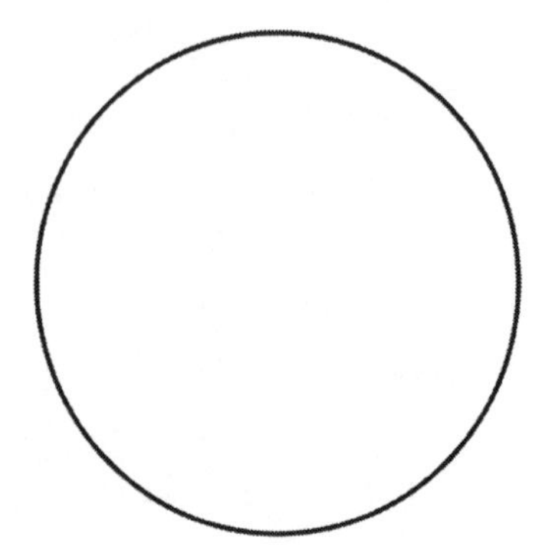

*"And the earth was without form, and void; and darkness was upon the face of the deep. And the Spirit of God moved upon the face of the waters."*

Joshua raised a hand, stopping Andy and drew another circle.

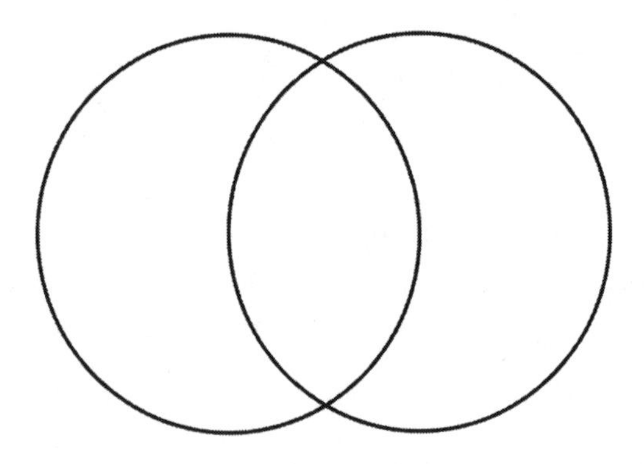

"It is important to realize the order of things. Here we read that *God moved upon the face of the waters.*" Joshua pointed from the middle of the first circle to the middle of the second. "So, the next thing the Spirit of God does is move to the edge of creation and repeats the process again, which forms two intersecting circles whose circumference crosses the center of the other. This forms the Vesica Pisces." Joshua pointed to the section where the two circles overlapped.

"It looks like an eye."

"Exactly! Read the next sentence."

"*And God said, Let there be light: and there was light.*"

"The Vesica Pisces has many different mathematical properties, but it also has to do with the properties of light, so this represents the creation of light. Also, if you look at it from another direction it looks like…" Andy craned his head around and nodded. "It becomes the womb of all creation."

"I see." Andy felt his cheeks flush.

"It is important to realize the order of things. First, there was nothingness, then God created a boundary around itself for 360 degrees, then God moved to the edge of creation and repeated the process, then there was light—the Vesica Pisces. Continue reading."

"*And God saw the light, that it was good: and God divided the light from the darkness.*" Joshua motioned for Andy to keep reading. "*And God called the light Day, and the darkness he called Night. And the evening and the morning were the first day.*" Andy looked up from the book. "So this shape represents the first day of creation?"

Joshua nodded. "And, for each day of creation, God repeated the process." Joshua drew more circles, "until—"

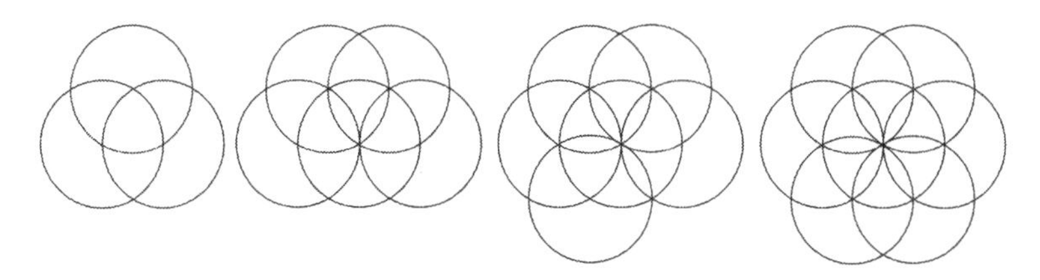

"I know that pattern. 'Tis the Seed of Life…" Andy stopped, noticing Joshua's deadpan expression.

"How do you… Well… it seems I have nothing here to share." Joshua stood. "I refuse to share any more knowledge with you until someone tells me how you all know about these secrets…

Excuse me." Joshua walked away, muttering something in Yiddish.

"Joshua," Andy called.

Joshua stopped mid-stride and looked at Andy.

"Thank ya so much for taking my mind off Charles for a bit. I needed the distraction."

"Physicians are meant to heal more than the body." He and Andy exchanged a nod, and Joshua continued on his way.

Andy returned his gaze to the Flower of Life. "So, you have something ta do with this." He patted the book on his lap. "I'm gonna figure ya out."

Etiennne took the afternoon watch. The Hospitallars could come searching for them at any time, and they had to be prepared. Etienne inhaled deeply, and the smell of earth and trees filled him. These woods held so many memories for him. This was where he had first kissed Isabella; it was also where he had first met Nazir and fought him.

Etienne walked to the grove where he and Isabella had first kissed. He closed his eyes and could almost feel the heat of her lips on his.

"You aren't very good at keeping watch, are you?" Raphael's voice startled Etienne out of his daydream.

Etienne laughed and shook his head. "Apparently not. These woods hold many memories for me."

"Memories can be dangerous if lived in too often."

"True, but memories are how we keep our loved ones alive after they are gone. They only truly die after we have forgotten them."

"Why must you people always live in the past and not see what is in front of you? The past should be left behind; it wasn't meant to be carried your whole life."

"This memory was worth holding on to."

"Was it worth losing your life for? If I was a Hospitaller you would be dead."

"At least my last thoughts would have been of someone I loved. Have you ever loved before?"

"What kind of question is that for someone you hardly know?"

"It is the kind of question that builds friendship and trust."

Raphael shook her head and walked away.

Etienne didn't know what to think of Raphael. He had never quite met anyone like her before. She was definitely a warrior, but she had a kind streak inside of her. He inhaled deeply and walked out of the clearing. There was one other place he needed to visit before they left the lake.

Etienne retraced his steps to where he and Nazir had first met. Etienne laughed. If he would have told his former self that he would mourn the death of Nazir, Etienne would have thought himself to have gone mad. Why would he mourn the person who tried to kill both him and Isabella? It is amazing how a shift in perspective can shift the whole world.

Besides nearly dying, something else happened in these woods. After Etienne had been stabbed by the poisoned blade, his father's angel had saved him. Etienne didn't know if it was real, or if it was just the effects of the poison. He had replayed it in his head several times, but everything was foggy. He just remembered the song that his father had sung. He hadn't heard it since his childhood.

Etienne hummed the melody, and a butterfly landed on his hand. He brought it to his face and smiled.

"Isn't it late in the season for you?"

The butterfly flapped its wings a few times then fluttered away. Etienne watched as it floated this way and that way.

*The butterfly can move in all directions.* Brother Philip's words rang out in Etienne's thoughts.

"Really?" Etienne looked at the sky and shook his head. The little butterfly danced in front of his gaze. Etienne knew he had to do the exercise Brother Philip had taught him at the Keystone Church, just before he retrieved the sword.

Etienne took a few deep breaths and walked very slowly. His heel touched the ground first, and he felt every movement as he rolled to the ball of his foot. At the Keystone Church, he had focused on the feeling of Isabella's hand in his. That was the magnet that pulled him to a time and place when she was there. He couldn't remember how he felt that day in the woods, but he did remember the song that had saved him. Etienne focused on the melody as he continued to walk slowly. The world became a single-minded focus on that song.

Etienne closed his eyes, and on opening them, he ducked behind a tree. Not ten paces away, Nazir held his lifeless body as a host of Moors watched.

"What have you done?" Nazir demanded.

"Only what you ordered." A Moor looked at his comrades for support, but they all stepped back.

"He is blood of my blood. Do you know how valuable his life is? If I die…he would be the only one left who could open…" Nazir pulled the dagger from Etienne's leg and threw it at the Moore, hitting him in the throat. The man dropped to the ground.

"Your horse, Commander," another Moor said.

"This is a good death, my boy. You died protecting your friends." Nazir closed Etienne's eyes and hopped to his horse on one leg. "I wish I could have known you." Nazir cracked the reins and rode away, followed by the Moors.

Etienne was left alone in the forest with his former self dying on the ground. He searched the forest, expecting his father to appear at any moment. He had so much compassion for his former self as he suffered. Etienne began to hum the tune his father used to sing to him, thinking that it would call him.

"Father," his former self said, looking straight at him with clouded eyes.

Etienne turned, but there was no one there; just him.

"Father," his former self yelled again.

Etienne sang louder. There was no one coming to save his former self. It was him. It had always been him. Remembering how the song felt in his past, Etienne sang even louder. He extended a hand and helped his former self to his feet. His former self was unsteady and unable to stand on his own, so Etienne scooped himself up. He had carried himself through the toughest part of his life. Etienne cradled himself as he walked back to where their camp had been.

He placed his former self on the ground gently and squeezed his hand. In a breath, Etienne found himself alone in the spot where their camp had been. Tears formed in his eyes. He had so much compassion for his former self. All he wanted to do was tell him how much he loved him and let him know everything would be all right.

Fransie had had enough of pretending like she was still sick inside the coach. It wasn't safe for them to stay here any longer. They needed to put as much distance between them and the Hospitallers as possible. She looked across at Charles and hoped the cross had healed him as well. She didn't know if they should move him, but if they didn't leave, they would be caught for sure. Fransie took a deep breath and stepped out of the coach.

"Whoa, lassie. Are ya sure ya should be standing?" Clair said, cradling Roslyn.

"I can assure you I am well. It was actually quite miraculous. Thank you for taking care of her when I was away and not well." Fransie reached for her child, and Clair reluctantly handed her over.

"Are ya sure ya are well enough?"

Fransie nodded. Roslyn took Fransie's finger and sucked on it gently.

"I bet you are hungry, aren't you?"

The child looked up at Fransie with large eyes. They couldn't quite focus, but Fransie knew she could recognize her voice.

"What are you doing up?" Joshua asked, with a furrowed brow.

"I am healed, Joshua. You are a wonder worker. See?" Fransie did a turn with the child in her arms. It was true though; she felt fine. The One True Cross had healed her.

"There will be some things we will need to discuss if I will continue in your company." Joshua's mustache pushed from side to side.

"We should probably discuss why you weren't in the prison with us." Michael crossed his arms. He, Emanuel, and Auriel were standing close to Binah, away from the others.

Joshua raised his eyebrows. "Even though I wasn't in a dungeon, doesn't mean I was any less a prisoner. They didn't see me as a threat, and knowing that I am a healer, they put me to work in the infirmary. I had to dine every night with that awful priest. Each night he tried to extract information about Fransie and"—he looked around at the others—"and about Kabbalah."

"Kabbalah," Auriel, Michael, and Emmanual murmured to each other.

Clair and Gerhart looked at each other and shook their heads.

"He means about the treasures and symbols we have been seein'." Andy placed a hand on Joshua's shoulder as he walked up beside him. "I think 'tis time that we are all on the same page. Everyone should have the same information. We need ta work together if we are ta succeed."

"Do you think Etienne will be all right with that?" Gerhart asked.

"Be all right with what?" Etienne appeared from a grove of trees, returning from the watch.

"I think 'tis time everyone knows what's going on. We need ta be on the same page ta succeed."

"We took an oath—"

"They can take an oath too." Andy held up the books of the Bible that Brother Bernard had made for him.

"But their beliefs are different."

"Technically, we all believe in the same God," Joshua said.

"I can vouch for each of them. Trust me," Fransie said, rocking Roslyn back and forth.

"I do. I trust you, Sister Franise." She and Etienne exchanged a smile. "And Andy is right, if we are going to succeed we all need to work together. Where is Raphael?"

"She hasn't come back from watch yet," Auriel said.

"Very well. She can take her oath later. Place your hands on the Bible and repeat after me," Etienne said.

"I want to take the oath as well," Charles said weakly from the entrance of the coach, holding his stomach.

"You're awake! Thank the Lord you're awake." Andy rushed to him with open arms, but Joshua stood in his way.

"I don't think he is quite that well yet." Joshua's broom mustache pushed back and forth as he spoke. "He needs more time to recover, though I am surprised he has recovered at all. It is quite miraculous."

Charles's legs gave out as he tried to step down from the coach and Andy and Joshua caught him.

"Oh, Charles, don't move. We will come to you," Fransie said. She watched as her friends all circled around Charles to take the same oath as she had. As a group, they needed this to bring them all together. They were all fighting the same fight, each a spark of light fighting against the darkness that was trying to consume the world.

"We will make this world safe for you, my love," Fransie whispered to Roslyn as the infant gripped her finger tightly.

"We must go now," Raphael said, tearing into camp.

"Are the Hospitallers here?" Etienne put his hand on the hilt of his sword.

"No, there is a caravan heading to Leon. We can join them and blend in."

"How do ya expect these ta blend in?" Clair motioned to the coaches. The gold of the Papal coach glinted in the sun, and the wagon attached to Blueberry looked more like a flowering tree than a coach. The branches and leaves from the severed head had nearly devoured the coach. There was even a small bird perched on a twig shooting from the top.

"We will have to leave the gold coach, but the other will blend in nicely." Raphael smiled widely. It was the first time Fransie had seen Raphael smile. It was one of those smiles that beams and is infectious.

## CHAPTER 31

In the distance were four ornately decorated coaches circled. They were painted with bright reds and greens, and one was purple and yellow. Etienne slowed as they approached, and the others did the same. On the roof of each caravan were people of all ages with crossbows trained on them.

A pear-shaped woman with silver-streaked black hair awaited their approach with her arms crossed. The shiny discs on her shawl reflected the sun in all directions. Next to her stood a man in his sixties with a scraggly beard and spectacles. His white hair was pulled back into a ponytail. He looked much more curious than concerned.

"That's far enough." The woman raised a hand stopping Etienne in his tracks. "Who are ya, and state your business."

"We are heading to Leon and would like to join your caravan."

All of the strangers burst into laughter.

"You hear that, Ma?" one of the archers shouted down. "They want to join our caravan." This sparked another course of laughter.

The pear-shaped woman placed her hands on her robust hips and shook her head.

"What's so funny about that?" Etienne asked.

"No one asks to join a Gypsy caravan—you have to be invited. And see, the thing is, we haven't invited you," the Gypsy woman said.

The archers re-aimed their crossbows.

Etienne had dealt with gypsies before as a Templar. They were notorious for robbing pilgrims on the Camino. They were nomadic people traveling all over the continent. Many people considered them a plague to the land. But Etienne also knew there was another side to Gypsies. One of the best nights of his life was spent amongst a Gypsy caravan when he first came to the Camino. They danced and sang all night long. He had also learned that in many places, it was illegal to hire Gypsies to work unless it was for their musical abilities, which was why sometimes they stole only to survive. Just as with everything in life, there were two sides to the story of the Gypsies

"And why do you want to join our caravan?" The Gypsy pulled her sparkly shawl closer around her shoulders, sending out a barrage of reflections in all directions.

"Wait a second, wait a second." The older man walked past Etienne with a look of disbelief. "I have never seen this species of tree before…or is it a bush?

He picked one of the leaves from the coach that was carrying the severed head and held it up to the sun.

"It could be a type of evergreen," he muttered. "They must be going to compete in the annual harvest festival in Leon." He looked at Etienne for confirmation.

"But, we always win that festival," a young archer said, with a look of disappointment on her face.

"If they enter, we may not this year sweetie; we may not. The man picked a flower from the tree. "Now six petals, but clustered like this?"

"Are you entering the festival?" the Gypsy woman asked.

Etienne nodded.

"Well, you can join us then on one condition." The Gypsy lady eyed Etienne.

"What is that?" Etienne asked.

"That if you win the festival—and by the looks of it you will—you give us the winnings."

"Can we agree to that, friends?" Etienne's companions nodded.

Etienne and the woman shook hands.

"I'm Ma DiLorenzo and this is Therese and Roberto, and their four children: Alafora, Haya, Dominic, and Hally." Each said hello in return. "Mary and Christoforo." She pointed to the next coach. "And their two girls Danja and Aryana." The kids all jumped down from the coach and surrounded Etienne. He felt a little hand go into his sporran. He grabbed Dominic by the wrist and the boy smiled at him as he let go of Etienne's gold.

"We have a condition as well."

"What is that?" Ma DiLorenzo asked.

"No stealing from us."

"Agreed."

"And are you Pa DiLorenzo?" Etienne asked the old man who was snooping around the wagon.

"No, I am Kevin." He pushed his spectacles up his nose. He craned his head around the back of the cart. "I must see inside."

"I can't let you do that." Gerhart lowered his ax between Kevin and the opening to their wagon.

"And why is that?" Kevin ineffectually poked Gerhart in the chest.

"Trade secret," Gerhart said, winking.

By sunset, the caravan had entered Leon; it was just as exciting as Etienne remembered it. The streets were filled with vendors, and the smell of food wafted down every alley. The caravan followed the Camino to the square in front of the cathedral, which was packed with people. Etienne admired the immaculate cathedral, and his soul longed to attend the evening service.

After traversing the crowd, Ma DiLorenzo led the caravan down an alley, which opened into a large plaza. The coaches lined up next to each other along the perimeter of the square. Etienne dismounted and tethered the horses of the coach to a pole. The whole plaza was decorated for a celebration. A giant stage was set on the western side of the plaza, and all of the surrounding buildings boasted evidance of a good harvest.

"Look at the competition." Kevin nudged Etienne in the ribs and pointed to the other wagons that sparsely lined the perimeter of the square. They were well decorated, but the Gypsies would definitely beat them in the competition. One reason alone was what pulled their lead wagon—it was an ox with the longest horns Etienne had ever seen.

"I can see why you won in the past years."

"This is only a fraction of the competition, but there is no way anyone will beat this." Kevin motioned to Etienne's wagon. "Although we do need to make it more festive. Would you care to join us?" Kevin handed Etienne a spool of ribbon. "Kids!"

Out of nowhere, all of the children appeared with spools of ribbon and other decorations. They climbed up the branches sprouting out of the wagon and threw ribbons to one another.

"I think it needs something else. It doesn't quite look like a Gypsy wagon yet. Dominic, go get the paint. You don't mind, do you?"

"Not at all."

"Eticnnc, look at my bow," thc youngcst Gypsy girl said.

"No, look at mine. She doesn't even know how to tie a bow," said the second to youngest.

"I do too!" said the first.

"No, you don't," said the second, hooking arms with Etienne. "You decide which is prettier." She looked up at Etienne with large doe eyes.

The bells for the evening mass rang and reverberated down the street and into the courtyard.

"I have to go," Etienne said. "But, I bet Gerhart would love to help you decorate."

"Which one is Gerhart?" asked the youngest.

"The really big one."

The girl smiled and ran towards Gerhart.

"Wait for me!" The other unhooked her arm from Etienne's and chased after the first.

"Saved by the bell," Kevin said, raising his caterpillar eyebrows.

Etienne smiled politely. "You will have to excuse me."

Etienne left the courtyard and retraced his steps to the cathedral, which was now bathed in a glorious orange and pink hue from the setting sun. Etienne joined the throng of parishioners entering under the statue of the Virgin Blanco.

Etienne had forgotten just how immense this cathedral was. The vaulted ceiling was so high, the light from the torches was devoured long before reaching the gray rock above. The arched columns supporting the massive cathedral were so thick, it would take him, Gerhart, Mariano, and Andy holding hands to reach around the circumference of one. Even then, he didn't know if they would reach.

Etienne followed the other parishioners through an opening in the gold gilded choir. He smiled at a Green Man carved in the edifice. The cherub face stared up at him with blank eyes and vines coming out of its mouth.

*These Green Men hold the secret of this cathedral. Their mouths have been bound with vines. However, Green Men are tricksters and reveal the secret in another way.* Ronan's words from the past made Etienne smile. They sure did hold the code, and he would never have been able to solve it without Andy.

Etienne thought Ronan would be proud of him. Standing in this very cathedral only a year ago, Etienne had been so naive. He had been just a boy. Now he was Seneschal of the Knights Templar, holding the same position that Ronan had held. Etienne had loved, he had lost, he had fought for what he believed in. He had been shaped by the Camino. He no longer was a boy; he was now a man with the responsibility of the world on his shoulders.

Ronan had held that same responsibility, and it had cost him his life. Why had Ronan chosen to lay this burden on him? Why had he shared the Templars' most guarded secret with him?

*He knew.*

Ronan had known there was a traitor in the Templars long before Molay. When Etienne delivered the message, Molay's pride had stopped him from seeing it. Now, look at the situation they were in: Ronan had died, Molay is trapped in Paris, and the Templars will be disbanded forever. That only left Etienne and his friends to solve one of the greatest mysteries of mankind and protect the treasure the Templars had hidden.

Etienne never asked for this responsibility, but he was willing to accept it. Ronan had been right about him long before he believed in himself. He had seen his potential long before Etienne could see it. The person Etienne had been the last time he was in this cathedral would have run away from this responsibility because he didn't feel worthy; but who he was now accepted it and all of the risks that came with it. How had he grown so much in a year?

"You were right," Etienne whispered. "You were right about all of it."

After mass, a clergyman that Etienne vaguely recognized approached him. "The bishop wishes to see you," the clergyman said, straightening.

"Why would he want to see me? I'm just a pilgrim," Etienne said, resuming his prayers.

"I know who you are. We have met before, and I know you are more than *just* a pilgrim, Etienne LaRue. Or should I say Seneschal LaRue?"

Etienne shot the clergyman a half-smile. "I guess you can't escape who you are."

"No, you most certainly cannot. Come, let's not keep the bishop waiting."

Etienne followed the priest down the corridor he had walked before. He remembered the bishop being more of a politician than a man of the cloth, but Isabella brought that out in people. She definitely had brought out the worst and best in him. It was she who had forced him to grow, almost more than the circumstances they had been thrown into. It was she, as much as anything else in his life, who made him the man he was today.

"So, we meet again," the bishop said, extending his hand for Etienne to kiss his large onyx ring.

Etienne followed custom and kissed the ring.

"I'm happy to see your rise in station hasn't given you delusions of grandeur."

"My predecessor taught me well."

"Congratulations on becoming Seneschal of the Knights Templar. That is quite an accomplishment."

"I would give up the title in a second to have Ronan back."

"True, he did seem a more appropriate candidate to hold the title than you. Which leads one to wonder, why has Etienne LaRue been made Seneschal of the Knights Templar? Why was Etienne LaRue accompanying Princess Isabella of France the last time you were in this room? Oh, did she make the transport that I informed you about?"

"Yes, she made it back to France safely. Thank you for informing us about it. And for your other questions—we do not choose our circumstances; we can only choose what we do when faced by them. I chose to accept this role when it was placed on me. There is nothing special about me."

"But, Molay seems to think so… And others don't… It is quite an enigma to figure out what to do with you."

Etienne's chest constricted, and he reflexively reached for his sword.

"Let's not have any of that in a house of God. We would be no match for you, and you would have to live with the fact that you slew two innocent servants of God. I would like to spare you that guilt. I am sure you have much blood on your hands already."

Etienne loosened his grip. "Who are these others?"

"Well, your own brothers to start with. Some support you, and others most certainly do not. It seems the Pope has taken an interest in you as well. Not to mention the Hospitallers, but why all of this fuss for you?"

"The best answer that I can give you is that Ronan believed in me."

"Yes, of course. The question now is do I believe in you? Should I help you or hinder you?"

"I think you should do what God tells you to do. It is by His will that I am who I am. I did nothing to deserve what has been thrust upon me."

"Well spoken. Will you be staying in our guest quarters tonight?"

"No, I have other accommodations, and I think I shall take my leave."

"Very well, I won't try to stop you." The bishop extended his hand again and Etienne kissed the black ring. The stone was cool and smooth on his lips.

"Choose wisely, for we both serve God," Etienne said, exiting the room.

Andy propped himself up against their wagon as person after person visited Ma DiLorenzo. She had set up a small table outside the back door of her caravan and had a line of five people deep, waiting to see her. Each person would sit, and Ma placed cards on the table. After a few minutes, people would pay her and either leave crying or smiling. Curiosity overcame Andy, so he joined the end of the line.

After fifteen minutes Andy sat in the chair, which had been warmed by so many people before him. Ma DiLorenzo shuffled the cards and smiled.

"Andrew Sinclair, I was wondering when you would join me."

"How did ya ken that I would join ya? Did you see it in them cards?" Andy nodded to the deck. "I heard you predicting other people's futures.

Ma shook her head. "I didn't need cards to see you staring at me for the past hour."

"Sorry about that. I'm just cur—"

"Curious." The metallic discs of Ma's purple scarf caught the light of the fire and danced in Andy's eyes. "Ask your question and let's begin."

"Actually, I prefer ta stay in the present moment rather than know the future. Everything important happens here and now."

Ma smiled even wider. "Well put, young man."

"I havenea been called young in a long time." Andy felt his cheek flush.

"Why are you here, then, if not to know your future?"

"I was curious about them cards and what you are doing."

Ma looked past Andy to make sure no one else was in line. "Very well then, I will still have to charge you."

"How much?" Andy reached into his sporran.

"Five coppers."

"But, you only charged the other three," Andy protested.

Ma clasped Andy's hands. "The others received a different service."

Andy reluctantly gave Ma the coppers; she put them in her overflowing pouch and separated the cards into two decks.

"There are twenty-two cards in the Major Arcana, which is considered the heart of the Tarot deck." Ma pointed to the deck on her left.

"So that's what these cards are called. How did you say it again?"

"Tarot," Ma repeated.

"Right, and what is the Major Arcana?" Andy nodded to the deck on Ma's left.

"The Major Arcana is a set of twenty-two cards that represents the Fool's Journey."

Ma laid out a card that had a fool on it, diagonally. The card also had a zero on it and the letter *Aleph* from the Hebrew alphabet.

"This journey parallels man's spiritual journey in life."

Ma placed down the second card mirroring the first. On it was a magician, the number one, and the Hebrew letter *Beth*.

"This story is the story of the innocent wonder, the Fool." She pointed to the Fool card; "to the realization of the oneness of everything."

Ma placed the third card down a ways from the first two pointing vertically at Andy; on it was a naked woman. Andy felt his cheeks flush once more. At the bottom of the card was written *High Priestess*. On top, was the number three and the Hebrew letter *Gimel*. She placed another card vertically above the High Priestess, which formed a triangle with the Fool and the Magician cards.

"Each of these cards represents a different step on the path. And, just as in life, if the card is facing one direction, it means one thing and if it is facing the other direction it means something else."

"What does the Fool represent?" Andy pointed to the first card Ma placed down.

"If the Fool is upright, it represents innocence, free spirit, new beginnings. If it is upside down, it represents recklessness, inconsideration, taken advantage of."

Ma placed down the remaining cards, and Andy nearly fell out of his chair as the pattern formed the Tree of Life.

"You look white as a ghost. Are the cards telling you something?"

"I just recognize that pattern."

"Interesting." Ma eyed Andy in a way that made him feel uncomfortable.

He wiped his sweaty palms on his pants and stood. "Right, I best be getting ta bed. 'Tis late."

"Sit," Ma ordered.

Andy followed directions like a school child and found himself back in the chair, more uncomfortable than he had been before.

"The Minor Arcana"—Ma pointed to the deck on her right—"are made up of four suits. Wands."

Ma placed down the first card, which had a hand holding a wand that was sprouting leaves. The card also had the Hebrew letter *Yod* written on it.

"Cups."

She placed down a card that had a cup, which resembled the Grail, drawn on it. It also had the Hebrew letter *Hey* written on top.

"Swords."

Ma placed down the next card, which had a hand holding a sword that looked like Etienne's sword. On top of the card was written the Hebrew letter *Vau*.

"And finally, we have the suit of Pentacles."

The final card had a five-pointed star inside a circle, held by a floating hand. But, more importantly, it also had the Hebrew letter *Hey* written at the top.

"Yahweh," Andy said, and reflexively crossed himself.

"Most people never see that. You are very clever, Andy. Beyond the face value of each of these cards, they also represent a different element. The suit of Wands represents Fire; Cups represents water; Swords represents air, and Pentacles represents earth."

"Well now, ya have that backward. Surely swords represent fire." Andy placed both hands over his mouth. "Sorry 'bout that. I donnae want ta tell you how ta do your job."

"I suppose you will tell me about the four worlds as well." Ma raised an eyebrow, and Andy shook his head.

"I didn't think so."

Ma brushed him off and placed the four cards, which also all had the number one on them, at the meeting point of the Fool and the Magician. They fit exactly where the Sephira Keter would be.

"In the Minor Arcana there are four suits, as you have seen, and each suit has ten cards in it." Ma took the cards that had the number two on them from each suit and placed them where Hokmah would be on the Tree of Life. She repeated the process with the threes and placed them where Binah would be. She continued until there were four cards at each Sephira.

"There, now you have the complete picture," Ma said as she gathered the deck together. All of the cards moved easily except one, which flipped upside down. Andy reached for it, but ma slapped his hand away. "You are not to touch another person's deck."

"Sorry 'bout that."

"You didn't know." Ma flipped the card over and froze. She placed it on the table so Andy could see. Andy looked from the card to her. "The devil, Andy. He is coming." Ma wrapped her shawl around her tightly as a cold wind blew through the square.

Fransie had spent a sleepless night inside the coach with Roslyn. She had made a cradle for her daughter amongst the roots that had sprouted from the head; it was a cocoon of blankets and love. Fransie didn't particularly like the head. She didn't think it was evil, but she also didn't think it was necessarily good. Looking at it had been part of the reason she had slept poorly. The other reason was the racket from all the animals and revelers who crowded the square. She looked forward to when they moved on—away from all of these people. She didn't like being around so many strangers.

"Good, you're awake," Auriel said, peeking her head through a flap. "Can I see the baby again? She is the most beautiful…the most precious…well, she is just wonderful."

"She is sleeping."

"That is just as good."

Auriel jumped into the covered wagon and sat next to Fransie with her back against the wood. She stared at the sleeping child.

"Why do I feel like this when I am around her? I have felt all of the other virtues, and none of them feel quite like hers."

"She is special." Fransie gushed on the inside. "She is of Jesus's bloodline." Fransie crossed herself. "Gabriel told me when we first met."

"Who is Gabriel?"

"He was the one who saved me when Luca attacked in Logronio. I actually thought it was you and Binah coming to my rescue. But instead, I got a tall, handsome, and broody Druid."

"I see. If I didn't know you were a nun, I would say you have feelings for him."

Fransie's cheeks flushed.

"I do have feelings for him—very deep feelings. He saved me. He saved us." Fransie looked from Auriel back to Roslyn. "But it's not what you think. As you said, I am a nun and have dedicated my life to serving Jesus. He will be the only man I will ever truly love."

"Right." The look on Auriel's face clearly showed her disbelief. "So where is this tall, handsome, dreamy man?"

"He got separated from us in a snowstorm. Etienne saw him a few days ago. Gabriel actually saved him from the Hospitallers and the Templars. But, the pull of the Harp was too strong. He is like us. He has True Scent. He tried to take the Harp from Etienne, but Sephira, his filter, stopped him. Etienne didn't understand why he did it. No one understands how hard these sins and virtues pull. Really, he is the only one who understands me. He is the only one who understands us." Fransie nodded to Roslyn.

Auriel took Fransie's hand. "I hope I get to meet him very soon." Tears welled in the corners of Fransie's eyes. "True Scent?"

Fransie nodded. "Well that means between us we almost have all five of the senses covered. All we are missing is taste."

"Actually, Andy has True Taste, and his animal is a centipede."

"A centipede? Yuck." Auriel stuck out her tongue and scrunched her nose. "Thank the Lord I have Binah and not a centipede."

Trumpets blew outside followed by the announcement, "Ladies and Gentlemen, welcome to Leon's Harvest Festival. For centuries this festival..."

Fransie didn't pay attention to the rest of the announcement. She rushed to Roslyn, who had been startled awake by the trumpets. She cradled the infant in her arms and rocked her back and forth.

"Have you seen all of the carts yet?" Auriel asked.

Fransie shook her head, and Auriel motioned for Fransie to follow her through the front of the coach to the driver's seat. Fransie followed cautiously with one arm cradling the baby and the other on the side of the wagon. Each step was carefully placed, avoiding the roots, which were now threaded through the floor.

Fransie's eyes adjusted to the sun, and a beautiful picture came into view. The perimeter of the square was lined with carts decorated with different colors, flowers, and even bread. Well, only Kevin's ox was decorated with bread; its mighty horns, which looked like they could do so much damage, were ringed with circular bread. Above Fransie, the branches of their cart stretched to the sky, each decorated with a little bow. Below, the cart had transformed from bare wood to a vibrant red with green accents.

"Do you like the way we decorated your cart?" one of the Gypsy children shouted up. "We did all of the bows ourselves. We did it for the baby. Can we hold her later?"

"We'll see," Fransie said. She didn't like the idea of children holding her baby. They were just babes themselves.

"What?" the child shouted up.

"We'll see!" Fransie shouted. The roar of the crowd surrounded them. There must have been hundreds of people all crammed into the square.

The child shook her head.

"Very soon, we shall begin the judging of the carts," boomed the announcer on the stage. Fransie turned her attention from the child back to him and saw someone run up the steps and whisper in his ear. The announcer nodded in understanding.

The announcer signaled to the trumpets and their bright sound bounced off the walls and quieted the crowd.

"Before we begin, there is a very important announcement."

Fransie watched in horror as Father Alexander walked onto the stage. She pulled her hood tightly over her head, covering most of her face. Father Alexander stood on the stage and waited until the crowd was completely silent. Even the beasts became mute in his presence.

"Good people." His raspy voice filled the square. "I am an emissary from the Pope. And as such, I bless this event and all who attend. Bow your heads and pray for God's blessing."

Fransie bowed her head but kept a vigilant eye on Father Alexander.

"Amen," Alexander said, and all of the courtyard looked to him. "As a messenger for the Pope, I order that all carts remain in the square after the festival for inspection by the Hospitallers."

"Like hell, we will!" Ma DiLorenzo shouted. She cracked the reins of the giant bulls who pulled her cart and took off across the square. The two other Gypsy carts in her caravan split off in opposite directions. Screams erupted, and the Hospitallers tried to stop them. The bulls put down their heads, and the Hospitallers dove for their lives.

"After them!" Father Alexander yelled over the crowd. The remaining Hospitallers chased after the caravans.

Auriel took the reins of their cart and cracked them but Blueberry didn't move; she just shook her head.

"Binah!" Auriel called.

Binah appeared with the other horses, and their companions tied them to the cart.

"We don't need speed!" Kevin shouted up. "We need invisibility, which Ma has given us."

"Why did she do that?" Fransie called down.

"The Gypsies and the Hospitallers don't get along. We are a free people and won't submit to their rules. Besides, we have some things in our carts that they may not like."

"Why did you stay?" Fransie asked.

"To show you another way out of the city, of course. I couldn't let them have this beautiful wagon."

Kevin calmly led Fransie and her companions through the winding streets of Leon unnoticed. From her vantage point, Fransie could see that the Hospitallers were guarding the entrance to the city.

"How will we ever get out of here? They are guarding the entrance to the city," Fransie called down from atop the wagon.

"Us gypsies have our ways." Kevin began to whistle, looking unconcerned. As he finished his song, it was answered by a whistle in the distance. He smiled at Fransie and winked.

The wagon stopped in front of a beautiful building with a large iron gate. Kevin whistled again, and the gate was opened. He took the lead horse by the reins and guided the wagon in.

In the courtyard, they were met by a man in his thirties with dark hair and blue eyes. He smiled, and his freckled cheeks rose.

"I didn't expect to see you here today," the man said, closing the gate. He stopped as a whistle echoed in the courtyard. The man whistled back, and it ricocheted down the alley. "You better move your wagon."

Kevin nodded and led the horses further into the courtyard.

"Yhaw!" Fransie heard, followed by a rumbling. Moments later, the three other coaches sped into the courtyard, and the man closed the gate—along with two wooden doors.

"Uncle Bruno! Uncle Bruno!" the kids yelled as they jumped from the caravan and nearly tackled the man to the ground.

"Thank you, son. It's good to see you," Ma DiLorenzo said. "Kevin, help me down from here." Kevin rushed to the coach and helped Ma down. Together they walked to Bruno and embraced him. "I wish we had more time to stay, but..."

"You need to use the back door."

Ma took Bruno's face in her hands. "That's my boy."

"Do we have to go already?" the youngest child asked.

"I'm afraid so," Kevin said, patting the girl on the head.

"It isn't fair," the girl said in a huff and walked away.

"Do you want to come with us? You know you are a Gypsy at heart," Ma said.

"You know my wife's family is here and..."

"You don't have to say anything else, son." Ma patted Bruno on the shoulder.

"You're right, though; I am a Gypsy at heart because all of you live inside it. No matter how far apart we are, you are right here, always." Bruno pointed to his chest. "Come on. Let's get you out of here before we all get caught."

Bruno led them to the far end of the square, which backed up to the city wall. He opened two cellar doors, and a ramp appeared.

"I'm going to miss you, son." Ma squeezed Bruno hard. "Kevin." Ma motioned for Kevin to help her back onto the coach.

"I'll miss you too. See you next fall." Ma nodded and drove the oxen down the ramp.

Fransie pulled Roslyn tight into her body as her wagon moved. She couldn't bear to think of ever parting with her.

# CHAPTER 32

Isabella lay staring at the plush canopy of the four-poster bed—the purple drapes hung and billowed. She had demanded to change rooms after Matilda's death. She couldn't bear to sleep where her cousin had died. The guilt was too much.

*Had I not left, none of this would have happened. Matilda, I am so sorry.*

Isabella turned and scanned the room. Her father had moved her to her mother's old chambers, which had large windows facing the tip of the island. The room was very royal, with its dark wood furniture and red velvet. However, Isabella's mother's decorations softened out all of the rough edges. It was comforting to be in here, but painful in another way. Isabella wished her mother was still alive. She would know what to say to comfort her. Plus, Isabella had so many questions for her about being a queen, a wife, a woman. Isabella felt cursed; everyone she loved at the palace had died: her mother, Gaston, Jessica, and now Matilda.

*It's my fault! I'm cursed! You are all dead because you loved me!*

Warm tears rolled down Isabella's face. She reached for the bedside table and took out a handkerchief. Isabella froze and inhaled deeply.

*It's her. It smells like her.*

Isabella pressed the cloth hard to her face and inhaled deeply. The smell of her mother brought back a flood of memories. The last time she was crying in this bed, her mother was stroking her hair and clearing Isabella's eyes for her. It was months after Etienne had been sentenced to death. Isabella had been so numb inside. She hadn't allowed herself to grieve. She was barely eating and was wasting away. Her mother had taken her into this very bed and held her. That embrace melted the sorrow that had bound Isabella so tightly. After Isabella had cried all the tears she could, her mother had said:

*"Etienne's death. It wasn't your fault. Don't put the blame of the world on your shoulders. Everyone is responsible for their own actions. Etienne decided to love you, knowing the risk. He is responsible for his own choice. As a queen you will have to bear many deaths. Don't take the burden of his on. His decision isn't your responsibility. Even if that decision was to love you."*

Isabella wrapped her arms tightly around herself and pretended it was her mother's embrace. Her words still held truth in them. Matilda had made her own choice, and Isabella wasn't the one who poured the poison. We are all responsible for our own actions and decisions. I will not blame myself for this, but I will take action.

Molay was right; the killer was still out there, and Isabella needed to find them. She pulled herself together and sat up in bed.

*Who would benefit the most from my death? And what enemies do I have?*

Isabella racked her brain, trying to find the answer to those two questions. The only person who would benefit from her death would be another woman who was in line to marry Prince Edward, or someone who wanted to hurt her father. Both of those were weak motives; anyone who lived in the castle knew that her father only loved himself, and there wasn't another suitable match for Edward in France.

That brought Isabella to enemies. Besides Molay, she didn't have any enemies that she knew of. Molay needed her; he wouldn't try to kill her—would he? Isabella thought of all the people she had wronged in her life, but she had done nothing worthy of death. Isabella flopped back onto the bed.

*What would Gaston do in this situation? He would start looking for clues since there are no suspects. Clues... Clues... The suicide note. I didn't write it, which means someone did.*

Isabella jumped from the bed, put on her dressing gown and slipped on her slippers. She had left the letter crumpled in Sainte Chapelle. She hoped it was still there. The killer wouldn't know the letter was in there, only she and her father knew. Isabella's footsteps echoed down the marble hall. She pulled the dressing gown tightly around her to keep the chill of the drafty night off.

The chapel looked completely different in the dark, but still had the feeling of being embraced by an angel's wings. Isabella walked to the confessional and brought the candle low to the ground. There it was, crumpled to the side of the wooden structure. Isabella sat on the cold hard floor with her back against the booth and read.

> *Dear father, I am sorry you have to find me like this. I have decided to take my own life rather than live in a world without Etienne. When you killed him, you killed me as well. Pray for my immortal soul.*
>
> *Isabella*

Isabella needed to find the intersection between those who could write and those who knew this information. News had spread like wildfire across the castle about Etienne when Isabella first returned. Matilda was a terrible gossip, bless her soul. Isabella made the sign of the cross. But, who would have known about her father saying that he had killed him?

Isabella thought back to the day her father had told her. She had only told Matilda and Katsuji. Could Katsuji have had Matilda killed to cover our tracks? It would have meant death for him if we were caught. Isabella shook her head. Katsuji was too honorable for that.

Isabella envisioned herself leaving the throne room. That's right, Sir David and Sir Richard were still outside the throne room flirting with the ladies as she exited. Perhaps the knights from England had overheard the whole thing. If so, that means they know about Etienne. Perhaps they tried to kill me to avoid an international incident. Everyone would know I'm not a virgin when we consummate the marriage anyway, but that was a problem for another day.

*I need to get samples of their handwriting.*

# CHAPTER 33

The wood in the fire crackled, and sparks flew into the air, mixing with the billion stars overhead. Etienne leaned back and watched the tiny orange dots disappear in the wind. He, Andy, and Mariano were the last ones awake. The colorful wagons were circled loosely around what had been an evening of singing, drinking, and dancing. It had been three days since they left Leon, and they hadn't seen a single Hospitaller. It was definitely something to celebrate.

"Right." Andy looked around. "Now that everyone is sleeping, there is something that I have been meaning ta tell ya." Andy produced a large book and papers from his satchel, which he carried at all times.

"What is that?" Etienne looked from the stars to the book on Andy's lap.

"'Tis the book of Genesis. Brother Bernard gave it ta me at the Templar castle. Molay had ordered him to make it for me before he left. He said it would help us in our quest."

"Have you figured out how it could help?" Etienne sat up and wiped the dirt from his hands. Andy handed him the book, and he thumbed through it.

"I was getting nowhere with it until Joshua showed me this." Andy pulled out a piece of paper and made a dot. "Here you have God in the eternal void; 'tis just being. One day God decides to expand its consciousness as far as it can go without moving and creates a sphere around itself." Andy drew a circle. "Next it moves to the edge of the sphere and repeats what it did the first time." Andy drew another circle and, where the two circles intersected, a shape resembling an eye appeared. "Let there be light!"

"What are you talking about?"

"God moved"—Andy pointed at the center of the first circle and then to the center of the second—"And said, 'Let there be light.'"

"Still nothing." Etienne raised his eyebrows.

"'Tis the first day of creation." Andy drew another circle. "On the second day, God forms the Trinity."

Etienne shook his head, and Andy continued to draw until the Flower of Life appeared.

"The seven circles of the Flower of Life represent the seven days of creation. It has ta do with the code!" Andy looked around to make sure no one was stirring.

Etienne shook his head in wonder. "Even then, Ronan was preparing me for this."

"Come again?"

"When I first met Ronan, he told me that each circle of the Flower of Life represented a day of creation."

"What do ya think it means?"

"I don't know, but I think it begins here." Etienne pointed from the first circle to the second."

"You are right," Mariano said.

"What do you mean?" Etienne asked.

When Mariano looked at Etienne, Etienne was filled with a concentrated presence and unconditional love that he had never experienced before. They locked eyes, and Etienne couldn't help but smile. For a moment, held in Mariano's gaze, Etienne felt the peace that he knew Mariano was experiencing.

"That is where it begins; as if there were such a thing as a beginning or an end—there just is."

"What are you talking about?" Etienne asked.

"That is where this world of illusion begins. The moment you go from nothingness to the concept of something, you automatically create not something." Mariano walked from the other side of the fire to join them. He pointed from the first circle to the second. "You create 'I am' and 'not I am'. This is where the illusion of separation begins. This is where the illusion of this world begins. This is where the illusion of you begins. You need a thing, and a something to compare it against, to make reality."

Mariano's words made Etienne uneasy. He dug his fingers into the dirt to ground himself.

"I'm lost. I hear what ya are saying, but I'm sitting right here. I'm not an illusion." Andy waved his hands in front of his face.

"Can you absolutely know you are sitting here by this fire?"

"It sure feels like I am," Andy replied.

"But can you absolutely know that you are, beyond a doubt—that you have a physical body and are sitting here by the fire?"

"I guess there is no way that I can absolutely ken, but I feel its warmth and my butt is sore from this hard ground."

"Are you sure those sensations and thoughts are yours? Are you thinking or are you being thought? Are you feeling or are you being felt? If you were unconscious right now, would you be feeling the warmth of the fire or sore from where you are sitting?"

"No, but when I regained consciousness, I would."

"Are you sure beyond a doubt that you would?"

"No, I guess the fire could have gone out, and I could have changed positions while unconscious."

"The whole world begins and ends with your perception of it—with the illusions you project and names that you tie to that which cannot be named."

"In the beginning was the word."

"Your whole perception of the world is made up of words. They try to give form and meaning to the formless. For example, you have the word "tree." This is first-generation thinking, then "tall tree;" then "tree I would like to sit under;" then "tree that bears fruit;" then "tree I will chop down for firewood;" then "stump where a tree was."

"There was no separation before a tree."

"Ya mean in the Garden of Eden. I havenea gotten to that part yet."

"When Man ate from the Tree of Knowledge, he saw himself as naked and separate from the world. You have naked and not naked. For the first time, Man felt shame in being naked; one was good and the other was bad. Then he felt fear. All of this stemmed from eating from the Tree of Knowledge, which created I am. I am naked. I am not woman, I am Adam, I am ashamed. The moment Man saw himself as separate from God, he fell from the Garden of Eden and into this world of illusion, where you have what you call good and evil, love and hatred. If Man could only see again that we are all one, he would return to Eden and know that eternal bliss once more."

"Right," Andy said. "'Tis too much for me ta take in after a night of drinking."

Etienne leaned back and looked at the billions of stars overhead, imagining that each was created from a single circle. He pondered both Andy's and Mariano's words deeply.

*More! I want more!*

Fransie was startled from her sleep. Beads of sweat dripped down her forehead as she looked desperately at Roslyn. He was coming for her. She clutched the baby tight to her chest and opened the door to the coach.

"Wake up! Wake Up! He is coming!"

Lanterns gleamed in the windows of the caravans, and one by one the doors opened. The horses brayed loudly; then there was silence.

"The horses! Quickly!" one of the Gypsies yelled.

"I feel him," Auriel said from the steps of Fransie's caravan.

"I have to leave! He is after her. I have to save her. Help me, please."

Auriel whispered and Binah thundered to them. Screams shot through the night air, and one of the caravans burst into flames.

"I can't let you go alone." Auriel helped Fransie onto Binah's back and jumped on behind her. "Run!" Auriel yelled, and Binah took off into the night.

The screams from camp faded, but the anguished cry from Gluttony chased on their heels.

"I still feel him." Auriel's body shook as she spoke.

"How is he keeping pace with us?"

"He is riding a horse."

*More! I want more!*

Fransie clutched Roslyn tightly in one arm while the other had a vise-grip on Binah's mane. Fransie's thighs were aching from squeezing for dear life, but she would hold on if it was the last thing she did. She would protect her child at all costs.

"More! More!"

Those weren't thoughts; they were words. At their left, Luca had caught up to them. In the moonlight, it looked as if his horse was possessed with Gluttony as well. Its eyes were bulging and nostrils were flared.

Luca jumped from his horse, and Fransie felt the warmth of Auriel's body disappear behind her. Binah reared up, and Fransie leaned forward to stay seated, praying the whole time.

"Go!" Auriel shouted.

Binah brayed loudly and shook her mane.

Luca rushed to Fransie and Binah, but Auriel pushed one leg so it tripped the other. The terrible mouth fell face-first into the dirt. In one movement it recovered and turned its attention to Auriel. The mouth gnashed wildly.

"Luca, I know you are in there. If you can hear me, stop," Fransie pleaded.

With the mouth facing Auriel, Fransie could see Luca's face clearly, hanging backward from his contorted torso. Everything that was still human left in his eyes begged Fransie for help.

Their eye contact was broken as the mouth lurched at Auriel. Binah turned and kicked Luca hard, sending him skidding to the ground once more. Auriel jumped on Binah's back. They started forward, but Luca recovered and latched onto Fransie's ankle, pulling her from Binah. As Fransie fell, she curled her body around Roslyn.

Fransie exhaled as the wind was knocked out of her then gasped for air. Roslyn was still in her arms. Fransie had managed to shield her from the fall. Things faded in and out, but her grip on Roslyn remained strong.

A warm liquid dripped on Fransie's hand. She was pinned on the ground and the mouth loomed over her. *Caroline, I join you now,* Fransie thought as a tooth sunk into her arm. Fransie pulled away, tearing her flesh. Was it that she pulled away, or was it that Gluttony was pulled off of her?

The pressure left Fransie's body and the putrid smell of the mouth's breath disappeared. Roslyn let out a cry. Her child was still in her arms.

The adrenaline in Fransie's body pushed her to her feet, and she ran.

"'Not that I speak from want, for I have learned to be content in whatever circumstances I am…'"

Fransie stopped. That voice was familiar, and so was the passage. Philippians 4:11-13 was Gabriel's mantra for overcoming his Gluttony. Behind Fransie, Gabriel's arms and legs were wrapped around Luca, forcing the mouth to face straight up to heaven.

"'...I know how to get along with humble means, and I also know how to live in prosperity; in any and every circumstance I have learned the secret of being filled and going hungry, both of having abundance and suffering need. I can do all things through Him who strengthens me.'"

"Ahh!" Luca's voice screamed. It was Luca, not the monster.

"Fight it, Luca. I know you are still in there!" Fransie ran to the two men pinned on the ground.

"'My grace is sufficient for you,'" Fransie and Gabriel said in unison. "'Those who seek the Lord lack no good thing,'"

*More! I want more!* The mouth continued to drool.

"Fight it, Luca. Fight it. Say the passage with us." She bent down and made eye contact with Luca. "'Not that I speak from want…'"

"'...for I have learned to be content in whatever circumstances I am…'" She and Gabriel said as Luca mouthed the words. Tears streamed down both Luca's and Fransie's faces as their eyes united.

"'...I know how to get along with humble means, and I also know how to live in prosperity; in any and every circumstance I have learned the secret of being filled and going hungry, both of having abundance and suffering need. I can do all things through Him who strengthens me.'" Luca's voice got stronger with every word as the three of them repeated the passage.

To Fransie's horror, Roslyn pushed out of her arms and landed on Luca's chest. Roslyn reached out and touched the mouth, as she did, the skin began to sew back together.

"'My grace is sufficient for you,'" the three said in unison. "'Those who seek the Lord lack no good thing,'"

Roslyn laughed joyously and patted Luca's stomach where the mouth had been. The only remnants of it was a scar that matched Gabriel's.

"Thank God, you both are all right!" Fransie wrapped her arms around her two friends. Releasing the embrace she looked from left to right. "Where is Auriel?"

"I'm going after them!" Etienne said to the others. He couldn't believe he had slept through the commotion.

"We are all going after them," Clair responded. "I'll willnea let anything happen ta that wee bairn."

A hawk screeched overhead, and a wide smile crossed Raphael's face. "All is well. They return now." She pointed to the east, and Etienne could barely make out a horse on the horizon.

He blamed himself for what had happened. Had he not been drinking with the others, he would have been more prepared for that monster—whatever it was. He could have sworn he saw a man's body hinged backward with a giant mouth leading from his midsection. He didn't know what it was, but he was sure it had to do with the treasure.

"See, Andy, the cards never lie. The devil paid us a visit." Ma's tan skin looked pale in the morning light as she placed a hand on Andy's shoulder.

"Wait, you knew this would happen?" Etienne asked Ma.

"The cards told us in Leon. Andy here didn't believe me."

"You knew too, and didn't bother to tell us?" Etienne stared squarely at Andy. "We could have prepared for that monster."

"He's not a monster; he's our friend!" Emanuel shouted, accompanied by vigorous hand movements.

"That was Luca," Michael said. "He has been possessed ever since he drank from that cup."

"A cup like this?" Ma shuffled through a deck of cards and produced one with a cup that looked like the Grail.

"We shouldn't speak of this anymore," Raphael said before anyone else answered. "Something isn't right."

Etienne looked back in the direction of the rider. Raphael was right; only Auriel and Binah were returning. There was no sign of Sister Fransie or Roslyn.

Binah raced into the caravan, and Auriel jumped from the horse's back straight into her sister's arms. Her body heaved up and down as she sobbed. Raphael held her and stroked her hair.

"Where is Fransie?" Etienne asked.

Auriel shook her head. Raphael and Etienne made eye contact and exchanged a nod. He jumped onto the back of the nearest horse and rode toward the rising sun. He had to see for himself. Fransie and Roslyn couldn't be dead. And, if they were, he would kill the beast responsible for it. He kicked the horse hard, willing it to go faster.

Etienne clenched his jaw as tears blurred his vision. Ahead in the rising sun, he made out a black horse, with two people walking beside it, and what appeared to be a body draped over the horse's back. Etienne was too late. These pilgrims had found Fransie first, but there was still hope, they would have left her body if she was dead.

Etienne cleared the tears from his eye and gripped the reins tightly with his other hand. As the ground disappeared between them, and Etienne's eyes adjusted to the sunlight, his heart leaped to his throat. It was Fransie, but she was walking, not draped over the horse's back. And next to her was Gabriel?

"Whoa!" Etienne pulled back on the reins, bringing his horse to a stop. He dismounted and swooped Fransie into a giant hug—careful not to crush Roslyn. "You're alive! Gabriel, thank you."

"I didn't do it for you." Gabriel looked straight ahead and not at Etienne. "I swore to protect Fransie and her child. I will do that until my dying breath."

"I'm sorry I doubted you."

"I forgive you." Gabriel turned to face Etienne and sighed heavily. "The Bible says to forgive someone, not seven times, but seventy times seven." Gabriel locked eyes with Etienne and smiled. "I think you are only up to about four."

A weight lifted from Etienne's shoulders that he had carried since the last time they had met. He had misjudged Gabriel, and Fransie had brought it to light. He was relieved that Gabriel could forgive.

"And, I suppose this is...Luca?" Etienne motioned to the man draped over Cash's back.

Fransie nodded.

"Is he dead?"

"No, he has been healed. The Gluttony that possessed him is gone, and the mouth is sealed. Thank the Lord." Fransie crossed herself and the other two followed suit.

"How?" Etienne asked.

"By the word of God." Gabriel placed a hand on Luca's back.

Fransie was rushed by everyone while they were still a good distance from the coaches. She was showered with hugs and laughter. Clair motioned for Fransie to give her Roslyn. Clair held the child high in the air and inspected her thoroughly.

"All seems ta be in order here. Jesus be praised," Clair said, satisfied with the inspection. "Ya must be tired. I'll look after the wee one if ya want ta rest for a bit."

"Thank you," Fransie said, feeling the strain on her body.

"Luca! Luca! Is that really you?" Emanuel shouted. He and Michael helped their friend down from Cash. "Wow! You donna look good."

Luca managed a weak smile as his friends wrapped his arms around their shoulders. They headed back to camp but were blocked by Ma DiLorenzo.

"This demon can't stay here." She crossed her arms emphasizing the conviction of her words.

"Please, he is our friend—" Fransie pleaded

"No! There are children here. My grandchildren; and if

anything were to happen to them, I would turn into a much scarier beast than him."

"If he can't stay, we won't either," Emanuel said defiantly, and Michael nodded.

"Nor I." Fransie stood by her friends.

"Well, I suppose that means none of us are staying then." Andy raised his shoulders and sighed.

"Yes, it seems that we will part, but let us part as friends." Etienne extended his hand.

"Before we can part as friends." Ma raised an eyebrow. "There is the matter of your payment."

"Payment?" Etienne asked.

"You promised us the prize money from the competition—"

"Plus the three extra days of accompanying you," Kevin butted in. Ma stared him down, and Kevin looked at her apologetically.

"But, we didn't win the competition and don't have the money," Fransie protested.

"Well, that does put you in a predicament." Ma looked from left to right. Fransie followed her gaze to see Ma's family armed with crossbows again. "We will accept this simple cup as payment." Ma held up the Grail.

"No!" Etienne said sternly.

"Where did you get that?" Fransie asked.

"I stole it from your wagon!" one of the kids yelled.

"You can't have that." Etienne placed a hand on the hilt of his sword.

"I wouldn't do that unless you want to die," Ma said.

"If you seek death, you shall find it at the end of my bow." Raphael stood protected by a wagon with an arrow pointed directly at Ma.

"I am old. If I die, my family will continue on, and they will take all that you have." Ma said.

"But she's not old." Fransie followed Auriel's voice; she had climbed one of the caravans and held Ma's youngest daughter at knifepoint.

"My child! Ma, we can't! Don't let her hurt my child!" One of Ma's daughters screamed.

"You wouldn't dare." For a moment Ma looked like an angry mother bear.

"No, I won't kill her, but I will take her. My horse is just behind this wagon, and you will never catch us," Auriel said. The little girl nodded confirming the presence of the horse.

"The horses!" Fransie shouted. "Take all four of the horses!" They didn't need the horses they had taken from the Papal coach.

Ma looked from Raphael to Auriel. "Deal," she said. Ma handed Michael the Grail, and everyone lowered their weapons.

# CHAPTER 34

"Floure, that is your name, right?" The young servant nodded. "I need you to do something for me."

"What is it, Your Highness?" Floure said, avoiding eye contact.

"It is all right, you can look at me. We will be seeing a lot more of each other now."

"Why is that, Your Highness?" Floure asked, stealing a momentary glance.

"With Matilda gone..." The words choked in her throat. Isabella felt that if they escaped, it would cement in the reality of Matilda's death. Isabella composed herself and straightened. "With Matilda gone, I will need someone to help me with specific things. Matilda trusted you, which means I can trust you too."

Tears rolled down Floure's cheeks. "I'm sorry, Your Highness." Floure brushed the steady stream from her face, and Isabella saw eyes that had shed more tears than just those.

"I miss her too; I think we all do. Matilda was the light that brightened this castle. She was a good friend. Now though, I need another friend that I can trust. Can I trust you, Floure? For the love of Matilda, can I trust you?"

Floure nodded, too ashamed of her tears to make eye contact.

"Good, this stays between us. Someone killed Matilda. She didn't take her own life."

Floure looked at Isabella with wide eyes."Why would they do such a thing?" Floure cleared her nose with the back of her sleeve.

"I think they were trying to kill me, and they are still out there."

"Does your father know?"

"Yes, but he doesn't believe me. That is why I need you to do something for me."

"What is it, Your Highness?"

"Sir Richard took a liking to you, correct?" Floure nodded. "I need you to get a sample of his handwriting."

"How do you expect me to do that? I am just a servant."

"Ask Sir Richard to write a poem for you or a letter. I don't care what. I just need to see something written by him."

"If you don't mind me asking, Your Highness, why?"

"No need to be timid, Floure, we are friends now. You can ask me questions." Isabella unlocked the drawer of the desk. "The killer left this." Isabella handed the paper to Floure. Floure looked at the paper and her cheeks turned red.

"Pardon me, Your Highness, but I can't read."

"Right, I'm sorry." Isabella put the paper back in the drawer and locked it. "That was a forged suicide note that I supposedly wrote. I need to find out who wrote it. I need to find out who wants me dead."

"What did the note say that makes you suspect Sir Richard? He is a good man."

"I know you like him, and want to protect him, but there were things in the note that only he or Sir David would know, and they are the only ones I can think of who would have a motive to kill me."

Floure nodded. "So it could have been Sir David? How do you expect to get a sample of his handwriting? I hope it's him and not Sir Richard... He has been so kind to me. I'm just a servant, and he was so kind and so gentlemanly. Sorry."

"No need to apologize. If he is such a good man, help me to prove his innocence by getting me that letter." Floure nodded. "As for Sir David, I am sure Matilda and he were courting, which means he wrote her letters. I will go through her personal effects and try to find them." Isabella placed a hand on Floure's shoulder, and they locked eyes. "Thank you for your help."

# CHAPTER 35

The march along the Meseta had been long and hot. Even in October, the Spanish sun was punishing. Fransie cradled Roslyn in her arms as they rode in the front seat of the coach. In the distance, Carrion de los Condes appeared on the horizon.

"That used to be Mommy and Auntie Caroline's home," Fransie said to Roslyn. "I wish you could have met her. She was brave and kind—but also incredibly stubborn. She would have loved you almost as much as I do."

Roslyn took Fransie's hand and sucked on her finger.

"Are you sure you want to stop at Santa Anna?" Etienne asked as he strode along Blueberry's side. "We could just continue to Castrojeriz."

"Yes. They need to know about Sister Caroline."

"I'm so sorry you both got caught up in this."

"And I am sorry you did as well. None of us chose this path. It was what God laid before us."

"I suppose it was just thrust upon us."

"And I couldn't think of a better group of people to accept the challenge. Etienne, look how far we have all come. Look at the family we are." Fransie stroked the top of Roslyn's head and the child cooed. "I wouldn't give her up for the world."

"That's the way I feel about Andy." Etienne joked. He made eye contact with Fransie and they burst into laughter, startling the baby. "Sorry, sorry." Fransie rocked Roslyn to calm her.

The convent of Santa Anna was just as Fransie had remembered it. At one time, her entire life was lived inside those walls, and the entire world came to them. She loved serving pilgrims. Every wound she treated was Jesus' wound. Every hungry mouth she fed was Jesus' mouth. She loved serving the pilgrims. It had been her calling until God called her elsewhere. She wondered if it was fair to have more than one calling in life. Had she abandoned God's plan for her own when she left the convent? She rocked Roslyn gently in her arms and knew the answer in her heart.

"Etienne, I have changed my mind. We should continue on to Castrojeriz. I will only need a moment."

Etienne helped Fransie down from the wagon as Clair held onto Roslyn.

"Do ya want me ta keep her when ya go?"

"No, thank you." Clair handed Roslyn back to Fransie and tickled her chin.

"Do you want us to come with you?" Etienne's eyes became large and soulful.

"No. This is something I have to do on my own."

Fransie took a large breath, marched to the door, and knocked firmly on one of the large wooden panels.

"No pilgrims will be admitted until after the noon hour," came the familiar voice of the guest master from the other side of the door. "The beds haven't been prepared yet. Come back when the sun is at its highest,"

"I am not a pilgrim," Fransie responded.

"Fransie? Sister Fransie? Is it really you?"

A small door within the larger door opened, and the kind old eyes of the guest master appeared—accompanied by a smile.

"Thank the Lord you have returned to us. Is Sister Caroline with you?" The guest master's eyes darted from side to side.

"I came to bring you the news of Sister Caroline's death."

The guest master's face turned somber. He shut the little door and opened the entrance to the convent.

"My poor child. You must be devastated." He went to hug Fransie but stopped when he noticed Roslyn in her arms. "Why, hello. Who is this?"

"This is my daughter, Roslyn."

The guest master nearly tripped as he stumbled backward.

"Your daughter. Oh, Sister Fransie. What has this world done to you?"

"It has been hard at times, but also kind and joyous."

"Well, you have returned home now, and we can put the child up for adoption. I'm sure you will be welcomed back into the convent."

"Adoption? No, she is my child, and I will keep her. I came here to tell you about Sister Caroline, but also to return these. Would you mind holding her for a moment?"

"I really would rather..."

Fransie handed Roslyn to the guest master and took off her habit. She had put on other clothes underneath in preparation for this, although she hadn't known her final decision until he had mentioned adoption. Fransie folded her habit neatly and exchanged it for her child.

"Sister Fransie! But, what about your vows?"

"I was only a postulant. I hadn't taken my final vows. I was still in a period of discernment when I left."

"I forgot that you were a novitiate. Are you sure this is the decision that you would like to make?"

"I am sure." Fransie looked at Roslyn in her arms. "God has shown me that I can do more good outside these walls than from behind them. He has called me to another purpose in life."

"Very well, Sister Fransie... I mean, Fransie. I will inform the others, and may God bless you on your new calling."

The guest keeper looked at Fransie's old habit in his hands and then at her with pleading eyes. Fransie shook her head, and the guest master closed the door.

Fransie. Her name seemed so naked without Sister in front of it. Being a nun had been her identity for so long. She didn't know how to be just Fransie.

# CHAPTER 36

Isabella had Matilda's personal effects brought to her mother's chambers. This was her safe space. She had barely left the room since she arrived, and going to Matilda's old chambers sounded unbearable. Isabella opened Matilda's chest and sifted through her things. Near the bottom, she felt paper—lots of paper.

Isabella pulled out a stack of letters about the size of a book, all bound together with a red ribbon. Isabella shook her head. These had to be the love letters from Sir David. He must have been prolific to write this much. Isabella untied the ribbon and read the first letter.

> *My Dearest Matilda,*
> *My heart yearns for you. When I think of you the world pales in comparison. Everything turns gray without the light of your sapphire eyes. I count the seconds on dreams until I arrive from Burgundy—*

"Burgundy?" Isabella skipped ahead to the signature. She didn't feel it was right to read Matilda's personal letters.

*With admiration,*
*Your Duke of Burgundy*

Isabella skipped to the next letter.

*To my little vixen,*
*I want to...*

Isabella skipped immediately to the signature; it was from Lord Devon.

Isabella looked at letter after letter, and all of the signatures were different. It would seem that half of France was in love with Matilda, but there was nothing from Sir David. Isabella put the letters aside and opened a small box; inside was a book with a letter sticking out of it. Isabella turned to the bookmarked page, and found Matilda's writing along with the letter.

*This must be her diary.* Isabella wasn't going to read what was written, but she saw her name. It looked like Matilda had been making a rough draft of a letter to her.

*Dear Isabella,*
*First off, don't be angry with me. I know you told me no British knights, but I couldn't help myself. Sir David was so deliciously handsome. I don't know if you are right or incredibly wrong. I didn't know how to tell you this in person, but Sir David and I have had a relationship since he first arrived at court, and well, I am carrying his baby.*

Isabella's jaw dropped. Why had Matilda kept this secret from her? Perhaps she had just found out. The entry was marked the day Isabella had left. Matilda had tried to tell her something, but Isabella was too preoccupied with her escape and Etienne's supposed death. Isabella felt wretched inside. She hadn't been there for her friend when she needed her the most. Isabella continued to read, savoring each of the words in this last message from her dearest friend.

*It is a joyous secret, and one I can barely contain. I want to shout it from the mountain tops. But, I told Sir David, and he urged me to get rid of the child. You see, the thing is, he has a wife. I know I am a ruined woman if I keep the child, but I love it already. That is why I am begging you to take me to London with you. I know he will leave his wife for me. I just know it. But, that won't be possible if I remain in Paris. If you don't take me I don't know what to do.*

*Love, Matilda*

*P.S. Your hair has been looking amazing.*

Isabella read the letter again and again. She wanted the words to change, but they remained the same. Isabella opened the letter that was marking the page.

*Matilda,*
*This is joyous news, but my heart is wrenched in two directions. I do love you as I have said many times before, but I am married. You knew that when we started this affair. I will provide for you and the child as best I can, but I will not leave my wife. She can never learn about you, nor the child. I urge you to save your reputation and deal with the child.*

*D*

Isabella didn't need a full signature. She knew this letter belonged to Sir David. Had he killed Matilda to keep her silent? Isabella took the suicide note from the bed and compared David's handwriting to the note. Isabella choked back tears—the handwriting didn't match. She wanted to hate Sir David. She wanted to blame him for Matilda's death. She wanted to be angry at someone besides herself.

Isabella looked at his letter again. Perhaps he was responsible, but indirectly. Isabella noticed that tears stained the letter. Had Matilda tried to perform the abortion and failed? Without Isabella going to London, there was no way for Matilda to go. Or worse, seeing no hope, had Matilda taken her own life?

## CHAPTER 37

The rising sun silhouetted the castle that perched atop the hilled city of Castrojeriz. From where Etienne stood atop Alto de Mostelares, the whole of the region opened below. The golden rays of sunlight moved across the ground like the sea tide pushing out the last remnants of night. Etienne closed his eyes as the wind whipped him in the face. Most pilgrims hated this wind, but Etienne loved it. He was home.

"I see why ya wanted ta leave." Andy pulled his cloak around him tightly to ward off the bite of the wind.

"I never wanted to leave. It seems to be the way of my life. Just as I am feeling at home someplace, I am called somewhere else."

"'Tis why I make my home in people, not in places," Andy said.

"What do you mean?"

"Well, see, you are my home. Clair, Gerhart, and Mariano are my home. When you left Santiago ta go with the Knights of Saint James, and Mariano left ta find himself, Santiago was the same place, but 'twasnea my home any more. I'm more at home in this very spot than I ever was there."

"I understand and feel the same way about everyone." Etienne looked over his shoulder at all of his companions on the flat mesa.

"What now?" Fransie asked, catching his eye.

"Now, we need to find a way around Castrojeriz to the Arc of San Anton. We don't know which Templars are loyal and which belong to the New World Order. I trust the Commandery Master at the Arc. I have known him for many years."

"We could wait until night and pass then," Andy said from Etienne's right.

Etienne shook his head. "There are night patrols…at least there were when I was stationed here."

"Perhaps some of us could pretend like we have the Fire of San Anton." Fransie offered. It was a good idea. Pilgrims came from all over the world to the Arc of San Anton to be treated for the disease that mimicked the plague.

Etienne looked from Andy back to Fransie, and his heart stopped. On the flat mesa behind them, a company of Hospitallers appeared on the horizon.

"Oh no. This can't be happening. We are so close." Fransie pulled her child into her chest tightly.

"We will have to take our chances with the Templars and sort out who is on our side later." Etienne took the first steps down the mesa and stopped as he turned the bend. Not more than one hundred yards below on the Camino was another host of Hospitallers.

Etienne looked around desperately. There was no place to hide on the flat mesa and no other way to descend the sheer drop. He could possibly make it, but he knew some of his companions wouldn't be able to. He couldn't leave them behind, not even for the treasure.

"Quickly, hide whatever treasures you can," Etienne ordered.

Before either set of Hospitallers reached them, all of the treasures, except for the head, were buried or hidden under piles of rocks.

"What now?" Andy asked.

"Now we are just pilgrims with the Fire of San Anton. The most conspicuous of us must hide in the cart and pretend like we are sick. "Who would the Hospitallers recognize?"

Everyone raised their hands except Clair and Mariano.

Etienne shook his head. "Blueberry couldn't possibly pull all of us."

"Let's just pull our hoods low and go forward. We don't ken if the ones commin' up the hill are after us or not," Andy offered.

Etienne hadn't thought of that. They had been chased for so long, it seemed like everyone was after them. He lowered his hood, and the others followed suit. They continued down the Camino until they encountered the company of Hospitallers.

"Hola peregrinos," a Hospitaller said from atop his horse.

"Hola," Etienne responded.

"It seems that we are at an impasse. The Camino is too narrow for us to cross each other. Your cart and our horses are too wide on this small road. I wouldn't want either of us to topple down. Will you be so kind as to back up to the top so we can pass safely?"

"Unfortunately, our donkey only goes in one direction." Etienne was at a loss for words, and this was the best he could come up with.

"That is quite a decorative cart," another Hospitaller said. "Are you coming from a harvest festival?"

"Yeah," Andy piped up. "And we would have taken first place if it weren't for them Gypsies."

"Gypsies?" the first Hospitaller asked.

"It's a long story," Etienne replied.

"Look, just unhitch your donkey, and we can all push the cart to the top. It can't be more than ten meters back.

"Stop them!" shouted a raspy voice. On the edge of the mesa stood the tall gaunt priest with long fingers. The Hospitallers in front of them drew their swords. Etienne raised his hands. A fight with this many Hospitallers would mean certain death.

"Now, I suggest we get that cart of yours back on the mesa."

Etienne nodded and unhitched Blueberry. Within five minutes, everyone stood atop the mesa. Etienne and his companions were lost in a sea of black tunics with eight-pointed silver crosses.

"Thank you, brothers, for your service. Which commandery

do you come from?" the priest asked the lead Hospitaller who had escorted Etienne and his companions back to the top of the mesa.

"We are from the Paris Commandery. We carry a message for Father Alexander Dumond from the Pope."

"I am he," the priest responded.

The lead Hospitaller produced a scroll with the papal seal and handed it to Alexander. The priest read and stopped about halfway through. He looked from the document directly at Etienne.

"Are you Etienne LaRue?" the priest asked.

"I am just a pilgrim," Etienne said.

"Take him, and pull back his cloak." The Hospitallers followed Alexander's orders and pulled back Etienne's cloak, revealing the Templar cross on his mantle.

"He is a Templar?" a Hospitaller said.

"We all are," Andy said.

"If that's true, the Templars must be getting desperate. You are the most raggedy bunch of misfits I have ever seen," another Hospitaller said, and the whole company burst into laughter.

"Well, we are," Andy replied. "And if you mess with us, you will be messing with all of them." Andy pointed over the edge of the cliff to a host of Templars massing in the valley below.

The Hospitallers all began to murmur, and the air became tense. Alexander raised his hand, silencing the discontent.

"I will ask you again, are you Etienne LaRue, Seneschal of Grand Master Jaques de Molay? Answer me, as my patience is growing thin."

"I am," Etienne said.

"Then we are at your service. Release them," Alexander ordered. "You are under Papal protection and the protection of the Hospitallers. Is that understood?"

Etienne couldn't believe what he had just heard, and by their persistent tight grasp, neither could the Hospitallers.

"I said release them! We all are under the command of Etienne by order of the Pope!"

The Hospitallers released Etienne and his companions.

"Luca! No!" Michael shouted, but it was too late. Luca had taken a Hospitaller's sword and stabbed Father Alexander in the chest. Alexander dropped from his horse.

A Hospitaller knocked the sword from Luca's grasp and ran him through. Luca placed both hands on the wound and fell to his knees. "Stephano! I join you now, brother. Your death is avenged and so am I for the torture I have recieved. Jesus, forgive me and take my soul."

"No!" Emanuel reached for his sword.

"Stop!" Etienne ordered, "It is done."

"Why should we listen to you and not kill you?" One of Alexander's companions asked with his hand on his sword.

"Because the Pope ordered it," said the Hospitaller who had delivered the message. "If the Pope orders it, then God orders it." The Hospitallers spoke among themselves and nodded their heads in agreement. "Good, what is it that you order?"

"First, we must bury these men. Then my companions and I must get past those Templars unseen."

Etienne repressed a smile. He knew in his heart that Isabella had done this. He had no idea how she turned the Pope to their side, but for the first time since she left, Etienne knew she had made the right decision. She hadn't abandoned them.

The Hospitallers moved off a small distance to bury Father Alexander, leaving the small group of pilgrims to bury Luca. Fransie didn't know if Luca had done it on purpose or not, but burying him had provided the perfect cover for them to retrieve the treasures they had hidden. They quickly transferred the stones and loose dirt from where the treasures were hidden to Luca's body.

"Is he really dead?" Fransie asked Gabriel.

"He appears to be," Gabriel responded.

"But he drank from the grail, which gave him immortality. When he was injured before, he healed quickly—remember?"

"I remember," Raphael said. "We tried to kill him again and again, but he wouldn't die."

"Perhaps when the Curse of More left him, so did the Curse of Eternal Life?" Gabriel's heavy brow dropped low. "Why am I still cursed with it?"

"Right, that does it," Andy placed the last stone over the place where Luca's face was buried. "Who would like to say a few words?"

All eyes turned to Fransie, and her face flushed. She looked around at her companions and knew the responsibility was hers.

"If you will bow your heads." Everyone followed Fransie's directions and she began, "God, we pray that you will take the soul of Luca into your hands. He was lost but found your son Jesus before he died. I pray that tonight Luca will be feasting in heaven with his brother Stephano and our Lord Jesus. Lord, we pray that you will watch over us as we complete our journey and that one day, we will all be reunited again in your Kingdom. Amen."

"Amen," everyone parroted back, making the sign of the cross.

Fransie was the last to leave the graveside. As she left, she whispered, "Luca, if you do come back—find us. You are as much a part of this family as anyone else."

"Clair, what has gotten inta ya? Ya didnea even ken Luca." Andy asked as he stared at Clair's tear-stained face. "Are ya afraid this plan willnea work?" Andy looked back into the coach to where

Etienne, Raphael, and Fransie were all pretending that they had the Fire of San Anton.

"'Tis a good plan. That isnea it."

"What is it then?"

"How can ya ask that, Andrew Sinclair?" Clair punched Andy hard in the arm. "She died right over there." Clair pointed a shaky finger to a clump of burnt trees on the plain below. "Our 'Eather died right there, and we couldnae even bury her."

Andy's heart sank. He had been so wrapped up in the excitement and planning, he had forgotten where they were. This was the very spot where Clair's daughter Heather had died two years ago. It was also where they had first met Isabella and Etienne. Etienne had saved him that day from the Moors, but Heather wasn't so lucky. When they returned to the grove of trees where Andy's coach had been hidden, it was on fire, with Heather trapped inside. All that was left now was these charred trees.

"I'm sorry, Clair. I ken it hurts." Andy wrapped his arm around his sister. "She was everything to us, wasn't she? Do ya remember the way she used ta sing? The bagpipes had nothin' on her."

Clair punched Andy again.

"Ouch!" Andy rubbed his arm. "Look, if we go that way round, maybe we can stop at the grove ta give her a proper burial?"

"Don't be daft, Andrew Sinclair. We cannea do that with everything at stake. I willnea put everyone at risk for my needs."

"Right. Then, after this whole thing is over, we will make sure she has a proper burial and a service ta match. I promise ya that, Clair."

A delegation from the Templars rode out to meet them at the foot of the hill. "What is this?" The lead Templar demanded. "Why have you brought this force here?" He pointed to the top of the mesa where the rest of the Hospitallers waited.

"Apologies, brothers. I know what this looks like," the Hospitaller who delivered the Pope's message said.

"It looks like Hospitaller aggression," the lead Templar snapped.

"We are just in the service of these pilgrims. They were attacked at a harvest festival in Leon by a band of Gypsies; who cursed some of these pilgrims with the Fire of San Anton. Our Brothers above agreed to protect them as they travel to the Arc of San Anton to be healed. We are dedicated to the service of protecting pilgrims as are you. Will you deliver these pilgrims the rest of the way to the Arc so we can continue our hunt for these Gypsies?"

"Of course. It is our duty to protect pilgrims as well. We will deliver them the rest of the way. But one question, why such a large force for a band of Gypsies?"

"The Gypsies have grown in number, and if they can create a curse such as this"—the Hospitaller pointed at Andy's wagon—"then we need all the help we can get."

"Would you like some of our men to aid in the search?"

"I would prefer that you protect these pilgrims. The Gypsies may return to finish the job."

"They will be well protected here," the lead Templar said.

"Let us part as friends then." The two men shook hands, and the Hospitaller escort rode back up the hill.

"Follow me," the lead Templar said to Andy. "I'm sorry to hear about your friends and family, but you will be safe here."

"I hope so," Andy said as he urged Blueberry forward. He also hoped that their story hadn't put Ma DiLorenzo and her family in danger, but they had to take that risk. Anyway, if the Templars in Castrojeriz were to follow Molay's orders, they would be disbanded in a few days. The thirteenth of October was just two sleeps away.

"Take them to the infirmary." Etienne heard from inside the wagon. He couldn't believe his plan had worked. No one had had to die, and they were within the walls of the Arc of San Anton—his former home. Etienne hoped that the Commandery Master was still loyal to the Templars instead of this New World Order. Etienne knew his best chance would be to convince him to join them.

The wagon jostled forward, and Etienne heard their Templar escort ride back toward Castrojeriz. Etienne smiled at Fransie and Raphael, who seemed as relieved as he was.

"Can any of them walk?" came from outside as the wagon stopped again. He didn't have to see to know they were now at the doors leading to the infirmary.

"Well, ah, you see," Andy fumbled with his words. They hadn't really planned what would happen when they actually got into the Arc, just that Etienne would talk with the Commandery Master.

"We can walk." Etienne stepped out of the coach. "My apologies for the deception, but—"

"Sound the alarm!" yelled the sergeant who was accompanying them. The bells rang loudly.

Etienne raised his hands, and all of his companions followed his lead. He had missed the sound of those bells. Adrenaline pumped through his body, not because he felt he was in danger, but because they were his former call to arms. Within moments, they were surrounded by Templars.

"Etienne, is that you?" a younger Templar asked.

"Nah, it can't be him. This is a man standing before us. Don't you remember? Etienne was just a boy," another Templar said.

"Nonetheless, it is our Etienne." The strong voice of the Commandery Master parted the Templars.

"Commandery Master." Etienne placed a hand on his stomach as a sign of fidelity and bowed his head. A hand rested on his shoulder, and he looked up.

"It is I who should be saluting you, Seneschal." The Commandery Master placed his hand on his stomach, lowering his head, and all of the other Templars followed suit.

Etienne took a step back and steadied himself against the coach. His Commandery Master and brothers who had once outranked him were now bowing to him.

"That isn't necessary," Etienne said, finding his words.

The Commandery Master smiled, took Etienne's hand, and they embraced as brothers.

"Templars!" The Commandery Master shouted. "Back to your posts!"

"Hugha!" the Templars responded, hitting their shields.

"Walk with me, Etienne," the Commandery Master implored.

Etienne looked back at his friends.

The Commandery Master motioned to the sergeant who had led their wagon in. "Escort our guests to the albergue and get them anything they need. I am sure their road has been long and hard."

"Yes, Commandery Master," the sergeant said, bowing. "If you all will follow me." He motioned for Andy and the others to follow, but they didn't move.

"Go on," Etienne said. "I will be fine."

"Right then." Andy placed an arm around the sergeant's soldier. "Do you have any food around here?"

"The last time you were here, you were no older than him." The Commandery Master nodded to Prince Charles who was talking to Joshua as a Templar led them away. "Now look at you—a man—and second in command of the Templars."

"I'm happy you got the message. We didn't know what we would find when we got here."

"You made the right choice coming here in disguise. We are the only commandery in Castrojeriz that is still loyal to the real Templars, not this New World Order." The Commandery Master shook his head.

"What is this New World Order? We encountered them in Ponferrada. A few loyalists were able to sneak us out, but it seemed that the whole castle had turned."

"That isn't a surprise. Edgar made Christan his Seneschal. He is the one recruiting all of the Templars."

"Edgar?"

"My apologies, I'm sure you weren't on first name terms when you were last here. Do you remember the Provincial Master?"

"Of course, he was the one who wanted me to spy on Isabella. He thought she had a hidden agenda for being on the Camino, and he was right. You aren't telling me—"

"That the former Provincial Master of the Templars is a high-ranking member of this New World Order," the Commandery Master interrupted, nodding. "Edgar tried to entice me to join. He showed me Jesus's Crown of Thorns and said it was one of the seven keys binding the One True Treasure. He said that he possessed the other six as well and that he now controls the One True Treasure. As it is said, the one who controls the treasure controls the Templars. I didn't believe his lies, though. It may have been the Crown of Thorns, but I don't think he controls the One True Treasure—at least not yet. Otherwise, he wouldn't be so obsessed with it."

"Ronan was right. He was right this whole time. There was a traitor in the Templars. Molay should have acted when he had a chance."

"This is bigger than just the Templars. This New World Order involves kings, and some say, even the Pope. It is a many-headed serpent infecting society."

"So you and this whole commandery will follow Molay's orders and disband in two days' time, along with all of the other Templars around the world?"

"Yes and no. We will no longer be Templars in the open, but we won't be going to Portugal to join the others. We will become the Order of the Antonians and stay right here. The service we provide to the pilgrims is too great to abandon. So we will take on a new name and mantle."

"And what will your mantle bear?"

"The Tau." The Commandery Master pointed at the T-shaped

cross set into the circular window above. It was Etienne's favorite window at the Arc. It had a large Tau in the middle and smaller ones circling it.

"It is fitting—a sign of protection and healing."

"So what brings you here?"

"A mission Molay sent me on. Do you think the Provincial—I mean Edgar—would try to recruit me as well instead of killing me on sight?"

"I believe so, but it is a dangerous gamble."

"It is one I will have to take to spare the blood of many."

"Molay made a good choice in you, Etienne."

"Molay didn't make the choice—Ronan did."

# CHAPTER 38

Isabella held Matilda's journal close to her heart. These words were the last thing she had of her dear friend. Not knowing what else to do, Isabella crawled onto the bed and began tying the linens to the four-post-bed to make a fort. She thought that Katsuji's technique would help her. She needed to feel safe. She wanted to leave her feelings of guilt and remorse outside. Isabella curled up inside her cocoon and read Matilda's journal. Isabella found a depth to her cousin in the pages that she had never known.

There was a quiet knock on the door.

"Go away!" Isabella yelled.

The knock persisted.

"I said go away!"

The door creaked open and the sound of footsteps came to the bed.

"Your Highness," a mousy voice said.

"What is it!" Isabella tore open the flap of her blanket fort. Floure stood at the side of her bed, holding a piece of parchment in her hand.

"I have the letter from Sir Richard."

Isabella stuck her hand out of the fort, and Floure gave her the letter. Isabella compared the writing to the suicide note.

"They match." Isabella tore down the fort. "Floure! Thank you. I knew he did it. Of course, Sir David wouldn't write the note himself. He had Sir Richard write it for him! How did I not see this? We must go see my father. There is a murderer amongst us. Help me into one of my gowns."

Once dressed, Isabella and Floure sped down the large marble corridor to the throne room. Isabella burst through the doors and marched to the throne.

"Father, we have a murderer among us."

"What has happened in my court?"

"Matilda's death was no suicide. She was murdered, and I have the proof right here." Isabella held up both letters. Her father motioned for Isabella to hand him the letters.

"Who has written this?" Her father looked up from the papers and his eyes burned like coals.

Isabella looked at Floure and nodded. "Go on. Tell him who gave you this letter."

Floure fidgeted and kept her head down.

"Speak! Or I will have you tried as a conspirator."

"It was Sir Richard. He gave me the note. Isabella figured—" Philip cut her off with a sweep of his hands.

"Bring me Sir Richard and Sir David immediately," Philip barked, and his guards sprang into action. Isabella watched as her father gripped the throne tightly. "This is treasonous. That poison was meant for you, Isabella. They attempted to kill my daughter. This will be war!"

Moments later Sir David and Sir Richard appeared, restrained on either side by guards.

"What is the meaning of this?" Sir David, asked as he struggled. "We are here as diplomats to the King of England. What you do to us, you do to him."

"Quiet, murderer!" Philip bellowed. "You will not speak again until spoken to." Philip's knuckles turned white as he gripped the throne tightly.

Sir David and Sir Richard nodded reluctantly.

"I am going to ask you questions, and you will answer. Is that understood?"

Both men nodded again.

"Did King Edward send you to kill my daughter?" Both men looked at the ground. "This is the part where you answer. If you choose silence we will do this the fun way in a very dark place."

Isabella was hoping they would remain silent. She wanted to see them suffer for what they had done to Matilda. Both men continued to hold their tongues.

"We know you killed Matilda!" Isabella blurted out. She couldn't keep it inside.

Sir David looked at her with remorseful eyes. They were the eyes of someone who had been mourning.

"No." Sir David shook his head. "Her blood may be on my hands, but I didn't kill her; she took her own life."

"You had her killed because she was carrying your baby. I read her journal. I read her last words, and they were wasted on you!"

"She was pregnant?" Sir Richard asked Sir David.

"Don't act like you didn't know," Isabella bit. "It was your handwriting on the suicide note, not Sir Richard's."

"What in the bloody hell are you talking about?" Sir Richard puffed out his chest.

"The suicide note Matilda left behind was written by the same hand that wrote this love letter to Floure, and that hand was yours." Isabella motioned for her father to give her the letters. He was beaming with pride at her and smiled as he surrendered the documents. Isabella held the two pieces of paper close to their faces.

"My dearest love, the moon pales in comparison to your beauty." Sir David started laughing uncontrollably. "There is no way that

Sir Richard wrote this. He hates poetry—and poets for that matter."

"Of course, you would defend him," Isabella seethed. "He was doing your bidding by writing that suicide note."

"He is right," Sir Richard said. "I do hate the buggers, and that most certainly isn't my handwriting. Who told you that it was?"

Isabella looked at Floure. "Her. Her?"

"I took it from your hand along with a kiss," Floure said, longingly to Sir Richard.

Sir Richard laughed almost as hard as Sir David. "I had a mild flirtation with you, Floure, but I would never get involved with a servant. And I most certainly wouldn't write you *poetry*."

"Silence!" King Philip bellowed. "Bring us a quill and some parchment." Within moments, both appeared. "Write!" Philip commanded.

"With pleasure," Sir David answered. Both he and Sir Richard wrote out the words on the suicide note and handed the papers to Isabella.

"They don't match. How can this be? It has to be you." Isabella looked directly at Sir David. "She was carrying your child. She wanted to keep the baby, and you killed her so your wife would never find out. You had him write the letter. I don't believe this. You are the only ones with a motive. Write with your other hand!"

"I loved her. I wouldn't kill her. She was carrying my child—my only child," Sir David said gravely.

"Write!" Isabella ordered.

Both men wrote out the letter again, and it looked like chicken scratch.

"Father, it was them. They were the only ones who could have overheard you telling me that you had killed Etienne."

"Daughter, perhaps Matilda took her own life. She was a ruined woman."

"No, I refuse to believe it."

"We weren't the only ones there, Your Highness." Sir Richard nodded at Floure. "She was there, too."

A look of guilt spread across Floure's face, and she ran for the door.

"Seize her!" Philip ordered.

The guards caught her and dragged her back to the throne.

"Floure? But why? Why would you kill Matilda?"

"I wasn't trying to kill her. I was trying to kill you!"

Floure's words petrified Isabella to the spot. Why would someone Isabella barely knew want her dead? What had she ever done to her? Isabella's heart wrenched. No matter what she had done, Matilda was the one who had paid the price for it.

Isabella slapped Floure across the face. "You killed my best friend."

Floure's features hardened into a sharp point. "And you killed the man I loved."

"What do you mean, 'I killed the man you love?' I haven't executed anyone."

"Tristan, my husband—you killed him. Had he not gone on that journey with you, he would still be alive. My child would have her father!"

Tristan was a father? Isabella loathed him even more. Not only had he betrayed her, but he had also pursued her when he had a wife and child waiting for him.

"We were going to go away together and raise our child. That is why he agreed to betray you. He needed money to provide for his family. "

"He would have never come back for you." The words came out of Isabella's mouth like ice. "His greed is what killed him. You are a murderer for nothing. You will lose your life, and your child will lose its mother."

"Hypocrite!" Floure spat. "That poison was yours. Who were you going to use it on? Your father?" Isabella took a few steps back. "That's right, I know the poison is yours. I know you got it from the Templar castle. People think we servants don't exist, but we see everything."

"Silence! Take her away," Isabella ordered. "Find her child, make sure it is cared for, and if it isn't, take it to the convent. The child is innocent in all of this. It shouldn't have to pay for the sins of its parents."

"Leave us," King Philip ordered, and the room was emptied. "Isabella." She turned to face her father. "Is this yours?" Philip laced the necklace through his fingers.

"It isn't mine—"

"I saw you wearing it at breakfast at the Templar Commandery."

Isabella's chest constricted. She wanted to run away, but there was no place to go. She had to face her father and tell him the truth.

"As I was saying, it isn't mine. Molay gave it to me. When we stayed in the Templar Commandery, he had me abducted. He gave me the necklace and said that if I killed you, the Templars would support my claim to the throne. That is why I tried to leave Paris. I couldn't bring myself to kill you."

"You said that you came back because you discovered that someone was trying to kill me. I never would have thought that someone was you, daughter."

"I came back to try to stop Molay from killing you! I have his confidence and know his plans. He and the Pope—"

"The Pope! That little weasel!" Philip gripped his throne tightly.

Isabella waited for the blood to return to his knuckles before she continued. "He and the Pope approached me at Matilda's funeral..." Isabella had a choice, probably the most important choice of her life so far. Should she tell her father the truth, or should she tell him what Molay had asked her to tell?

"Go on." Philip tapped his fingers on the throne.

"The Templars are moving all of their treasure in two days, on the thirteenth. It will be when they are the most vulnerable. That is your time to strike, Father. Fill the pockets of our country with the wealth they have stolen from so many."

Isabella hoped she had made the right choice. It had never occurred to her that Molay could be laying a trap for her father by delivering this message. Maybe the Templars weren't disappearing. It was too late now, though; she couldn't take back her words.

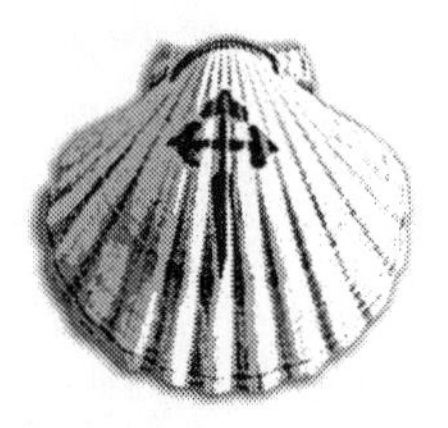

# CHAPTER 39

The clip-clop of Etienne's horse's hooves echoed up the lonely street ahead of him. Castrojeriz seemed so much smaller than it used to. When he was a sergeant, this town seemed so large. He passed the two skulls and crossbones carved into the Church of Santo Domingo.

*O death, O immortality,* Etienne translated the Latin phrases above the skulls.

The last time he passed this way, he had thought of all the millions of pilgrims who had passed on the Camino before him, now he thought of the person he was. He had died to the Etienne that passed this way before him. It seemed he had lived several lives since the last time he walked these streets.

He thought of his conversation with Brother Andre when they first met in Ponferrada. Brother Andre had said, *life is like a running river. People come and go like a leaf on the current, yet you stay the same, unchanged, always the river.*

Etienne had responded, *There are some people who shape the course of the river of your life. They are like the rocks that plant themselves, diverting the flow of the water.*

He thought of all the people and events who had shaped his life to this point here and now. He was the sum of every decision he had ever made, each leading him like a tributary to this moment—this one moment he had to make a difference in the world or die trying.

Etienne stopped outside of the Iglesia de San Juan—the Templar Commandery where Edgar had taken up residence. It was also the place where they had escaped the mob by going into the secret Templar tunnels Ronan had led them to. Everything started here, and it will end here as well.

"I must speak to the Provincial Master," Etienne ordered on entering the Commandery.

The guards scrambled to their feet and pointed their weapons at him. "And who are you?" A scraggly toothed Templar asked.

"I am Etienne LaRue, Seneschal to Grand Master Jaques de Molay."

"Bravo." Etienne heard along with slow clapping. To his left, Edgar entered the chapel from the cloistered garden. "Bravo." He waved the guards off and beckoned for Etienne to join him. "Etienne LaRue, come and join me. The last time I saw you, you were just a boy. Now, you are Seneschal of the Templars—an honorary title that will only last for one more day."

Both guards snickered at the comment.

"None of you are worthy to wear the mantle of a Templar." Etienne bumped shoulders with the scraggly toothed Templar as he passed, silencing him. The man rubbed his shoulder and glared at Etienne.

"We shall see about that, my boy. Come. Come." Edgar tried to place an arm over Etienne's shoulder, but Etienne shrugged it off. "Let me show you something that might change your mind about our worthiness."

At the altar stood four armed Templars each facing out toward the cardinal directions. Edgar made a brushing motion and the Templar closest to them moved, revealing the Crown of Thorns.

"Beautiful, isn't it?" Edgar lifted the Crown and looked at it from different angles. "The one who wears Jesus' Crown rules the world." Edgar placed the Crown on his head, and little droplets of blood streaked his sandy-blond hair.

"Who taught you such blasphemy?" Etienne demanded, his insides churning.

"The one who gave it to me. When I became Provincial Master, I learned of a door in Burgos that led to this treasure. I opened that door and—"

Etienne covered his ears as the sound of scraping nails pierced the air. From behind the altar, the hag—who Etienne knew was Pride in physical form—approached.

"Because, I gave it to him," The hag cackled. "All hail the leader of the New World Order."

"All hail its supreme commander," the Templars parroted back.

"You fool, you let your pride deceive you!" Etienne shouted.

"Look behind you. What do you see?"

Etienne glanced at the back of the church where the pentagram stained-glass window reflected the torchlight. Etienne had seen it before but never knew why it was on the church.

"I see a symbol that shouldn't be on a church." Etienne crossed himself.

The Provincial Master laughed hard and turned to the closest guard. "He doesn't know. He is Seneschal of the Knights Templar, and he doesn't know." The Provincial Master shook his head.

"It could mean many things," Etienne said defensively. "The five points could represent the five wounds of Jesus, and it is pointing down to represent the Holy Spirit descending on the earth.

"Or."

"Or it could represent Lucifer—the devil." Etienne's shoulders tensed as he said it.

"I prefer to say bringer of light. Do you know why that is?"

Etienne shook his head.

"That symbol represents Venus, the morning star; every eight years it traces the pentagram across the night sky. Lucifer, just like Venus, was the bringer of light. Light is another name for wisdom, as I'm sure you know."

"Wisdom...Baphomet....Surely you aren't implying that the Templars worship the devil?"

"You decide for yourself. Even in this small town, there is this." The Provincial Master pointed at the window. "And, tell me, what is the name of the church when you enter into town?"

"Iglesia Viergen del Manzano."

"Right, the Virgin of the Apple. Who do you think that represents?"

"Eve."

"And what did Eve do?"

"She convinced Adam to eat from the Tree of Knowledge."

"She is the one who set us free. She is the one who gave us knowledge. 'And the serpent said unto the woman, Ye shall not surely die: For God doth know that in the day ye eat thereof, then your eyes shall be opened, and ye shall be as gods, knowing good and evil.' She made us equal to God."

Etienne laughed. "You have it backward. Don't you see? This was the first deception that all other deceptions came from. Truly, Lucifer is the Father of all Lies. All other deceptions come back to the belief in an *I* that is separate from God. You can't have the illusion of *good* and *evil,* unless there is an *I* that is seperate." As he said this, Etienne understood Mariano's words from the Gypsy camp. *"Here O Israel the Lord God is one."*

"What are you talking about?"

"The suffering of mankind started with this *knowledge.* This belief that *I am.* The moment you have an *I,* you have an *I am not;* this is where the suffering of mankind began; this is where *Good* and *Evil* begin. This wisdom that you claim has set you free—made you equal to God—has deceived you into believing that you are separate from God. Separate from the Giver of Life. That is why Jesus' first commandment was 'Hear O Israel: the Lord thy God is one.' As soon as you have an *I* that sees itself as separate from God, then you have: I am naked; I am ashamed; it is women's fault, not mine… The suffering goes on and on from there. This *wisdom* has trapped mankind into a prison of its own making."

"Silence! You will join the New World Order that worships the true light."

"I will never join you! I believe as most Templars do, that Jesus is the one true light that came to take away the sins of the world. I just never understood what sin really was before. Without understanding sin, you can't fully understand Jesus. Why do you think he preached to love your neighbor as yourself? It is because you are one and the same. I will not be deceived into serving false gods. I will not serve the cult of good and evil. I will never join you!"

"Is that so? Come closer, and look into my eyes."

Etienne tried to resist, but his body was compelled forward by the hag. She was in two places at once. Her clammy hands and sharp fingernails wrapped around his head, and she yanked it up so he was eye to eye with Edgar.

"You will join us," Edgar said.

Etienne cringed at the hag's moist breath on his ear, and her whispering began. Pride told Etienne of everything he could be. She told him he could take Edgar's place.

"You will tell me everything you know about the treasures," Edgar said, staring intently at Etienne.

The hag whispered even more incessantly, and Etienne closed his eyes, trying to resist the pull of her words on him. She was invisible to the others; they were oblivious to her. They must have believed that the Crown of Thorns gave Edgar mind control, when in actuality, it was Pride.

*The Lord is my shepherd; I shall not want. He maketh me to lie down in green pastures: he leadeth me beside the still waters. He restoreth my soul: he leadeth me in the paths of righteousness for his name's sake. Yea, though I walk through the valley of the shadow of death, I will fear no evil: for thou art with me; thy rod and thy staff they comfort me.* Etienne recited Psalm twenty-three in his mind repeatedly as a shield to block out the call of Pride.

"Thank you." Edgar wore a look of satisfaction on his face.

Etienne didn't remember saying anything. Had he told Edgar everything he knew about the treasure? Had he fallen prey to the pull of Pride?

"Let's go to the garden, and you can show me what Ronan showed to you."

The two guards from the door grabbed Etienne and dragged him to the garden.

"Which one is it?" Edgar stared at Etienne intently, as the little trickles of blood emanating from the crown streaked his face.

Etienne felt his arm lift without his control. The shadow of Pride was pointing his finger directly at the small disc on the ceiling with the Flower of Life on it.

"Of course, why didn't I see it sooner?" Edgar clapped his hands together and walked below the disk. He snapped his fingers, and a guard lifted him. With sure hands, Edgar tapped the pattern of the Tree of Life. In response, the handle of the well in the middle of the courtyard spun frantically, and the sound of stone scraping and gears moving bounced off the walls of the cloistered garden. Soon, the well transformed into a set of spiral stairs leading down.

"Ingenious," Edgar mused. "Bring him." The guards dragged Etienne to the edge of the stairs. "Take us to the door." Edgar's eyes burned with a tinge of insanity.

The tunnel was damp, and the torchlight was devoured by the darkness in front of them. Etienne smiled at the thought of how cunning Isabella had been. She had tricked Ronan into leading her down to this door. She had even pretended that she had pricked her finger on the door when she had actually unlocked it, releasing the Shadows. A breeze blew down the tunnel, and the hairs on Etiennne's neck rose. The Shadows had almost killed them before.

They were pure wrath. Had Mariano and the Alchemist not taught them how to defeat them, they surely would have died.

Etienne laughed uncontrollably, and the company stopped.

"What is it?" Edgar grabbed Etienne's arm tightly.

"I see...I see now... I will lead you to the door. You don't have to use that crown any longer. I will join the New World Order. There is no way for us to defeat you. You are too powerful. What can one man do against so many?" Etienne motioned to all of the guards accompanying him.

"Release him," Edgar ordered, "Brother LaRue has finally come to his senses."

"Are you sure?" asked the scraggly toothed Templar.

"You dare question me!" Edgar's voice echoed down the tunnel until it disappeared into oblivion.

"This way," Etienne said, excitedly as he picked up the pace.

The door was just as Etienne remembered it. Roots climbed through the old wood, and the face with a slot for a mouth was staring right at him. He touched the spot between the carved eyes where there was a remnant of Isabella's blood in a zig-zag pattern. This was the closest he had been to her since she left. Etienne's heart churned for a moment.

"Stop!" Edgar demanded. "I must be the one to open it!" Edgar shoved Etienne out of the way and touched the door himself. "Finally."

"Do it. Just as I taught you." The hag's voice seemed to come from all dircctions.

Edgar poked his finger on a thorn of the crown and drew the backward Z between the eyes. He stepped back, and nothing happened.

"Why isn't it working! Why isn't it opening?" Edgar slammed Etienne against the wall.

"I don't know. Last time we walked away, and they came after us."

"They? Who is they?"

"The Shadows." Etienne grinned widely.

"Shadows?"

"Yes. Don't you know there is both a trial and a treasure behind each door? Edgar, she fooled you. Pride led you here for its own purposes."

The door moaned as the roots unthreaded themselves from the door. It looked like hundreds of giant snakes moving in all directions.

"What is this trial? You are lying. She helped me every step of the way." Edgar pointed to the hag. "She helped me come into power. Tell me it isn't so."

"The trial of the door of Burgos is Pride, and you failed." Pride lunged forward and tore out Edgar's throat with her terrible nails. He dropped to the ground and the Crown of Thorns pressed deeper into his head.

Pride cackled, and the other Templars ran.

"It is too late for you as well," she called after them.

The vines had unbound the door and the mouth stretched wide. Unlike the other doors, instead of light, darkness poured out. The darkness ate the light of the torch that had been dropped by Etienne's foot and consumed the whole tunnel.

Etienne focused his mind on the present moment. He let any thought of the future or the past disappear into the power of the here and now. Muffled screams came from down the tunnel, followed by silence.

Sparks shot off the wall as the hag scraped her nails on the wall. The sparks landed on a torch and brought light back to the tunnel. Etienne looked to his left, and the light couldn't penetrate the darkness behind the door.

"Now it is just you and me," Pride said. "Take the crown; it is yours. You deserve it. You will be all powerful."

"No," Etienne said firmly. "Fransie defeated you first. It is hers to take. I will not touch it."

"Oh, you will," the hag cackled.

"Why are you doing this? Why did you lead Edgar here, only to kill him? Why did you hunt us for the treasure we possess?"

"I thought Edgar would be the one to release him, but it turns out it will be you." The hag cackled again and was gone.

"I think the tree is trying to tell us something," Joshua said.

Andy looked up from his food and smiled. The two of them had become thick as thieves after their first conversation at the river. Andy had told Joshua everything about the treasure and their adventure. In return, Joshua had told him everything he knew about Kabbalah. From their conversations, Andy had gained a deeper understanding of the Sephiroth, learned about the four worlds, and how all of it relates to the Tree of Life.

"What is it?" Andy asked with a mouthful of food.

Joshua looked left and right then leaned across the table.

"Remember when I showed you how the leaves that had sprouted from the head looked like the Seed of Life?"

"Aye, then you showed me how the flowers that came next looked like the Flower of Life."

"Good, I'm happy you were listening." Joshua rubbed his hands together. "As I was taking out supplies from our wagon tonight, I noticed that the tree had begun to fruit."

Andy laughed. "Now it's a fruiting head." By the look on Joshua's face, Andy could tell he wasn't amused. "Sorry 'bout that." Andy took another spoonful of his porridge.

"I shouldn't be telling you this." Joshua waved his hands in dismissal and leaned back.

"Ya cannea do that. We had a deal. I tell you everything I ken." Andy pointed to himself with his spoon. "And you tell me everything that ya ken." He pointed the spoon at Joshua.

"People have been killed on sight for transferring this knowledge outside of the proper channels. I could be killed for this. I want you to take it seriously."

Andy pushed away his bowl and looked Joshua in the eye. "Ya have my full attention."

"Good, hand me the drawing of the Flower of Life."

Andy rifled through his bag and produced the paper and some charcoal for drawing.

"You know me so well," Joshua said, taking the charcoal from Andy's hand. "So, as I showed you before, the Flower of Life is always drawn with nineteen circles and one circle surrounding it. Why do you think we put the circle around it after nineteen circles?"

"I suppose 'twould go on forever if ya didn't."

"True, but it is also to hide the knowledge that people are killed on-site for if they share." Joshua looked around.

"Relax, I donnae ken that there are other Kabbalists here. Well, maybe Clair; she has always been a little suspicious." Andy rubbed his chin as he looked in Clair's direction.

"I'm serious, Andy." Joshua raised his eyebrows.

"So am I. 'Tis just us here." Andy raised his eyebrows as well.

They both broke out in laughter, and all of their companions in the kitchen of the Arc's guest house looked at them.

"Andrew Sinclair, are ya drunk already?" Clair crossed her arms and glared at him from across the room.

"Mind your own business, Clair." Andy waved her off and leaned across the table to Joshua. "See? suspicious." Both men laughed again.

"Are you ready now?"

"Aye." Andy cleared a tear from his eye.

Joshua darkened the outline of the center circle in the Flower of Life, the circles above and below it, as well as two circles on either side of it.

"The second image to appear in the Flower of Life after Genesis is what the ancient Egyptians called the Egg of Life."

Joshua redrew the seven circles on another sheet of parchment.

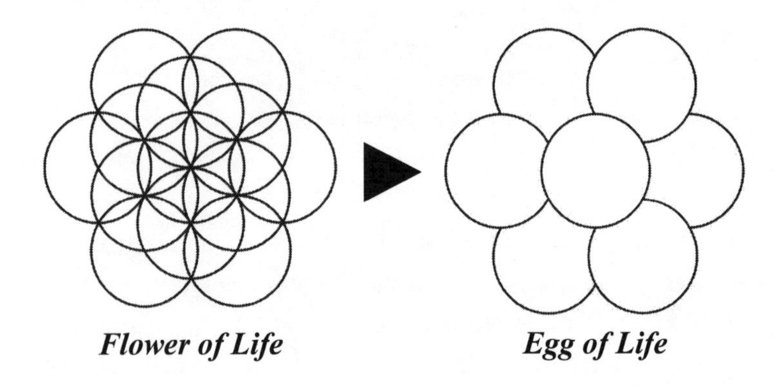

***Flower of Life*** ***Egg of Life***

"If you connect all of the center points you make a cube."

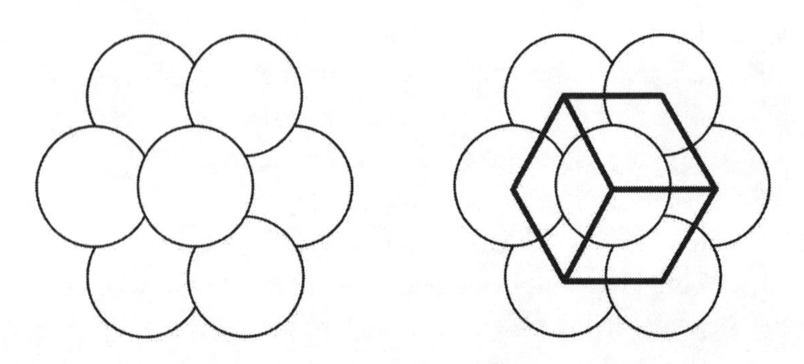

"Also known as a Hexahedron by the ancient Greeks." Andy drummed his fingers on his stomach—proud of the knowledge he had. "See, I ken a thing or two."

"So you do my friend, so you do. But, do you know why the Flower of Life is cut off after nineteen circles?"

"I donnae ken, but I think ya are gonnae tell me."

"Ungrateful." Joshua shook his head.

"We have a deal." Andy crossed his arms.

"Because there is hidden knowledge beyond the perimeter that they don't want you to see."

"Who is 'they'?"

"Does it matter?"

"I guess not."

"If you complete the circles cut off by the perimeter you will have the secret."

"Well, donnae keep me in suspense."

Andy leaned his full weight on the table as Joshua drew one more layer to the Flower of Life.

"You get the final secret."

Joshua darkened four more circles creating what looked like a six-pointed star. He redrew the star shape made up of thirteen circles on another sheet of paper.

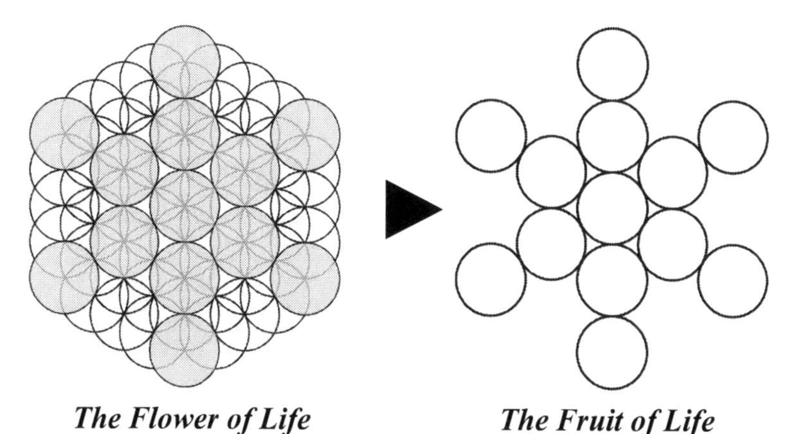

***The Flower of Life*** ***The Fruit of Life***

"And what is that?"

"This is what I have been trying to tell you. I think the tree is trying to tell us something." Joshua produced a twig with thirteen purplish berries that looked exactly like the image Joshua had drawn.

Andy took the twig from Joshua's hand. "Amazing! So, what does this shape mean?"

"It means"—Joshua took back the twig—"...everything. This shape was known to the ancients as the Fruit of Life. This is one of the most sacred forms in existence." Joshua held up the twig.

"So…why is it so sacred? I donnae get it."

"Because everything in reality can be made from this shape. But, it takes both male and female to make it happen. This image is female, it doesn't contain any straight lines. But if you connect the middle point of each circle with straight lines, something amazing happens. I'll let you do the honors."

Joshua handed Andy the piece of charcoal. As Andy drew, shape after shape appeared.

"What is this?" Andy asked, staring down at the beautiful image.

"This is Metatron's Cube. It is one of the most important information systems in the universe."

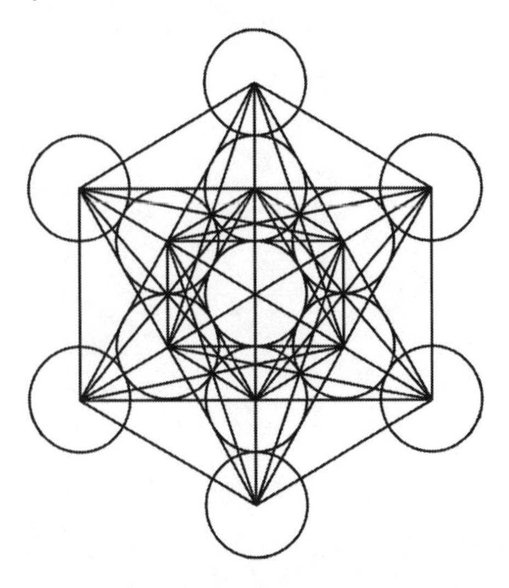

"I see it now…the four Platonic Solids."

"My gift to you, my friend." Joshua spread his hands out above the drawing.

"You can get the four unique shapes in existence from this. We already created the Hexahedron, but I can also make out the Tetrahedron." Andy drew the pyramid shape. "The Octahedron." Andy drew the mirrored pyramid shape. "And, yes, there is even the Icosahedron." Andy drew the many triangle shape.

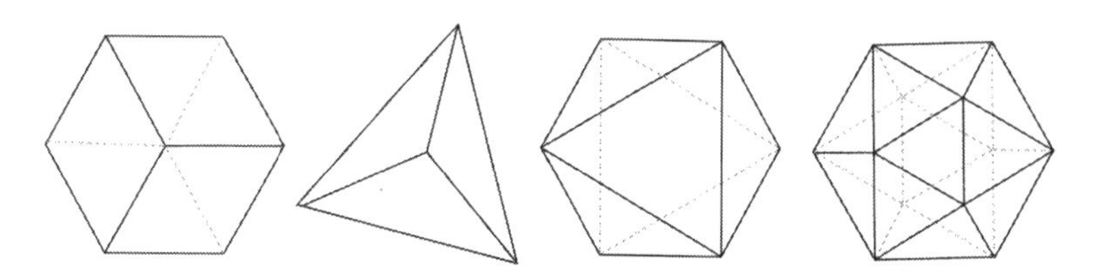

"And what are the requirements for a Platonic Solid?"

"Well, all of its faces have ta be the same size. All of its edges are the same length. All of the interior angles are the same size. Finally, when put inside a sphere, all of the edges touch perfectly."

"Are you sure you found all of the—"

A scream came from the door, cutting Joshua off.

"Dear God, what is that?" Joshua asked, looking over Andy's shoulder.

Andy turned. "Remember them Shadows I told ya about? Well, that is one of them."

"Why aren't you afraid?"

"Fear and pain feed them."

"Look at it. It's huge." As Joshua finished, a Shadow darted like black lightning across to Joshua and picked him up from his seat. Joshua looked down at Andy with cowering eyes. "Help me."

"Help yourself. All you have ta do is bring your consciousness inta the present moment. They can't hurt you there. Just look at it. See it for what it is."

"I can't." Joshua closed his eyes tightly.

"Then you will die. Your own fears and pain will kill you when there is actually nothing in this present moment that can hurt ya. Face your fear, and see it for what it is: just a past that may or may not have happened or fear of a future that may never come. Joshua be here! Now!"

Joshua took a deep breath and looked directly into the face of his Shadow.

"These fears and pains of the past can't hurt you in the present moment. This moment is all that truly exists. Don't let fear rob you of your life."

"You're right. I see it now." Joshua began laughing. "I have held onto you for too long… I forgive you; find peace. You are dead… you aren't real, just a memory." The Shadow melted into the table, and Joshua dropped to the floor.

"Joshua? You all right?"

Joshua rose like a man drunk on life. He smiled from ear to ear and looked at the wood of the table closely. "I'm better than alright. I feel free—free of a past that has haunted me. I see that you experienced it too."

"Nah, I defeated my Shadow ages ago."

"Why are you smiling like that then?"

"Because this means Etienne's plan worked!"

"What plan?" Joshua asked.

"Etienne planned ta lead them ta the door with the Shadows behind it, knowing that after 'twas opened, the Provincial Master and all who sought the treasure with him would have to face their own Shadows. My guess is none of them survived."

"But what about Pride? From the stories you have told me, no one could resist it for long."

"True, but Etienne had the Cape of Humility to protect him." Andy stood. "Gather your things, we are going ta meet him."

# CHAPTER 40

On the eve of October 12th, 1307, Isabella found herself in the Templar Commandery, in the same bed she had been in months earlier. This wasn't going according to plan at all. Her father had used the same rebellion trick to gain access to the Commandery. He wanted to be the first to enter the Templar vaults before anyone else.

Isabella sighed. She punched and kicked the bed, sending sheets and blankets everywhere. She had promised Molay that they would attack on the thirteenth. That was the plan. The look he had given her on entering the commandery gave her the chills. Isabella knew for sure that he was going to kill both her and her father in their sleep, and there was nothing she could do about it; it was all her fault.

Stone scraped against stone. This was it; they were coming through the secret passage to kill her. Isabella took the dagger from her bedside and lay still. She would stab them before they had a chance to kill her, and run to her father's chambers. They would escape together before Molay knew they were gone.

"Isabella." It was Molay himself who came to do the deed. Isabella lay as still as she could. If she was going to die, he was going to die with her. "I know you are awake."

Isabella threw off the covers and brandished the dagger. "If you come any closer I will kill you."

"I believe you would, but there is no need for that." Molay walked to the candlestick on the table and lit the charred wicks.

"I believe you would do the same to me... and perhaps you already have to my father."

"Your father is well. Both of you will get what he deserves in the morning."

"So, you are going to kill him? Kill us?"

"I have no intention of doing either."

"What do you mean, both of us will get what we deserve in the morning?"

"You will see."

"I didn't have a choice! It was my father's plan. I told him to attack on the thirteenth. It was his idea to come here tonight."

"I'm sure it was." Molay walked back to the passage. "Sleep well, Isabella. Who knows what tomorrow may bring."

## CHAPTER 41

Fransie rode in the back of the wagon with Gabriel and Roslyn. He had refused to leave her side since the attack. Fransie couldn't explain what had happened at the Arc, but she was happy Mariano had been sitting right next to them. In the Shadow's face, she had seen Roslyn's death over and over again. It was her biggest fear. She had fought as hard as she could against it, but it did no good. Since becoming a mother, she had been racked with the fear of Roslyn getting hurt—or even worse, dying. Mariano had helped her to see that the Shadow wasn't real and couldn't exist in the present moment. She was afraid of a future that may never come, and it had paralyzed her in some ways. Now she felt at peace with it. Before facing this fear, she would have stayed at the safety of the Arc, but now, here she was in the wagon once more with Roslyn in her hands. They were heading to a danger she couldn't imagine, but she knew Roslyn was a part of this as much as she was.

"Why is the city empty?" Andy asked from the front of the coach.

"The Commandery Master had told me that the Provincial Master and the Baron had the city evacuated," Gabriel said loudly from her side.

"But why?"

"They said that a threat had been detected under the city, and they were digging for it to destroy it," Gabriel shouted.

"That's clever," Fransie heard Andy say over the rattling wheels. The rattling got louder. It wasn't coming from the wheels, it was coming from all around them. The rattling turned into a cracking.

"Fransie!" Gabriel dove over her and Roslyn, shielding them from the falling debris.

The cracking continued, and the roots of the head strangled the boards under Fransie. The floor split and the ground appeared. Fransie's stomach lifted to her throat as she rose in the air. Gabriel's arms tightened around them, and they dove through the back of the coach. Gabriel wheezed as they landed. He had put his body between them and the stone road.

Andy and Clair, who had been driving the coach, were also on the ground with wide eyes. They all watched as the roots and branches of the head tore the coach apart. The rubble of the coach let out its final death groans, and Andy approached cautiously. He cleared some debris and lifted the head from the wreckage; it had freed itself from all of the branches and roots.

"Are you and Roslyn all right?" Gabriel asked as Fransie rolled off of him.

"We are fine, thanks to you, Gabriel. Why do you think it did that?" Fransie asked as Auriel took Roslyn, and Gerhart and Mariano lifted her to her feet.

"Because it had delivered its message." Joshua proudly held up a twig with some berries on it.

"And because we are here." Andy pointed to a set of stairs on their left, leading down to the entrance of a church.

The inside of the church looked like a battlefield. Andy noticed Fransie dig her face into Gabriel's shoulder. He didn't blame her;

it was a lot to take in at once. Body parts were strewn everywhere, and blood painted the large columns. Andy tried his best to ignore it as he scanned the church for his friend.

"Etienne, thank the Lord you are all right." Andy rushed to the altar steps where Etienne was sitting. "That was brilliant, absolutely brilliant. Your plan worked."

Etienne looked up at Andy. "This isn't brilliant—it is a travesty. How many more lives will have to be lost in the pursuit of this treasure? Was anyone else injured at the Arc?"

Andy shook his head.

"Good, that means they can be trusted."

"Etienne, did you do this? And what do you mean plan?" Fransie asked.

"In a way, I did do this, but not directly. It was the Shadows."

"You mean those things that attacked us?"

"They did this?"

"Yes, they are the trial of this door—Wrath. I knew that going in there, and I led all of these men to their death. I even put your lives at risk. I knew the Shadows would attack anyone who was trying to find the One True Treasure. They each would have had to pass the trial just as you did—but, by the looks of it, none of them did."

"Laddie, ya did what ya had ta do. You didnea kill them. Their own Shadows did."

"I think I know what this treasure is." All eyes turned to Joshua, who stood with his hands behind his back. "After experiencing one of these trials, I understand; they aren't here to hurt you, but to prepare you—to purify you. For anyone who stands in the Lord's presence who is not pure will surely die. These trials are preparing us to stand in the presence of the Lord; to stand before the Ark of the Covenant."

"Why didnea I see it sooner? 'Tis the holiest relic of the Jews," Andy said.

"That is true," Joshua added. "It holds the Ten Commandments that were given to Moses on Mount Sinai. It is where one can speak directly to God. It has the power to wipe out nations. I don't know about all of you, but I should be fine. I belong to the line of Levi. My ancestors were the only ones who could carry the Ark. Still, though, none could touch it lest they die."

"Are you sure we should find it? I mean, why don't we just give up now?" Fransie asked.

"If you knew King Philip, you would understand why we are doing this. He is the type of person who would use the Ark to destroy nations," Etienne said.

"Well, what are we waitin' for? Let's find this treasure." Andy rubbed his hands together.

"We don't even know where to start," Etienne said.

"Let's re-assess everything we ken about it. Did ya collect the treasure from the Shadows?"

"No, I left it below, along with the Crown of Thorns. I don't want to touch that thing."

"Does that mean Pride is defeated as well?" Fransie asked anxiously.

Etienne nodded. "As far as I know, Pride is gone, but defeated, I'm not sure about. She wants us to unlock this treasure. She told me I would be the one to wake him..."

"What does that mean?" Fransie asked.

Etienne shrugged his shoulders.

"Well, whatever it is, I'm sure we can take care of it together. Let's take inventory."

Andy produced the head he was hiding in his cape, along with the Harp strapped to his back.

Fransie held out the Grail.

"Good, and I have the Shard of the One True Cross, the Flaming Sword, and below are the Crown of Thorns and whatever the Shadows possessed."

"So now what?" Gerhart crossed his arms and leaned against a column.

"What was the code again, Andy?" Joshua brushed his mustache from side to side as he finished his question.

"Where five become one, here I lay under a field of stars, at the feet of the saints. At least that is all we have of the code. There may be more."

"So why did you choose to come here?" Joshua looked between Andy and Etienne.

"Two reasons," Etienne responded. "First, we knew we had to come here to collect the treasure for defeating the Shadows. And secondly, the sigil for the city is the Cross of Jerusalem, which has four smaller Templar crosses surrounding a middle larger one. We figured this was 'Where five become one.'"

"Why is that the sigil for the city?" Joshua asked, pushing his mustache from side to side again.

Etienne shrugged his shoulders. "Maybe because of the five Templar Commanderies."

"I know the Arc of San Anton. What is the name of this one?" Joshua asked.

"Iglesia de San Juan."

"I see where you are goin' with this," Andy said. "We passed Santa Maria del Mansano when we entered the city, and the Iglesia de Santo Domingo; 'twas the church with the skulls and crossbones."

"Right, I remember that one," Joshua said. "And what is the name of the church that the final commandery is in?"

"Santa Clara," Etienne said.

"And there you have it—at the feet of the saints: Santa Clara, Santo Domingo, Santa Maria, San Juan, and San Anton. Five saints!" Joshua said, excitedly. "All we have to do is map out the meeting point of these churches and start digging." He nodded his head triumphantly.

"What about under a field of stars?" Andy asked.

"It's the pilgrims." Etienne looked up at Andy. "'For every pilgrim on the Camino de Santiago, there is a star in the Milky Way,'" Etienne quoted. "The pilgrims are the field of stars. It is buried below the Camino."

"Right!" Andy nearly burst into a jig; they were onto something here.

"I still don't understand why we had to collect all of these?" Fransie held up the Grail. "If all we had to do was dig where these five churches intersect."

"As I said before, the trials were there for purification, in order to stand in the presence of the One True God of Israel." Joshua looked certain of his theory.

"I think there is more to it than that," Andy said. "You were never there when one of these doors was opened—'twas like entering a different world. Etienne, didn't Ronan tell you that these were the keys to unlocking the One True Treasure?" Andy gestured to the treasures.

Etienne nodded.

"So, if they are the key, where is the lock?" Andy asked.

"My guess is the intersection of these churches," Joshua said. "The better question is, how do we use them to unlock the door?" Joshua punctuated his sentence with his mustache once more.

"Before doing anything, we have to go back down and collect the Crown, and the treasure from the Shadows. I wasn't sure if the plan was going to work or not so I left them down there." Etienne stood. "Fransie, will you come with me? You defeated Pride first, it is only right that you collect the crown."

"Are you mad?" Andy said. "We cannea let the two of you have all of the fun. We are coming with ya." He looked at all of his companions and they nodded in agreement. "Besides, 'twould be good for Joshua here ta see what these treasures are all 'bout."

Etienne led his friends through the tunnels hollowed out below Castrojeriz. He was surprised he had found the door; it was a maze down here. He had made a mental map when Ronan had led them through last time—just in case he needed to find their way back—but that was nearly three years ago now.

The air was cold and moist; pressing against his skin; it reminded him of Pride's breath. He had told the others she had been defeated, but he didn't know for sure. He didn't know anything for sure. Ronan had told him that after a trial had been defeated, or when the person who opened the door was killed, that the door would shut again. But, was this true? That is why he wanted the others to wait above with the treasures and only have Fransie accompany him. Was he leading them and the treasures into a trap, or even worse, certain death? For all he knew, the Seven Deadly Sins were just appetizers for the main course. Who was this *him* Pride said he would awaken?

Etienne stopped at the ajar door, with the gnarly vines crawling in and out of the carved face. It was still open…

"Eek!" Andy let out as he spotted Edgar. "Ya didnea tell us that the Crown was still on his head. What happened?"

"Pride ripped out his throat."

"Why would she do that? Since he opened the door in Burgos, wouldn't his death imprison Pride behind it? Tell me again why you didnea take the Crown, Etienne."

"The Crown is Fransie's to claim. Humility told her that it was hers should she ever find it."

"It is true, but you can't expect me to…"

"I'll get it for you, Fransie." Gabriel moved to get the Crown, and Etienne blocked him.

"I'm sorry, Gabriel, but I think Fransie is the only one who can claim it. We don't want to take any more chances with Pride."

"Etienne is right. Clair, will you hold Roslyn for me?" Clair took the child, and Fransie cautiously removed the Crown from Edgar's head.

"Wait a minute, if the Shadows were defeated, why is this door still open?" Andy asked.

"That is why I only wanted Fransie to join me. I would have preferred to have you all stay above with the other treasures."

"And where is the light?" Fransie asked.

"Here you go." Gerhart handed Fransie a torch.

"No, the light from behind the door. All of the others had either a green or blue glow to them. I just see blackness here."

"Maybe because we defeated the trial, the door stops being magical?" Andy offered.

"No, it was this black when I opened it. Even the light of our torches couldn't penetrate it.

"A Shadow can only exist where there is light. You are the light you bring into this void," Mariano said.

"Void," Andy mumbled.

"How do we proceed?" Fransie asked with a tremor in her voice.

"With this." Etienne pulled the flaming sword, and thrust it into the door; it cast a halo of light ten feet in front of it, then was devoured by the darkness. "Wait here. I can just see it there." Etienne pointed to something shiny.

"What is it?" Fransie asked.

"I think it's a spear," Etienne said.

"If this is the Crown of Thorns, then maybe that is the Spear of Destiny," Fransie said.

"The spear that our Lord was stabbed with, and blood and water ran out from the wound?"

Fransie nodded.

"Void," Andy muttered again.

"Void," Joshua echoed.

"What are you two talking about?" Etienne asked.

"'In the beginning God created the heaven and the earth. And the earth was without form, and *void*; and darkness was upon the face of the deep. And the Spirit of God moved upon the face of the waters.'" Joshua quoted.

"'And God said, Let there be light.'" Andy and Joshua said in unison. A rumbling noise filled the tunnel, and a great beam of light shot forth from the mouth of the severed head Andy was holding. The light filled the entire cavern, but was concentrated on a spot on the far wall.

"And there was light!" Andy said.

"So there was, so there was." Joshua patted Andy on the shoulder. "I told ya we had ta do more than dig."

Etienne could clearly see what looked like a keyhole on the far end of the cavern. The light was shining directly on it.

"None of you have to come with me, but I must carry on." Etienne took his first steps into the cavern, and to his dismay, he heard everyone file in behind him.

"I ken that ya are trying ta be noble and protect us, but, can't ya see, we are all in this together. We took an oath, remember?" Andy stood next to Etienne and winked.

Etienne shook his head and walked to the spear; where it lay on the ground looked shimmery. It was almost as if the floor was made of water. As Etienne picked up the spear, a pedestal rose from the void beneath them.

"Well, old friend. I think here is where we part ways," Andy said.

"Finally some sense has gotten into you." Etienne was relieved. He didn't want to put Andy, nor anyone else at risk.

"I wasnea talking to you. I was talking to Balphy."

"Balphy?"

"Aye, the severed head." Andy pointed to the pedestal. "'Tis just like the one he was resting on in Santiago. "I'm gonna miss ya, creepy head. Thank ya for all of your help." Andy placed the head on the pedestal, and Andy fell backward as a light shot out of its mouth and focused on the spot Etienne had noticed before.

"I think he is trying ta tell us one last thing. Good old Balphy," Andy said, picking himself up from the ground.

Etienne and Andy walked to the spot on the wall followed by the others.

"May I?" Andy took the spear from Etienne and fastened the head of it into the keyhole in the center of the light. He smiled at Etienne and turned the wooden handle with both hands.

The earth quaked, and Etienne steadied himself. "Is everyone all right?" he yelled, and everyone answered in the affirmative. Where the keyhole once was, a gaping hole opened, and the light from the head shone down a long corridor.

"Well, that's two treasures down. Only five more ta go," Andy said, marching forward.

Fransie regretted bringing Roslyn. Why had she brought her? They could have just stayed at the Ark of San Anton. She shook her head as she followed her own shadow down the tunnel cast by the shining light behind her.

"Gabriel, why did we come?"

"'Where you go I will go, and where you stay I will stay. Your people will be my people and your God my God. Where you die I will die, and there I will be buried. May the LORD deal with me, be it ever so severely, if anything but death separates you and me.'" Gabriel quoted Ruth 1:12.

"We all feel that way," Michael said.

"Yea, even into a dark creepy tunnel." Emanuel overdramatically pretended he had the chills.

"Fransie, if you want to leave, Auriel and I will join you as well," Raphael said. "Their quest is not ours."

"Their quest is ours; it belongs to all humanity," Fransie said. "That is why I continue. Don't you feel it pulling you forward too?

Not like the Harp or any of the other treasures, but it is that thing that pulls you forward, that thing you know is your purpose. They will need us."

The tunnel led into a chamber with six doors, including the one they just entered through. In the center was a half-opened sphere sitting on a metal base. The light shining in from behind them illuminated a thin line in the ground that passed beneath the sphere and stopped at one of the six doors.

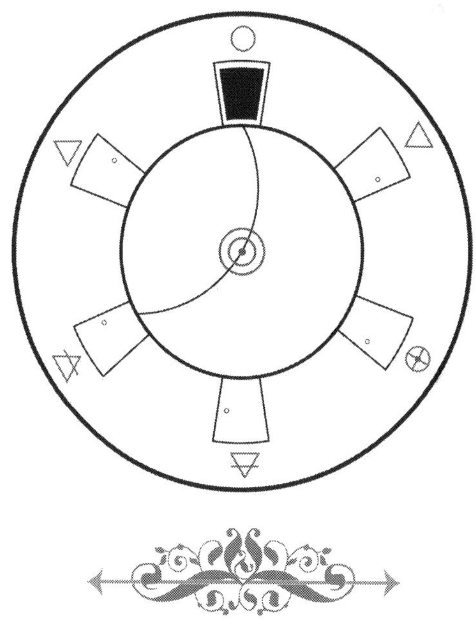

"What in the world do ya think this is?" Andy said as he cautiously approached a half-sphere basin on a pedestal in the middle of the room. Actually, upon closer inspection, it was six half-sphere basins, stacked inside one another like bowls. The innermost contained a relief of the sun, and was solid. Andy peeked into the largest basin, and besides holding the other basins, there were four notches carved into it that resembled a square.

Etienne pulled Andy back. "I don't know, but let's be careful before we figure it out."

"Move over, move over," Joshua said, squirming his way between Andy and Etienne.

"The thing is round, ya could have gone ta the other side."

"I just wanted to inspect all of it." Joshua shot Andy a smile.

Andy looked at Etienne with pleading eyes, and Etienne shrugged. "Now you know how I feel."

"What are these markings?" Fransie asked as she walked to the far side of the sphere.

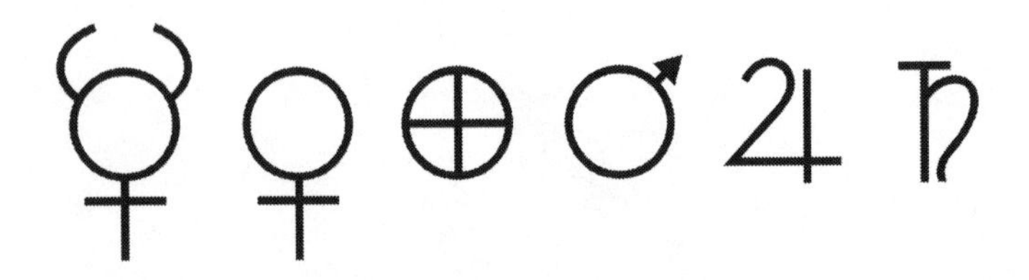

"Those are the symbols for the planets," Gabriel responded. "The man with horns is Mercury." He pointed to the carving on the first ring outside the sun. "The second is Venus."

"It looks like a stick figure person," Gerhart said, leaning his tall body across the sphere to get a better look.

Andy wished he would have walked around to that side. He could have been making this discovery, instead of them. Fransie didn't even care about the code.

"The circle with the cross in the middle is Earth—then Mars." Gabriel pointed to the circle with an arrow in it. "These last two arc Jupitcr and Saturn."

Andy stood on his toes to see the image of a four with a curvy end on the left side and a lowercase *H* wearing a hat.

"The rings must represent the orbits of the planets." Gabriel furrowed his weighty brow.

"If those are the planets, then this diagram is all wrong. Everyone knows the Earth is the center of the universe, not the sun. Next ya are gonna tell us the earth is round, not flat." Andy crossed his arms in a huff.

"I have met some people on my travels who believe both those things. I, for one, do too," Gabriel said.

"There are markings above the doors as well," Raphael said. She had followed the beam of light to the second door on the left from where they had entered. "This looks like a triangle pointing down, with a horizontal line through it."

Andy shot Joshua a look, and Joshua shrugged.

Gabriel walked to the marking. "This is the alchemical symbol for Earth." He moved to the next door. "This one with a triangle pointing up is Fire." He passed the door they had entered, which had a plain circle. "This one with the triangle pointing down is water." He walked to the next door. "The circle with a cross inside represents both Earth and Spirit." He pointed at the last door. "Which means that one must be Air." He walked to the door and smiled. "Yes, it has the triangle pointing up with a horizontal line through it."

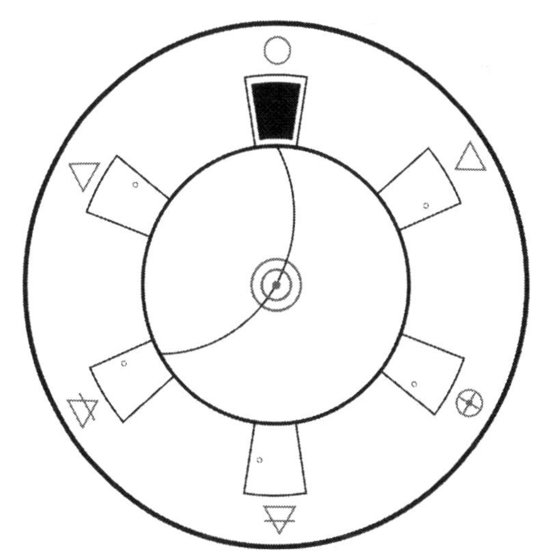

"Show off," Andy said, even more flustered than before.

"Yes! Yes!" Joshua said, excitedly. "It all makes perfect sense now."

"What does?" Andy clenched his jaw and took a deep breath

through his nose. He had worked years on this code, and now these two outsiders were figuring it out.

Joshua pulled the twig and berries from his pouch. "This."

"What is that?" Etienne asked.

"'Tis the last message the tree gave ta us before it decided to self-destruct," Andy said, before Joshua had a chance to answer.

"Go on then, ya big drama queen; what's the message?" Clair said.

All eyes turned to Andy, and he felt shameful. "Joshua discovered it. I think he should be the one ta tell ya." Andy pulled out the paper with the drawing of the Metatron's Cube from his satchel and handed it to Joshua.

"Thank you." Joshua spread the paper out on the ground and kneeled next to it as the others gathered around. "This shape is called Metatron's Cube. If you extend the Flower of Life beyond the traditional boundary of nineteen circles, you get the Fruit of Life. Then if you connect the center of all the circles with straight lines—bringing together the male, straight lines, and female, circles,—you get the building blocks of life. You also get the five Platonic Solids."

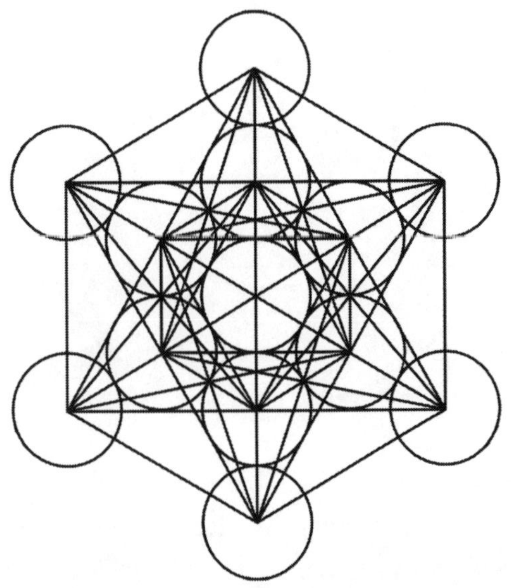

"I thought there were only four," Andy said.

"I was trying to tell you about the fifth before those Shadows attacked us."

"Ahh, I see, carry on."

"You have the cube also known as a Hexahedron, which correlates to the element of Earth." Joshua pointed to the door with the light streaming to it. He drew the cube; next to it, he drew the triangle facing down with the line through the middle.

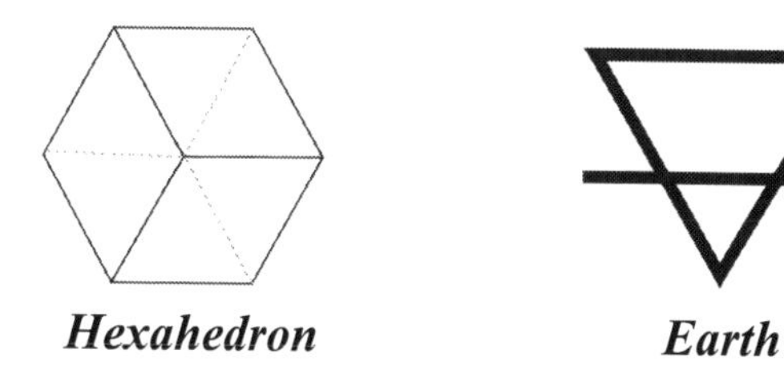


"Next is the Tetrahedron, which represents Fire." Joshua drew the pyramid shape and next to it the triangle with the point facing up.

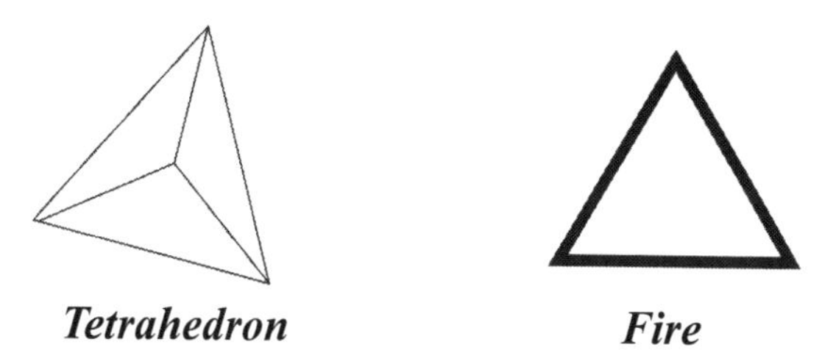


"The Octahedron, which represents air." Joshua drew the diamond shape and the triangle facing up with a line through it.

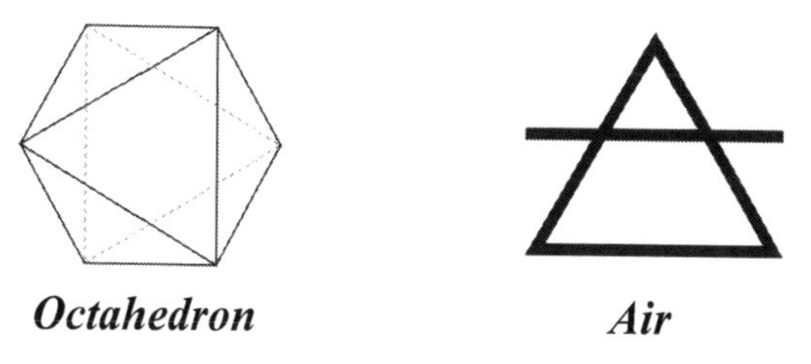

"The Icosahedron, which represents water." Joshua drew the many triangled shape and next to it, he drew the triangle facing down.

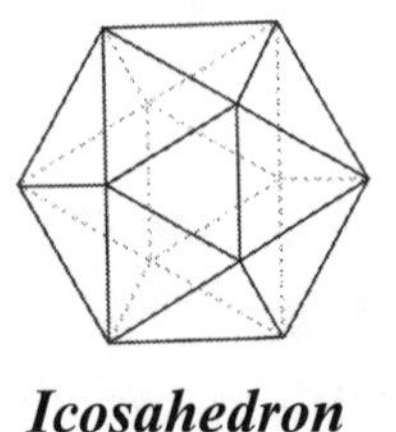

***Icosahedron*** ***Water***

"And finally—I could be killed for telling you this—well, I may die anyway."

"You're just as dramatic as Andy. Get on with it." Clair crossed her arms and raised an eyebrow.

"Very well. The last shape is the Dodecahedron. This shape represents Aether—the creation force of the universe. I believe this correlates to spirit from the Alchemical symbols." Joshua drew a shape made of many pentagons, and next to it, the circle with a cross in the middle, which had two meanings.

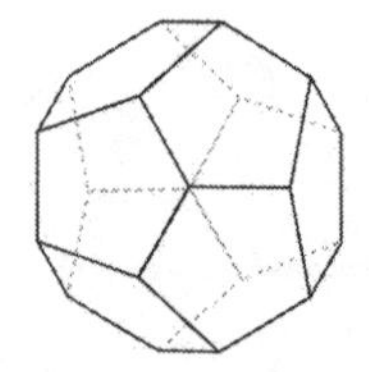

***Dodecahedron*** ***Eather***

"So now what?" Etienne asked.

"I don't know," Joshua answered.

"Ya may not, but I do." Andy led everyone to the half-sphere in the middle of the room. "If ya look here—" Andy pointed to the notches in the outermost sphere. "There are four of them; a cube would fit nicely in there. And on the next one in"—Andy pointed to the next sphere—"there are three, just like the points of a pyramid."

"Great. So where do we find these shapes?" Fransie asked.

"My guess is that we will find them behind each door, and I think we should start with this one." Andy strutted to the door that the ark of light was leading to.

"So how do we open it?" Auriel asked. These were the first words she had said since they entered the tunnels. Andy had noticed that she and Raphael had been keeping to themselves.

"Well, there are five doors, and we have five treasures left. Balphy and the Spear led us here. Now I think we have ta figure out which treasure is related to which element. So of the Harp, Grail, Crown of Thorns, Shard of the One True Cross, and Flaming Sword, which do ya think represents earth? Didn't Ronan say that the treasures acted as both the lock and the key?"

"He did," Etienne said. "And I think I know which one opens this door." Etienne pulled the Shard of the One True Cross from his sporran and placed it in a notch carved into the door. It fit perfectly, and the door slid open.

"See, I told ya. Let's go find a cube."

The tunnel led to an iron gate and stopped. Through the bars, moonlight bathed a crypt. Etienne sheathed his sword to douse the flames, just in case anyone was still in the chapel above.

"Gerhart, would you mind helping me with this?" Etienne requested, looking over his shoulder.

Gerhart walked up to the rusted iron gate and put both hands on it.

"Quietly, please," Etienne said, before Gerhart began.

"Right, quietly." Gerhart shook his head and pulled. The rusted metal gave way and made an awful screeching noise that was so loud Etienne had to cover his ears. The noise echoed in the crypt and eventually died into oblivion.

"Nice work," Andy said sarcastically as he patted Gerhart on the shoulder.

Etienne led the crew to a set of stairs at the far end of the crypt. "We don't know what we will find up there. We might be entering a commandery full of Templars, or an empty church. Be ready for anything. Everyone knows what we are looking for, right?"

"Aye, the cube," Clair said. "We just went over this not ten minutes ago."

"Let's search in groups of two." Everyone followed Etienne's orders: Clair and Gerhart paired together, Andy and Joshua, Auriel and Raphael, Michael and Emanuel, and Fransie and Gabriel.

"That leaves us," Mariano said, placing a hand on Etienne's shoulder.

"What about me?" Prince Charles said. In the moonlight, he looked as pale as a ghost. "You don't expect me to go alone?" Etienne wasn't sure about bringing Charles along, but Andy had convinced him that he was a changed man since his encounter with Greed. After Charles's help in Hospital de Orbigo, it was hard to argue with Andy's point.

"You can join us, laddie. I'm sure we will be the winning team," Andy said, boastfully.

"It isn't a competition," Etienne said.

"Life is a competition, and we will win this one, especially with Charles on our team." Andy winked at the young prince, who still looked scared out of his wits.

"It will be all right, Charles." Etienne placed a hand on Charles's shoulder. "We will take care of you. I promise."

The young man nodded, and together they ascended the stairs.

The moment they reached ground level, the small stairwell opened to a cavernous church. Etienne smiled. He knew exactly where they were. "This is the Iglesia de Santa María del Manzano. We don't have to worry about being quiet here;

the chapel is empty this time of night. The Templars are either in the refrectory or the sleeping chambers."

The pairs filed into the chapel; each split off in a different direction. Etienne and Mariano passed the altar to an alcove on the south side of the chapel. Inside was a giant book sitting on a ledge and some large wooden doors with iron works. Etienne pulled his sword from its scabbard slightly and its flames lit the room.

"It is a music book," Mariano said, leaning over the pages.

Etienne scanned the room. "I don't see anything here that represents Earth."

"Me neither. How wonderful that we get to continue the hunt."

"Wouldn't you rather just have it done?"

"Everything happens in its perfect time—in its perfect way. I would only suffer if I was to fight and argue against the way of things. Reality wins every time."

"Right… I understood what you told us at the Gypsy camp—"

"We found it!" Andy shouted.

"As I said, everything happens in its perfect time and way. If it was meant to happen another way it would."

As they crossed the altar to the northeast side of the chapel, Mariano's words made Etienne think of Mathew 6:32 *For your heavenly Father knows that you need all these things. But seek first the kingdom of God and His righteousness, and all these things shall be added to you. Therefore do not worry about tomorrow, for tomorrow will worry about its own things.*

"Now, why did ya have ta go shouting like that?" Clair said, with her hands on her hips as Etienne and Mariano approached.

"Sorry, I just got too excited," Andy said, with large eyes.

"What did you find?" Michael asked as the others all congregated in the northeast corner.

"Young Charles was actually the one to find it," Joshua said.

"All I did was say 'that's weird."

"And then we took it from there." Andy patted Charles on the back.

"So, what is this weird thing you found?" Etienne asked.

Andy motioned to a sarcophagus behind him. "It was hard for our old eyes to see, but young Charles saw it right away." Andy winked at Etienne.

"What is it?" Gerhart crossed his mighty arms.

"On the shields," Charles said with a tremor in his voice. "There are two left hands with pentagrams carved into them."

"Actually, one is carved in, and the other is a relief," Joshua corrected.

"I just thought it was strange, and these two were nearly jumping up and down."

"See, when Ma DiLorenzo was telling me about the Tarot deck, she said the pentacle was a sign of Earth—"

"Also, in Christianity, it represents the five wounds of Jesus," Etienne interrupted.

"I was just getting ta that. 'Tis perfect, a sign for Earth and also for the crucifixion—the Shard of the Cross opened the door."

"So, now what?"

"Now that you are here, I was thinking we should try ta open it. The three of us couldn't do it alone."

"Gerhart, Gabriel, Michael, Emanuel," Etienne nodded to the sarcophagus, which had a sculpture of two knights on the lid. Gerhart and Gabriel took the ends, and Michael and Emanuel took the middle.

"On the count of three," Gabriel said. "One, Two, Three." The men pushed with all of their might. Even Gerhart was getting red in the face, but the lid to the coffin wouldn't budge. Etienne and Mariano joined them; they all pushed together, and the lid still didn't move.

"The will to give and to receive is both the lock and the key," Fransie said, almost in a trance.

"What was that?" Etienne asked out of breath.

"It was in the Cathedral of Burgos. Gabriel—I mean Pride posing as Gabriel—read it to me."

"Who here is good at carvin' wood?" Andy asked, and all eyes turned to him. "What? I have an idea." He brushed Emanuel and Michael out of the way. "If ya look at these pentacles, one is carved into the rock and the other is sticking out. I figure, one is the will ta give and the other is the will ta receive. We should carve two stars that mimic these out of wood and place them in this one." Andy pointed at the engraved star on the left. "And around this one." He pointed to the star on the right.

"Hmm. That might actually work." Joshua said, scratching his chin. "I have been known to whittle a thing or two. If someone will lend me a dagger I can give it a try."

"I can too," Auriel said, "but where will we get the wood?"

Gerhart swung his ax and chopped off part of a pew. "What, we don't have time." He handed the wood from the pew to Joshua and Auriel.

Auriel was the first to finish. She handed Etienne her carving; it was a perfect raised five-pointed star. Etienne took the piece of wood and placed it inside the carving of the pentacle.

"Nice work. It fits like a key," Etienne said.

"There, that does it." Joshua blew sawdust from his carving.

He went to hand it to Etienne, but Etienne stopped him. "I think you two should do the honors." Etienne beckoned Auriel to the sarcophagus and handed her the piece of wood.

"All right, now what?" Auriel asked.

"Let's try pushing both of them in." Joshua placed his carving around the star on the right, and she placed hers into the star on the left. "One, two, three."

They both pushed, but nothing happened.

"Why don't you try turning them," Charles said.

"Good idea, laddie," Andy ruffled Charles's hair. "But which way?"

"The will to receive is feminine, and the will to give is masculine." Joshua brushed his mustache from side to side. "The left is considered masculine and the right feminine. I am receiving the star, and Auriel is giving the star. So, if I turn to the right, and she turns to the left, this should work."

"Let's try it again," Auriel said.

"One, two, three," Joshua counted.

A rumbling noise filled the church as the lid to the sarcophagus slid open. Andy rushed past everyone else and climbed up the ledge that the coffin was on. His upper half disappeared, and moments later, he reappeared with a cube made up of equal length wooden rods.

"We should close this so no one knows we were here," Etienne said.

Once Andy was down, Auriel and Joshua turned the stars in unison. The same awful rumbling noise filled the chapel, along with voices and the rattling of keys.

"Quickly, to the crypt," Etienne ordered.

Andy aligned the corners of the cube perfectly inside the sphere in the center of the room with the six doors—two of which were now open. The moment he let go, light radiated from the base of the sphere, arcing in two directions.

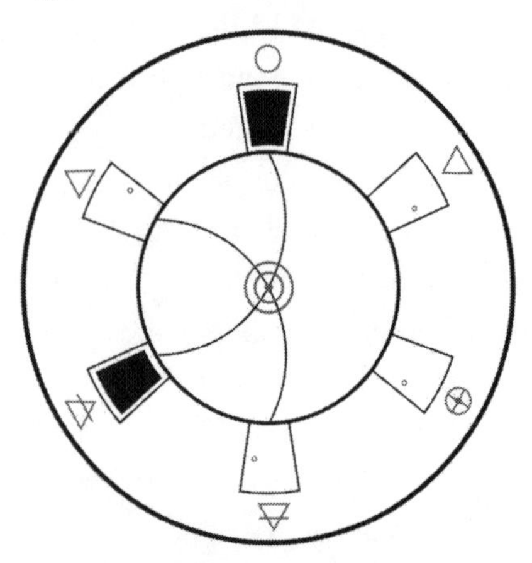

"Looks like we have a choice now," Andy said.

"This one leads to fire," Gabriel said, pointing to the triangle above the door.

"What was the Triangle facing up with the line through it again?" Michael asked, standing at the door on the other end of the arc of light.

"That symbol represents air," Gabriel answered from across the room.

Andy looked inside the second sphere and saw three marks. "I think we have ta go for fire next. The platonic solid that represents fire is a pyramid, and there are three notches inside this next sphere."

"Well, it is pretty obvious what treasure we collected that represents fire." Etienne drew his Sword and blue flames licked the metal.

"I never noticed that before." Andy pointed to the hilt of the Sword where a pyramid shaped sapphire was glinting.

"Neither have I." Etienne examined the jewel closely. "It must be the key to opening that door." Etienne used his dagger to pry the gem free. "It is a perfect pyramid." He held open his palm for all to see.

"There isn't a pyramid-shaped marking on the door, like the last one." Gabriel said, running his hands over the wooden door.

"'Tis because it's up there." Andy pointed to the alchemical symbol above the door, and sure enough, it was exactly the same size as the sapphire.

"Gerhart, do you mind?" Etienne handed Gerhart the sapphire. Even at his full height, Gerhart had to stand on his toes to fit the gem in place.

Andy smiled widely as the door rumbled open. "That's two more for me." Andy nudged Joshua in the side.

"There are still plenty more to go. The game isn't over yet," Joshua said, rubbing his side.

"This is the end," Etienne called back to the others. He had come to a set of steps leading up to what appeared to be a stone lid. "Gerhart—"

"Yeah, yeah, Gerhart do this, Gerhart do that," he muttered as he passed Etienne. Gerhart placed his shoulder on the lid and pushed up. The lid cracked open, and he gently slid it to the side, creating an opening large enough for them to go climb through.

Etienne placed his sword on top of the lid, and he hoisted himself up. He immediately recognized where they were: it was the crypt below the Arc of San Anton. The passage had led them to a coffin with a false bottom. Etienne threw a leg over the rim of the coffin and stepped down. He smiled at the tombs lining the crypt as if he was smiling at old friends. He had attended several internments in the crypt. It was strange; he felt a sense of peace being among his fallen brothers.

"Help me up, laddie." Andy stuck a hand through the opening. Etienne grabbed him by both armpits and hoisted him over. "Thanks," Andy said, brushing himself off. "Not another crypt."

"This is the crypt below the Arc; we are among friends here."

One by one, Etienne helped his friends climb up and out of the coffin, until all were present. He was amazed that little Roslyn had been able to sleep through everything. She was still tightly cocooned in a fabric wrap, close to Fransie's body.

Joshua rubbed his hands together. "So, what are we looking for here?"

All eyes turned to Andy.

"Ma DiLorenzo said that the card for fire was the wand, so I suppose we are looking for a wand. I thought it would be a sword, but the sword was for air; and of course, the cup was water—that one made sense."

"Right you heard, Andy; we are looking for something that could represent a wand. And remember, we are among friends."

Etienne opened the door from the crypt and was met by a blade pressed into his chest.

"Who are you? And what are you doing down there?" a Templar demanded from the passageway outside the crypt.

"I am Etienne LaRue, Seneschal to Grand Master Jaques de Molay."

"We have been looking for you murderers. And to think, the whole time you were cowering down here."

"We are not murderers!" Etienne's hand reached for his weapon.

"I wouldn't do that if I were you." The Templar dug his blade into Etienne's chest for emphasis. "You may not be a murderer, but one of your companions killed the Commandery Master. We found him in his chambers with his throat slit, and this lot all mysteriously disappeared." He nodded to Etienne's companions.

"We didnea kill him. It must have been a Shadow. That means he belonged ta the New World Order."

"Shadow? What do you take me for—a fool?"

"Calm down. We know you are no fool. Who is in charge?"

"Juan-Diago is. I will take you to him in the tower—"

Etienne rolled away from the blade and slammed the young Templar in the jaw with his elbow. The Templar dropped, and Etienne caught him before he hit the ground.

"I'm sorry, brother. It was never my intent to hurt you."

"Well, I guess we donnae have friends here either," Andy said.

"This will make things more difficult, but not impossible. Who else here can climb?"

"I can." Raphael stepped forward.

"Good, I know where the pyramid is; all we have to do is reach it. You all stay here—guard him and our escape. You come with me."

Etienne and Raphael moved stealthily through the commandery to the kitchen, where they slipped through the back door. Etienne knew it would be the least guarded place in the commandery. After it was latched for the evening, it was not thought about until morning.

Outside, Etienne felt the bite of the wind on his face. He looked up and smiled.

"Now is not the time for stargazing; what are we doing out here?" Raphael whispered harshly.

"I'm not looking at the stars, I am looking at that." Etienne pointed to the tower above them. "There are two towers on the Arc of San Anton—the one where the Commandery Master sleeps, and this one where the signal fire is lit. If you use your imagination, the tower could be a wand, but more importantly, the signal fire is housed inside a metal pyramid. When the fire is lit, it looks like the metal itself is aflame. There is one guard up there and a bell. If it is sounded, we are done for."

"What are we waiting for?" Raphael fastened her bow around her tightly and climbed.

Etienne was a good climber, but he found it difficult to keep up with Raphael. At times he was using brute force to lift his body to the next stone, while Raphael seemed to consistently find hand and foot holds. Her flexibility was amazing. She disappeared over the lip of the wall, and Etienne urged his muscles harder to catch up with her.

He gripped the edge of the wall tightly and pressed up. Leaning forward, he rolled over the ledge and took a few deep breaths. He glanced at the open door to the tower. Inside, Raphael had her arms and legs wrapped around a guard. She held him tightly, but the guard's fingers were barely brushing the rope of the bell. Etienne threw his dagger and pierced the man's hand. Raphael wrapped her forearm tightly around his mouth to stifle his scream. The guard gasped for air, but Raphael's arm cut off his air supply, and he went limp.

"I had it," she said, releasing her grip.

"I can see that. You didn't kill him, did you?" Etienne looked at his brother Templar on the ground and his conscience gnawed at him. He withdrew his dagger and bandaged the man's hand.

"No, he just passed out."

"Good. That doesn't give us much time though."

Etienne had been right, the framed pyramid with the pyre inside was roughly the size of the three points in the sphere. He gripped the metal frame tightly and pulled with all of his might, but it didn't move.

"Help me with this."

Raphael nodded and took the other side. Together they pulled, but it didn't budge.

"Both the lock and the key," Raphael said, pushing away the pyre.

"What are you doing?" Etienne asked.

"Looking for the keyhole."

Etienne helped Raphael move the logs and other combustible material. As the logs disappeared, Etienne could see clearly that the pyramid had a clamp on each side, and in the center of the pyramid, there was a slot.

"Give me your sword," Raphael said.

Etienne unsheathed his sword and the tower glowed with its light.

"Whatever you are going to do, do it quickly."

Raphael took the Sword and placed it into the slot. As the hilt reached the base, the clamps holding the pyramid released.

Bells reverberated through Etienne's body. The Templar had regained consciousness and was pulling on the rope attached to the bell as hard as he could.

Etienne took the pyramid from its platform and tried to retrieve his sword, but it was stuck in the slot.

"Leave it; we don't have time."

Raphael took Etienne by the arm, and they ran to the door.

"Etienne LaRue," a voice said, stopping them. He would know that voice anywhere. He thought he had recognized the Templar on the ground, but the man's voice confirmed it.

"Brother Demetre. I'm sorry… I didn't…"

"I know." Demetre stood and yelled to the courtyard below. "False alarm! False alarm!" Demetre turned to face them.

"You are so much older. I didn't recognize you." Etienne didn't know what to say to one of the four Templars who had helped him escape from Paris all those years ago.

"And you have become a man. What were you, twelve, last time we met?"

"Something like that."

Demetre extended his uninjured hand and the two clasped their forearms and shook.

"Seneschal of the Knights Templar. You have come a long way. There are many here who are still loyal to Molay. I am one of them."

"Then you know about this New World Order?"

Demetre nodded. "The Commandery Master tried to recruit me himself. I refused, so I was put on tower duty."

"We didn't kill—"

"I know, but, I bet she could have if she wanted to." Demetre nodded toward Raphael. "Why are you two risking your lives for that?" Demetre pointed at the pyramid in Etienne's hand.

"The less you know about this the better."

"Understood."

"Will you help us to escape?"

"You were never here."

"Thank you. I'm sorry about the hand again."

"It's my own fault. I am the one who taught you how to throw a dagger."

Etienne and Demetre exchanged a smile.

Roslyn had awoken, and Fransie was doing everything possible to keep her quiet. She had fed her and changed her cloth diaper.

She didn't understand how Roslyn could sleep through all of the action and then start to fuss the moment they sat still. The others weren't helping either, especially Andy. He kept making goo-goo noises at Roslyn, which only seemed to upset her even more.

"I donnae understand," Andy said, sticking out his finger for Roslyn to grasp. "I'm usually really good with babies."

Roslyn pushed Andy's finger away and started wailing again.

"'Tis because you are a big baby yourself." Clair elbowed Andy in the side. She extended her finger and Roslyn sucked on it. "See, that's how 'tis done."

The door to the crypt rattled, and Fransie's heart jumped to her throat. Had Roslyn's crying given them away?

Everyone was silent, and the door rattled again—this time more violently.

"Everyone back down into the coffin," Gerhart whispered.

Gabriel climbed into the coffin first and helped Fransie inside. The others were soon to follow. Once everyone was in, Gerhart closed the lid on them.

"Is he not coming?" Fransie asked Clair desperately.

"That big oaf." Clair banged on the lid, but her small fists were ineffectual.

A muffled crashing noise came in through the coffin lid followed by voices. Fransie couldn't make out the words, but she didn't like the sound of that crashing. Whoever it was had broken through the barricade they had constructed after Etienne had left.

"Help!" A voice cried. Then silence again. Everyone around Fransie drew their weapons, and she backed further down the tunnel.

The coffin lid rumbled again, and Gerhart appeared with a large smile. "They made it back with the pyramid!"

"What was that cry for help?" Fransie asked.

"It was the Templar guard. He slipped his gag, and we had to re-tie him."

Andy and Joshua chattered the whole way back to the room with the six doors; Fransie was happy they were becoming good friends. Joshua had been alone in Burgos—sure, he had his patients—but from their conversation, it sounded like he didn't have any good friends close by.

Fransie's eyes adjusted to the light in the room with the six doors. The tunnel had been especially dark without Etienne's sword. Fransie stood by the wall of the round room as Etienne placed the pyramid in the sphere inside the cube.

"Ouch!" Etienne withdrew his hands as the pyramid burst into flames.

"I wasnea expecting that," Andy said to Joshua.

"Neither was I. But we were expecting that." Joshua pointed to the two new arcs of light emanating from below the pedestal of the spheres. One arced to the door they had just come from, and the other shot over to two doors to the right of it.

"Looks like we have two choices now," Fransie said.

Gabriel walked to one of the doors with a new beam of light leading to it. "This is the alchemical symbol for water."

"Well, that doesn't make sense," Joshua said, getting as close to the spheres as possible without being burned. "Perhaps I'm counting wrong. Andy, how many notches do you see in the next sphere?"

"Five."

"That's what I counted too. The next one should be the dodecahedron, which correlates with Spirit, not Water."

"What's the symbol above the other door with the light shining to it?" Andy asked.

"It's the triangle facing up with a line through it," Michael said.

"That's the symbol for Air," Gabriel said.

Andy started pacing with his hands behind his back. "Perhaps we were supposed ta start on the inside and work our way out."

"No, the Cube was definitely first," Joshua said.

"Does it really matter? None of us can know for sure, and it is already too late. All we can do now is to figure out what to do next. It is pretty obvious that the Grail represents water." Fransie said.

"That leaves either the Harp or Crown for Air," Andy said.

"I would place my money on the Harp," Joshua said.

"And why is that?" Andy crossed his arms.

"Because of the name for thc Platonic Solid that represents air—the octahedron—"

"All we have to do is play an Octave on the Harp," Fransie said.

"I was just about to say that," Joshua sputtered.

"Sure ya were," Andy said. "That doesnea count as a point for you."

"But—"

"'Twas Fransie's point, fair and square."

"Do any of you know how to play this?" Michael held up the Harp.

"I do," Fransie said, "but I'm not going anywhere near that thing."

"With Rosalita, you should be able to resist it."

Rosalita? Fransie hadn't thought about her since they entered the tunnels. Usually, she felt her scurrying around from time to time. But she hadn't felt anything. Fransie patted her body frantically.

"She's gone."

"Sephirah!" Gabriel called. The dog was nowhere to be found. "She did come down with us, right?"

"I don't remember." Fransie placed a hand on Gabriel's shoulder.

"Bartie! No!" Andy yelled, dropping to his knees. "He's gone, he is really gone."

"There, there." Joshua patted Andy's shoulder.

"We won't know about Binah and Hokmah until we leave this place. God willing they are still with us," Raphael said.

"I'm sorry for your loss—all of you," Etienne said. "But, the sooner we figure this out, the sooner we will know for sure."

"He is right, Fransie," Raphael said. "Play the Harp. We can pray that it no longer has an effect on us."

Fransie nodded. She gave Roslyn to Clair and took the Harp from Michael. Raphael was right. The Harp no longer had an effect on her. She positioned the Harp, and when she played the first note, the door vibrated. With each progressive note, the vibration got stronger. She didn't know if she should continue or not. Fransie didn't know if it was vibrating from the music or if something was trying to break through. She couldn't let her fear stop her; they had come so far. She plucked the last string, and the door burst open. Fransie was knocked to the ground along with everyone else. A song carried on the wind whipped through the room and caused the flames to turn bright blue.

*O God, come to my assistance; O Lord, make haste to help me*

*O Lord, Thou wilt open my lips, and my mouth shall declare Thy praise,* the voices sang.

There was a suction noise, and everything in the room was silent.

"Fransie, are you all right?" Gabriel called from across the room. He and Michael rushed to her.

"I am well," Fransie responded as they lifted her.

"What in the world was that?" Andy asked, sitting up.

"That was Matins," Etienne said, helping Andy to his feet. "It is the morning prayer of the nuns at Santa Clara. It must have been their voices that blew into the room. If you listen closely you can still hear them echoing down the tunnel."

"That was one heck of an echo," Andy said.

Fransie brushed herself off and walked to the object in the center of the room. In the innermost sphere, light particles in a gust of wind blew continuously in a diamond shape. Two rays of light arced out from the pedestal holding the object; one led to the door with the alchemical symbol for Earth and the other led to the door marked with Spirit.

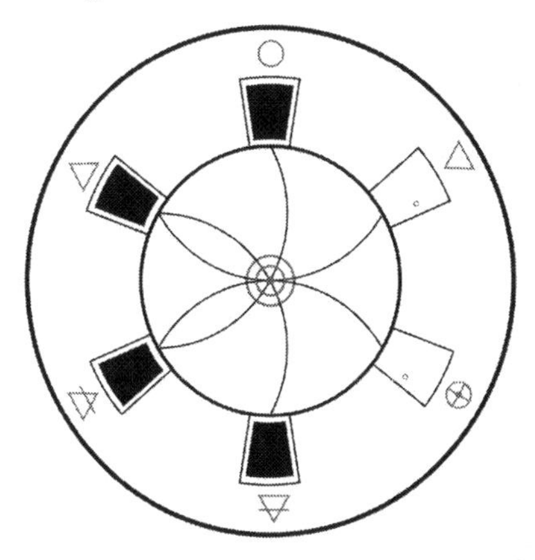

"That definitely is the Octahedron," Joshua said, admiring the shape.

"I know what to do with the Grail," Fransie said. The song had made her think outside of the box. "I need some water and wine."

"I have some water." Gabriel handed Fransie a bladder.

Everyone looked at Andy.

"What? Ya donnae think that I have wine, do ya?"

Clair tapped her foot and stared Andy down.

"Fine, take it." Andy handed Fransie a small gourd.

Fransie poured the water and wine into the Grail, but nothing happened. Everyone looked at her expectantly, and Fransie shook her head.

"What were ya expecting ta happen?" Andy asked.

"In O Cebreiro, when the priest performed Mass with the grail, the water and wine turned into the blood of Our Lord Jesus." Fransie crossed herself.

"Well, I suppose we need ta find a priest then. No use letting good wine go ta waste though." Andy reached for the Grail, and Fransie jerked back sharply. The entire contents of the cup spilled out all over the door marked with the upside-down triangle. As the liquid dripped down, it seemed that the door melted away.

Fransie looked at the door then at her friends. "Let's go find a priest."

Etienne led them through the tunnel on the other side of the door that had just opened. After a few yards, the tunnel pitched up into a steep vertical climb. He didn't like not having his weapon, but he had a suspicion he knew where they were going. He knew the city better than anyone else and had made a mental map. The only commandery they hadn't been to yet was the Iglesia de Santo Domingo. If Etienne was right, that meant the chamber with the spheres was right below the section of the Camino that passed the two skulls and crossbones.

*Here I lie below a field of stars,* Etienne thought of the riddle. When they had first decoded that section, he imagined the treasure in the middle of a field or under a painting of stars. He never imagined that the stars were the pilgrims. There was so much truth in the old saying that *For every pilgrim who walks the Camino de Santiago, there is a star in the Milky Way.* The pilgrims were the field of stars. He loved the beauty in this.

When he had passed that spot on the Camino, he had often thought of the centuries of pilgrims who had walked that way before him. He had also thought of the strange inscription above the skulls and crossbones: *O death, O eternity.*

"What are you thinking about?" Mariano asked. "You have been very quiet."

"I'm thinking about death and eternity."

"That which has never been born can never die, and that which is eternal can never be born. Life is an illusion. The first illusion. As you told me earlier, you understood that original sin was the creation of an *I* seeing itself as separate from God. And what did God tell Adam and Eve the punishment for eating from the Tree of Knowledge was?"

"Death."

"Right, 'the wage for sin is death,' as it is later said in Romans. But, that didn't mean that God would strike them dead. How can something eternal, something that knows itself to be a part of God die? You can't have death without the illusion of being separated from God. That *sin,* the illusion of an *I* that is separate from God, also brought in the illusion of death."

"I'm not sure if I understand you."

"What do you think of when you think of eternity?"

"The way I can best imagine it is a straight line continuing on forever."

"Good, now imagine an arc in the middle of that line. That is the creation of the, *I*—the personality that sees itself as separate from God. Both its life and death are an illusion. It is still a part of the same line connected to God. God gets to experience this world through Etienne—through all of us. God gets to experience love through your love for Isabella. God gets to experience friendship through your friendship with Andy and all of us."

"Did I just hear my name?" Andy said, quickening his pace to catch up to them. What are ya two going on about?"

"Death," Etienne said.

"Sounds rather morbid. I think I'll focus on stayin alive. Thank ya very much."

"I think that is a good idea. We are here." Etienne signaled for the others to stop, and everyone grouped together. "I think I should go alone. I'm pretty sure we are below the Iglesia de Santo

Domingo. If I am right, I know the priest here, and think he will be willing to help."

"We cannea have you taking all the risk." Clair crossed her arms.

"I don't think it will be much of a risk. We heard the morning prayer from Santa Clara, which means we are approaching the time for Mass. Father Ignatius knows me, and I believe he would be willing to help us without too many questions. The church should be empty except for him and maybe an altar boy."

"How sure are you that it is the church and not the middle of the commandery?" Fransie asked.

"I have been making a mental map of all the places we have been. I know this city well and am ninety percent sure this will lead to the church."

"I trust you." Fransie handed Etienne the Grail. "You just need him to consecrate the wine inside the cup."

"Thank you for your belief in me."

"We all believe in ya." Andy patted Etienne's back. "We also love ya and don't want anything ta happen ta ya. So, if ya aren't back in thirty minutes, we will come lookin' for ya."

"I love all of you as well." Etienne placed a hand firmly on both Mariano's and Andy's shoulders and looked at the others sincerely.

"Wait a second." Gerhart raised a finger. "Wasn't the town evacuated except for the Templars?"

"Father Ignatius is a Templar. He will be preparing Mass for his brothers."

"Ya better hurry then, before they arrive," Andy said.

Etienne followed the passage the rest of the way to a metal grate. He removed it as quietly as he could and slid through the wall into the chapel. The morning light was streaming into the chapel as Etienne stood. It had that certain quality that only morning light has, making everything crisp and fresh. The tan stones seemed to glow in the light. The ceiling looked like a bouquet of flowers opening to the morning sun. Etienne stopped. Above, to his left, there was a pattern that mimicked the Seed of Life, or rather several seeds of life spanning the length of the church. He had never noticed that before.

"Can I help you? How did you get—"

Father Ignatius stopped speaking as Etienne turned around.

"Are you who I think you are?"

Etienne nodded. He was unsure where Ignatiuses's loyalties lay, but he didn't really have a choice. Ignatius was a broad man, and if it came to it, Etienne didn't know if he would be able to take him in a fight. He was a man of the cloth, but also a Templar with years of experience.

"I heard you were back, but I had to see it with my own eyes." Ignatius began to circle Etienne. "You left us as just a boy, now you are a man, and by the looks of it, life has hardened you."

Etienne stood firm as Ignatious circled behind him.

"And Seneschal of the Templars. Who would have ever guessed this?" Ignatius' footsteps continued to echo around Etienne. He stopped in front of Etienne and stepped forward. He looked Etienne directly in the eye. "I'm proud of you." Ignatius pulled Etienne into a hug.

"Thank God you aren't part of the New World Order."

"I never said I wasn't."

Etienne's body tensed. He reached for his sword that wasn't there as Father Ignatius crushed him in his embrace. The air squeezed out of Etienne as Ignatious tightened his grip.

"I never said I was either." Ignatius released Etienne, and he gasped for air as he stumbled backward. "My loyalties are with God. So I am going to ask you again, what are you doing here?"

"I need your help," Etienne said, regaining his composure. "I need you to consecrate the communion wine in this." Etienne pulled the Grail from his belt. "After you do that, you will see which one of us is sent from God."

"Very well."

Ignatius walked to the altar with his hands behind his back, and Etienne followed. The altar was draped in white cloth and was prepared for Mass. A small pitcher of water, and another of wine, sat next to the communion bread. Ignatius walked around the altar, and Etienne stood in front of it.

"Where should I begin? We don't have time for the full Mass. In a few minutes, the chapel will be filled with Templars; some of them will side with you, some of them won't. I would prefer to avoid a civil war in my church."

"You are the priest. Let's start from wherever you choose."

"The Lord be with you." Ignatius spread his arms.

"And also with you."

"Lift your hearts."

"We lift up our hearts to the Lord."

"Let us give thanks to the Lord our God."

"It is right and just."

"It is truly right and just, our duty and salvation, always and everywhere to give you thanks, Father most holy, through your beloved Son, Jesus Christ, your Word through whom you made all things, whom you sent as our Savior and Redeemer, incarnate by the Holy Spirit and born of the Virgin. Fulfilling your will and gaining for you a holy people, he stretched out his hands as he endured his Passion, so as to break the bonds of death and manifest the resurrection. And so, with the Angels and all the Saints we declare your glory, as with one voice we acclaim—"

The next part they said in unison. "Holy, Holy, Holy Lord God of hosts. Heaven and earth are full of your glory. Hosanna in the highest. Blessed is he who comes in the name of the Lord. Hosanna in the highest."

Ignatius continued. "You are indeed Holy, O Lord and all you have created rightly gives you praise, for through your Son our Lord Jesus Christ, by the power and working of the Holy Spirit, you give life to all things and make them holy, and you never cease to gather a people to yourself, so that from the rising of the sun to its setting a pure sacrifice may be offered to your name."

Ignatius placed his hands over the wine and bread, closing his eyes. "Therefore, O Lord, we humbly implore you: by the same Spirit graciously make holy these gifts we have brought to you for consecration, that they may become the Body and Blood of your Son our Lord Jesus Christ at whose command we celebrate these mysteries."

Etienne waited for Ignatius to continue, but he had stopped speaking. Etienne opened his eyes to see Ingatius's hands trembling. He was white as a ghost.

"Forgive me for ever doubting," Ignatius found his words and made the sign of the cross. "This truly is a miracle. Take it! Take it and go quickly."

Ignatius handed Etienne the Grail, and inside, viscous blood moved from side to side. Etienne took the cup carefully, trying not to spill the most precious blood of his Lord Jesus Christ.

"Did it work?" Fransie asked Etienne as he entered the tunnel.

Etienne nodded, not taking his eyes off of the cup.

"Thank the Lord ya are back, laddie. We were just about ta come look for ya. What took ya so long?" Andy went to pat Etienne on the back, but Etienne stopped him with a glance.

"Let's go," Etienne said.

Fransie was the first to enter the room with the six doors. She looked at the sphere in the middle then at Etienne entering cautiously with the cup.

"Give me the Grail," Fransie said.

Etienne slowly handed her the cup, and she walked to the spherical object in the center of the room.

"Now what?" Etienne asked.

Fransie smiled and poured the contents of the cup directly over the middle of the spheres.

"What are you doing? That is the blood of Christ!" Etienne pulled Fransie's hand back, but the contents of the Grail had been emptied.

"This." Fransie motioned with her eyes to the spheres.

Etienne released his grip when he saw the blood circulating in mid-air, creating a shape. Below them, an arc of light shot from the spheres to the door Etienne had just come from and the door that represented Air.

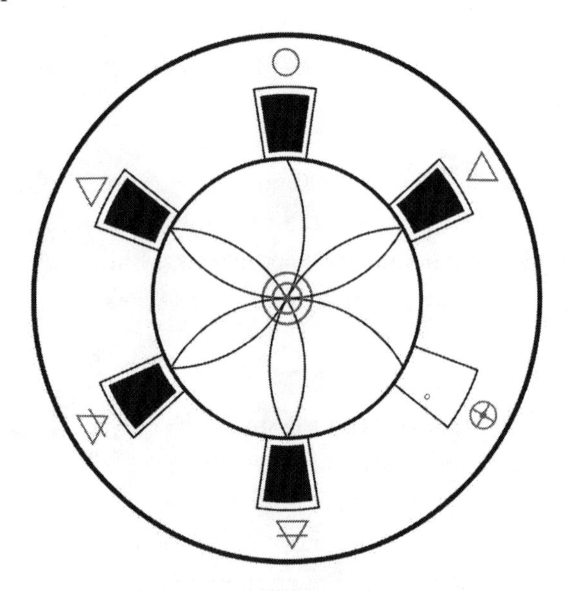

"Well, I'll be." Andy pushed his way between Fransie and Etienne. "'Tis the Icosahedron." He counted to himself. "Yep, it has twenty equilateral triangles. Fransie, you are a genius!"

Fransie's cheeks reddened. She wasn't used to that kind of praise, nor did she like it. "So now what?" she asked, changing the subject.

"We only need the Dodecahedron," Joshua said, joining them at the spheres.

"And the Crown." Andy held up the object. "I have been examining it since you left." Andy handed the Crown to Etienne. "And I donnae ken how it works. It isn't even shaped like a Dodecahedron."

"Joshua, what does the Dodecahedron represent?" Fransie asked.

"It represents Aether; the substance that fills the universe outside of Malkuth, the lowest Sephira on the Tree of Life. It is the substance that holds the heavens together."

"It makes sense that it would be last; perhaps it will be the bridge that takes us to where the Ark is."

"Are you sure we should be doing this?" Gerhart asked. "If this thing is so well hidden, and in a different universe, do you really think Isabella's father would be able to get it?"

Fransie was surprised that Gerhart was the voice of caution. He was always the first to rush into battle.

"You haven't met my father," Charles responded. "He will stop at nothing to get what he wants. He may not be able to get it himself, but he is cunning enough to trick noble people into getting it."

"Is that what he is doin' ta us?" Clair poked Charles in the chest. "Is that why you are here? You sneaky little—"

"Now, Clair, ya ken that Charity took away his claim to the throne. Leave the lad alone, he is one of us." Andy put his hands on his hips.

Everyone started arguing, and the noise bounced off the walls. Fransie looked to Etienne to see why he wasn't stopping it. She placed her hands over her mouth. Etienne was wearing the crown and a misty, iridescent, white substance was streaming from between his eyes into the spheres, where it was interlacing to create the Dodecahedron. Etienne opened his eyes and smiled at her as the shape was completed. Below Fransie, an arc of light shot out from the spheres. As it reached the final door, she noticed the shape the light had been making; it was the Seed of Life. A bright blast of light filled the chamber, then darkness.

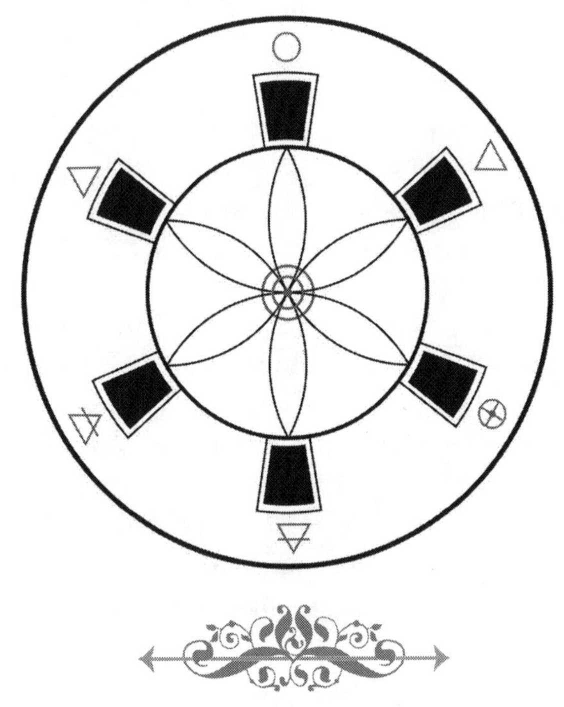

Etienne stood—if you could call it standing. Perhaps he was floating—he didn't know—darkness went on in all directions for infinity. His heart raced; where were his friends? The void was terrifying. He looked for his own hands, but he couldn't make them out. They were his hands but not his hands.

*I want my friends.* As the thought passed, the shape of his friends formed from the nothingness. He didn't know how he was seeing them, there was no light in this space—only a void. Perhaps his friends were the light.

"Etienne, where are we?" Andy asked, but Etienne felt himself asking the question. It was as if he was inside each of them.

"We are home," Mariano said. "This is where we have always been and will always be."

"I don't like it here," Andy said. "I want to find the Ark." The vibration from Andy's words formed into a golden box just over four feet long, by two and a half feet wide, and two and a half feet tall. On the lid sat two golden cherubim; their front wings stretched back nearly touching, obscuring the view of the lid.

"The Mercy Seat..." Joshua moved to the object.

Etienne smiled. Before they arrived, there was no movement in this space. Etienne was everywhere and nowhere at the same time. He was all things and nothing.

"Between those two wings is where God sits and communicates directly with man. This is holy ground." Joshua lay prostrate, and the ground appeared under him.

"I want ta take the Ark and go." Andy's words filled the void. Etienne's body became whole and the circular room reappeared.

"We're back," Etienne said, remembering how to breathe again.

"What do ya mean? We never left this room. I think ya put on that crown too tight—although it worked." Where the spheres oncc stood was the Ark Etienne had seen in the void.

"I didn't do that. You did. Your words formed it from the void." Etienne was trying to grasp onto the reality he had just experienced.

"Void?" Joshua said, turning his face from the ground.

Mariano laughed heartily. "You are still there, Etienne. Although, when you bring God into this world"—Mariano nodded to the Ark—"You also bring the devil. We are in the world of illusion, the world of opposites. The world the I Am created to know itself."

Etienne was petrified to the spot. What had he done? Pride had told him he was the one to wake *Him.* Did she mean the devil?"

"Of course," Andy said. "The book Brother Bernard gave to me had Genesis in it, but it also had John 1:1—

*In the beginning, was the Word, and the Word was with God, and the Word was God. The same was in the beginning with God. All things were made by him; and without him was not anything made that was made. In him was life; and the life was the light of men. And the light shineth in darkness; and the darkness comprehended it not,"* Andy quoted.

Mariano laughed again. "Andy, you don't know how right you are."

"When I was there…" Etienne said, "I thought the words *I want my friends* and you all appeared. Then Andy said he wanted to find the Ark—"

"And it appeared." Andy scratched his chin. "Then I said—"

"You said you wanted to take the Ark and go. That is when I returned."

"I don't know why you aren't lying prostrate," Joshua said, his face still pressed to the floor. "You have spoken directly to God. I'm surprised God hasn't struck you—"

"Stop!" Fransie yelled. "If speaking directly to God has the power of creation, it also has the power of destruction."

"'Tis true," Andy said. "Remember the story Ronan told us about the battle of Montisgard? Odo used the treasure to kill thousands, but the treasure also eventually killed him and all of the Templars who accompanied him."

"As I said, the world of opposites," Mariano said. "We are all just made up of words turned into thoughts. Or thoughts turned into words turned into thoughts once more; who can only know ourselves if compared to something that isn't us."

A rumbling came from deep in the belly of the first tunnel they had entered.

"What was that you said about the devil?" Andy asked.

"You brought it here," Mariano said.

"We must move the Ark and leave this place at once." Joshua stood. "I can try to move it on my own." He tried with all of his strength to lift the Ark by one of the two long poles laced through the rings on either side, but it didn't budge. Gerhart moved toward him, and Joshua stopped him with his hand. "Only the Levites can approach the Ark."

The rumbling grew louder down the tunnel accompanied by teeth gnashing.

"We must leave it and go." Fransie looked desperately at the tunnel.

"We can't. We brought the Ark here. It is our responsibility to move it to safety," Etienne said. He stepped toward the Ark.

"Stop!" Joshua yelled. "I wish we had the Arch Angels here."

Raphael screamed out in pain, followed by Gabriel, Michael, and Auriel.

"It hurts! What have you done to us!" Auriel yelled, her back bulging.

Gabriel ripped off his cape and leaned forward. The back of his shirt tore open and two giant wings came forth. He expanded them and stood straight; the sight was magnificent.

"The devil isn't after the Ark." Gabriel's voice sounded like a legion of soldiers talking all at once. Etienne had to cover his ears to muffle the sound. "Take the woman clothed with the sun, and the moon under her feet, who wears a crown of twelve stars, and go."

Fransie shone brilliantly. Looking at her was like looking at the sun, yet Etienne could behold her. On her head was a crown of twelve stars.

"'Tis just like the clue in Astorga," Andy said, pulling on Etienne's shirt. "Revelation 12:1." Andy turned white. "That means that there is a twelve headed—"

Emanuel let out a blood-curdling scream. Etienne turned from Fransie to see him suspended in the air by a spiked red tail. His body shuddered as the last of his life left it.

A roar reverberated off the walls and shook Etienne to his core. Raphael shot an arrow that was lit with a blue flame down the first tunnel they had entered. By its light, Etienne beheld the beast. It was a red, seven-headed dragon with teeth larger than broad swords.

"Go!" Gabriel commanded.

Gerhart swooped up Fransie and ran down the tunnel leading to Santo Domingo, the Church Etienne had just come from. Andy, Clair, Joshua, Prince Charles, Mariano, and Etienne followed Gerhart as Gabriel, Auriel, Michael, and Raphael fought off the beast, whose heads and tail were reaching in from the doors on the other side of the room. Just as Etienne was about to leave, Michael left the fray and flew like lightning through the tunnel leading to the Arc of San Anton.

They ran blindly through the tunnel as up and up they rose. Etienne was surprised it was taking so long. They should have already reached the church by now. Andy had fallen to the back of the group as he didn't have the stamina that the others did.

"Etienne, I'm scared," he panted.

"I won't let anything happen to you. Just stay in front of me."

Chills ran up Etienne's spine as the tunnel rumbled behind him. The sound of one gallop after another came chasing after them, and it was gaining quickly.

"But, if this is the passage from Revelation, it says that the devil's tail cast down one-third of the stars from Heaven."

"So."

"Etienne, there is a star in the Milky Way for every pilgrim who walks the Camino. We are those stars, which means three more of us will die."

"We don't have time for thoughts like that. Focus on running forward and don't look back. No matter what you hear."

Etienne thanked God that the tunnel narrowed as they climbed. It bought them some time. Had Gabriel, Auriel, and Raphael been defeated by the beast? Were they the stars who were to fall? They must not have succeeded because the beast was still chasing after them. The whole ground shook as the beast tried to push through the narrowing hole.

A shaft of light appeared ahead. "This way!" Gerhart yelled. Etienne could make out his mighty form propping open a large stone lid.

"Thank you, my friend," Etienne said, patting Gerhart on the back as he passed. "Why aren't you coming?"

"I can't."

Above the stone Gerhart was holding, was a pile of rubble weighing tons. The thrashing of the beast below must have caused the side of the castle to fall on the stone.

"You have to try!" Etienne yelled.

"I can't move," Gerhart said, with a strained voice. He smiled at Etienne gently. "Tell Clair I love her."

"Gerhart!" Clair screamed. She ran back to them, and Andy grabbed her.

"Clair, I can't let ya," Andy said.

A shaft of dust blew out of the tunnel. It was warm and smelled foul.

"Is the tunnel caving in?" It was the first time Etienne had ever heard Gerhart's voice quake.

Etienne slowly shook his head. A hideous yellow eye that resembled a goat's had appeared behind Gerhart as the dust settled.

"Back ta hell with ya, ya beastie!" Clair grabbed Andy's dagger and jumped in the hole past Gerhart, stabbing the devil in the eye.

The beast made a sound worse than nails scraping, and thrashed around, causing the earth to quake. The rocks tumbled and the small hole closed, swallowing Clair and Gerhart into the earth.

"No!" Andy yelled. "Clair! No!" Tears tore down his cheeks.

The ground shook again and raised beneath Etienne's feet. He took Andy by the arm, but Andy didn't move. Etienne pulled harder, and Andy shrugged him off.

"One more of us has ta go. It may as well be me."

"Andy." Etienne shook him by both shoulders. "Clair wouldn't want you to just stand here. We have to go. Now!"

The ground shook beneath him.

"The others are gone. We can still protect them," Etienne insisted.

"And how do ya suppose we will protect them against the devil without any weapons, Etienne?"

"I don't know. But we have to try. Help me, Andy."

Andy shrugged. "What difference does it make if I die now or ten minutes from now?"

"It makes a big difference to me, my friend, and to them." Etienne pointed to their friends who were climbing the tower of the castle.

The earth shifted underneath them, and Etienne pulled Andy by the shirt to the stone entrance of the castle. A horn was the first thing to appear out of the ground, followed by a head, whose eye was pierced by Andy's dagger. To their right another head appeared, followed by another.

Etienne and Andy fell into the main courtyard of the castle. The beast disappeared momentarily behind the stone wall, but the ground shook as it freed itself from the rubble.

"Run!" Andy yelled. "Run!" He scrambled to his feet and ran to the tower the others had climbed.

Etienne followed close behind. The higher ground would give them a better chance. Etienne hoped that only the heads could attack the top of the tower. A shadow spread across the land as day became night, and a wind like a hurricane swept up the spiral staircase, pinning Etienne to the wall.

"Etienne! It can fly," Andy shouted from above.

A talon tore through the stone wall like it was paper. The tower swayed for a moment, then half of it gave way. Etienne climbed up the remains of the stairs to the top where the others were. From there, Etienne could see the full might of their foe. The dragon's wingspan was twice the size of the castle and its twelve heads reached above the tower. They had no hope.

"Jesus, save us," Etienne prayed, clasping his hands together. He couldn't save his friends, but he would die trying. "Everyone stand behind me," Etienne ordered. Andy, Fransie, Charles, and Joshua hid behind him in the protection of what was left of the tower, but Mariano stood by his side.

The dragon took to the air, and Etienne used all of his might to shield the others from its force. In the distance was the Arc of San Anton. Etienne's features softened as he caught one last glimpse of the place that had been his home.

A streak of fire shot from the Arc of San Anton, and one of the beast's heads dropped from the sky. The force of its impact caused the tower to quake.

"What was that?" Joshua asked, peering from behind Etienne and Mariano.

"I think Michael has the Flaming Sword. I saw him head down the tunnel leading to the Arc," Etienne said.

"Thank the Lord." Fransie made the sign of the cross.

Michael squared off with the dragon in the sky. The devil's heads encircled him.

"That isnea fair," Andy said, peeking through his fingers.

"Mariano, why aren't you afraid?" Etienne asked.

"Why aren't you?"

"I am afraid, but I am acting in spite of it."

"How can I fear something that isn't true?"

"What are you talking about?"

"Original sin. You said you understood it?"

"Yes, the original sin is when you believe the thought that you are separate from God."

"True, and if you can never be separate from God, that means that nothing can be separate from you. The supposed good, the supposed bad." Mariano pointed to the beast. "Is that separate from you?"

"How could that possibly be a part of me?"

"Then you haven't understood. Etienne, there is no you. There is no dragon. You both are imagination from the same source. Imagination misunderstood and misidentified."

"How could that be true? I have a body; I can see Michael fighting with the dragon; I can smell the sulfur coming off of the beast."

Tell me, does your leg exist?"

Etienne looked down. "Of course it does. It's right there."

"But did it exist before you brought your attention to it?"

"Of course it did, otherwise I wouldn't be standing."

"Are you actually standing? The senses cannot be trusted; they all come from the mind, which creates them. That doesn't make them real. Once you understand they come from beyond you, you understand that your perception of them is imagined as well."

One of the heads from the beast tore through the sky toward them. The beast opened its mouth, and the smell of brimstone was repugnant.

"We are gonna die!" Andy yelled.

Etienne held his ground with Mariano. He had never experienced such fear before. The devil was coming to consume his soul. He grounded his feet firmly and braced for impact. Instead of teeth, a gust of wind and spattering of blood painted Etienne's body. It took his mind a moment to process what he was seeing: Gabriel had flown up and stabbed the beast through the mouth with the Spear of Destiny. The angel took the spear protruding from either side of the head and twisted hard. A cracking sound like a felled tree came from the beast, and its massive head fell to the ground, taking out the side of the castle with it. The other heads let out a terrible howl, and all of its goat-like eyes turned to them.

"Why are you smiling?" Etienne asked Mariano, in disbelief.

Mariano locked eyes with him. "It is only when you accept the worst parts of the world—the worst parts of yourself—that you lose this world of opposites. You cling onto this world of opposites to hold onto your identity. Etienne could never exist without not Etienne. Evil cannot exist without Good. If you want to be free, you must let this go. Etienne must die."

"I get it," Etienne said, focusing on the peace Mariano's eyes held in the chaos around them. "'If anyone wants to come after Me, he must deny himself and take up his cross and follow Me. For whoever wants to save his life will lose it, but whoever loses his life for my sake will find it.' Jesus, emulating God's pure love. He loved both the good and the bad, the just and the unjust, because his eyes weren't veiled by the original sin of seeing good and evil. To him, he saw God inside every person."

The wings of the beast flapped, causing a hurricane-force wind, pushing Etienne backward. The beast shot up into the sky with a flaccid neck where the twelfth head had been, and all four angels chased after it. The beast spun like a tornado and threw the four angels in all directions. It narrowed its body like a spear and dove to the tower.

"Jesus knew he was never separate from God. Nothing and no one can ever be separate from God. Hear O Israel, the Lord God is One" Etienne said as the beast barreled into him and Mariano.

Etienne expected to feel pain but there was none. He felt like he was falling, yet there was nowhere to fall to, no body to experience it. He focused his consciousness where his hands should be; they flicked in and out of existence, as did everything else around him. At that moment, Etienne knew that every experience he had ever had, or person he had ever met, had never existed; for he himself had never existed. Every thought, that he had belived was his own, was never his to begin with.

*I am you, and you are me. We created each other. How could we have ever truly known ourselves, without knowing each other?* Etienne wondered if he had spoken those words or if they were spoken through him. As if such a thing as Etienne existed anymore.

"...without you," a different voice said. He recognized that voice, but weren't all voices his own?

## CHAPTER 42

Isabella hadn't slept at all. Molay's cryptic warning repeated itself again and again. *She would get what she deserved.*

As dawn broke, so did the silence. The bells of war rang out from the walls surrounding the Commandery, accompanied by the sound of soldiers in heavy armor filling the hallway outside her door. Isabella was dressed and ready for whatever was to come. After Molay had left, she had barricaded the door and figured out how to open the secret passage. As the pounding started, she ran to the passage and closed it behind her.

The sound of the door breaking from its hinges was muffled by the stone wall she was hiding behind. Isabella was tempted to run, but if it was Molay, he would send soldiers to capture her on the other side. She would wait until these soldiers were gone then sneak back into the empty room and wait until nightfall to escape.

"Isabella!" voices cried.

"What has he done with her?" It was her father's voice. He was alive. He had won.

Isabella pulled on the lever to open the secret passage, and the stone rumbled. Isabella was met by the points of ten blades on the other side.

"Father, thank God it is you!"

"Good, you are alive. Come, there isn't much time. We must find him." Her father's voice was devoid of affection. It sounded like getting her was almost a nuisance.

"Your Majesty." A soldier appeared at the door, panting. "We have him."

Her father sheathed his sword. "Good, it is over. If I would have known it would be this easy, I would have attacked long ago. How many casualties have we sustained?"

"None," the soldier returned.

"There were only twenty Templars in the whole Commandery, and they gave up without a fight—including Molay."

"Take us to him," her father barked. The joy of his victory quickly disappeared from his voice.

Molay was bound in the same chair that Isabella had sat in the night Molay had abducted her. He had a black eye and blood trickled from his nose, blotting the gag in his mouth. Isabella was confused; hadn't the soldier said they surrendered? Why was he so badly beaten? The brutality he had sustained was equal to the compassion he had once shown Isabella in that very seat. Isabella's father removed Molay's gag, and they locked eyes.

"Congratulations on your great victory, Your Majesty," Molay said, mockingly.

Philip backhanded Molay, and little droplets of his blood splattered across the room.

"Where are all of the Templars?" Philip demanded.

"A better question is why have you attacked your neighbor?"

"You know why, you heathen." Philip cleaned Molay's blood from his hand. "You are a heretic—all Templars are! You spit on the Holy Cross in your initiation ceremony amongst other unspeakable things. Worse of all, you worship Baphomet—"

Molay shook his head.

"Don't try to deny it! You worship the devil! I hereby declare all the Templar treasures, both here and elsewhere, will be confiscated by the French crown. Untie him."

"What?" a guard said, reflexively.

"Don't question your king."

The guards untied Molay and took him by both arms as he stood.

"Now, you will take me to your vaults."

"With pleasure." Molay smiled, revealing blood-stained teeth.

Isabella couldn't help but wonder why Molay had a glint in his eyes. Did it have to do with his cryptic message from the night before—*that they both would get what they deserved.* Was this a trap? Were all of the Templars lying in wait inside the vaults?

"Father, perhaps we should go back to the palace," Isabella said as they stood outside the vaults. "We don't know what could be on the other side."

"I know exactly what is on the other side…" The look in her father's eyes said, *how dare you question me*? "Gold, silver, gems, everything this country needs to sustain itself—to secure your future."

"But, we don't need to be here!"

"Why do you think we stayed here last night? I didn't want a single piece of treasure to go missing."

"But—"

"Silence!" Philip's words bounced off the stone walls surrounding them. "Open the vault now!" Philip demanded.

The guard pushed Molay to the massive vault door. He smiled back at Isabella and her father.

Isabella didn't like this at all. Something didn't feel right. She placed her hand on her dagger just in case she needed to use it.

Molay went through a number of steps, and the massive door clinked open. Her father took a torch from one of the guards.

"Father," Isabella protested. She tried to grab his arm, but he shrugged it off and entered the vault.

Time slowed. It was silent for too long.

"No!" Her father's scream echoed up and down the tunnel.

How could she have ever trusted Molay? She had led her father to his death, and hers would be next. Isabella ran into the vault with the soldiers—weapons drawn.

"Father—" The vault was completely empty, except for her father, who knelt on the ground, pounding it. Isabella rushed to him, but he pushed her away.

"This is no way for the King of France to act!" Isabella's words stopped her father from pounding the ground.

"You are right." Philip rushed to Molay and pummeled him. "Kill them! Kill them all!" Philip demanded.

"Kill me, but do not kill my men. Innocent blood will be on all of your hands." Molay looked directly at her. She understood his warning from the night before. The lives of his men would be on her hands because they were a day early. The plan had been for only him to be at the commandery when her father attacked.

"No! You will stay where you are." Isabella's words were so firm, the guards froze in place, looking from her to her father. "By French law, these men need a trial."

"She is right, Your Majesty. As much as we hate the Templars, by both French and Papal law, they deserve a trial." Pope Clement stood at the entrance to the vault, arms crossed. "Besides, he is the only one who can explain what happened."

"What do you mean?" Philip seethed through clenched teeth.

"They are gone. They are all gone."

"What do you mean, they are all gone?" Philip glared at the Pope.

"The Templar Commanderies, and their vaults, are just as empty as this one. I have been receiving reports from the papal forces I dispatched that all of the Commanderies in France, and beyond, are empty. It is like magic; both the Templars and their treasure have disappeared. He is the only one who knows what happened." Pope Clement pointed at Molay.

"Where is the treasure?" Philip shook Molay violently and threw him to the ground.

Isabella placed her hand on her father's as he tried to draw his sword. His whole body was shaking with rage. "Father." Isabella looked at him with pleading eyes. She stood on her toes and whispered in his ear. "There is a much more important treasure than what was in the vault. If you kill Molay, you will never be able to find it."

Philip's breathing steadied. He looked from Isabella to the Pope to Molay on the ground. "You are right, daughter. You will make a good queen. Take him prisoner," he commanded, pointing to Molay.

# CHAPTER 43

"Etienne, we cannea do this without you." Andy shook Etienne's limp body.

The moment Etienne had put the Crown on his head, a blinding light filled the room, and where the spheres had been, the Ark appeared. Andy had been filled with joy until his friends dropped one by one. Moments after Etienne had put on that Crown, Emanuel was thc first to fall, followed by Clair and Gerhart, and then Mariano just disappeared completely. All of this had happened in a matter of seconds. Andy was afraid that he would be next.

"Please come back ta us, laddie." Andy took the Crown of Thorns off of Etienne's head, trying as hard as he could not to stab himself or cause any more injury to his friend.

Etienne's eyes shot open, and he gulped for air.

"Thank the Lord! You're alive!" Andy wrapped his arms around Etienne tightly.

"What happened?" Fransie asked, looking up from Gerhart and Clair's bodies on the ground. "And where is Mariano? He just vanished."

Etienne's laughter filled the cave as tears filled his eyes. He laughed so hard that he started hyperventilating.

"Right, he has gone mad. This cursed thing did it to him." Andy tossed the Crown aside.

"Don't speak such blasphemies." Gabriel dove to catch the Crown before it hit the ground.

"Perhaps if we sit you up." Fransie gripped Etienne's arm and nodded for Andy to do the same. Together they lifted Etienne to a seated position. "Charles, fetch him some water."

"Here you are." Charles handed the bladder to Andy, and he pressed it to Etienne's mouth and tilted it up.

"Sitting, lying, standing, it is all the same," Etienne said, wiping his mouth.

"What happened ta you?"

"I found the way back home. The truth will set you free, my friend." Etienne placed a reassuring hand on Andy's shoulder.

"Will they come back home?" Andy pointed desperately at Clair's limp body on the floor.

"They are home as well, but they won't come back here—as if they ever left."

"No!" Andy yelled. He brushed off Etienne's hand and ran to Clair. He cradled her limp body in his arms and cried harder than he had his whole life. Andy knew the others were watching him as he grieved, but he didn't care. Andy cried until his eyes were raw and his clothes damp.

"Andy," Fransie said, placing a hand on his back, "we have to go."

Andy clutched Clair even tighter and shook his head.

"She is right, my old friend. It is time," Etienne said, sounding like himself again.

Etienne placed a hand on Andy's other shoulder, and Andy took it. He looked up at his friend who had become like a brother. "We cannea leave them down here—not like this."

"I know." Etienne's soulful eyes were filled with compassion. "I have an idea."

Andy nodded through blurred eyes. He wiped his nose with his sleeve.

"Michael, Gabriel, Raphael, and Auriel, you carry the Ark," Etienne ordered.

"But—" Joshua protested.

"They are the ones to carry it. I have seen what is inside them."

"Fransie and Joshua, you carry Emanuel."

"Charles, you help me with Gerhart. He has carried us all so many times, now it is our turn to carry him."

"But, he is so big. How can two of us possibly—"

Etienne silenced Charles with a smile. "We will be fine."

"Andy, that leaves Clair. Are you all right to carry her?"

"I would like nothing more." Andy draped one of Clair's arms around his shoulders and cradled her as he stood.

"Etienne, are you sure about this?" Gabriel looked at the Ark tentatively.

"Yes. But first, we must cover it." Etienne unfastened Gerhart's large cloak and draped it over the shining golden Ark.

Etienne recounted the tale of what had happened as he led them through the maze of tunnels, including how Clair had stabbed the devil in the eye. The story had distracted Andy from Clair's body in his arms. When she was alive, she was a force to be reckoned with. Now she seemed so small.

"Stop here," Etienne said, leaving them in the darkness. There was a rumbling, and sunlight filled the cavern. Etienne returned and picked up Gerhart again with Charles. "This way."

"I recognize this palace," Andy said, after they had climbed out of a small ravine.

"That is the bridge I first saw you run over as you were being chased by the Moors," Etienne said.

"That feels like a lifetime ago." Andy shook his head. "Wait a minute, that means that charred section of trees is—Oh my God, Etienne."

Etienne nodded.

"'Tis where our wee Heather died. We never gave her a proper burial. Ya see that, Clair?" Andy said to her limp body, resting on his lap. "Ya can all rest in peace as a family." Andy's eyes welled up with tears again.

"Heather was Clair's daughter, right?" Fransie asked, placing a hand on Andy's shoulder.

"Aye, that she was, and the light of our life. Ain't that right, Clair?" Andy smiled remorsefully at Clair's body. "Heather contracted the Fire of San Anton. 'Tis why Clair and I were on the Camino in the first place. We tried to cure her disease back home, but nothin' worked, so we decided to bring her to the Arc of San Anton to be healed. But we only made it this far. We were attacked by Moors. Etienne saved us that night, but our coach caught fire and Heather died trapped inside. The Moors were coming back, and Clair and I never got to say goodbye. We never got to bury our wee Heather. Now all that's left of her is this ash around us."

Fransie squeezed Andy's shoulder, and he grabbed her hand. "We have time to bury them now, Andy."

"Aye, that we do."

They spent the better part of the afternoon digging graves in the charred ground with what tools they had. New life had sprung up in the grove, but the burnt stumps were a reminder of what had happened there nearly two years ago. They placed Clair, Gerhart, and some of Heather's ashes into one grave, and Emanuel in another some distance away. They filled the graves and placcd wooden crosses on each. They also put up a cross for Mariano, whose body was nowhere to be found.

"Someone should say a few words," Fransie said, looking at the others. "Very well then, I'll—"

"I have this one, lassie." Andy stepped forward and cleared his throat. "Gerhart, I was scared of ya… It wasn't your strength or your size, I was scared of how much I loved ya. You were, and always will be, my brother. You were the strength of our group, and ya lent it whenever we needed ya. I will always think of ya in moments when I need ta be strong. Even in death, ya will still lend me your strength.

"Clair, what can I say about ya? Ya were my heart, not just my heart, but the heart of our Camino family. Your love, though it could be harsh at times, kept us together. It made us inta a family that didn't need ta be bound by blood. It figures that ya would go stabbing the devil in the eye ta protect those ya love. I will think of you every time I think of family and home. It will take more than death to separate us. Ya will always be with me." Andy took a handful of the ashen dirt and threw it onto the grave. "Ashes ta ashes, dust ta dust."

The others said words about Mariano and Emanuel, but Andy didn't listen. One by one, his friends left the grove, but Andy remained. He stood for a long time just looking at the mounds where Clair, Gerhart, and wee Heather lay together as a family—his family.

"Andy, it's time." Etienne walked back to him and wrapped an arm around Andy's shoulders.

"I cannea believe they are gone."

They stood together in silence for a few more moments then Etienne gently led him back to the others.

"There are coaches approaching," Michael said, as they reached the edge of the clearing. He pointed to the Camino, which wasn't too far away.

"It cannea be," Andy said, looking up at Etienne.

"The Camino always provides, my friend." Etienne ran to the Camino and flagged down the coaches. They slowed to a stop, and the driver of the first coach jumped down and hugged Etienne.

"Katsuji!" Andy yelled. Katsuji waved at Andy and beckoned for them all to join them.

"I cannea believe 'tis you," Andy said, shaking his hand, then embracing him.

"In the flesh," Katsuji said, doing a small turn. "Andy, may I present my bride, Akari." Katsuji helped a woman unlike any other Andy had ever seen down from the wagon.

"'Tis a pleasure ta meet ya." Andy hated that his blushing cheeks always gave away his feelings.

"My friends, where are the others; where are Gerhart, Mariano, and Clair?"

Etienne shook his head, and Katsuji bowed.

"I am so sorry for your loss." After a few moments, he rose again.

Andy turned away and cleared the tears from his eyes. He didn't know he had any more to shed.

"What are you doing here, my friend?" Etienne asked.

"Looking for you."

"Me?" Etienne asked.

"Yes, Isabella ran away from the palace to find you, Etienne. She chose you over everything else. She was going to throw away her marriage and throne to be with you."

"If that is true, why isn't she here?"

"Because of me," Akari said. "When I first met her, I misjudged her relationship with Katsuji. I forced her to return to the palace. After Katsuji explained the situation to me, it was already too late. We couldn't find Isabella before she was trapped back in the palace. Forgive me for hindering your love." Akari bowed.

"There is nothing to forgive; everything happens exactly as it should."

"Isabella urged me to find you to deliver her message. I am sorry I wasn't able to deliver her in person."

"Ya hear that, laddie? Isabella chose you. Clair would be so happy. Well, what are ya gonna do about it?"

"Katsuji, will you help us once more?" Etienne asked. "We need to get to the Port of Santander in the north. Will you bear us and our cargo there?"

"I am at your service."

Andy waved the others over, and they approached carrying the

Ark. After everyone was introduced, and the Ark safely stored, Andy pulled Etienne aside.

"What are ya gonna do about Isabella?"

"I am going to attend a wedding."

"What!"

"Life is showing me exactly where to go to next. Charles can't know where the treasure goes, and we must fulfill our promise to deliver him back to his family. The ship will drop him and me off at Boulogne-sur-Mer, where Isabella is to be wed, and you will continue on and take the treasure to its new home."

"Alone?"

"Andy, the quest for the treasure has always been yours, not mine; now it is up to you how that story ends."

"But, I cannea do this without you."

"You will be well guarded. It will be as if God's angels walk with you. My fate lies elsewhere."

"Ouch!" Andy rubbed his backside. He turned and was met face to face with Blueberry the donkey. "Blueberry, ya bit me! What are you doing here?" The donkey blew its lips, getting spittle all over Andy's face. "Now, donnae be mad. I didnea leave ya. I was gonna come back for you."

The donkey lowered its head, and Andy petted it. "At least yea won't be leaving me. The question is, where should we go?"

Andy looked at the others, and the Ark—they were all his responsibility now. Blueberry blew her lips, spraying Andy with spittle again.

"What is it?"

The donkey brayed loudly.

"Aye, you're right, I made a promise to take you back home… Aye, 'tis it." Andy kissed the donkey on the forehead. "Etienne said something about finding the way back home. Perhaps that's just what we should do as well."

# CHAPTER 44

***Boulogne-sur-Mer, January 25, 1308***

The damp seaside air penetrated the many layers of Isabella's clothing and dug deep into her bones. The frigidness in the room matched her feelings. She was frozen inside—her heart encased in ice, ready to shatter at any moment. She pulled a fur shawl tightly over her silken blue and gold wedding gown and dug her hands deep into her fur muffler. This was the worst day of her life—the moment she had been dreading since she was engaged to Edward.

The room Isabella had been given in the Cathedral of Notre-Dame de Boulogne was large and decorated beautifully. However, all Isabella saw was what her father estimated her worth to be. She was surrounded by her dowry, which she had been told was worth 21,000 livres.

*How could you put a value on a person?*

Isabella looked at the dagger on her vanity next to where she sat—it had tempted her all morning. *I would be worth nothing to either of them if I were dead.*

Her father burst into the room. "Isabella, what a great day!" He was emanating joy; a characteristic Isabella seldom saw in him.

"Is it?" Isabella responded, coldly.

"It is. Not only are you getting married, but your brother has returned to us victorious."

"Charles is here..." Isabella nearly knocked over her chair as she stood. Her brother was alive? Nothing had been heard of him for months, but her father's last word sunk in, "What do you mean *victorious*?"

"He has returned with the Templars' treasure"—Philip held up a crown of thorns—"and he has killed Etienne."

Isabella's frozen heart shattered into a million pieces.

"No! It can't be."

"Charles thought you might say that. Hold out your hand."

Isabella hesitated.

"Don't make me ask twice." Her father's voice became sharp.

Isabella held out her hand, and he dropped the Shard of the One True Cross into her palm. Isabella clenched her fist around it tightly. She knew her father was speaking the truth; she had stolen this from Andy. There was no way he nor Etienne would have given it up without a fight.

"I am adding that to your dowry," Philip said dryly, "under the provision that it will be kept in your supervision at all times." He held up the crown. "This though, I will keep on display in San Chapel[15] so all can see the might of France."

"Leave me," Isabella whispered.

"Daughter—"

"I said leave me! I am a queen in my own right, and I demand that you leave."

"You aren't queen yet, but I will honor your wishes. However, our returning hero wishes to see you in private, and I won't deny him an audience with you. How can I, with all he has accomplished?"

Her father left the room, and Isabella grabbed her dagger. Its point and her anger were all directed at Charles now. She would kill him and suffer the consequences. Isabella waited patiently, facing the vanity with her back to the door.

"Isabella." Her brother's voice had an apologetic tone.

She would wait until he was close enough, then she would strike.

"Isabella." He said again, standing behind her. "I brought something else for you, as well."

Isabella turned and stabbed hard. A strong hand wrapped around her wrist and pulled her arm back.

"I told you she would try to kill you," a familiar voice said.

Isabella looked at the hand on her wrist and then at the face of its owner.

"Etienne!" Isabella dropped the dagger and wrapped her arms around him. Etienne held her tightly and swooped her off the ground in a circle. Etienne set her down and Isabella touched his face. "Is it you? Is it really you?"

Etienne nodded and gave her his half-smile. She pulled his face to meet hers, and they exchanged a kiss that melted the ice around her heart. For the first time in months, Isabella felt warm. She was whole again.

"Charles, thank you." She took her brother's hands. "We must go quickly. How are we going to get out of here?"

"We're not," Etienne said.

Isabella looked to Charles for confirmation, and he shook his head. "Half of Europe is out there waiting for you to get married. There is no way we could possibly escape."

"Why come here only to leave?" Isabella turned from both of them and crossed her arms. "Why don't we steal the almighty powerful Crown of Thorns from my father and use it?"

"The Crown isn't the One True Treasure," Etienne said. "It's only one of the keys—like the shard of the One True Cross. Only when they are all brought together can the treasure be found. What better way to make sure the treasure is never found than by giving one of the keys to each separate kingdom? Our father will have the Crown, you will have the Shard, and other kings will be given the remaining keys. They would go to war and kill each other before they would ever be united again. "

"That is quite brilliant, Etienne." Isabella's anger subsided for a moment, and she faced them again.

"It wasn't me who came up with it; it was Andy."

"Of course it was." Isabella laughed. "I have missed all of you so much." Etienne moved in for another kiss, and Isabella stopped him. "I am still angry with you. Why are you here?"

"I chose you over the treasure." Etienne looked at her with his soulful eyes. "I had to see my wife again, if only for a few moments. You are where my destiny lies."

"Oh, Etienne." Isabella kissed him tenderly. "What are we to do?"

"Sire a child, of course," Charles said quickly.

"Charles!" Isabella couldn't believe her brother had just said that.

"I'm serious. And Etienne is dead. You are speaking to Lord Roger Mortimer,[16] an English Lord with lands in Wales and Ireland."

"How?" Isabella's mouth gaped.

"Our mutual friend, Gabriel, arranged it," Etienne said. "As a Lord, I will be invited to court, and when the time is right, we can be together as lovers. You are my wife, Isabella."

"I know." Isabella placed her hand on Etienne's chest. "And it pains me so much to even think of being with another man. How is this plan even going to work? Won't you be recognized?"

"We have taken care of that," Charles said. "I have spent the last hours introducing Etienne to all of the nobles in Europe as Lord Roger Mortimer. Your wedding was the perfect opportunity to do this. Everyone is here. Our friend Gabriel provided us with Etienne's pedigree going back generations, including his very fortunate inheritance of late. Even our father didn't recognize him."

"Plus, only a small handful of people have ever actually met me in person," Etienne said, "and most of them are in Spain."

"Look, I will help in any way possible," Charles reassured her. "It was the best plan we could come up with."

Isabella wrapped her arms around them. "I love you both so much."

"I will take my leave. You don't have much time." Charles left the room quickly, leaving the two of them alone.

Isabella and Etienne's eyes locked, and she saw their future. The plan wasn't perfect— there would be difficult times—but it gave Isabella hope. They didn't need to say any words; their bodies spoke for them. As their lips met, any doubt that Isabella had disappeared. This would secure their future.

THE END

# EPILOGUE

So, you may ask, where is the treasure? Rumor has it that Andy took the treasure to his ancestral lands just south of Edinburgh. He changed his name from Sinclair to Saint Clair. After many years, he finished construction on a chapel, which they named Rosslyn Chapel, or Rosslyn's chapel, as he liked to call it.

How do we know this? One day Chelsea was working in the fields when a messenger approached riding a blue and gray donkey. She immediately recognized the donkey as Blueberry. The messenger gave her both the donkey and a letter from Lord Saint Clair. All the message said was, *Ya have ta come to Edinburgh ta see Roslyn's Chapel.* The gossip in Santiago de Compostela was that Chelsea packed her bags immediately and never returned to Santiago again.

Katsuji and Akari traveled east and had many adventures along the Silk Road. When they returned to the land of the rising sun, Katsuji presented Akari's father the jar of sand he had collected from Finisterre, which was known to be the end of the world. Both of their families were overjoyed to see them. The two were wed and had many children.

Jacquess de Molay was imprisoned and tortured. On October 24th or 25th 1307, at the University of Paris, where he was under forced interrogation, Molay confessed that the Templar initiation ceremony included denying Christ and trampling on the cross. King Philip ordered that any remaining Templars throughout Christendom be arrested.

In a later confession ordered by the Pope, Molay retracted these claims. This caused a power struggle between Pope Clement and King Philip. Molay endured several years of imprisonment and torture. In March 1314, Molay was executed on the Ile des Javiaux, which is located in the Seine River, at the tip of the Ile de la Cite. Legend has it that Molay cursed both the Pope and King Philip, as well as all of his descendants, as he burned to death. Within a year of Molay's execution, both King Philip and Pope Clement died. Over the next fourteen years, the male bloodline of King Philip died out, collapsing the three hundred-year rule of the House of Carpet.

As for Etienne and Isabella, she held true to her promise. By 1325 Isabella's marriage had become unbearable. Her brother, King Charles the IV, had taken some land that belonged to the English crown. Isabella returned to France as a delegate from Edward to negotiate a peace treaty. Isabella was joined by Roger Mortimer (Etienne), her lover, and together they put together an army to oppose King Edward. Isabella and Mortimer returned to England with their mercenary army and took the country by storm. They forced King Edward to abdicate the throne, and Isabella ruled as Queen Regent until 1330 when her son took the throne.

It is also said that just outside Castrojeriz, pilgrims on the Camino de Santiago stop at two unmarked graves to leave a flower for all of the fallen pilgrims on the Camino de Santiago.

# NOTES IN CLOSING

If you enjoyed this novel, please consider leaving a review wherever you discovered and bought the book. Reviews are the lifeblood of independent authors, and can often make an enormous difference in how successful we are at making sure our stories are read or heard by the people who need them most. We would be incredibly grateful for your help in sharing this story as far and wide as possible.

For more information about the Through a Field of Stars series, visit www.throughafieldofstars.com.

Thank you for reading.
Buen Camino,

B. J. S.

# APPENDIX

**PRINCESS ISABELLA OF FRANCE** was born to King Philip IV and Joan I of Navarre sometime between 1290-1295, and died in 1358. She was their youngest child and only daughter. Her nickname was the She-Wolf of France. She was notable for her intelligence, beauty, and diplomatic skills. She married Edward II of England in 1308 and ruled as Queen of England until 1327.

**JACQUES DE MOLAY** was born in 1243 and died March 18th, 1314. He was the 23rd and final Grand Master of the Knights Templar. He led the Templars from 1289 to 1312. His main goal as Grand Master was to rally support for another crusade in the Holy Land.

**THE KNIGHTS TEMPLAR** were a Catholic military order that operated from 1119 to 1312. The order was among the wealthiest and most powerful orders in Christendom. They were renowned fighters and never left a battle until their flag left. They also were arguably the first organization to be a multinational corporation, with over a thousand commanderies and fortifications across Europe and the Holy Land. They also served as the first banking system for pilgrims. The Templar legacy is shrouded in speculation, secrecy, and legend. Part of the Templar leadership was imprisoned in Paris in 1307. However, a majority of the Templars and their wealth disappeared and has yet to be found. The order was officially disbanded by Pope Clement V in 1312.

**THE CAMINO DE SANTIAGO** was one of the most important pilgrimages in the Middle Ages, along with the Roman and Jerusalem pilgrimages. In English it is known as the "Way of Saint James." It is a system of pilgrimages that spread across Europe, leading to the remains of the apostle Saint James the Greater, which are housed in the Cathedral of Santiago de Compostela. Pilgrims would walk thousands of miles on the Camino to receive a plenary indulgence for the forgiveness of their sins. Today the Camino de Santiago is still incredibly popular, attracting over 250,000 pilgrims a year.

**POPE CLEMENT V** was born Raymond Bertrand de Got in 1264 and died in 1314. He was Pope from June 1305 – 1314. He is known for suppressing the Knights Templar and for moving the Papacy from Rome to Avignon, which started the Avignon Papacy. When elected Pope, he was neither a cardinal nor Italian; this caused many to speculate that he was tied with King Philip IV.

**KING PHILIP THE IV OF FRANCE** was born in 1268 and died in 1314. His nicknames were Philip the Fair, and the Iron King. He reigned as king of France from 1285-1314, and was married to Joan I of Navarre. Philip waged many wars and expanded the power and territory of France. He borrowed heavily from the Templars for these wars and became very indebted to them. In 1307, Philip arrested the Templars, which in turn cleared his debt and eased his fears of them creating a state within France.

**SANTIAGO DE COMPOSTELA:** The city of Santiago de Compostela was built up around the cathedral, and is now the capital of the Galicia region in the northwest of Spain. It is believed the word Compostela comes from the latin Campus Stellae, which translated means Field of Stars.

**SANTIAGO** *(also called St. Jacob or St. James the Greater)* was born around 3 AD and died 44 AD. Saint James was one of the 12 apostles of Jesus, along with his brother John. They were the sons of Zebedee. James was the first apostle to be martyred. St. James is the patron saint of Spain. According to the 12th century Historia Compostelana, St. James preached the gospel in Spain as well as the Holy Land. After he was martyred by King Herod, his disciples brought his body back to Galicia, Spain.

**THE ORDER OF KNIGHTS OF THE HOSPITAL OF SAINT JOHN OF JERUSALEM (*AKA: HOSPITALLERS*)**: The Hospitallers were a Catholic military order formed in the 11th century. Originally, they were associated with an Amalfitan Hospital in Jerusalem. During the first crusade in 1099, they received their own papal charter and were charged with the care and defense of pilgrims. After the Templars were disbanded, they were charged with the care of many of the Templar properties. In 1530 they took up residency in Malta and became known as the Knights of Malta.

**THE CROSS OF JERUSALEM** is the coat of arms and emblem for the Kingdom of Jerusalem from the 1280s. It has one large cross in the middle and four smaller crosses in each quadrant of the larger.

**THE WORK** is a system of four questions and a turnaround developed by Byron Katie. This section, and others in the novel, were inspired by her philosophy. The author highly recommends you visit her website www.thework.com and read her debut novel *Loving What Is.*

**PRISCA SAPIENTIA** is the belief that there is one "lost pure knowledge" that would connect all sciences.

**PRINCE CHARLES THE FOURTH OF FRANCE** lived from 1294 - 1328. Charles was the third son of King Philip IV and the last in the direct line of the House of Carpet. He ruled from 1322 - 1328

**JUAN SANTIN:** this story is based on an actual legend about the Holy Grail in O Cebreiro

**CROWN OF THORNS**: The Crown of Thorns was housed in the Sainte Chapelle beginning in 1238

**LORD ROGER MORTIMER** was an English nobleman who had an affair with Princess Isabella of France (Queen Isabella of England) and helped her to overthrow her husband Edward II in September 1326. Isabella and Mortimer were successful and Isabella's son Edward III was crowned on the first of February 1327 at the age of fourteen.

There are many experiences, books, and conversations with friends (both new and old) all over the world, that have inspired my philosophies and ideas in my life. As I wrote this novel, and walked the Camino, some of the books that have inspired me are listed below. I highly recommend reading these books if you found theconcepts in this story interesting or meaningful to you.

*Buen Camino,*

*~ B.J.S.*

## SUGGESTED READING LIST

***THE WAY: THROUGH A FIELD OF STARS***

Book one in the Through a Field of Stars series.
https://linktr.ee/throughafieldofstars

***BACK: THROUGH A FIELD OF STARS***

Book two in the Through a Field of Stars series
https://linktr.ee/throughafieldofstars

1. ***THE BIBLE***

2. ***LOVING WHAT IS,* by Byron Katie**

   "The Work" is a system of four questions and a "turnaround" that Katie created to help you question your thoughts, which can ultimately help you escape from damaging or painful patterns of belief and thinking.

   To learn more about "The Work," read *Loving What Is,* or go to www.thework.com, to discover how to use this process to confront and overcome your own thoughts.I have personally gotten some really life-changing results from engaging in "The Work," and I know many others who have as well. I highly recommend it.

3. ***THE POWER OF NOW, by Eckhart Tolle***

   This book is amazing and really helps you to be in the present moment. It is perfect for those who want to explore meditation. www.eckharttolle.com

## ACKNOWLEDGMENTS

I like to say God has a sense of humor. When I was young, I was obese and I became a dancer; I have dyslexia, and now I am an author. You can never tell what you will be called to in this life. I would like to thank God for inspiring this novel and helping me to achieve a task that I thought was impossible.

Writing this series has been an exciting and humbling journey. It forced me to face a lot of my fears and to turn something that was my weakness into a strength. It has been a long road, but I have been fortunate enough to have had many companions along the way.

"Every Camino is like a lifetime: some people walk with you for a day, others a few cities, still others come in and out at the perfect moment. But, there are a rare few, who will walk with you until the end of the world."

My journey as an author has paralleled my journey on the Camino. Many people influenced and helped this novel along the way, but I feel blessed to have found a partner willing to walk to the end of the world with me. My wife, Chelsea, has not only helped me with every aspect of the series, but she also walked over 500 miles on the Camino with me until we reached Finisterrea— the end of the world.

Chelsea has been with me since I wrote the first draft. I thought it was perfect, but she kindly let me know it needed a little work. Here we are, three years and many versions later, she is still my constant companion and support. I hope everyone has the opportunity to feel as loved and supported by their partner.

I would like to thank all of the pilgrims who walked countless hours with me and inspired the characters in this novel. I would like to thank all of the mentors that led me down the path of becoming an author. I would like to thank all of my beta readers and editors. You took this novel from an ordinary book into an amazing novel.

To get this novel out into the world, there were numerous individuals who mentored and encouraged me along the way. They were generous with their time and helped to give feedback, or edit. Some of these people include: Carol Scheppard, Howling Whale, Malina Dravis-Tucker, Ethan Okura, Josh Lieberman, Valeria Fox, and all of our beta/gamma readers.

There were also a whole slew of people who believed in me enough to support my Kickstarter campaign. Thanks to their generosity we have funded all the costs of editing, creating an audio book, printing, and distributing the first set of novels! To thank those individuals who financially supported the novel, I'd like to give a special shout out here! Oh, and of course a big thanks to my supportive family who planted adventure and spirituality into my heart.

Made in the USA
Middletown, DE
16 September 2024